My Gun Is My Passport -
The First American Gun Fighter in Afghanistan

By W. Hock Hochheim

About the Author

W. Hock Hochheim is a former U.S. Army investigator and Texas police investigator, patrol officer
and a former private investigator. He currently
owns and operates an international combatives
training company and teaches in eight allied
countries around the world. He is the author
of six non-fiction books and countless articles
on policing, the military, street survival, close
quarter combat and conflict psychology.
He lives in Texas.

Published by:

Lauric Press
1314 W. McDermott
Ste. 106-811
Allen, TX 75013
817-805-3068
www.LauricEnterprises.com

Copyright 2010 W. Hock Hochheim

ISBN No. 978-1-932113-38-9

Printed in the United States.

This is a work of fiction. Names, characters, places, and incidents either are the product of the author's imagination or are used fictitiously, and any resemblance to actual persons, living or dead, businesses, companies, events, or locales is entirely coincidental.

While the author has made every effort to provide accurate telephone numbers and internet addresses at the time of publication, neither the publisher nor the author assumes any responsibility for errors, or for changes that occur after publication.

Further, the publisher does not have any control over and does not assume any responsibility for author or third-party websites or their content.

Prologue

President Theodore Roosevelt slid the inch-thick, international import file across his desk to the other side. "I am sorry, Randolph, but the United States Government cannot help you on this one."

"But, it does concern commerce, Mr. President," Randolph commented.

"True, true. But the actual acquisition of these fine crystal products inside Stockholm does not officially concern our laws on international commerce," Teddy said with a broad smile.

"But I cannot stress enough the ruthlessness of these men, sir. They have a stranglehold over this cut-glass business. They've threatened and even beaten my representatives, demanding a huge share."

"High seas, Randolph. High seas. We can only be concerned with the high seas. Pirates, and so forth. Transportation. Not acquisition. Not the original purchase of goods on foreign soil."

"It's blackmail! Whatever shall I do, sir?"

"Sounds to me like you need some private protection all right, Randolph, right there in Sweden. Well, I do know of someone who might help."

"Who, sir?" Randolph asked.

"Well, sir, his name is Johann Gunther. Born in Baam, Germany. Do they speak any German in Sweden, Holden?" The commander in chief shouted to an aide across the room.

"I don't think so, Mr. President," his aide, Holden, replied. "Swedish in Sweden, sir."

"Yes." Roosevelt stood and walked over to a large framed photograph on the wall—a picture of his Rough Riders atop San Juan Hill.

He squinted at the faces. "There…there he is, right there," and thumped a finger at a blond-headed figure in the unit photo. "Gunther emigrated here from Germany as a young boy with his family. Married way too young. Suddenly, the boy had two children! As if he weren't barely a teenager himself. Living in the slums of Brooklyn. Bleak life! Bleak. Went out for cigarettes one afternoon and never once returned. Joined the Army!"

"Sounds untrustworthy," Randolph declared, as he joined Teddy beside the photo for a look.

"Oh," Teddy peered over the top of his spectacles, "he has grown up quite a bit since. Mr. Gunther was an Oklahoma lawman, a West Point grad, saw action in Africa and the South Pacific. And of course, volunteered with me in Cuba. I myself have used him a time or two for problems not unlike yours. I like to use him because he is not handicapped by the…rules."

"Is he a retired officer?"

"He was an officer, but not retired. He mustered out at the rank of major. He's about forty years old."

"Mustered out for business?" Randolph asked.

"Yes." Teddy sighed and sat down. "Money is the song he sings."

"Where is he located?"

"He lives in Fort Worth, Texas."

"Texas! He's a detective? A cowboy, a gunman?"

"Well, all of those, Randolph. He is a bully, son of the dying West, maverick son of a bitch, and they just don't make 'em like that anymore, that's for sure."

Randolph Hearst stood. "How may I reach him?"

"He has a troubleshooting company in Fort Worth called Remedies Unlimited, but I happen to know right now he is in Montana or Wyoming somewhere. He took a job with a ranching consortium out there. The ranchers have been plagued by a band of renegade Indians and half-breed outlaws—led by Cochise's grandson." Teddy lit up a cigar and continued. "They ramped up a bit of an old-fashioned posse. Gunther is in on it. When he's through, he'll be back in Texas. Contact him there."

"I will, Mr. President." He stood, shook Teddy's hand, gathered his file, and left his office. Holden shut the door after him.

"I have one thing for Mr. Gunther to do before you get a hold on him," Roosevelt muttered to himself and crashed back down into his leather chair. His gaze dropped to the world map on the desk. He drummed his fingers over Afghanistan.

"Okay, Holden, send in the next pain in the ass."

1
Feather of the Hawk

"You know…" Gunther startled the life out of the sleeping teenager, "…in the King's African Rifles, if they caught a guard asleep at night, the watchman would receive twelve lashes from a Kiboko."

The boy coughed and sat up. Johann Gunther dropped cross-legged beside him, adjusting his long leather jacket to shield him from the frozen Wyoming ground. He positioned his Browning pistol handle to protrude from the overcoat's side slit.

"Ahhhh….Will you tell my pa I fell asleep?" the boy mumbled, running his hand over his face.

Gunther ignored the teenager's question and stared out across the Wyoming plain. Snow fell lightly around them. "The Kiboko is a bullwhip made from rhino hide. Each lash of the Kiboko whip sounds out like a pistol crack and will cut an ass open like a knife." Gunther rested his Mexican Mauser rifle across his thighs. The butt of his second long gun, the Winchester lever-action shotgun, slung over his back, touched the ground behind him.

"A posted guard is the most important chore next to battle itself. A guard protects his men as they eat and sleep, so they are fresh for the fight. A guard's turn to sleep will come later, at rotation," Gunther reported and glanced out into the darkness.

The boy repositioned his rifle. Small hands in giant gloves.

"You been to Africa?" He peered sideways at Gunther from under his giant hat brim. Small head in a big hat.

"Yes, helping the British fight against North Africans, much like these men we now hunt here. Indigenous men—where the word Indian itself comes from."

"Did they raid ranches and take away the livestock, and the mommas and babies, too?"

"Yes. They did. We were after a man named Tippu Tal, a legendary African slaver. He captured and sold his own people to slave traders from all over the world."

In the distance, a lone, hunched figure bore down on them at a dead run, his footsteps muffled by the light snow. As the man ran through the blurry haze, the startled boy gulped and clutched at his rifle, but Gunther rested a heavy gloved hand on the stock.

"It's…it's your friend," The boy gasped.

"Yes," Gunther spoke quietly.

The Filipino man strutted up to them, dropped down crosslegged beside Gunther, and turned back to face the darkness. He sucked in deep breaths.

"Dey' are very busy tonight, Major Jo," the dark-skinned man said. "After midnight they no sleep. Tonight dey dress up. Dey sharpen up dey knives and arrows and load up dey guns. One put on a bandoleer of shotgun shells. Dey have a bow-wow."

"Powwow," Gunther corrected.

"Yup. Powwow. I am thinkin' dey are coming to kill us tonight in this snowfall."

"Tell the others, Jefe," Gunther said calmly.

The short man took off for the cold camp about fifty yards behind them.

"He from Africa?" The boy asked.

"No, from the Philippines. Islands in the South Pacific Ocean."

"My pa says your friend is a heathen."

"Jefe is not a heathen. He is a Muslim. He speaks four languages and is a war hero." Gunther rolled up to one knee. He shook his head in frustration at the darkness before him. The falling snow was not wet, but frozen dry flakes, and dropped as in a swirling fog. It was a *pogonip*—a Shoshone word for white death, a heavy fog with flying bits of snow.

"Will you tell my Pa I was asleep?" the boy asked again as Gunther stood.

"Kid, if you fall asleep again and you let Yatook Taza and his gang sneak in here ... if he doesn't gut you alive...I'll kill you myself."

Gunther trotted back to the encampment. He overheard the small group of men clustered around Jefe for news of his spying on the enemy camp.

"We'll lay out in a circle. There are thirteen of us!" Long John Shaw drew in the dirt.

"They's eighteen o' them!" Toenail Johnson scratched his cheek with his knife.

"We'll march to their camp," Art Benning motioned in the direction of the dirt drawing.

"Dey's already coming here, Art. Dey got the jump on us," Jefe warned.

"We should ride on back to Tucker's Turnaround. We'll have a rock wall behind us," said another. Long John and the others murmured agreement.

"Ohhh! They'll strip us naked…ohhh…and split our guts while we watch!" Toenail said.

Fear reflected in the eyes around him.

Gunther knelt into the rabble with an eye on the nervous men, familiar with their backgrounds and experience, just as he was with the enemy aiming to kill them. Only three months ago, some Arizona and New Mexico renegades banded together under a half-breed named Yatook Taza, rumored to be the grandson of Cochise. The gang tried to test their old criminal tricks on new victims and migrated north. The local lawmen of Montana, Idaho, and Wyoming said they had no jurisdiction over this traveling band, especially as they raided over state lines. The lawmen passed the onus over to the Army because a Chiricahua Apache led the gang. "This is a federal problem!" they declared, backing away from the trouble.

The Army in turn, said the band was a pack of criminals, and they had no jurisdiction fighting crime. Frustrated by this lack of military action and by the "citified, three-piece suit" lawmen of the neighboring cities, The Plethcart, Wyoming Beef and Agricultural Consortium took action, rounding up a team of mostly ranch hands to hunt down the brigands. At the last moment, they hired Johann Gunther to ride shotgun over the posse, offering him $500 to participate in their little militia against Yatook Taza.

Ride alongside is exactly what Gunther did. In the last ten bitter cold days they had swapped hunter/prey roles, in and out of Wyoming and Montana in a dance of death with Yatook Taza and his band. All the while the gang hauled around their kidnapped women and children. But, it looked as though this icy night they were all just too cold and cranky to sleep, and both groups craved a hot fire, coffee, and well-done deer meat, enough so to kill their enemies and put an end to this chase.

Gunther impatiently focused on Caribou Bob Pyle, the official ramrod of their human hunting operation. Caribou was the lead foreman of the Verner Ranch, one of the spreads raided by the Yatook gang. The outlaws had butchered six men, kidnapping three women and five children. Pyle was a caribou hunter and once a U.S. Army cavalry private in Georgia, but saw little real action, except for a fistfight or two. Caribou just sat stone still, glaring at the frozen ground.

"Caribou? What's next?" Lincoln Grant implored. Gunther knew Grant had seen a few Indian raids and range skirmishes. All these men were hardened plains types. But few, if any, had stared down the guns, faces, and war cries of savage, charging madmen. Nor had they fought against a snakelike, throat-slitting invasion the likes of which they were about to see within the next hour. Minutes maybe.

"What do you think, Mr. Gunther? You're an old Army man," Schoolyard Winston asked in the vacuum of silence that followed Caribou. All heads turned to the former U.S. Army major.

"Build a fire, Schoolyard. A big one. Near the horses," Gunther said matter-of-factly.

"What?" Lincoln said.

"We will spread out in a circle as you suggested, Long John," Gunther said, "but we'll move so far out that the light from the fire won't give our positions away. This way we have a fix on where we all are. Without that fire, in this dark, we would be lost to each other, isolated and…easily killed. The fire will also be an attraction point for them. Our horses, saddles, and the silhouettes of our gear by the fire will be their point of convergence. It will be an irresistible draw on this dark flatland. If they break our circle and get behind us? We'll see them thanks to the fire. I do know they will kill every one of us, and slowly if we don't do something and I mean…right now."

Jefe took the hint and dashed to the woodpile near the fire mule—the creature hauling around the cooking wood. Another helped him build a fire.

"Gather your saddles and gear in a circle around the fire," Gunther added. "They'll assume we're all there, and this small area will be our last vestige and fallback point."

Several men got busy with the saddles and blankets.

"After we get into position," Gunther told Jefe, "raise that fire higher." He turned to the group with more orders, "Stay low. I suggest you wrap a thick, spare shirt around your neck to deprive these savages of a quick-kill, throat slit."

"Bob," Gunther said. "Best get your son and the other lookouts back in and privy to our plan."

Caribou Bob Pyle stood and nodded in agreement, with a sense of surrender. Any real leadership power he had, he handed off, and rightly so. War such as this was out of his expertise. He ran for the mound where his son waited. Gunther lifted the shotgun off his back and hung the Mauser over his shoulder in its place. This was a short-range shotgun night.

Gunther had more advice for the collective. "I suggest you all take a piss, gentlemen. A stomach wound may poison your system. But not all at once. We can't let Yatook catch us all with our pants down and our dicks in our hands."

The group halved in turns, urinated while the other half guarded. Next, they all knelt in a makeshift circle around the small fire. At Gunther's word, they slowly moved out into the dark. Walking first, then hunched, then trotting, then crawling. Gunther settled in a natural indentation, reminding him of the classic military motto he'd heard at West Point: "The infantry loves the ground." The ditch he chose wasn't deep enough for true love though, just a fast tango and good-bye. With the men in place, Jefe poured on the kerosene, whipping the fire behind them into a hellish blaze on the wild night.

Moments went by. Then an hour…

Suddenly, there was an unnerving, pathetic wail of a cry in the distance. Gunther knew instantly it was the boy, and he guessed by the nature of the gasping pleat the teen was run through with some kind of edged weapon. The weakest link of the chain was now broken.

"John? John!" Caribou Bob shouted out in the snowy darkness, his voice quivering in a sobbing plea.

The sound and the silence meant many frightening things. Death of a boy. Loss for a father. Loss of a perimeter. Killers before them. Killers behind them. Gunther wondered, "Had the poor boy fallen asleep again? Dammit!"

"AGHHHH!" Came another scream, this time from an adult. Gunther envisioned with it, a sudden stab in the back. This circle was surely broken.

There came an ever-so-slight crunch behind him, the sound of snow compressing? How close? Who? A step? Yes! Another…the steps stopped. Then started again. Closer. Gunther rolled over, shotgun barrel up, to see a black figure just three feet away outlined like a monster in red from the fire. The monster's hand, held high, gripped the shape of a long knife. Gunther pulled the trigger, sending a powerful buckshot blast deep into the chest of the man. He exploded backward from sight with a pitiful yelp. The plains went quiet, except for the mechanical sound of Gunther's lever action. The downed attacker dug his boot heels into the dirt, kicking at the icy turf as he struggled and gurgled in the throes of death.

Since his gun flash revealed his hiding spot, Gunther dashed twelve feet to the right. Another gunshot rang out some forty yards to his left. Another invader fell to the cold ground with a thump. As he dove into a new indenture, three pistol shots rang out to his right.

A series of arrows zipped through the air, dropping into the circles of saddles and gear by the fire. That ruse worked. One hit a horse in its hind flank. It bucked in shock and bleated out in pain.

Muffled voices were all round. Another shotgun discharged some thirty yards away, but this interrupted darkness flashed a red outline of much closer horror. Gunther spotted a brigand as he jumped on top of Jefe, long knife in hand, and Jefe wrestling on the ground for his life.

Gunther stood and let his shotgun fall to his side the full length of its sling. He drew the .45 semiautomatic pistol from the slit in his jacket and cracked off a round at the moving head of the killer. He missed! He immediately charged at the fighters for a closer shot. Suddenly, his own head became a target, as a rifle reported from the darkness and a round zipped past his ear. Gunther continued his charge.

The killer bore down on the wiry Filipino as Jefe deflected and blocked each Bowie knife stab, trying to grasp the weapon arm. The action robbed Gunther of a clear shot. But, the distant rifleman took his shot, firing as the blaze briefly revealed Gunther's silhouette. Gunther turned his aim and fired off a classic shot in the dark to distract this rifleman from another attempt.

Gunther raced closer but there was still no way he would take such a shot at two men in a chaotic wrestling match. Plus, at this range, a .45 round could enter the savage, hit a bone, and ricochet into Jefe! Gunther smashed his .45 across the attacker's head instead. He snatched a handful of the wild hair, yanked the stunned man's head back, and shot him point-blank in the face. The bullet blew out a portion of the man's head from the jaw to the ear and he lifelessly tumbled back, aided by Gunther's shove and Jefe's desperate push.

Gunther dove to the ground next to Jefe. "You all right?"

"Yeah, Major Jo," Jefe huffed. "Dis crusty bastard, he did get the Jim Dandy jump on me..." Jefe reached over for the dead man's loose Bowie knife and turned it over and over in his hand. "Nice knife! I keep."

"You do that." Gunther rolled to his left and tried to retrieve the Winchester shotgun from his back. Its sling was tangled up with the Mauser sling. Jefe leaned over and cleared the long guns from each other.

"Tell you what," Gunther said. "You stay there on your back and watch behind us. I'll watch the front door."

"Sure ting," Jefe laid his shotgun across his chest. Gunfire erupted like a sporadic nightmare, like lightning and thunder all around them. But, it was Lincoln Grant, far off to their left, who would receive the full fright of the icy night.

At first Grant heard the faint thumping of galloping horse hooves. Then came the wet, snorting sound of a horse sucking and expelling the frigid air. Grant rose to one knee, bringing his rifle to his cheek. Fear unlike any other bear-hugged his chest. Still, he aimed into the dark.

First he saw the billows of smoke from the horse's nose. Then the whole figure suddenly appeared like a ghostly visage in the gray snowfall not twenty feet away. He fired a bullet center mass of the monster and, as though the creature's legs had crashed into a brick wall, the horse's head fell forward, its eyes wide with shock. The body of the horse tumbled over, pitching its rider headfirst. Gear and guns followed, rotating in the night air as the rider collided with great force face first onto the icy ground. The horse flipped and rolled and screamed until it landed on its back. It struggled to rise. Lincoln Grant charged his rifle with another round. The rider lay moaning and then ceased all movement or sound. Grant lay back down.

<>

Three hours passed. The horse bled to death. The slightest dot of a red, blurry sun appeared off on the horizon, under the breaking snow clouds. With this illumination, the sporadic attacks ended. This new yellow light cast itself across the rocky and flat terrain and a wicked, whistling, cold wind kicked up. Gunther and Jefe stood about the same time as did the other survivors, taking stock of the costly night. In the distance, they discerned tiny figures returning to the small mountain range that harbored the enemy camp.

Gunther spotted Caribou Bob Pyle slumped over the body of his son. He and Jefe trotted over to Pyle. His son was frozen solid.

Small shafts of ice formed on his lips, but there was something else in his mouth.

"Whatever…will I tell his mother?" Caribou whispered as he sat up near his son.

Gunther leaned over the boy's face. A hawk feather was shoved in the teen's mouth, as some kind of bizarre ritualistic calling card from the murderer.

"He thought this would be some kind of grand adventure," Bob continued.

Gunther remained silent for a moment. He leaned over and removed the feather from the boy's mouth, then flicked it into the brisk wind. It was gone in a second, like a small bird set free.

Over his shoulder, Gunther told Jefe, "Set a guard with a long gun. Get the rest of these men to saddle their horses. We need a body count. No buzzards are here in this snow and wind, but wrap the dead in their blankets. We'll be back to carry them home."

Jefe took off, shouting orders. Gunther stared at the mountain range ahead that concealed his enemy.

"We need to raid their camp as soon as possible," Gunther yelled over his shoulder to the men.

"I can't leave…him,' Bob said.

"I know," Gunther answered quietly. At the campsite, the men saddled up. They gathered their dead friends' sleeping bags and shoved the frozen bodies into them, a chore much like bagging heavy logs.

Jefe saddled up both Bob's and his son's horses and led them to the stricken father. Jefe and Bob stuffed the teen's quilted blanket around the body. The blanket was sectioned off with elaborate stitches and drawings of young children at play around a piano. A Christmas blanket. They laid the corpse over the saddle.

Gunther walked over to Lincoln Grant as the cowboy inspected his sprawled targets. The dead horse was broken legged and disheveled, as was the motionless rider, a full fifteen feet from the animal. Gunther approached the still body, his Winchester primed upon him for a surprise, but as he neared he could tell by the unnatural and painful positioning of the limbs that this rider was dead. The body was clad in a strange mix of Sears catalog finery and animal skins. Gunther grabbed the head hair and pulled back the rubbery broken neck.

"I musta' shot that poor horse right dead center into his brain," Lincoln said as he looked over the animal.

"Broken neck," Gunther declared of its rider. The head lay flipped completely back over onto the shoulder blades, frozen into the awkward position. He studied the face. "This dude here? Is Ya-took Taza. Mr. Lincoln Grant, you have bagged yourself the ring-leader."

"Oh, oh dear, sweet Lord of Mercy," Grant said exasperated, as he knelt near the corpse beside Gunther.

"You well may become somewhat famous. The man who killed the renegade grandson of Cochise." Gunther searched the pockets. "Of course, he just claims to be the grandson. No one can prove that for sure. But it is one helluva story!"

"Should we scalp 'im?" Grant wondered aloud.

" Oh, nooo," Gunther mumbled, as he pulled a package of or-ange rock candy from Taza's breast pocket. "We don't need to do such a thing."

"I…ahhh….I hope there is not too much notoriety doing this." Grant angled closer to Gunther. "I, ahhh,…I had just a peck of a problem back in Illinois? I am wanted on…some misdemeanors back there. Nothing big! There is no extradition authority to pull me back ya understand. But I'd rather be forgotten."

"Your secret is safe with me," Gunther smiled. Jefe and most of the men rode up. Jefe had Gunther's stallion and Grant's roan in tow.

"Yatook Taza!" Gunther pointed. By the scowls and bewilder-ment on the faces of the men, now missing five more of their old friends due to this scoundrel, it was apparent they didn't know whether to celebrate or shoot the damn corpse full of lead.

"You get him?" Toenail asked Gunther.

"No. Not me." Grant nervously wiped his nose.

"We can't leave this body behind," Gunther added. After some shared glances, three dismounted and hauled the killer over to a spare Palomino. By now, the other men were saddled up, circling and ready to ride.

Gunther climbed on his horse and said to his friend, "Jefe, you know where they camped last night. Lead the way." He turned to the men, "Now let's go kill those sons a bitches."

With this mandate and a fresh dawn to their right, they rode off.

◇

Jefe lay flat on his chest, hatless, with Lincoln Grant and Gunther alongside him, peeking over the rocky edge of the mountain range. The morning cold robbed the moisture from his eyes. Below, thirteen leaderless men, fresh from a lost skirmish, scurried about, breaking down their camp in an apparent hope to escape. Five female prisoners helped, following barked commands from their kidnappers. Some small children wandered aimlessly between them.

"Lincoln, are you as good a shot as that horse-brainer from last night?" Gunther crawled back from the ledge and slipped the Mauser rifle off his back and handed it to Jefe.

"Yes, sir," Grant said, "Fair, I am."

"Who in your group is also a good shot?" Gunther handed Jefe some Mauser ammunition magazines from his coat pockets.

"Toenail is," he answered.

"Go get him. Get Caribou, too," Gunther added, his hand forcing his long blond hair back against the wind and shoving his hat back on his head.

Grant back-crawled away, got himself clear of the ledge and scrambled down a pass in the rocks to the rest of their waiting posse. Jefe took the Mauser, laid the magazines on a rock, and settled into a sniper position. In a moment Caribou, Grant, and Toenail Thomas were crawling toward them on the ledge.

"Gentleman, the plan," Gunther said. "We are going to ride in, guns blazing. This shindig will begin upon my first pistol fire. Caribou, you and I will charge the men from that dirt turnpike right over there." Gunther pointed out an opening to the valley floor to

Page 17

the east of the gang. "It's the only quick way in. Jefe, Lincoln, and
Toenail, the three of you will nest up here with your long guns.
You will each pick a separate target. Tell each other your targets.
No sense wasting time and rounds accidentally double-shooting at
the same man. Next, you will pick apart the enemy. First, shoot the
ones that do not scatter, but rather stand their ground instead and
shoot back at us as we charge in. Also, shoot those who get behind
cover that we cannot hit easily."

Gunther continued. "Imagine now where they will run for cover.
Talk about it. That rock. That wagon. Plan ahead. We need to hit
'em before they saddle up."

The men nodded.

"If it all goes to hell," Gunther added, "we will scramble back
up here and defend ourselves from these heights. You will cover
our ascent. But, I sincerely doubt these scumbags will do anything
but run ragged and die. They haven't even posted a guard that I can
see. Taza must have been the brains of this team."

"So, we should just keep on shooting?" Toenail asked nervously
as Gunther turned to leave.

"I sincerely hope to hell you kill all of 'em before I get close,"
said Gunther with a wry smile, and he and Caribou left for the
main group.

"Who-we! Did Army generals teach your friend how to sketch
this out?" Toenail asked Jefe.

"No. Major Jo always says sergeants taught him the real
fighten'," Jefe said.

The ragtag snipers blew warm air nervously into their bare
hands.

Jefe started selecting targets.

"You look real comfy with that military sharpshooter. Where'd
you learn this?" Toenail asked Jefe as he tried to settle in.

"Major Jo and I fought together in the Philippines," Jefe answered.

"The Phillio-penes. I read about them in Bible," Toenail said.
"Who in hell was ya' fighten' over there?"

"The Moros."

"Morons, ya' say?"

"Moros. Let's pick our targets like Major Jo said." Jefe changed the subject to the work at hand.

◇

Within minutes Gunther and Caribou Bob were back down on the lowlands, approaching their anxious men who were already on horseback, poised for the attack. He could tell Caribou was intent on their mission, and somewhat distracted from the painful loss of his son. Revenge. The horses stutter-stepped as he and Caribou ran toward them. Even the packhorses, laden with gear and the two bodies of young John and Taza, tied in a cluster of pine trees to the left, shuffled about, tugging on their ties. Gunther and Caribou mounted their horses.

"May we stop and say a quick prayer?" Long John Shaw asked Gunther.

"No time. Another second and they might be mounted and moving. Attacking a mounted force is one of the worst things I've ever experienced. Lots of crossfire," Gunther said, turning to Long John. "Let your pistolas do the praying, Long John." Then he added with a smile, "And may God bless our snipers."

With that, Gunther yanked a rein and turned his horse toward the gorge down the rocky road. He spurred the animal, a .45 in one hand, his shotgun slung across his chest. The men, clearly bedazzled and frightened with the thought of such a front run, the likes of which none had done before, lifted their weapons and blindly imitated this austere Texican who became their leader.

Agitated by this commotion, some of the packhorses, including the two bearing the corpses of the young boy and Taza, yanked on their reins, which were wrapped on bare branches. They bucked and danced free from the trees, compelled to follow their herd. Within a moment, five caravan horses clamored behind the advancing war party, two of them carrying the dead.

◇

It was not a mere warning or signal shot into the frigid air that started the fray. That would waste a bullet. Gunther fired first at the closest marauder, his .45 kicking the man off his feet as he tried to mount his horse. He tumbled into the legs of the animal. The creature leaped and snorted, and the battle for life and death was on!

Among the ducking kidnapped women and children, the remaining thirteen renegades scrambled for their guns. The snipers from above began pouring lead into the confused enemy. The posse spread out in a line and fired at every man as fast as they could.

Long John fell in the dust, hit by an enemy Winchester round. He tumbled shoulder-first onto the frozen ground, whereupon he started praying, wishing he'd started a moment earlier.

Gunther charged into the encampment's center, blasting away until his semi-auto ran dry. He raised his Winchester shotgun and let the empty .45 roll forward on his trigger finger. No time to re-holster. His long finger bridged across the .45 trigger and onto the trigger of the shotgun. A man took aim at him but was cut down by Jefe's eagle-eyed shot from the ledge.

Gunther closed in on one thug as he dashed behind a woman prisoner, snatched her by the hair, and put his revolver to her throat.

"I'll shoot her open!" he screamed. "Yeah!"

The female, gray and skeletal from her captivity, now prepared herself for anything. She grimaced at Gunther and shook her head. It was a license-to-kill expression. Even her! She had had enough of this and the monster needed killing. Gunther halted his horse. He knew a shotgun blast from his Winchester would take a corner out of the poor woman. A young child cried. Random gunshots rattled the wide canyon, but were dispersing. The horses carrying the dead boy and Yatook Taza ran amok, crisscrossing through the carnage.

"I will shoot her throat open!" the man threatened again. Gunther remained silent. He bent his shoulders over the horse's neck to gain every last bit of cover. He let his horse take slow steps toward the pair, the barrel of his scattergun aimed at the outlaw.

Gunther sized up the skunk, the southwestern half-breed. He noticed a series of hawk feathers stuck in the outlaw's hatband. The hawk-man didn't look to see the rider approaching from his left. That cowboy held a Colt pistol aimed at the criminal's head.

"I got him in my sights," growled Caribou Bob Pyle to Gunther. The thug whipped his head to Pyle. He sneered, huffed, and then suddenly seemed to become very calm. That was not a good sign.

"I'm leaving!" He said to Pyle in a tone as cold as the day, backing away with the woman.

"Drop that cannon, feather man!" Gunther bellowed loudly. "There's nothing but hundreds of icy miles behind you! You have nowhere to go!"

The man kept backing away, hauling the resisting woman. At the right moment Bob shot the man in the lower leg.

Bam! And snap! The leg bone cracked and the skunk spun and fell away. The thug discharged his revolver skyward as he dropped. Bob fired again, catching the killer in the upper left shoulder, knocking him completely off his feet. Released, the gasping woman dove forward into Gunther's advancing horse, hugging its neck. Bob rode in the last few feet, methodically blasting rounds into an already exploded body. The last one hit the killer's head like a glancing, heavy rock. It tore open the hat, spread loose the feathers from the hatband, opened the skull, and spread the contents across the ground. The last shot. The plains fell silent but for the whistling wind. Loose hats from dead men bounced across the ground and disappeared with the wind.

Bob turned his horse and galloped through the site, his teeth clenched, his pistol up, desperate for one more to shoot, one more to kill. His barrel scanned the thirteen bodies. Then, the full painful pallor of Bob's dead son fell back over him like a deep sickness, the moroseness forgotten for the few seconds of savage violence.

They's all through, Bob," Steven Simpson shouted.

"I ain't!" shouted Long John Shaw.

Gunther peeled his horse off toward the man. He jumped off his mount beside Long John.

"They caught me unawares from my blind side," Long John

gasped.

"I think it hit your shoulder, John. If you are still breathing and thinking, that is an awful good sign. You pray, and I'll work on it," Gunther said and started opening the clothing near the wound.

'Ohhh, ohhh…our father…he thwarted heaven…" John babbled.

"Make sure everyone's down and dead!" Gunther shouted while tending the wound.

Jefe, Toenail, and Lincoln Grant stood on their precipice, jumping and hollering victory cries, to which the men below returned their own vocal salutes. Gunther motioned to Jefe to bring his medical field kit, and Jefe jogged down to his horse to retrieve the bag.

"…and so hollered be his name…" continued John.

Schoolyard Wilson gathered up the two horses carting the dead teen and Taza.

"You both had to be here for the grand finale?" he commented solemnly.

"They kingdom come. They's will be done…"

The freed woman snatched up the wandering three-year-old boy. Caribou Bob dismounted and walked to her.

"Lois McIntyre?" Bob looked the woman up and down. "Weren't you taken from the McIntyre Rail and Ranch three weeks ago?"

"Yes," she answered. "I know I'm a sight. It's a wonder you can recognize me with the bruises and such. Is…my husband—"

"No Ma'am," Bob said painfully. "He is dead. Everyone...has passed."

She stood for a few seconds and then dropped to her knees. With this descent, the blond-headed boy's feet hit the ground and he started to wander off again, the woman suddenly powerless to act. Bob knelt beside her and quietly asked, "Where is your daughter, ma'am?"

"She's dead," Lois murmured.

"On earth, as it is in holy heaven above…" Long John Shaw prayed loudly.

Jefe galloped up with the medical kit, followed closely by

Toenail and Grant.

The rest of the women collected the other children and gathered around Bob, sharing questions and answers. Soon, the men collected to see their neighbors' wives and daughters. They wrapped them in their arms. There was much exasperated crying, even wailing by many of the group, menfolk included. Jefe and Gunther swapped looks at them and at each other, while running the white bandages around Long John's bloody shoulder. The round passed right through him. Lock the torso still and pack the wound was the first-aid protocol. Jefe took a rope from his saddle and tied the arm across his chest. John winced with every touch and forgot he was praying.

"Who is this boy?" Bob asked the women.

"We don't know. They had 'em before they took us," a woman said.

"He was kidnapped and his parents killed," Lois added.

Bob walked up to him, saying over his shoulder, "Anyone know his name?"

"Nobody knows his name," A woman said.

Bob sat cross-legged before the boy and smiled at him. "Who are you, boy?" Bob whispered in wonder into the child's face. There was no answer, only a withdrawn stillness. "Where is your home?"

<>

Within an hour, every dead man was sacked and tied on his saddle. The women and children prepped and loaded the gang's covered wagon. They still had to trudge back to last night's camp and package up the four men killed there. Next, they proposed to ride on to Tucker's Turnaround—the small cliff that would offer some windbreak and finally light a fire for the first hot food in days. Gunther and Jefe faded back into simple, quiet travel companions, strangers and outsiders to the group again as they had started out. In the elation of rescue and winning, in the horror of close calls, bloodletting and death, Gunther recognized they suffered the shock of war burn.

The group left the plains with Caribou Bob Pyle in the lazy lead. Straddled across the front of Bob's saddle was the boy with no name, wrapped in a horse blanket against the cold. On the horse tethered to his forearm rode the frozen corpse of his teenage son stuffed in his Christmas blanket. Bob could only imagine what his wife would think. One dead boy. One alive.

<>

Johann Gunther passed the time of the trip to Tucker's Turnaround making his plans. Once back at the prospering city of Plethecart, he would receive $500 from the rancher's consortium. Jefe would receive a slice. A posh passenger train would take them back to Fort Worth, Texas. He watched over the rest of these poor, scarred souls, wondering how they would manage to pick up with their lives again. For a decade to come, there would be stories of how Caribou Bob Pyle led his men into hell itself, guns blazing in a daring rescue. This was the pulp embellishment of the old, Wild West, not the fodder for this new 20th century! But, these amazing tales would eventually vanish, too, as is the nature of such things.

<>

Plucked from the mouth of the dead teenager and pitched from the fingers of Gunther the night before, this vicious calling card of murder, this hawk feather, had flown on the crisp dawn air. Dried, discolored, and disconnected from life itself, it bounced from rock to gorge to winter tree. Another bird, a sparrow, snatched it and flew it to a lofty pine branch, carefully knitting it into a nest of mud, needles, and stems, from which eggs of life where to be hatched. There this feather, this nest would disintegrate over the summer, lost for all time, still…yet…in its way, giving a full account of itself.

2
Buscadero Opera

Handguns. In the later 1890s and early 1900s, you could often define a city limits by the rules of open or concealed handgun carry. In most cities in America, even the rowdiest men could not wear their handguns in open display. The once common practice of weapon confiscation at the city limits was, for the most part, unnecessary and over. Most city dwellers and travelers concealed their pistols under their clothing as a matter of routine, anyway. Out of sight? Out of law enforcement mind. But, as you wandered to the outskirts, those who did brandish carried their firearms openly on or in their belts as their jobs, survival, or fancy dictated. It was not uncommon for a rancher to ride just inside a city borderline for quick supplies or other business, even pleasure, wearing his revolver in a classic, open cowboy rig, but such sights were not typical as you moved closer downtown.

Fort Worth, Texas, was a kind of border city in and of itself, called the "cowboy" side, west of the more sophisticated Dallas. It truly was a gateway to the dry, flat, hot southwest. The southwest side of this cow town was a transition zone, a no-man's land of confused borders and disputed legal jurisdiction. While loosely called Fort Worth, it really wasn't in the city limits officially. Largest of these smaller townships was a place called Middlefield. It contained scores of local officials on the take, unpaved streets, soused rowdies, hookers, and unemployed lawmen with plenty of violence, homicides, other felonies, and racial brutality.

Headed for this raucous zone of sin, Johann Gunther could have worn his brown leather gun belt and the John Browning prototype

.45 semi-auto pistol if he so wanted. And, maybe he should have, considering where he planned to go. Gunther opted instead for his city gun, his German Luger. And, instead of traveling by horseback, or even his Remedies Unlimited company horse and carriage, he went as a passenger on the noisy, smoky, rubber-wheeled automobile.

This newfangled contraption belonged to the new Fort Worth Opera House Company. Opera President Max Dozier had recently hired Gunther to do a fast job! This duty required a quick search, heavy lifting—as in a fat, drunken man—and a very quick return. Barring flat tires, the automobile could help him accomplish his mission in two or three hours, providing he could find the fat, drunk man. Gunther might return to his office in time for an afternoon Earl Grey tea, a habit he picked up from some of the roughest British soldiers he'd worked alongside in Africa.

There were so many of these autos putt-putting around Fort Worth that they no longer frightened citizens, who once dodged the cars on sight thinking them monstrous runaway trains. Even the so-called motor truck, the bigger autos, appeared on the streets frequently these days, delivering beer and boxes of products of all types to stores. So Gunther's noisy, late-morning arrival went largely unnoticed—as he preferred.

In his jeans, white shirt, tan boots, camel sporting jacket and hat, his Luger resting on the right side of his tooled leather belt, Gunther outfitted himself for the city, not the range. As a world traveler, he felt comfortable in both worlds.

"I think this is it, William," he shouted to the driver and pointed to a roadside bar called Aguardiente's, named after a fiery brandy made in El Paso. "This is where I found him the last time."

The driver, in goggles and a tight leather skullcap, nodded and yanked the steering wheel to the right—directly into a deep wagon wheel rut. Gunther grimaced with the jolt. Before the hissing and shaking of the vehicle stopped, he jumped from the rig and stepped up on the wooden sidewalk. He pounded his boots upon the planks to shake free the area's cantankerous, glue-like mud then pushed open a half-door to enter the establishment. With his thumb, he knocked his hat back on his head, released a deep, impatient sigh, and glanced over the faces.

Mostly men rested at the tables this early afternoon. They ate brisket and drank, or sat mesmerized from an overnight drunk. Gunther immediately detected the smell of the fine barbeque curling through the stale beer air. He sucked in a deep sample of the spicy odors, smiled, and walked to the bar.

"That smells like the best brisket I will find just about anywhere," he told the barkeep, who acted too preoccupied to look away from his chores.

"Buffet's one bit per person. You'll find it against the back wall," the man mumbled.

"Thank you, sir." Gunther dropped a silver coin on the bar.

He made for the buffet serving tables, eyeing the customers on the way. As predicted, Peter Rollendale was hunched over a table and looked as ossified as a four-day drunk. Gunther raised an eyebrow as he walked on by him. A smile formed on his lips as he grabbed a plate and began spooning beef, beans, and sweet potatoes aboard. He grabbed some biscuits and covered it all with a sweet, rascally red sauce. Following a wink of approval, a lovely, female server of this fine spread pulled him a beer from the keg.

Armed with a plate and beer mug, Gunther walked to Peter's table, took a seat next to the drunk, and spread the food before him. Peter and his two acquaintances looked Gunther over. The three men at the table were a sorry lot. Obviously up all night. Oily clothes. Stinky. Unshaven. One of Peter' friends had a boil the size and shape of a thimble near his left ear. The other had no front teeth. Gunther preoccupied himself with the pit-simmered meat. He took a draught from the icy beer mug.

"Ahhhh," he moaned, delighted.

Peter smirked and shook his head. Gunther ate more.

"Peter," Gunther said with a mouthful. "They are looking for you down at the opera house." He never looked at the drunken builder, just the food.

Peter shook his head again, eyes downcast. He clutched a glass of whiskey. A near empty bottle rested at his knuckles, both surrounded by piles of crushed eggshells and peanut husks.

"I don't think he—" the man with the boil started to interrupt.

Gunther yanked the Luger from his holster and, with his elbow on the table in a very casual manner, pointed the weapon right between the man's eyes.

"Mister," Gunther growled, "I don't know you. And I don't want to know you. And you would do well for yourself…to shut the fuck up." Gunther let his eyes and the barrel linger for a second and then laid the gun on the table near his beer. He continued to eat. No one in the bar reacted with any surprise at the display.

"Max sent me to get cha'," Gunther continued. "The opera's grand opening is tomorrow night—well, you know this—and about half the seats are unfinished. Your carpenters are standing around without lumber and are like little lost children without their head honcho."

"Tell 'em to…to…to get some wood. Nail the wood…together. What I need to be…beeezzz there for?" Peter said, too liquored up to make or finish a sentence.

"Well, that's just it, Pete. You know where the wood delivery is, and they don't. They are just standing around with a bunch of nails and nothing to hammer them into. You are the boss. This is your contract. Your job."

"I told that…that…" but Peter really had no answer. No excuse. His gruff tone trailed off into silence.

Gunther dropped his fork into his food, "Dammit, Pete! This is the third time I've had to find you and take you back to work. Each time I find you, drunk as an armadillo. Now, when I finish this plate, we are off to the opera, and you can explain yourself to Max. I just wish you would dry up and take advantage of your position. This is a great contract."

Peter had no answer. It was the same speech he'd heard from Gunther the last time. Peter stared down at the table. Gunther's lip curled and he looked up at the man with the boil, and then jammed the Luger violently back into the holster.

"You some kinda' buscadero?" the man with the boil asked.

"Partly," Gunther answered quietly, but that question told Gunther a lot of the boiled man's background. A buscadero was a little-known old border term for a gunfighter.

This pair of low-life strangers were unlikely compadres for Peter Rollendale, the redheaded son of an Irishman whose family built ships for Britian. Peter was once an officer in the U.S. Army Corp of Engineers. He resigned his commission in 1903, got married to a Hispanic beauty from El Paso, and opened a construction company in Austin. Good connections and recommendations from Governor Batson himself landed Peter several lucrative municipal contracts. His most recent building contract was the Fort Worth Opera House, currently without enough seating for the rear ends of tomorrow's grand opening attendees.

But, Gunther also knew the seething, underbelly biography. The cow town tabloids would reveal Peter's life was peppered with pot-holes. Rumor and scandal had it that his wife had cuckolded him repeatedly with his younger foremen, and the governor actually threw him as a discount contract, trading card for votes and contri-butions. Gunther read the Austin-Statesman's investigation, peeling each crisp newspaper page back to read more and more on Gover-nor Batson, who would promise great, cheap, building deals for city projects to gain grass-roots local support. The reporters claimed the governor would shovel Rollendale in for work. Rollen-dale was always unavailable for interview.

The opera contract was good, but not as lucrative as it should have been. These affairs and disappointments paved his penchant toward whiskey into a real problem. In short, Gunther surmised, Rollendale was rapidly cracking apart at his own foundations and the flow of hard liquor was eroding what stability he had left.

"It's time we go, Peter." Gunther stood. Rollendale remained seated, and Gunther had to grab the scruff of his collar with his left hand and pull him up. He kept his right hand free in case Mr. Boil and Mr. No Teeth needed another quick flash of his Luger, or worse.

They marched outside. The white glare of the Texas sun must have hit Peter's bloodshot eyes hard because he ducked, gasped, and squinted as they climbed aboard the automobile. The driver gave the car a few hand cranks. As the engine fired up, he jumped behind the wheel, lowered his goggles, released the brake, and they chugged off for downtown.

"It's all just a godamn sham," Peter blurted out. Gunther stared at his pale profile for a few seconds, smirked, and turned away.

◇

"I give you Mr. Rollendale. Again," Gunther declared to Max Dozier, the portly head of the opera house. Rollendale crashed into a plush leather chair in front of Max's desk. Gunther back stepped to the office door and waved a finger at Betty, Max's French assistant. "Coffee," he whispered. She winked and nodded her understanding of the predicament.

"Peter, where have you been? Construction is at an utter standstill!" Max complained dramatically. He and Peter bantered. Betty tiptoed in with two cups of Columbian brew, one for Peter and one for Gunther.

Gunther listened for a few minutes, daydreamed for another few, and announced at a quiet hush in the heated conversation, "Well, gentlemen, I will be leaving."

"Ahh... wait, will you, Gunth?" Max said breathlessly, stepping around the desk. "Ahhh, there's another ten dollars in this if you will get Peter off to collect that wood shipment for his men at the lumberyard."

Gunther pondered the offer.

"The load needs Peter's signature for release and delivery. The automobile will be at your disposal. Two tickets to our dignitary box for the show tomorrow night?" Max added, curling one end of his gigantic handlebar moustache.

"Where's the wood, Peter?" Gunther growled.

"At the yard. Glenrown's Lumber Yard." Peter sipped the coffee. He seemed to be coming back to life.

"Okay," Gunther agreed. "Just let me call my office." He turned for Betty's room, cranked up the wooden box, and asked the city dispatcher for the Remedies connection to report his delay to Jefe.

◇

It was after 5 P.M. when the roar of the auto brought a curious Jefe to the heavy oak front doors of Remedies Unlimited. He was wearing his office uniform, the barong, the traditional long, white, Filipino shirt over slacks and black shoes. Gunther jumped from the vehicle.

"Look at the car! Hurry! Come on!" Jefe shouted. His two young children, a boy and a girl, ran to the doorway for a look. They admired the auto with round mouths agape. Gunther rubbed both their heads as he walked by.

"You missed tea!" Jefe said. "But! You have barbeque!" He swatted at a small, red stain on Gunther's shirt. "Any good?"

"Really good," Gunther said as he walked past him. The vehicle belched itself down the street and the kids shut the front door.

"Where you go?"

"A bar in Middlefield. Aguardiente's," Gunther answered.

"You get the drunk man back to work again?"

"Yep, yet again. He is almost done with the opera, and that will be the end of that. Anything going on here?" Gunther asked.

"No. I cancel the two o'clock appointment. He will come again tomorrow. You go home?"

"Oh…." Gunther scanned the large multiple-room suite. Jefe's children returned to their board game in a lobby corner. "I guess so."

"Good! I get coach. I got big surprise!" Jefe said, stirring the air with a pointed finger. He hurried to the back as Gunther grabbed up his leather satchel and the afternoon newspapers from his office. Jefe dashed out the back door to the stables, where another Filipino in a dark suit sat on bench.

"Go! You go now," Jefe declared to the man, who nervously stood up. The two hitched Darlene, the carriage horse, to the company's three-person coach. With the reins in hand, the skinny man climbed into the driver's seat.

Jefe held Darlene's harness and helped lead the rig out the back gate. "You remember where to go? Yes?" Jefe asked in Spanish.

"Si! Si. Si," the driver answered.

"Get around da' front. Go on!" Jefe ordered in English, remembering his promise to consistently talk in English and help the man learn the language. Then he scrambled back in the building and through the lobby.

Gunther stood at the open front doors and turned with surprise at Jefe's reappearance, expecting his partner to be at the reins of the coach. Jefe met Gunther's raised eyebrow by grabbing his elbow and escorting him to the curb. Their open carriage turned the corner and advanced down the red brick city street with a skinny, grinning stranger wearing a top hat at the helm.

"My cousin Luis! From Manila!" Jefe declared. The coach stopped. Both Darlene and Luis turned and stared at Gunther. When Gunther turned back to Jefe, he spotted the two kids at the door giggling and waving at their "uncle." Jefe opened the coach door and waved a majestic hand for Gunther to ascend.

"Hmmph," Gunther growled and stepped up. "He knows how to get to the hotel?"

"Oh, yes, yes," Jefe said proudly. "He knows everything! He has studied the maps. Everything."

Gunther sat in the rear, waved good-bye to the kids, and the carriage whisked off into the busy horse and carriage traffic of Throckmorton Street, then on to the Dunston Hotel, where Gunther rented a suite as his residence.

"Luis, do you speak English, ah…speak United States?" Gunther asked.

"Si…ahhhh…yes. Quite some, Major Jo."

"Quite some! Goooood," Gunther responded, staring at the oddly shaped, knobby head and ghastly thin neck visible underneath the big felt hat. "Good."

Gunther looked back and saw Jefe standing proudly on the street watching the transport. As office manager of Remedies Unlimited, and in fine Filipino fashion, Jefe had given himself a verbose, grandiose title, "The Supreme Secretariat General" of the company. He was capable of making such personnel decisions. Soon, Gunther believed Jefe's entire family would immigrate over, one job at a time. Jefe's wife and oldest daughter were already the office cleaning crew and caretakers of the horses, and soon his other children would grow into important corporate positions. But, to Gunther, they were like his adopted family, and there was, in the end, no man on earth he trusted more than his old Filipino war veteran friend, Jefe Kokoy.

Halfway to the hotel, Gunther patted his breast pocket, remembering his extra present from Max Dozier. He leaned forward to rest his arms on the backboard of the driver's seat.

"Turn to the right. Right here, Luis!" Gunther ordered, and the driver yanked the reins to the left.

"Right! Amigo. The other way! This way!" The carriage swayed hard again on its springs and cut off the coach behind them. Their horse bucked. A foul curse hit the air. Gunther waved to the angry driver as they trotted past the Antebellum-style homes of Victoria Street.

"Okay…okay, see that house right there? Okay. Stop." Gunther guided, but the buggy didn't stop.

"Stop! Halt! Luis! Aqui!" There was just enough classical Spanish in the Philippines to use Texican terms and get the communication job done.

"Si, Major Jo!" He pulled the rig to a skidding stop, pitching Gunther against the seats. It was obvious Darlene didn't care for this surprise maneuvering. She turned her head and gave them both the big eye.

"Quite some!" Gunther muttered as he stepped from the carriage.

"Aqui, uno momento." He pointed demonstratively to the ground, "Aqui!" then turned for the stately house.

The tutor Annalee Gish leased rooms in this mansion, and she was busy in open parlor teaching mathematics to her Wednesday group of college-bound teens. Gunther stepped into the den and looked through the glass panel doors and white lace curtains to see Annalee. She spotted him and excused herself from the tutoring.

Annalee shook her head at his untimely arrival as she approached, but then, Gunther was often untimely.

"Yes, mister?" she said in a tone reminding him she was working.

"In my pocket are two tickets to tomorrow night's opera. Box seats…and I think the governor will be right among us. Interested?"

Her displeasure over his lack of timeliness faded and a smile curved her lips.

"Yes. Yes, but I've got to finish this prep class." She guided him back to the front door.

"I will call you tomorrow, ma'am." He gave a short bow. Then left. He bounded across the yard and back into the carriage.

"Okay, 'Quite-Some!' To the Dunston Hotel," Gunther said, and with this order, Luis had an official nickname. Now, an important question still remained…would Darlene take to him?

◇

The opera hall was a golden mix of wood and steel, with both gas and electric lights. Gunther and Annalee marveled at the craftsmanship as they took a quick stroll down an aisle toward the stage. After their inspection, they climbed the hall stairs to the balcony for a look at their royal dignitary box seats. In the middle of a section of twelve seats a slanted door led to a descending stairwell. A small bar and sitting area provided exclusive entertainment to pampered, elite patrons. A piano player produced calming classical music. A bartender and chef served up the wine and sandwiches. Present were most of the evening's guests and introductions were handled by Max, who was sweating profusely from opening night nerves. He announced the arrival of Gunther as a local businessman and Annalee as his companion, a prep school teacher.

As they moved forward, a beautiful Hispanic woman behind them in line refused to wait her turn in the unofficial line of handshaking. She approached Gunther with a gregarious smile.

"My name is Rosaletta Rollendale." The raven-haired lady presented her gloved hand to Gunther.

He smiled, gave her a short bow of his head, and to the white-laced hand, the proper light kiss. She added a secret delay, pushing and rotating her hand ever so slowly on his lips, a linger with a message.

"Rosaletta Rollendale. Such an international name," Gunther remarked—so, the cuckolding wife.

Next to him, he could feel Annalee stiffen.

Rosaletta giggled slightly. Several men in the room cast jealous looks his way. Peter, her husband, and the next young man stepped abruptly forward to interrupt the handshake.

Gunther squeezed Annalee's arm and offered her a reassuring smile. "That was awkward." Gunther tugged at his tight collar. "You look quite pretty, dear," he said to Annalee.

She gave him an intelligent yet mysteriously wise smile, but any additional exchange between them had to wait.

"Roy Wise," the man announced, pumping Gunther's hand. "I am Peter's foreman on this job."

Introductions were made.

"Well, sir, you have done an excellent job. This place rivals any opera house I have ever seen. You both should feel very proud tonight."

The men nodded, and he noted that Peter seemed sober and held a cup of coffee in his hand.

With that, six people marched in, led by Texas Governor Bullard Batson. Batson looked red-faced and from his swaying stance appeared somewhat touched with alcohol. He glad-handed and half-hugged Peter Rollendale with a giant grin, and they exchanged whispered pleasantries.

Despite the rumors of discontent between the two, Gunther thought Peter seemed glad to see Batson. Max rushed up and stuck to the governor's side like horse glue, steering him around to meet the guests. Gunther noted the other five men in their wake were probably state police officers with pistols under their jackets. He saw one twist around surveying the room, and Gunther spotted the telltale clothing print of a pistol handle pushing against his jacket. Bodyguards. No one bothered to introduce any of them. They were simply there, with deadpan expressions. Gunther had played the part of invisible man himself many times and knew the role. He gave them a quick nod of the head. Now they knew he knew.

Batson's gaze drifted over Gunther and Annalee as he worked past them and down the line glad-handing.

With glasses of French wine in hand, Gunther and Annalee slipped out of the room and back into the theater.

"Mrs. Rosaletta Rollendale wanted you to eat her glove for dinner," she commented. "She needs a very large hand fan to cool herself down."

"More like a fire hose," Gunther added.

◇

Within the hour, everyone was seated in the theater and stilled with anticipation. The opening act was perhaps the most entertaining and popular of the whole evening. The Beautiful Jim Key! Jim Key was not a man, but a horse, and far from any normal horse. Advertised as the smartest horse in the world and under the guidance of Dr. William Key, Jim astounded Gunther and the audience with feats of reading, writing and mathematics by selecting proper answers with his hoof. The Beautiful Jim Key was smashing box office records in opera houses all over the United States. Jim Key basked in the rounding applause offered by his enraptured audience.

Then the Italian opera began. As an obese Italian woman bellowed an aria from a white chariot, a sudden motion diverted Gunther's attention from the stage. Down and to the left, a well-dressed man stood and stepped over the polished shoes and around knees, making his way over to the aisle. Gunther straightened at the sight of the boil on the man's cheek. It was the man from Aguardiente's bar! A strange heat flowed through Gunther's body. What was this pus bag doing here? And in a tuxedo?

Then down and to the right, the man with no teeth—his partner—also dressed to the nines, stood and walked toward the aisle. Both men glanced up into the box seats furtively as if to see whether their advances were detected. Gunther clutched Annalee's forearm, and she turned to him with a look of surprise.

"What?" she asked.

He grimaced and watched the men advance toward their box of seats.

"Get down," he ordered, pushing harshly on her upper arm.

"What?"

Annalee gasped when she noticed the advancing men. Gunther grabbed Annalee and shoved her down below the seats.

To cover her, Gunther stood. Both men appeared to see Gunther at the same moment. Their heads rose further as they focused on his face. Gunther could read their surprised expressions. They seemed to recognize the "buscadero" who snatched Rollendale from the bar just the day before. They locked eyes on him as Gunther's shifted back and forth. All three froze. Then all three slapped leather!

"Down!" Gunther hollered, as he yanked his Luger from its holster. The man with the boil yanked a revolver from his belt line, but he did not aim at Gunther! Instead, his barrel fanned off to Gunther's left. To the governor? The confused armed guards stood as if in slow motion, each flapping their jackets aside to reach their arms. Mr. Boil discharged a deliberate round into the section. The bullet struck Rosaletta Rollendale right in the throat. Her clavicle ruptured in a small red explosion, and she raised her hand to clutch her neck. She gasped, as much as her destroyed pipe could gurgle. The .45 slug blew out the back of her neck and hit a state guard seated behind her in the thigh, knocking him out of his chair as effectively as a strike in the knee with a two-by-four beam.

Gunther unloaded three rounds almost in a straight line into the Boil's head, chest, and belly, in that order as Rosaletta's head struck the seat before her. The boiled man tumbled back. His gun hand dropped slowly and fired each inch of the way down. Bullets tore into two seated spectators as they squirmed to escape. A barrage of state police fire rained down on the falling shooter, some of their rounds indiscriminately gouged through the fleeing bystanders as they vaulted over the seat backs and pitched themselves to the floor screaming.

At this point, the opera house crowd went mad. The performers dashed for exits stage left and right. Patrons shrieked. The orchestra members flattened to the floor amid a chorus of chaotic notes as instruments and music stands tumbled like dominoes.

Gunther spied a balding man crouched low. He moved forward. Gunther aimed but could not get a shot. Innocents jumped or leaped in his way. He jerked right, then left. The man with no teeth charged, head down, up the stairs. No one but Gunther noticed. Gunther moved toward the governor. From twenty paces away, he watched Peter Rollendale stand and turn toward the governor, who was still seated behind him in a state of frozen shock. Peter smiled. Peter pulled a small revolver from his vest pocket and aimed it at Batson. An alert state officer fired at Peter, hitting him twice in the shoulder and picked him right up off his feet, pitching him over the seat back. With this mule-kick impact, Rollendale's gun fired, missed the governor and struck Max Dozier in the shoulder. Max just sat there gasping, his great bulk absorbing the small round. Peter landed heavily on a couple hunched over in the seats below him, the man and woman there dashing aside and pleading for God's mercy. On his back, his legs draped over the seat back, Peter stared up at the beautiful curved mahogany wood ceiling above him. The chandelier came all the way from Sweden. He took up his pistol, put the barrel into his mouth and blew his own brains out.

Mr. No Teeth dove flat on the stairs. He crawled upward among the customers' pounding feet to escape. Gunther ran to the right aisle. The thug lost himself in a sea of legs, gowns, pants, shoes, and boots.

He spied a head weaving in and out between the boots! "Hey!" Gunther barked, pointing his pistol at the criminal.

The man froze, flat on the red carpet. Gunther spread his left arm out to stop the flow of escaping people. The man peered over his shoulder and saw the threat. He grimaced and shook his head.

"You don't have to," Gunther suggested in a plea for surrender.

Several state police officers scrambled to Gunther's side, their silver Navy Colts pointed at the man. Once surrounded by them, Gunther dropped his pistol hand to his side and stepped back shaking his head.

"Have to," the man replied. An officer cocked his pistol.

"Oooohhhhh, hell," No Teeth growled and rolled over, pulling his gun up. Three officers opened fire and bullets pelted the man. Eleven bullets flew until parts of the man's body seemed to melt into the carpet. Gunther sat back on a seat arm trying to comprehend all that had just happened, in less than fifteen seconds. He turned to see the astonished Annalee, still crouched in front of her seat in a puddle of satin gown, mouth agape, and staring back at him in horror. Below her, lay the body of Peter Rollendale, upside down and dead, a chunk gone from the top of his head. Rosaletta lay slumped over, and Roy Wise sobbed beside her, holding her head and rocking. Then, evening dress and all, Annalee jumped over the seat, stepped around the bloody Peter and worked her way over to the wounded Max.

"Summon an ambulance," one wounded officer pleaded, writhing in pain and clutching his thigh.

"Get the doc wagon!' echoed a voice at the exit doors.

Wounded patrons stumbled into the aisle, shrieking for help. Orchestra members began to slowly peer over their pit wall.

Gunther followed Annalee's path to Max, passing in front of Wise. "You…are very lucky to be alive," Gunther told the wide and wet-eyed Wise.

He climbed up a row to sit beside Annalee and Max.

"I am sorry Max," Gunther tucked his handkerchief in and around the shoulder wound. "I never saw this coming. These two men were drinking with Rollendale when I found him yesterday. No doubt he'd hired them to kill his wife and her boyfriend, while Peter himself would turn and shoot the governor. Then kill himself."

"Is…is Peter dead?" Max uttered, his eyelids fluttering.

"Deader than hell, Max."

"Is the governor okay?"

"I am in one piece Max!" Batson interjected, leaning into Max's view and tapping the side of his head affectionately, "Thanks to you! All of you." But the politician looked straight at Gunther.

Max just moaned, "Ohhhhh." He was beyond words. His premier

night was a bloody nightmare. "This opening night—this opening premiere—will go down in Fort Worth history as ah…ahhh…"

"A Buscadero Opera," Gunther said quietly, dabbing the wound with his handkerchief. Nobody else seemed to know what that meant. And now, there were two less men who did. It was a sign of the times.

3
Stringing Penelope's Bow

In the lobby, Gunther spoke with Fort Worth detective Leslie Green. He related the events of the past two days as Green listened intently. Then Gunther and Annalee stepped arm in arm from the front doors of the opera hall, weaving among the Fort Worth police, the ambulances, the traumatized patrons, and the annoying reporters from the *Star Telegram Newspaper.*

Police Chief Hallie "Snowtop" Griffin arrived in his new automobile, shouting for Detective Green across the plaza as the flashbulbs from Telegram cameras popped away. The governor emerged from the opera house and the newsmen flooded his way, seeking any comment about the night's events.

Gunther's plan was to sneak off for a much quieter walk back to Annalee's house, just a few streets away. He clutched her tightly against the events of the evening and whisked her from the scene. He wondered what she thought of him now, having witnessed him shoot down a man. She knew well his occupation, but actually seeing the ugly truth explode before her, the blood of it splashed on her evening dress...

"Major Jo!" came a familiar shout.

Gunther turned to see the Remedies' coach, pulled by Darlene, clopping down the brick street, with Jefe seated beside his cousin Quite-Some, the driver. Both emphatically waved at Gunther.

Gunther grabbed Darlene's halter rig as the wagon bounced to a halt at the curb, "Anything wrong?"

Jefe looked around, "What has happened here?"

"An attempt on the governor's life," Gunther answered.

Jefe leaned down to them for a whisper, "The president called us. He wants to talk with you."

"The president of what?" Gunther asked.

Jefe leaned even further down, "President Teddy! The president."

"What? What does he want?"

"He said he will telephone our office again at twelve midnight. I told him you were at the opera and I would have you back by then," Jefe answered.

Gunther contorted his mouth and turned to Annalee in frustration. Jefe spotted the blood on her dress.

"You okay? You hurt, Missy? You near the governor?"

Annalee shook her head, but her face still looked white.

Gunther guided her to the door of the coach and Jefe offered her his arm and helped her in.

Gunther opened his pocket watch and reported, "We've got half an hour."

"Johann! Johann!" two elderly men cried out. Gunther saw two reporters running their way. He quickly stepped aboard the wagon.

"Let's get out of here." He dropped, exhausted, into the leather seat next to Annalee. Then he continued the report to Jefe. Astonished, Jefe grilled them about every second of the night as they rode back to the Remedies office.

◇

More than a dozen telephone dispatchers connected with each other, call-by-call, city-by-city, all the way from the White House through Indianapolis, Cincinnati, Nashville, and on down, like a cable chain to get that small bell in the wooden box on the table of the Texas office of Remedies Unlimited to clang. Gunther lifted the bell-shaped receiver from the hooks and leaned into the voice piece.

"Mr. Gunther?" the last and local dispatcher asked, "We have a call from Washington, D.C. for you."

"Yes, please send it through." A series of clicks resounded.

"Hello? Hello?" Teddy bellowed.

"Mr. President!" Gunther said.

"Yes. How are you, Gunth? I hear you wrapped up that Yatook Taza mess quite well! Still got your scalp?"

"Yes, sir. I'm fine, sir. And you?"

"Well, Gunth…truth be known…I am having trouble seeing out of one eye. But other than that, I am fit as a fiddle. I expect to be hunting with you and the boys again next spring. I cannot wait to get out of here and back in the high country."

"Good, sir. And I will be there. How can I help you?" Gunther replied.

"Gunth, do you remember Colonel Vito Latissimo? You served with him in Oklahoma according to our record."

Gunther's head rocked back, as did his memory. "Yes, sir. I do."

"Well, he has gone missing," Teddy said.

"Missing?" Gunther spent at least fifteen minutes huddled over the phone. His other hand tightly cupped his left ear to enhance the poor volume. Then, he hung the phone back upon its metal arms and leaned back in his leather chair, staring at the floor with both hands resting on his kncccaps, palms up.

Annalee entered the office. Jefe carried a silver tray of brandy and glasses behind her and snapped Gunther from his trance.

"Teddy says good night to you, Jefe. Wishes you well. Said he couldn't wait for another stick fighting lesson when we go hunting. He wanted me to tell you that he and General Leonard Wood have been bashing the hell out of each other with Filipino sticks every chance they can."

"Good that he practice!" Jefe said quietly while pouring the brandy. "What does he want?"

"For me to help chase down a missing U.S. Army colonel."

"Missing? Where? Mountains? Forests? Or desert?" Jefe asked.

"Afghanistan."

"Aph-where-istan?"

"Very far away, Jefe. North of India. Near Russia. East of China actually. British India."

"Ooooooh," Jefe howled, as he handed Gunther a glass.

"Well," said Annalee, "the president must really need your help!"

Annalee had recovered some of her color. She understood the nature of Gunther's travels. If she resented his absences she carefully kept her feelings to herself.

Gunther sipped the brandy and ran his hand over his head and through his long blond hair.

"Presidents are not supposed to need my help. This is not a good thing. This really means trouble. Presidents will eat you up… and spit you out." Gunther stared at the floor, more as a reminder to himself than a commentary for Annalee.

Then he swallowed the whole shot of hot brandy, enjoyed its smoky flavor and even the slight burn as it went down. "The first thing Roosevelt himself ordered me to do was to belly crawl up a hill in Cuba, toward a Spanish Gatling gun. I lost four good friends in my unit. I have a scar from a bullet on the back of my left calf. Apparently, I wasn't crawling low enough." He set his glass on the desk and leaned back in his chair and crossed his arms. "That enemy bullet, by the way?" he continued, "was bought from a Michigan gun dealer."

Annalee's eyes widened. "Complicated."

"Always," he answered. "And, everything Teddy has asked me to do since has been complicated and leaves me with a scar."

"You go?" Jefe asked.

"First, I'll travel to Washington, to the War Department. They'll brief me. Then and there, I will decide whether to go or not, to Af-where-is-stan."

"I go too?" Jefe asked.

"No. If I do go, it will be for a long time. Six months at the very least? Maybe more." He cast a sad look at Annalee, and then to Jefe, "I will need you here to work cases and run the outfit."

"Gunther?" Annalee said. "So soon? You only just got back? I was looking forward to some time together."

"I know, so was I. But when the president calls…"

"You must listen," Jefe finished.

Gunther shrugged his shoulders in defeat.

Annalee took the glasses, placed them on the tray, and left the room—her exit speaking louder than words.

Gunther watched her retreating back and sighed.

"When will you leave?" Jefe asked.

"Afternoon train tomorrow," Gunther replied.

"They pay for train ticket? Hotel? How much they pay you?" Jefe asked directly. After all, he was the business manager and Supreme Secretariat General of Remedies Unlimited.

"Yes, they will pay for the ticket and hotel, but the overall fee? That mi amigo, will be the key question I will ask in Washington. I tell you right now it is going to cost them dearly to hire me." He pounded his index finger on the table to make a point.

"Tomorrow morning," Gunther continued, "the president's aide will call us with the train details. Can you collect the information and come get me at the hotel as early as possible? I need to pack my full travel kit. Everything. If I take the job? I will go from D.C. straight to India." He knew this would be painful news for Annalee receive. It was painful for him to say.

"Oh sure. Sure," Jefe said.

There came a knock on the front door. Jefe answered. It was Detective Green and a partner with more questions. The final victim of the night would be his last hours with Annalee.

◇

One-thirty A.M. and holding hands, Gunther and Annalee strolled down her home street. Quite-Some slowly walked Darlene, pulling the coach some forty feet behind them for privacy. The night air was brisk and some condensation trailed each of their words.

"Helluva night," Gunther mumbled. "Are you sure you are all right?"

"I'm an old farm girl, remember? We killed something every day to eat it," she said in her own melodious way. But, then she added, "Truly though, I am not completely all right, Johann. It is both amazing and exciting that the president of the United States

Page 45

calls you for help. I am more than impressed."

"It's not that simple, Anna," Gunther interrupted. "I no doubt will be a pawn in some game of his."

"Tell him no," she said matter-of-factly.

"I can't. He is the president of the United States. He calls? You go."

"That is what's good about you, Johann, you have a sense of duty," she added. They walked silently for a few seconds. She stopped, turned to him, and continued, "If I were to stay with you—as your wife. Become your wife. What would I become exactly? A military wife? A policeman's wife? A Pinkerton's wife? A…a…gunfighter's wife?"

He had no quick answer for her frank question. He was instead taken aback for a second by her beautiful brown eyes, piercing into him for a crucial answer. They were—she was—too powerful for him to utter a word of any sense. They had danced and flirted around the word marriage a dozen times. Wife! She said it so frankly this time. This was no dance. This burned down to the very wick of life.

"If I knew which one," she broke the hypnotic trance, turning away to continue their walk. "I could make sensible plans. I could justify to myself, say…waiting for an Army soldier. A military wife understands that her husband would be gone for months at a time. A year. Years, maybe. I know this. I understand this. A good woman knows these circumstances, and with love and commitment, she survives." She chopped the air with a gloved hand to emphasize each point. "I know what police and marshal spouses face. Of course, a lady would be wrong to be the wife of a gunman. I couldn't imagine…"

"I am not any of those things, Anna. I assume that when such time comes, I will not be doing any of those things. I hope to have enough money saved, a really substantial amount, to quit it all someday," he said.

"Some day? Quit it all? Can you? Can you give all that up? You so seem to thrive on it."

"Oh I don't like it that much, Anna! I hate it most of the time. I just seem to…do it really well."

"Oh…I know you do. I saw you tonight. You saved a lot of lives tonight. You saved the governor of Texas! He needed you. The police need you. The president needs you."

He guessed she was about to say that she needed him, too. But she didn't. He said, "I saved some, yes. But not those poor people who were shot tonight just watching an opera. Just regular people, just sitting there, their only crime being too close to killers."

"Not like in the books, is it?" She said. "Not like in the dime novels and books."

"Nope. Not at all," he mumbled. He had a sudden flash of Rollendale's head blown open. A brain that once contained the mechanics of architecture, his skill to dream, to conceive and bring about a hall of music and creativity, the essence of which exploded into pieces of gray matter and bone fragments coating the back of a chair seat.

"And the hero saves them all," she added. "In the books, the hero has his woman and together they live happily ever after. Ulysses comes home, unstrings his hunter's bow, and lives with Penelope happily ever after."

They embraced and lingered in their kiss on the sidewalk in front of her house. Without another word, her hand drifted slowly from his as she walked away to the front porch. The coach rolled nearby. Gunther remained on the cobblestones, watching her go inside and shut the door softly. The last thing he saw of Anna was her gloved, tapered fingers. Then he climbed aboard his coach.

The Filipino rolled the reins in a small delicate wave over Darlene's rump. This was the night. A night right before a global departure, when a star-crossed man should propose marriage. But the moment drifted off into the air like the condensation from their breath, their words, and their unsaid thoughts.

Gunther did not feel sad. He could find more pain in *The Odyssey*. It was truly a heartstring not a bowstring that hooked Penelope's bow, and for Annalee this night, this man, it shall remain undone.

Gunther rode off into the very cold night with one last wave from the figure of Annalee Gish through the frosted window in her doorway.

4

The Last Train to Capitol Hill

At 11 a.m. Jefe appeared at Gunther's hotel suite with a Haversack.

"You will meet a Sergeant Major Kelly Homestead at the Washington, D.C. train station in two days," Jefe advised and handed him a handwritten record of the phone call. He picked an apple off the breakfast tray by the couch and gnawed out a chunk while inspecting Gunther's progress. Then, they both started packing Gunther's two large travel trunks.

"Missy Annalee?" Jefe asked while organizing jackets and pants into the steamers. "She gonna' miss you somehow?"

"Well, Jefe. It is hard on a very respectable lady to hog tie herself to a rake like me."

"Humph! Rake. Yeah," Jefe mumbled. He pulled a round stick from the duffle bag. "You take this stick with you. I bet you the mountain people up there fight with sticks, too. You need a good stick buddy!" Jefe tapped the kamagong weapon three times on Gunther's shoulder. Gunther turned, took the stick, and tossed it into the trunk beside his .45 pistol and Bowie knife. His shotgun and Mauser rifle were broken down in their respective carrying kits.

"My wife made this beef jerky. She said this is only for you. A secret. She said to carry it in your stinky armpit, where no one wants to look. When everyone else is starving to death in the mountains, you sneak this jerky out and only you eat it. Hide it!" He threw the wrapped package into the trunk.

"And Isabella has a gift for you." He threw a book from his

Page 48

youngest daughter into the trunk. Gunther reached in and picked it up. He thumbed through it.

"Jefe, this is in Arabic…I think. I can't read this."

"It is the Koran. It maybe is not for reading. It may be for good luck? If you have a big question? You lie down and put the Koran on your heart. Best way to think. You know the big eyes of Allah may be watching. Anyway, Isabella wants you to have it. You take it or break her heart."

Gunther shook his head and dropped the book in the trunk. "You know I could turn this job down and be back by the weekend."

"Big talk, Mister Ulysses! You are a crazy man, and you like to go to crazy places."

"Ha!" Gunther laughed at the coincidence. "You know the topic of Mister Ulysses came up last night with Annalee."

"She nice girl, but you need to marry Cleopatra or maybe the president's daughter, Alice. You like a special girl. Lots of shine. I know you."

"Yeah, well, 'Princess' Alice just got married in the White House. She is quite a pistol all right. She married a congressman from Ohio."

"You stay away from her! We can't make any scandals, bad for business," Jefe warned, as he inspected the weapons cache. "You got…your Mauser rifle. Your Winchester shotgun. Your gun belt. Your Bowie knife. Your .45 Browning semiauto. Your .45 Colt revolver. Your Filipino stick. You got bullets. You got magazines. You got German Luger?"

"Right here," Gunther said, tapping his left chest, where the pistol resided in a shoulder holster. The two finished packing, and Gunther rang the bellboy on the room phone. He took one last look around. When the bellboy arrived with a handcart, the three hauled and balanced the two trunks full of clothing and gear down the stairs. The new elevator was under construction. Gunther hoped it would be up and running upon his return and the mess and noise gone. He stopped at the lobby desk and reported that he would be gone for an indeterminate amount of time. The bill would be paid the usual way during his occasional absences, by Jefe.

Gunther left Dunston's Hotel and climbed aboard the coach as Quite Some and Jefe tied off the last straps securing the luggage. They were off to the train station, but they made one quick stop on Throckmorton Street—at Delahorne's Book Emporium.

Gunther dashed in and scanned the history book titles, picking up a British military tome on the campaigns of India. A quick scan revealed it included battles, maps, and information on Pakistan and Afghanistan. It was the only book on the subject in the whole store.

"Going somewhere, Mr. Gunther?" Delahorne asked as Gunther approached the counter. The owner peered out the framed window at the trunk-laden coach waiting outside.

"Going here," he said, tapping the cover of the book.

"Oh, may the Lord be with, Mr. Gunther. You may as well be going to the moon, sir!"

"Yeah," Gunther reached for his wallet.

"Speaking of the moon!" Delahorne declared spontaneously, "or thereabouts…we just got this new book in. Very popular book in Europe and the East Coast." He handed Gunther a volume from the front window display to his left.

"*War of the Worlds,* by H.G. Wells," Gunther read the title out loud. "I've heard of this." A huge metallic animal of some sort, a spider perhaps, stood tall on the cover. It fired a red flame upon the buildings of London. "I'll take it, too," he said. "Anything but Homer."

Tickets bought, trunks aboard the train by a rail man, Gunther shook Jefe's hand, made a tough face, and rolled a light fisted punch across Jefe's jaw.

"Good-bye with you! You will do all your daily exercises!" Jefe declared. Gunther smiled, nodded, and turned for the train.

"Send telegrams," the Filipino shouted as Gunther boarded the last train of the day for the nation's capital. "May Allah be with you, mi amigo."

The train lurched from the station. Gunther found his private room, flipped off his hat, propped his feet up on the empty seat across from him, and opened his briefcase. He extracted the two new books, keeping the military one on his lap. As in the book-store, it cracked open like the sound of small breaking twigs. A red ribbon was stitched into the lining as a bookmark. It even smelled good.

"Ahhh, those Brits sure know how to make a book," Gunther said to no one. But his mood changed quickly as he read the opening paragraph.

"In this wretched land of rock and sand and jagged stone, of bitter cold, dizzying mountain heights, and isolation, our intrepid troops were faced with marauding, cut-throat tribesmen and a harsh, corrupt government, all…."

Gunther sighed. He kicked off his snakeskin boots and rapped on his door window to catch the attention of a porter in the hall.

"Hey porter! Porter!" he yelled.

"Yes, sir?" the man answered, opening the door.

"Whiskey… a bottle that is. Something good."

"Yes, sir," and off he went.

Gunther leaned back and through the window watched the landscape of his adopted hometown, Fort Worth, evolve by. It seemed he saw construction everywhere. Newly tarred roads, buildings, houses. Street poles webbing electricity and phones everywhere. Sections of water pipes shoved into huge ditches. Cranes, some not unlike the creatures on the front of H.G. Wells' book, hoisted and moved iron beams and materials skyward. Within ten minutes he was in the flat, virgin countryside. Cowboys herded cattle on horseback, and farmers plowed their crops.

"Whiskey, sir," the porter said while sliding open the door, balancing a tray with a bottle, a thick, crystal glass, and an ice bucket. He poured Gunther a drink. Gunther passed the man some coins as a tip and spooned two cubes into the glass.

He looked at the books on the table. "Cutthroats or monsters?" he pondered aloud. Then he selected the British military tome. He reopened the book and took a good, stiff drink and braced himself for the next depressing page about the alien, hellish lands for which he was bound.

5
Uncooked Biscuits

"Wilson Station!" The car agent bellowed over the blasting steam and screeching iron. Two porters stood ready to haul Gunther's luggage off the train. Gunther buttoned his brown leather jacket in preparation for the February weather of the nation's capital. It had snowed a foot, and the train station was only partially enclosed. The last sudden gasp of the engine lurched nearly everyone off his or her feet.

The car doors opened, and a fleet of men, some thirty of them, dressed in red velvet suits scurried to the doors of the cars with small wooden step contraptions to bridge the gap from the last train step to the ramp. Gunther was reminded of a dance hall chorus line.

With the help of porters, Gunther established himself near a newspaper stand, away from what seemed to be hundreds of travelers. He sat on a trunk and stood watch over his gear, waiting for a certain Sergeant Major Homestead to appear.

"Major Gunther!" Came a call, and he turned toward the voice. A tall, somewhat overweight man in his late fifties, in a brown United States Army uniform, a flat trooper hat, and large moustache bounded toward him, followed by two soldiers less than half his age.

"I am no longer a major," Gunther said, returning the smile.

"What then should I call you, sir?"

"Oh, Gunth. Gunther. Johann. They make my head turn," Gunther answered.

"Sergeant Major Kelly Homestead," he announced. They shook

hands and the man pumped a hearty handshake accompanied by a genuine smile. "This yer kit?"

"That's it," Gunther said.

"Corporals, get busy," Homestead ordered, and the young men grabbed the trunks and headed for an exit.

"I must warn you, about our transport. The damn thing is not fully enclosed. And it is colder than a well digger's ass out there."

So it was—and it was as busy as it was frigid. Washington, D.C. was ten times the size, congestion, and din of Fort Worth. The carriage, clearly marked "United States Army" and steered by one of the corporals, swayed around narrow streets, challenged the very lives of pedestrians, wrestled with other coaches, even automobiles, and disregarded corner traffic cops posted inside yellow stands, waving their hands and blasting whistles like madmen. None of this interested Homestead at all, but Gunther found it entertaining.

"West Point are ya' sir?" Homestead asked.

"Yup."

"Ahhh, I have to admire a soul from the Point. Lots of book learnin,' lots of harassment and torture. Makes a lot of tough eggs," Homestead said.

"And a lot of pricks," Gunther added, and the sergeant major nodded his agreement. Gunther could already tell Kelly Homestead could smarm his way around the most obnoxious officer, look respectful, do his job, and then piss in the officer's empty boot at night for revenge.

"How long have you been in, Sergeant Major?" Gunther asked.

"Twenty-nine long years."

"Where have you been?" Gunther asked.

"All over stateside. Infantry. Cavalry. Indian fighting and wasting time painting rocks and polishing cannon balls. Then, like you, the Philippines for that little dandy war party."

"You know where I've been?' Gunther asked, surprised.

"Know where ya' been and where ya' going," Homestead said with a smirk, looking at the view, then he turned to Gunther and smiled, "cause I'm a going with ya'!"

"You are? And why have they selected you for this trip?" he asked.

"I, like yourself, have served with this uncooked biscuit—Colonel Vito Latissimo. I was his personal aide-de-camp in New Orleans for one whole year," Homestead said. "And, it was a long year. The boy is crazy. You know in New Orleans he studied and practiced Caribbean Voodoo!" He leaned over to Gunther to make the point. "One night he shot a Cajun hooker in the ass with a dart from a blowgun! Damn near went to prison. He was running up and down the Gulf of Mexico in steamships all the time. Be gone for days. Come back with what he called "business deal" shipments—wagons full of clothes and furniture. But, he always had a hoax going to make money. He came by it honestly! He was with the Black Hand, I think."

"The Black Hand," Gunther repeated, but, as a former New Yorker, Gunther knew well of the Black Hand and the crime gangs operating on the northeast coast.

"Yes, sir, the Italian criminal families. Sicily. Latissimo always had a few Italian soldiers close to him," Homestead explained.

"Is Latissimo from New York?" Gunther asked.

"Boston." Kelly said.

"The son of a bitch wasn't a bad officer! He did a good job as a commander. He also graduated West Point!" Gunther said. "And there are a few stories about him at the Point too. But, he graduated with honors."

"Where are you from anyway?" Homestead asked.

"Texas, more or less. Mostly. I was born in Germany, but grew up in New York City," Gunther answered. "Moved to Oklahoma and then to Texas.

"Ahhh. That explains it. You have three accents fucking each other when you talk."

Both men broke out in laughter. So too did the one corporal in the coach until the sergeant major shut him down with a stern look.

They pulled up in front of the War Department's Officers Quarters, a large stone and marble building not far from the White House. Gunther would spend the night here. The men hefted the trunks to the bellboy's waiting arms. Gunther and Homestead dismounted and shook hands.

"I don't know Latissimo that well. Not as well as you," Gunther said. "You could certainly identify him better than me. I'm not sure why I'm here, or if I'm even going along on this hunt. It depends on how tomorrow's meeting goes. But, either way, this blowgun and the dart-in-the-ass story? You'll have to tell me more, sergeant major."

"It's a lulu! I will be here, and in this miserable, half-open, cold coach at 9 A.M. for you. Dress warm. It'll snow tonight. We'll have us a sit-up with the bigwigs at 10 A.M. And then you can decide if yer in or if yer out! Dinner tomorrow night, I'll tell ya' all about the blowgun and French/Cajun ass," Homestead said with a grin.

Neither Gunther nor Homestead spotted the three swarthy men with black hair and long dark coats watching them, huddled together in the cold across the snowy avenue.

6
Sharing Moses

Morning rose with the predicted hard frost and two feet of snow, confounding D.C. traffic. On the coach ride to the War Department, Gunther winced in empathy with each slip and skid of the two Army horses pulling their wagon. At one point, traffic came to standstill, with little hope for progress.

"We're gonna be late!" Homestead moaned, trying to spy down the street at the lines of stationery coaches, wagons, and automobiles, whose shrill horns were making the horses shy and people dodge to avoid being trampled.

Gunther asked, "Sergeant Major, when was the last time you took a little bareback horse ride?"

"Oh, hell, must be…" then he got the idea. "Are you suggesting we do so, sir?" he asked with a smile.

"I suggest we do so. Wouldn't want to be late." He slipped a leg over the side of the coach and dropped into the snow.

"You are dressed for the part, cowboy," Homestead commented on Gunther's wardrobe of brown duster jacket, white hat, scarf, the ubiquitous Western gun belt, and boots. "Boys," he told the two corporals in the driver's bench up front, "unhook these horses."

They followed orders and with their fingers in the bridle rings of the halters, led the two horses to the sidewalk, where Gunther and Homestead waited.

"What'll we do with the wagon, Sergeant Major?" one asked.

"Well ya silly fucker, what ya think you'll do? You park that crate, walk to the War Department, collect these horses, get 'em back here…sweet Jesus! Do I have to tell you everything?" Homestead bellowed.

"No, Sergeant Major," the men said in chorus.

Gunther and Homestead jumped on the backs of the old stable horses, grabbed some mane, and heel-tapped the beasts onward.

"You lead the way," Gunther said. "I'm lost in this jungle."

They walked in, out, and around the snarled traffic, on down the avenue, even going for stretches on the sidewalks. Gunther took a few good-natured taunts from the passengers in their cars, wagons, and trolleys.

"Get lost, cowboy?"

"Hey! The rodeo left town last week, Buffalo!"

"You got a license for that thing, buddy?"

Gunther just smiled and tipped his hat.

"Yeah, well, we're moving and you're not!" Homestead pointed out to more than a few of them and received blaring honks in reply.

Once at the Army stables headquarters, Kelly and Gunther slipped off their animals and passed them to very surprised stable hands. Then they hustled into the War Department lobby. With Homestead in the lead, they jogged through the marble hallways and straight into the Andrew Jackson Meeting Chamber. It was an enormous room where at least fifty or more people congregated making loud conversation. An aide guided Gunther and Homestead to seats at a large wooden table in the center of the room. Gunther admired the huge, stately chamber as he slipped off his jacket and hooked his hat over the large ornamental knob on his seat back.

Apparently, they were waiting on him to arrive, because the group also took their seats. Several other men sat at this main table, but most settled into rows of chairs lined up to their left. A mature, attractive woman with black hair sat against the far wall, dressed in the latest fashions Gunther had recently seen while in San Francisco. A small officer with mutton-chop sideburns stood across the table and positioned himself before a giant map of Europe and Central Asia, breaking Gunther's curious gaze on the lady.

"Hello everyone, my name is Captain James Marigold, Headquarters Company," he addressed the group. "And I work under the direction of the White House and the Army Chief of Staff. We have asked you here today for this mission briefing. But first, let me take care of the most important business. The mess hall is in the basement, Room 233B and breakfast will continue until eleven hundred hours. We have eighty-five minutes to get this damn thing done!"

The men laughed and commented with agreement on the importance of that piece of intelligence.

A smiling Marigold continued, "We are here for a mission, we have come to call Operation Passport." He strolled the length of the table. "I will introduce your fellow first-line personnel of importance in this operation. You will take it upon yourself to meet their seconds later."

He began with a civilian seated not at the table but by a window under a six-foot tall oil painting of Andrew Jackson. "This is the good Reverend Silas Verne, from Georgia. Reverend Verne has recently returned from a seven-year pilgrimage to save the poor lost souls of Afghanistan on behalf of the Southern Baptist Union. He is adept at the local language, the mountain passes, trails, and the natives and their customs."

"Of Georgia?" a soldier in the peanut gallery called out. The room full of people erupted in laughter. Even Marigold held back a burst. Gunther had to take a look at this man with so bold a sense of humor as to disrupt such a meeting. His smile evaporated. The soldiers seated behind him were all about fifty years old or more. One man looked to be sixty! Some were as fat as they were old.

A young man with lieutenant bars on his collar bolted to attention and declared, "Silence!" The men contained their laughter, diminishing the rabble down to a few moans and foot shuffling.

"Thank you Lieutenant Kerry," Marigold said. "As I mentioned, the good Reverend Silas Verne."

Gunther eyed this man of God, who dressed entirely in black. He too was in his fifties, dried, wrinkled, and wispy thin. His lanky arms and legs sprouted from the chair like those of a praying mantis. He smiled shyly at the group. Abe Lincoln with red hair. Gunther thought.

"Captain Lewis Boston," Marigold pointed a finger at the officer at the table. "Captain Boston will lead the American contingent of three hundred Calvary troops. He is a veteran, like so many of you here today, of various skirmishes on our frontiers."

In his brown and impeccable uniform, the 30-something-year-old commander remained still as a statue in his seat, his bald head and face shaved within a fraction of massive blood loss, Gunther could see that stubble, or any other infringement of rules, was simply not an option for his troop.

Marigold pointed at Kelly, "Sergeant Major Kelly Homestead, United States Army. He has been assigned to this mission as the top kick NCO." To which Kelly smiled, nodded, and waved a hand at everyone. It was apparent to Gunther that several of the men already knew the amiable NCO by the return shouts of approval and loud whistles.

"The happy fifty NCOs seated to the left are seasoned cavalry-man, all with a special skill," Marigold said. "Each one has been in combat, and each one has served as a camel-riding instructor in that grand U.S. Army experiment, incorporating the humped, ship-of-the-desert beast into our forces. And as we all know…the camel won that one!"

The men laughed, with permission this time, since a commander had made a joke.

"These sergeants will supervise two hundred fifty cavalrymen." Then Marigold pointed out the young officer. "That is Lieutenant Kerry, company XO, seated on the end. He has already made his presence known."

The young man stood again and declared, "Lieutenant Jack Kerry, West Point 1905, from the state of Florida." The man sat down. Gunther quietly sighed. All these old saddle tramps being led by a Dixie greenhorn, but his own introduction recalled his attention back to the table.

"And, this is former Army Major Johann Gunther, West Point graduate, class of 1896, former Oklahoma lawman, former Rough Rider under the command of our President Roosevelt. He is here as a consultant and advisor. He is a very experienced problem solver and comes with the very…highest…recommendations."

There was no doubt in the room those highest endorsements came from Teddy the Great Bear himself. Gunther nodded to them and saluted with a short turn of his right hand. He could feel their gazes taking in every aspect of his appearance. He could tell they found him a mysterious consultant with his big Stetson hooked on his seat, his long blond hair brushed straight back like George Custer almost touching his shoulders, his bolo necktie and Western cut suit, and that Texican gun belt!

Marigold moved up the table with his introductions. "Captain Milton Perryweather of Her Majesty's British Army. Infantry. The captain will bring two hundred of his British soldiers, and a promise of some five hundred more Indian sepoys! He is a decorated veteran of several skirmishes and wars on the Afghan frontier. Captain Perryweather and Captain Boston will share overall command of this mission."

Gunther sized up this peacock. He didn't look much like the command-sharing type. He sat with an indignant sneer, dressed in a red velvet tunic with a hat as tall as his head propped on the table. From where Gunther sat, he spied a long sword with an elaborate European handle and hilt that hung from the Brit's belt. His long stark face, framed in curly black hair, had a scar that ran up from his neck over one eye. He held an expression of elite arrogance. Boston and Perryweather did not exchange glances. Boston only rotated one brown leather glove over and over in his hand and stared at the table.

"And this is William Harrigan. He is a reporter with the *World Geographic Society Magazine*. He and his team will go along to chronicle this enterprise in both word and photograph."

Gunther saw a bearded man in his forties in a three-piece wool suit stand and smile. He said to all, "Please just ignore me and my partner, as we wish only to bring photographs back from this wild, unexplored area for our society and magazine." He returned to his seat. Where was his partner, Gunther wondered? Then he saw in the corner a black man in a three-piece suit, seated by a suitcase made for cameras and related gear. A camera stood at the ready on an open tripod.

Captain Marigold continued, "We are all here because of…horses. Giant horses. Exceptional horses." He let that remark float through the room. "In summary, gentleman…and lady—" He gestured to the raven-haired woman—still no introduction—and continued, "—three years ago Colonel Vito Latissimo, in conjunction with a British Colonel Sean Glow, led a contingent of U.S. and British troops deep into Afghanistan in search of a breed of extremely powerful horses, legendary in size and strength, in hopes that our armies might capture and breed them for all our military purposes. Two years ago, both colonels and all of their men…disappeared. I have asked Captain Perryweather to brief you on this history."

The English Commander stood, nodded, and replaced Marigold at the table. Marigold took a seat.

"We are off to Afghanistan," Perryweather began as he drew his sword and pointed with it on the map. "As you see here, Russia runs across the top of it. Persia to the west. China and Pakistan to the east. British India to the south. We go there to solve a mystery." He slammed the sword dramatically back into its sheath as his left hand steadied the sheath. Only Gunther was close enough to see that this ostentatious display of cutlery had cut a small gash on the web of Perryweather's left hand. Perryweather hid his hand behind him and continued.

"One of the great mysteries of recent years," Perryweather began, "is the disappearance of our Colonel Glow and your Colonel Latissimo. In 1903, they left on a grand expedition to Central Asia, together with a small band of British and American soldiers, not at all unlike the group we have here. Their quest, as Captain Marigold explained, was a quest for these magnificent horses.

"But first, I must take you back eighty years. You see…since the 1820s, members of the British government have been…seduced…with the legend of a breed of horses capable of magnificent strength and size to rival no other. These horses were believed to run wild in the wilderness beyond the Hindu Kish, still a very unexplored, unmapped and quite savage area. They believed these horses could be captured, tamed, trained, and even crossbred into our stocks. Used in the cavalry, transportation of artillery…the military uses for such powerful creatures are numerous.

"The first British expedition sent in search of these horses was launched in 1820. The expedition failed. Its members were believed killed within a year by slave traders and murderers of the northwest frontier beyond the Khyber Pass. It is true that one of the members—a William Moorland—was also a British spy, working in the confidences of several import/export businesses. We suspect Moorland may have been murdered by agents of the Russian government."

Perryweather tapped Russia on the map—with his non-bleeding hand. "The Russians, you see, want all of Central Asia in the empire and they wish to thwart any European contact whatsoever. They have their Cossack hearts set on establishing a strategic railway system throughout the region. They want seaports to the south. In my country, we have called the whole bloody thing the Great Game. Who wins Afghanistan?

"In 1900, the respected journal called *Science* published the works of Dr. Fairfield Osborn, who claimed that Central Asia is the origin point for most present-day mammals. Such a horse may not have migrated out and still could be unique to that region. Rumors of sightings of these animals grew. By 1902, your President Roosevelt became deeply intrigued.

"In 1903, Colonel Glow, Colonel Latissimo, and their men took off through the Khyber Pass to find these horses. But they also…" he hesitated, "meant to spy, …gentlemen. Their mission was twofold. Not unlike Moorland eighty years earlier, they meant to spy on the Russians and Chinese. Document their presence, if any. Discover trade routes. Learn who among the tribes were taking influence and where. And, also to find these legendary horses, if at all possible. If they were questioned or stopped, they would claim they were on a simple horse-hunting expedition. Indeed, I do put it to you that the Americans were far more interested in finding these horses. The British? Well, they were more interested in the spying."

Perryweather shoved his cut hand into his pocket. "We have been in countless small wars and skirmishes with the religious madmen and tribes in that godforsaken country. To make matters worse? Gunrunning! In the last year and a half, there's been a steady increase in the quality and quantity of the tribesmen's firearms. They've always exhibited expertise in stealing rifles from our most fortified garrisons and rifle factories, but a whole new supply of rifles of all types—even a large cache of Martinis discarded by the Australians and New Zealand forces have reached the frontier. Many believe these weapons have been smuggled in by the Russians to do battle with my country. It seems the deeper we penetrate into the Centrals, the more madmen and tribes we find. They are better armed than ever before."

Perryweather walked back to his chair. "Because of this, Lord Kitchener himself, the commander-in-chief of India, has granted us a small escort from the ninth Bengal Lancers and some units of the second Punjab Infantry. In all, tabulating the Americans, the British, and Indians, we should have a contingent of some one thousand men. Such is important for safe passage that we look large enough to intimidate predatory, indigenous warlords." With a flourish of coattails, Perryweather sat.

"Thank you, Captain," Marigold said.

Gunther was amused that as soon as Marigold took the attention of the group, Perryweather drew a white handkerchief from a breast pocket and fumbled with his cut hand under the table. Perryweather looked up and noted that Gunther was privy to this secret medical attention.

"The expedition of Glow and Latissimo vanished by 1905," Marigold continued. "We've heard reports of vicious murders. Another report had Glow as a slave to a sheik. Another had our colonel alive and the leader of a wild gang of religious zealots. Our expedition, this Operation Passport, is to solve the mystery of their whereabouts and bring closure to their assignment."

One thousand men to bring back two? Gunther thought. Either they were related to Teddy, or something else was afoot.

"And if we find them horses, bring them back to stud!" Kelly

Homestead declared. This broke the solemnity of the room, and most of the men laughed. Marigold smiled and shook his head. Perryweather sneered at the frivolity.

Boston flipped his glove again, no longer able to stay quiet, "All this talk of horses!" He stood and partially faced the troops. The room fell into a hush. "As we speak, gentlemen, the Department of the Army is designing mechanical horses! In five years the cavalry will be driving armored automobiles to battle. Mechanized wagons with canons screwed on the top. Then we will be shooting down our precious horses, giant, magic, or otherwise, to save the feed bill!"

The room remained silent, as not a troop among them was without a love for their horse. Nor could anyone argue against his disgusting prediction. Boston sat.

Marigold broke the silence. "Be that as it may, we must still recover the colonel and our men, if possible, and the British troops. And there will always be a need for the horse in our Army!"

He pointed to the woman across the room, "Gentlemen, this is Mrs. Lydia Latissimo, the colonel's wife. She has been a tortured soul now for years…" She lowered her eyes as all turned to her. Marigold continued, "…wondering and waiting for any word on her beloved, missing husband. She has requested attendance on this search and was granted permission—"

"Preposterous," mumbled Captain Perryweather, just loud enough for Gunther and the closest men at the table to hear.

"—from the White House," Marigold added emphatically with a cold glance at the Brit. "Mrs. Latissimo is an accomplished equestrian and outdoorswoman of some regard and is well prepared for the trip."

Gunther, and probably every other man in the room, had a personal definition of her eventual involvement on this trip.

"Finally, I have asked Reverend Verne to inform you of a brief history of the country you shall be exploring," Marigold gestured to the man. Verne stood slowly, cleared his throat, and unfolded a piece of yellow paper.

"Good day, all," the Reverend Verne said with a timid smile and a heavy Southern accent." I have lived in Afghanistan. This country is a landlocked nation, between many nations, as Captain Perryweather has described…"

"Could ya' speak up, sir?" bellowed a voice from the rear.

"And therefore serves a crossroads for commerce should the good peoples of the world ever get to pass through it safely. Through the centuries, Persians, Greeks, Arabs, Mongols, and many others have invaded. Alexander the Great. Genghis Khan." He smiled again. "So many. And, many settlers have remained, creating the diverse tribes of today. It is a warlike stock. They speak many languages. I speak a few of these.

"Afghanistan is covered with mountain ranges and deserts. Many of the peaks are insurmountable. Some stick straight up out of the ground miles high. At their base are hundreds of tons of loose rocks for miles that you can't even walk over without getting a sprained ankle. A horse would fall crippled in a moment. There are also fertile plains hundreds of miles in the north. Rich farmland. In and around the mountains you will find lush forest as thick as jungles. We are bound to the northwest of this great plain. We will get there by traveling through the Khyber Pass."

Verne stepped up to the map and pointed the location. "I …I lost my daughter there. The pass has many gangs setting up tolls or robbing or raping. I set up a place of worship farther northeast… and I lost my wife there."

Gunther stared at the reverend, this Ichabod Crane–looking character with a shock of red and gray hair, trying to perceive something beyond that passive demeanor and whispering voice. Lost his daughter? Lost his wife? Going back? Why?

Verne continued, "Ah…ah…I have seen God's animals and some birds the likes of which I have never seen before in Afghanistan. It is not impossible that on God's green earth there exists such a horse. I have not yet seen such horses. Mostly," Verne said with a smile, "many of the regular people there are nice, friendly people. But tribal and ethnic loyalties will always come first. They will worry if you are hungry at night and feed you their last crumb, but they will slaughter you in the morning if a leader decides it.

"They live by a code of honor they call the Pakhtunwali. This code imposes three important obligations, which an Afghan must observe or face lasting dishonor and ostracism. Fugitives must be offered safety and protection. Hospitality must be offered at all times, even to a deadly foe. Any insult, whether it be real, imagined, or by default, either to an individual, his family, or clan, must be avenged no matter how long it takes. Any quarrel about zar, zan, or zamin—gold, women or land—and a war will ensue until sufficient blood has been spilled to expunge the insult."

These were fighting words that grasped the attention of Gunther and every man in the room.

Verne continued, "I have witnessed many atrocities not just by the criminal elements, but by the Muslim fanatics who feel that Allah is their God and all non-Muslims are infidels. This alone is your death sentence. Certainly Christians. We do share Abraham, Ishmael and Moses. But they do not believe as Christians do. No other place on Earth needs more of God's work than there." He blinked his eyes several times, smiled at the men, and at Marigold. Then he sat down in his chair with an insecure pumping motion.

"Now!" Marigold ordered. "Everyone! Everyone line up over there. Mr. Harrigan is going to take a photograph."

Harrigan and his partner busied themselves extending the legs on cameras, lights, and reflectors. Meanwhile, Marigold's aides positioned the key personnel, Captain Perryweather, the Brit and Captain Boston, the American in the center. Kelly Homestead and Lieutenant Kerry stood beside Boston. They guided Gunther to the side of Lieutenant Kerry and stood the Reverend Silas Verne beside Perryweather. The rest of the men shuffled into three lines behind them, with the back line standing on chairs. Lastly, an aide took the forearm of Mrs. Latissimo and escorted her to the very center between Perryweather and Boston. Her plumed hat towered, but the men behind never bothered to let their faces be seen.

Gunther had been framed in several of these group photos. Sometimes more than half the people in them ended up framed in a casket. With the sound of this expedition against Pakhtunwali and zealot Muslims, many in this pictorial would also die.

Boom!

A bright and smoky flash.

The living group was memorialized for all time.

"This meeting is adjourned," Marigold declared. "Your supervisors will brief you directly as to your exact orders."

The men picked up their jackets and belongings from their nearby chairs. An aide opened the double doors. Gunther was the only one to sit again at the table as he watched Marigold step to Mrs. Latissimo's side and walk her to the hall.

Homestead rested a hand on Gunther's shoulder. "I'll see ya in the hall, cowboy."

Gunther nodded and Kelly mingled with the men as they filed out. Marigold returned to his papers at the table and smiled at Gunther.

"And what is my reason for going?" Gunther interrupted the silence.

Marigold walked around the table and half sat on it in front of Gunther. He smiled. The smile of a man formulating a sales pitch. His bent leg swung nervously in the air like the timing weight on a clock.

"Mr. Gunther!" Marigold declared. "President Roosevelt has authorized me to inform you that you will fully regain your officer's commission and rank of major in the United States Army."

Gunther stared at Marigold's happy expression. He remained expressionless, put his hands on the table's edge, shoved the chair back, and stood. "Captain, I can make the entire yearly wage of a major…in your United States Army….in one afternoon." He reached for his jacket and finished with, "Have yourself a successful Operation Passport."

"Now wait. Wait, sir," Marigold said as he slid off the table. "The president has another payment plan for you, should you find his re-enlistment offer unsatisfactory."

Gunther sat back down and said, "I, too, have a payment plan. Two thousand dollars a month."

"That is a lot of money," Marigold said with a gasp.

"Yup. I might have to bed down with a camel," Gunther added.

Marigold returned to sit and shuffled some of his papers, but it was another ruse for a stall. He looked up and admitted, "I can tell you that the president will offer you…this fee."

Gunther stood. "The first installment of two thousand dollars should be forwarded to the bank of England. I will retrieve it in India." Gunther walked to the table, opened Marigold's file, and wrote banking names and numbers. "The rest of the money will be wired monthly to my bank in Fort Worth."

"Two thousand is a lot of money to be carrying about the Northwest Frontier," Marigold said.

"That region operates on bribe money. Always has, probably always will. I want to have sufficient funds on hand to solve any problems."

"Yes, that can be arranged."

"If the money is not in the British bank, I return home. If the money does not reach my Texas Bank by the fifteenth of each month, I stop what I am doing and return to Texas."

"That is not very patriotic, Mr. Gunther," Marigold said.

"It would be very unpatriotic not to pay me on time, Captain Marigold. Now that you have my interest, what exactly is it that I am supposed to do atop this camel, surrounded by these veterans?" Gunther asked.

Marigold started stacking and packing his papers. "I don't exactly know, Mr. Gunther. I believe the president…believes in you…that you will do what you have always done for him in the past. And whatever that is, he expects you to do it again. I believe the term he used for you in my meeting with him yesterday was…insurance."

Still confused, Gunther stood and slipped on his jacket.

"Speaking of insurance," Gunther added. "I want some."

"Yes?" Marigold asked.

"Ten machine guns and teams in ten wagons," Gunther said.

Marigold raised a quizzical eyebrow.

"I want them, and I want them under my command, not Boston's or Perryweather's."

"We were not authorizing automatic weapons on this trip."

"Of course you weren't. That would make too much sense," Gunther commented.

"Machine gun teams. Ten. Ten wagons."

"You'll have them, sir.

"And, I want dynamite. I also want bows and arrows."

Marigold's eyes widened with the request. "Bows and arrows?"

"I'll have two from the U. S. Army Olympic Archery team along. With powerful bows. We will be unable to lug cannons through those passes. Sticks of dynamite on arrows will reach far."

"You shall have them also, sir. You'll be leaving by military transport tomorrow morning," Marigold said, relieved the Texan had fully signed on. "I will inform the president. I am sure he…"

"Military transport?" Gunther froze. "As in, hammocks in the basement of some rotting ship?"

"The USS Kentucky!" Marigold said.

"Like I said, hammocks in the stinking bowels of a crude ship. Slop for food and chores for the idle. Where does this rat ship put into port over there?"

"First Cairo, down the Red Sea, then Karachi. The British Navy has a fort there in Karachi, and the land expedition will launch from there," Marigold answered.

"Do tell me, Captain Marigold, how is the Lady Latissimo getting to Karachi?" It was Gunther now who took a half-seat on the table.

"I believe she sets off from Annapolis on a British cruise ship tomorrow, on Her Majesty's Treasure. It will take port in Karachi with a brief stay also in Cairo."

Gunther grabbed his satchel. "Her Majesty's Treasure. I believe I have heard of her. Beautiful new ship. Sergeant Major Homestead and I will need two round-trip, first-class tickets on that commercial liner," Gunther said.

Marigold seemed speechless, so Gunther continued, "You know, make that three tickets. I am sure Reverend Verne has never seen a day without self-imposed suffering. He needs to experience some forced luxury," Gunther added, holding three fingers in the air as he turned for the door. "Master Sergeant Homestead will be in touch with you later today for the details."

"Three tickets," Marigold repeated, half-amused at the power play.

"First class," Gunther reminded, with a nod and wink over his shoulder.

As Gunther shut the door and entered the hallway, he was suddenly stopped by a harsh, crisp voice from the hall behind him.

"Did you accept your special payment plan?"

Gunther stopped and turned slowly to see Captain Perryweather. The Brit struck a match to his pipe.

Sergeant Major Homestead remained at the end of the hall.

The Brit sucked on the pipe and stoically placed his left fist in the small of his back, then slowly approached Gunther.

"Ever get that bleeding to stop?" Gunther asked, looking at the hand. But Perryweather ignored the remark.

"You see Gunther, I know about you. All about you. I have been thoroughly briefed." Perryweather circled the cowboy.

Gunther stood still, now curious to see what this new game was.

"You, sir," the Brit growled, "left your wife and family in New York..."

Damn Roosevelt! Gunther thought to himself, knowing how much Teddy loved to tell that story.

"Just walked away from your children. You left that policeman's job in Oklahoma after you caught that gang of desperados, all because you couldn't collect the reward. You left the Army after only seven years, looking for more money." He continued to circle Gunther. "Here today, you won't serve your country unless you're paid a cutthroat's ransom."

Down the hall, Homestead crossed his arms, leaned against the wall, and watched.

"Oh, we have been dealing with you madmen Germans for centuries. Your Kaiser is cooking up a good war in Europe right now. And you sir, are nothing but a mercenary." Perryweather continued with a scowl. "You'll do anything for money. You are untrustworthy, and I won't lose sight of you for an instant. If I catch you taking a bribe to thwart this mission, I will skin you alive myself!"

Gunther looked at the cutlass hanging at Perryweather's side and then back up to his face, "You'd better bring a bigger sword."

Gunther walked down the hall and stopped by Homestead. He smiled at the soldier.

"I guess yer in?" Homestead asked.

"I'm in," Gunther said reluctantly while shaking his head, not believing it yet himself. They started for the lobby. "Ever been on a cruise ship, Homestead?"

"No, sir," Kelly answered quizzically.

"When you pack tonight, Kelly? Have your wife pack a dinner jacket…"

7

Hell and Havoc

"MISTER. Gunther!" a man outside his door shouted, hammering on its panels. Gunther popped up from the desk where he'd been writing a telegram to Jefe. He swung open the door to see a breathless, white-faced corporal from the front desk.

"Mr. Gunther, it is absolutely urgent that you follow me! I—I cannot tell you how urgent." He realized he'd been shouting and dropped his voice to whisper, "—that you follow me. Please sir, get your coat and come."

Gunther grabbed his leather duster and dropped his Luger in an outside pocket when the soldier's head was turned. He topped his head off with his Stetson and followed the eager troop down the hall, the stairs, and across the lobby of the Officers' Quarters and through another hall to a side service entrance. The corporal shoved the metal door open, but Gunther stopped at the door. The soldier beckoned him out into the dark alleyway, one blanketed in snow, bordered by wooden crates and trash barrels.

"Well, where in hell are we going Corporal?" Gunther gripped the handle of his pistol in his pocket.

"There, sir." He pointed to the street, to an ornate black coach parked by the curb. Gunther slowly stepped forward to see more. Two black horses calmly stood while a large man in a black suit held one horse's harness. Another man slowly walked a circle around the transport. Yet another man sat on top.

Gunther sighed, grimaced, and walked to the coach, leaving the corporal shivering with his arms folded. The patrolling man opened the door. Gunther climbed in. Before him was the president of the United States. Theodore Roosevelt sat with Captain Marigold.

"Hello, hello my friend," the president warmly greeted Gunther with a giant smile, taking Gunther's hand in both of his.

"Hello, Mr. President," Gunther said as warmly, yet somewhat perplexed. He nodded at Marigold and took off his hat.

"You look as fit as a fiddle, Gunth! Been hunting?" he asked.

"Just people."

"Ha!" he exploded with his infectious laugh. "Captain Marigold has informed me that you are an official member, albeit a damn expensive one, of the Operation Passport expedition."

"Yes, sir."

"Sure we can't interest you in regaining your Army commission?" He handed Gunther a cigar from his tuxedo pocket and then lit it for him.

"No, sir. "Gunther drew in the flame to ignite the tobacco, "I have done my time."

"Cubans," he said with a wink and a smile. He lit one for himself.

"Captain Marigold informs me that your first paycheck will be used for bribery over there."

"Probably, sir. But I'd rather keep it."

"The White House has no official budget for bribery," Teddy said.

"But my house does, which I suspect is yet another reason why I am here?"

"Sadly," the president continued, "we won't have time to finish them here. I have, more or less, sneaked over here to see you between a Japanese state dinner and the unveiling ceremony of some goddamn museum statue of a naked woman fingering a harp." He drew a satisfying dose on his cigar. "Ha! Nobody knows I'm here. Well, I appreciate your help in this Gunth. Something has gone seriously awry in Afghanistan, and I am not sure how to handle it."

"How so, sir? I still do not know exactly what I will be doing."

"Colonel Latissimo…is not dead. In fact, far from it. The son of a bitch is very much alive and well and wreaking havoc and hell over there. We have found out, from some intercepted Russian telegrams, that our colonel has become some kind of criminal, a tribal leader of sorts! Yes! He has his own pack, a militia of natives, and is running a whole territory in the northwest. He may or may not have some of his former U.S. Army commanders and soldiers still working with him."

Gunther listened in surprise.

"Yes!" Teddy roared again. "I have asked you along on this operation, Gunth…" a blast of smoke left Teddy's mouth, "…because I want your expertise in assessing the situation, and then I want you to kill him."

"Kill him?" Gunther repeated quietly.

"Yes. We cannot have this U.S. Army officer, traitor, and trespasser running amok over there, conspiring with those Cossacks and irritating our British friends. We simply can't."

"I…," Gunther started to respond.

"I cannot openly order my regulars to do this, Gunth," the president interrupted and took off his black top hat. "You know this, boy! I can't tell Captain Boston this. Hell, I don't even know Boston. And I certainly can't tell the Brit Captain Perryweather this is what I want done. But…I do know you, Gunth, and I can tell you. And I know you will think and act outside of the rule book on this and do the right thing."

"Can I bring him back alive?"

"Rather you didn't," Teddy said abruptly.

"What if he surrenders?"

"Don't let him," Teddy said.

"What of Mrs. Latissimo? She is coming along you know."

"What of her? She wants to see her husband. She has asked me and several Washington newsmen and her local congressman if she could go. I have been wriggled into a blasted position. I can't say no. I'll look like a damn boot heel if I tell her no. Work around her."

"Around her?" Gunther said.

"But, let me warn you," the commander in chief leaned forward. "Watch out for her, Gunth. I have heard she is a conniving, selfish, overbearing, tricky…well…just watch out for her. She has boxed me into this, working the newspapers and politicians like a…like a snake charmer."

"I presume Captain Marigold has informed you that I need ten machine guns."

"He has."

"And archers."

"That he has."

"Dynamite."

"Aplenty."

"Three round-trip cruise tickets to Karachi."

"Three."

"And, two thousand dollars each month to my bank account in Fort Worth."

"You have a mercenary's heart!"

"So I have been told, and only just this morning."

Teddy rapped his cane on the coach wall. The guard yanked opened the door.

"Without any one of those things," Gunther looked at Marigold, "I will turn right around and head for Texas."

"The naked lady awaits!" Teddy reported, nodding his head in agreement, "God bless you and good luck, you cowboy son of a bitch. I hope to see you and Jefe in Montana in ten months. You can tell me up there all about this trip over whiskey and another Cuban. And my God, I surely wish we were up there now, man, sittin' around a campfire, drunk as hell."

Their heads were but two feet apart, and Gunther saw his president's eyes begin to tear up, then he snorted and continued with a new vigor, "And then you can tell me about that Indian chase in Wyoming too. I want to know every detail! Please give that crazy little jungle-man Filipino my best."

"I will, sir." Gunther stepped out into the brisk, night air. Teddy affectionately tapped his cane on Gunther's back on his way out. The two guards boarded the coach, and the driver pulled the team away. All the while, Gunther saw Teddy's face in the window glaring at him. It was the saddest expression, until he forced a smile.

On the sidewalk, Gunther watched the magnificent coach off, but he was not alone in his observation. A ruddy-faced man in black had been spying intently on him and the coach from behind a tree across the avenue. The man cursed quietly in a foreign tongue. He could only wonder who was in the coach. What rich man? What American robber baron, prince, or king? The guards had held him at bay, but as the protectors boarded the wagon, he stepped onto the icy cobblestone street. In his coat pocket he fingered his own handgun, a short-barreled .45 revolver.

Gunther looked up to the cold, clear night sky and took a draw on the cigar, then he turned and wandered slowly back down the alley to the lodge. The man in black started a trot across the street, bound for the alley to catch up. What a great place to kill this Yankee, he thought to himself. His eyes zeroed in on the back of Gunther's head. He gripped the handle of his pistol and started to pull it from his pocket.

But the young corporal suddenly appeared in the man's view and both his hands were in his pockets. This young soldier had also been spying on the coach the whole time? With guns in his pockets? The stalking man stopped dead where he stood, turned, and walked off down the sidewalk, as would a pedestrian.

"What did the president want?" the corporal asked as Gunther neared.

"Why, to give me this cigar, Corporal." He rolled the Cuban in his fingers and smirked at the wonder in the young soldier's face as he stared at the presidential cigar fresh from the hands of his commander in chief. Gunther impulsively aimed the lit end on the brick wall beside the door and stabbed out the flame with a few taps. It was only one-quarter gone.

"And now," Gunther said," I give this cigar…to you." He handed it to the corporal. The man held out both his hands and accepted the cigar as though it were a tube of gold from the Denver Mint.

"It is a very fine cigar!" Gunther advised and he passed him bound for the doorway.

"I will never smoke it!" the man declared.

"Do as you wish, Corporal," Gunther said. "But, as you will find in life, it's a lot more fun smoking it once than just looking at it," he added over his shoulder as he disappeared down the service hallway. He had a telegram to Jefe to finish.

8

Atlantic Manhunt

"No, No! Sir? Sir!" cried the ship's porter with an Egyptian accent. "You gentlemen are not in the first-class group. You are in the regular group! You are all in the coach rooms. Please! Your suitcases need to be removed from here and taken over there," he insisted with gregarious hand motions to punctuate his words. Apparently, three swarthy men dressed in identical black suits didn't understand the mixed English/Egyptian accent.

"Horsy, ain't he?" Homestead commented as he turned his collar up against the brisk sea air.

Gunther and Homestead watched the wrestling display with amusement as the ship's porter tugged on a suitcase from a confused traveler's grip. Gunther thought the men looked like triplets, as he and Kelly dropped their footlockers off by the growing mountain of first-class luggage. Another porter laced tags sporting room numbers through the handles.

Gunther scanned the people arriving at the dock to board the ship, passengers in all kinds of clothing and of all nationalities. "I imagine they have quite a language problem."

"Hey, there's Harrigan, the photographer and his assistant," Kelly said. The men were towing several large suitcases and footlockers. They walked to the cameramen and helped them hoist the gear to the first-class passenger luggage.

"Name's Johann Gunther," he said to the assistant as he grabbed one handle of a camera case.

"John Smith," the black man replied with the smile.

"This thing is about as big as a coffin," Gunther added.

"It has two camera stands and our biggest camera, the latest Folding Kodak."

"We've got the heaviest!" Kelly Homestead said, as he and Harrigan hauled another huge piece. A porter ran toward them. "We know!" Kelly winked to him as they set the load down in the proper pile. With gear stacked and tagged, the men stood on the dock and took in the enormous cruise liner.

"God, I wish I could take a quick pictorial here!" Harrigan said while catching his breath. He whisked his tweed cap off and craned his neck to stare up at the magnificent ship, putting both hands on his hips. "Look at her! She's a beauty. One of the biggest in the world! I didn't know you were on this ship, too?"

"Yes," Gunther said as the men started up the long passenger gangplank to the towering ship, "we are, and so is Lady Latissimo and Reverend Verne."

"Oh good. Good," said Harrigan with a smile. "This will be a very entertaining trip."

◇

Gunther and Kelly Homestead in their suits and ties—Gunther's a Western bolo—strolled into the dining room reserved for their first meal in first class, a splendid eatery as opulent as any found in Europe. A maitre'd guided them past a string quartet playing classical music to an empty table in the crowded room. Through the restaurant windows, Gunther could see the gray sunset coastline of frozen Virginia fading out of view. Aboard another ship, a navy transport, steaming out of that harbor somewhere, were hundreds of Army soldiers, horses, and supplies. And, some machine guns, he hoped.

"Mr. Gunther!" a voice called out, and Gunther stopped and turned. It was Harrigan waving a red napkin, half-standing from his seat. At the table with him were Mrs. Latissimo, another younger woman, the Reverend Silas Verne, and an elderly couple.

"Here! Here, sir," Harrigan said. "We have two more places." Gunther excused the maitre'd.

Page 79

"Evening all," Gunther said as the men sat with their group.

"Spectacular room, isn't it?" Harrigan commented.

"Mr. Gunther," the reverend spoke up. "I…I do want to thank you for arranging this first-class passage for me. It was most unnecessary…I…"

"Think nothing of it, Reverend," Gunther interrupted. "I hope you will enjoy yourself."

"Ahh…" continued Silas, "this is Mr. and Mrs. Abel Svenkunland from Norway! You know Mrs. Latissimo, and this is Miss Marilyn Bloom, an employee of the Latissimo family."

They nodded, and Verne reversed the introductions. "Our friends are…Johann Gunther. He is…ah…a businessman, and U.S. Army Sergeant Major Kelly Homestead. He is out of uniform, of course. The Svenkunlands are on a world tour and wish to see the sphinx and pyramids."

"You'll be getting off in Cairo then," Homestead said. Gunther eyed the blonde-haired Miss Bloom, Latissimo's handmaiden? Assistant? Daughter-in-law? Now, not only was there one woman, but two on this nightmare trip.

"Ja!" Abel Svenkunland said with a smile. "Ve are looking fovard to seeing …the…the ancient buildings."

"Your English is very good!" Gunther commented, "I have never been to your country, but I have heard it is very beautiful. I myself am from Germany…ah…you know…Deutschland? But, I barely remember much of it. My family moved to the Americas when I was very young."

"You are a…cowboy? Cowboy?" Abel asked, pointing at Gunther's bolo tie. "Is that the vord said correct?" Abel asked.

"That is correct. Although I do not know if I am a real cowboy," he answered slowly for them. "Cowboys work with cattle? Cows. I do not."

"He is from Texas," Homestead declared with a teasing tone.

"Texas!" The Swede erupted. Both his hands flew up. Then he translated for his wife. "JA! Ve know Texas. Cowboys and Indians. Buffalo Bill Cody! Ve have seen his Vild Vest Show in New York City last week."

"And I'll bet it was a humdinger," Gunther said with a wink and a smile.

"Do you know Bat Masterson?" Abel asked.

"No, sir."

"Vyatt Burps?"

"No again."

"Annies Oakleys?"

"Never had the pleasure," Gunther said to the disappointed man.

"And, you are an Army man?" Abel asked of Homestead.

"Yes, sir, I am. Twenty-nine years with the United States Army," Kelly answered.

"Twenty-nine years!" Lydia Latissimo interrupted in shocked manner, "My! That is such a long time, don't you think?" She looked over the faces at the table. "And at a job where people shoot at you, and I know for how little pay. Do you think that a job where people shoot at you…is a foolish job…Mr. Svenkunland?"

Gunther noted two things quickly. One, she was drunk. Two, she had a thick Southern accent, possibly enhanced by the wine, possibly not.

Homestead spoke right up, sparing the Swede an answer. "Now, would you be calling your very own husband, the colonel, a fool, Mrs. Latissimo?"

"My husband's record stands for itself, my dear sir," Lydia replied in a curt tone. She turned to Gunther.

"Our Mr. Gunther was once in the Army, and was wise enough to get out when he could," she said and took a quick sip of her drink. "What I wonder sir, is why are you back in bed with the Army? What exactly do you do for the Army, Mr. Gunther? I am sure we would all be very interested in knowing," she said, nodding her head and scanning the faces at the table, as if trying to also get infectious nods from them. "I am sure that Mr. and Mrs. Svenkunland would like to know how a Texas cowboy works for the Army?"

Gunther smiled and lit a cigar. "I am a travel expert, Mrs. Latissimo. I have traveled a lot. However, I expect on this trip I will do little more than watch over the horses and decide which way is north."

"And you need guns to watch the horses…and look at your compass?" she asked, but she glared at the left side of his dinner jacket, as though she knew a hidden pistol hung at that very spot.

"Vill you all see The Great Train Robbery?" the Swede asked.

"Oh yes!" Marilyn Bloom announced, but the men around her seemed befuddled. "There is a new moving picture film theater aboard ship. And they are playing the moving picture, The Great Train Robbery," she explained.

"I have heard about this," Kelly Homestead remarked. "And, we will go." He cuffed Gunther lightly across the shoulder. "Won't we, Johann?"

"Okay."

In the table discussion of moving pictures, Gunther leaned over to Harrigan, "Where is your assistant, John?"

"We were politely informed that this restaurant will not serve Negroes," he answered, as a black waiter beside him poured tea and coffee at the table.

"Hmmm…" Gunther growled as he sipped his coffee from a cup too dainty for his liking.

"John runs across this. We run across this problem. It's a shame, too," Harrigan continued, shaking his head. "John is a most excellent photographer and a great assistant to me as well. He is more than an assistant. His work stands alone. He has put together several of his own exhibits. Well received at first, then, when it is revealed that he is a Negro, his reviewers ignore him."

"Oh, just as well, really," Mrs. Latissimo interrupted again. "Perhaps he should put on only Negro photo exhibits in Negro halls?"

"Well, where is John now? How is he eating?" Gunther chose again to ignore Latissimo.

"He is taking his meals in our room."

"Hmm," Gunther growled again.

"And, what will you be eating tonight, ma'am?" the waiter asked of Lydia Latissimo.

The group ordered. Meals of the finest international cuisine, wine, and brandy were set before them, held at bay for a moment while the reverend said a prayer of some depth and considerable length. The Svenkunlands Norwegian life was the subject of meal-time conversation, some out of genuine interest, but mostly to avoid the stress of their upcoming harsh and dangerous mission; that, and to steer the Lady Latissimo away from any more remarks that might cause a fistfight.

As the conversation drifted, Gunther leaned back in his velvet chair, tuned out the idle talk, and let his mind wander to the quartet's Boccherini's Cello Concerto in G Major as it lofted through the room. He took a study of Lydia Latissimo, a woman in her late forties, possessing a pretty face and long black hair with touches of gray. When quiet and still, she looked innocent and beguiling enough. Her eyes fell vacant periodically as if she too dropped deep into her own thoughts. She glanced at Gunther frequently. Was she somehow suspicious of the president's plot that would have him murder her husband?

Then his eyes lingered on Marilyn Bloom. Twenties? Twenty-five at the most? She did not look the hardy type, ready to fend off the rigors of jagged mountains and bleaching deserts, astride a horse. She ate her entire meal with bright white dress gloves and they remained pure even after a strawberry sauce dessert. Her table setting was as clean as when she started, not a careless tumbled crumb or a carefree drop of lost water. It was hard to tell any more of these women as they were strapped up in the layers and bustles of dining gowns from jawline to toe. Marilyn caught his exam of her, smiled politely, and turned back to the conversation.

In a quiet break, Gunther stood, "Gentlemen, I believe we run the risk of boring these ladies to near tears, shall we adjourn to the cigar room and let them flee our disinteresting company?"

"Aaagggh!" a stuffed Homestead groaned as he stood, the old chuck wagon habit getting a chuckle from Gunther.

"As I do not smoke…or drink, I think I will retire to my room," Silas Verne said.

"Spoken like a good reverend," Gunther said, patting Silas on the back.

"And, I will join my friend John," said Harrigan.

The group wandered out to the lobby. They exchanged their room numbers. Lydia reminded the men that she and Marilyn were in the same suite. Gunther and Homestead carried their drinks and smokes to a leather sofa in the nearby Turkish Emporium and Smoking Bar, adjacent to the dining room. It was getting late and only the last few diners lingered. Gunther spotted the "foreign triplets" at a table in the corner, still dressed in their black suits like a singing trio.

"Sounded to me like Lydia Latissimo was pushing for a cat fight in there," Homestead remarked.

"Yup, and who is the blonde?"

"She is probably a maid! Purty thing though. Man, my wife sure would've enjoyed this meal," Kelly said and sipped from his glass.

Gunther smiled.

"So is this thing I hear about your wife and kids true?" Kelly asked.

"Hmm?"

"About you leaving them in New York City and never seeing them again?" Homestead clarified. "What Perryweather accused you of yesterday in the hallway?"

Gunther sighed with an added grimace. After a few seconds he answered, "Yes, it is. I was very young. Sixteen years old with a kid! Three! In a tenement in New York City. Trapped. Trapped like the greasy rats that walked across our beds at night. I walked out one afternoon. Said I was going out to get some cigarettes. I went straight to an Army recruiter's office."

"They let you into West Point like that?"

"Oh no. No. Not yet. First I did three years, like you, a saddle tramp. Parading around. Fighting Comanch' and Apache. I mustered out in Fort Sill, Oklahoma, and signed on as a deputy in a town down around Paris, Texas. Deputy for about four years. Then, the governor of Oklahoma recommended me to the Point."

"Favor?"

"Yes. He got re-elected more or less because I shut down a gang of murderers working Oklahoma and Texas. There was even a price on my head from the gang's family. He knew I couldn't stay in the district. The clan would surely bushwhack me. He made me an offer. West Point!" Gunther sipped his brandy.

"Ever think about seeing those kids of yours?" Kelly asked, studying the cowboy's profile.

"No, Kelly. That was another life. I…I just don't think about it. When I left, she and the kids went straight to her parent's house, and they were way better for it."

"I've got five kids," Homestead continued, "and they are the very joy of my life." He tapped his jacket over his heart. "I got their picture right here, and I miss 'em already."

"I worked with a deputy named Jerry Van Cook in Oklahoma," Gunther said. "He told me once that there were two kinds of people in the world, settlers and explorers. Bred to be such. Makes a lot of sense. I figured out back then which side of the fence I was on."

"Outside lookin' in?" Kelly asked.

"Outside lookin' in." Gunther confirmed.

"Well, it doesn't always have to be that way! Maybe someday?" Kelly stood and stretched. "Well hell, I'm drunker than a damned old skunk. Guess I'll hit the cot. Much thanks for getting me aboard this ship. Ya know, I could be eating shit-on-a-shingle and swinging in a rope hammock, shoulder to shoulder with the rest of the boys. That was a fine meal. I wish my wife were here for it, and she could see this ship. My my."

"Maybe someday…sergeant major, there might be some tickets from Santy Claus to take the whole Homestead troupe on a floatin' shindig such as this one," Gunther said with a smile.

"Oh, sure," Kelly murmured sarcastically and wandered off to the double doors to the deck, "See ya at breakfast! Tough life, ain't it? Livin' meal to meal."

"Mañana!" Gunther shouted over his shoulder, and right there made a mental note on how part of his monthly $2,000 paycheck would be spent—a special Homestead family surprise. He didn't even notice the three men leave the bar. He sat for a moment, finished his drink, stood up, and stretched. He decided to walk a few rounds on the deck if it wasn't too cold and then turn in for the night.

"Good night," the man polishing the bar said as he left.

"Good night to you."

He pushed open a set of double doors with both hands to step out into the cold air. He looked skyward. The ship's running lights mixed with the fine falling snow, almost ice, creating a slight glowing gray hue that encircled the ocean liner. Not a bad chill, especially with the warm brandy running through him. He threw up the collar of his dinner jacket and stepped to the rail. He could not see the ocean water below, just an ominous fog.

He started aft. The decks appeared quiet and empty. Gunther could not see a single passenger nor even a crew member on the entire side of the ship, even the two upper decks above him appeared empty. Well, just a few folks. He smiled as he heard some hurried passengers suddenly jogging up behind him, probably a young couple on their honeymoon leaving the ship's dance hall.

He turned to…smack….a jarring blow hit him in the back of the head.

He was suddenly three years old. Standing on a hill overlooking the Rhine River and the green hills bordering the winding blue water. Boats of many colors traversed the waterway. It was such a beautiful, sunny afternoon. But strange…he had his Luger on his side, in his tan leather shoulder holster! It was very heavy and the giant pistol took up most of the length of his little body.

"Johann," his mother said and leaned in front of him, her unforgettable long blonde hair cascaded in layers before him. He smiled. Her hand caressed his face.

"Johann, draw der Luger," she said calmly with a smile. She grabbed his small, chubby hand and placed it on the giant handle. He stared at her, confused.

"Johann!" She screamed violently. Her eyes bulged monstrously. Her teeth clenched and became yellow, spiked with points and bloody, "Draw der Lugahhhh!" In horror, his tiny hand reached for the weapon…

When Gunther opened his eyes he saw two men towing his

body across the walkway to the railing, each with one of his legs! The man holding his right leg was trying to hook a foot over the railing! They were about to pitch him overboard!

Gunther's hand was on his pistol, as his mother had ordered. He yanked out the gun and shot one man right in the mouth. The man's head bolted back. His back arched violently, hands to his throat, and he slipped silently over the rail and plunged into the wet darkness below.

The second man wasted not a second. He released Gunther's leg and dove straight across his body with outstretched arms to capture Gunther's gun arm. The weight of this large beast crashing upon him knocked the air from his lungs. The man climbed like a scram-bling animal across Gunther, hand over hand on his arm, scaling it like a rope, with the pistol his prey. Gunther acted out of his own animal reflex, still not even sure where he was. A boat? A boat? The Rhine? But he knew in a second this man would have at his Luger, so he flicked the pistol away with his hand as far as he could.

Then he rolled out from under the man as his attacker crawled on all fours toward the gun. Wracked with blinding pain, Gunther's vision blurred. Yet somehow he crawled hand over hand up the man's back as the thug reached for the loose gun still feet away. Gunther got to the man's head with his left hand to haul him back. He hooked the man's face, catching inside the cheek with his curled fingers. With a desperate pull, he ripped back and a large section of the man's cheek tore from his face. It flapped back and fell forward, hanging down like an open peel of an orange. The man shrieked.

With both hands, Gunther banged the man's head against the frozen wooden deck. Once. Twice. But the man was strong! He pushed and squirmed his way around to come face-to-face with Gunther, scratching and pounding on Gunther's neck and jawline. The man's torn cheek fell back, exposing raw gums, teeth, and free-flowing blood. He roared like the werewolf he resembled!

"You are dead, you freak!" Gunther yelled. He stood straight up and leaped headfirst for the gun. But the man clutched Gunther's ankle just as he disappeared from above him. With this sudden capture Gunther slammed straight down on his face and chest. He kicked furiously to release his leg, and yet again the man was climbing Gunther's body, hand over hand, like a rope to get to that gun.

He twisted his torso so he could see the attacker. When the man's head crossed Gunther's belt line, Gunther tore the cheek completely from the face in two harsh yanks. Then Gunther pelted the animal's eyes and nose with his fists. The beast arched back somewhat to escape the blows, backed up enough for Gunther to slide his right boot across the man's stomach. He kicked hard and it pitched the man onto his back, three precious feet away. Gunther spun and lunged for the pistol. He got it! He rolled to his side and pointed the firearm at his slobbering enemy.

"Who are you?" Gunther growled. It was suddenly clear to him now that this monster was one of the three dark-suited men. The man he shot and who tumbled overboard was the second of the trio. Gunther could not trust his balance to stand and just lay on his side, awaiting an answer. "Who are you?" he repeated with a coughing gag.

The foe plugged a hand over the stinging, wet gape of his mouth. Blood drained through his fingers onto his neck and chest. He howled and gasped like a beast in shock and pain, his neck outstretched like a yelping, mad wolf. With a knee and a hand on the deck, and a red-tinged evil eye on Gunther, he pounced again for one last assault!

Gunther shot him twice in the head and chest. The face ruptured, the head jacked to the side, and the blasted body tumbled onto Gunther's legs in a lifeless heap.

"Freak!" Gunther roared inside a coughing spit. He violently kicked his legs to toss off the corpse.

His back stopped against the wall. His head ached and he patted the blood-matted hair of his head. His probing fingers could feel that the skin of his skull lay wide open. He'd been struck from behind. But with what? He looked at the flooring where he might have been attacked first for a pipe or a stick. Nothing. He pinched the teeth in his mouth with two fingers. All were there. None were loose, though his mouth and jaw felt swollen, sore, and battered.

He patted his wallet in his back pocket. Still there! No doubt these robbers were not at all prepared for an armed Texican. They had probably jumped many an unarmed city dweller. But, when were they going to rob his wallet? It seemed like they just wanted to toss him overboard and kill him.

His stomach roiled. He pushed slowly to his unsteady feet using the wall as a brace, took one step, and fell flat down on his face. Gunther lay there for a few seconds, legs and arms askew. Where were the sailors? Crewmen? Where was help? Hadn't anyone seen or heard this mess? Where is some help? Granted, the 9mm round of a Luger was not that loud. Slowly Gunther rolled onto his back and stared up at the light snow falling from under the light above. The cold deck felt good on his head.

Again, he tried to rise, but only to his hands and knees this time. Crawling to the body, he sat beside the corpse and searched the pockets. No wallet. No identification. No papers. American cigarettes and matches. Ripping out the collar label of the jacket he shoved it in his jacket pocket. Too dark to read. Then he yanked free a religious medallion from the man's neck, but it was too dark to scrutinize the jewelry's markings. He found folded papers in the man's back pocket. He shoved jewelry and papers into his jacket pocket as well.

Then he took a good look around and pondered his next step. Still not a soul to be seen! The fine snow fell a bit harder and with a new velocity affected by the winds. Was that the very ghost of his mother, he wondered, or just a twisted dream of an unconscious man? He tried to shake the question from his head.

Fuck the help! Gunther said to himself. He clutched the jacket of the man and while still seated on the ground, he hauled the body across the walkway, towing it in one-foot increments over to the railing. Dizzy and careful not to tumble over himself, he stood. He looked at the deck above, then left and right. No one. He hooked the dead man's left arm over the railing, then a stiffening leg over the top piping. With an exasperated grunt, he rolled the bastard over the rail. He watched the corpse drop into the dark gray oblivion. The hum of the ship and parting ocean hid any splash. He slid downward, sitting on the deck resting his back against the rail, scanning for witnesses. Empty. Silent. Gray. Cold. Icy snow.

He wiped the melted mist from his face. How long before the salty sea air would erase the blood from the deck? The snow was now building in the coldest patches. And, where was the surviving third partner of this greasy wolf pack?

He knew he had to make it back to his room without passing out so he waited until some strength came back to his legs. He sucked in the cold air and it breathed strength into his system. He stumbled only slightly as he tried to leave, then spotted the man's torn cheek still on the deck, collecting just a bit of icy snow. It reminded him of a dead, pink fish.

He carefully stooped to pick it up. "Here," Gunther growled, as he picked up the flesh and flung it overboard. "You forgot this."

Back in his bathroom, Gunther opened both the hot and cold faucets of the bathtub, stripped, and stepped in. As the water level rose, he slid completely under and massaged around his head wound. Sore, but no stinging pain. Toiletries of Epsom salts and other foreign, indefinable powders and balms lined up the back wall of the tub. He dumped all of them into the water.

He sat up and reached for his crumpled jacket on the floor in the pile of clothes by the tub. He pulled out the clothing label. Sears. He pulled out the man's piece of jewelry. It was a religious medallion of a woman's image, perhaps the Virgin Mary? He looked on the back to find an inscription. It was in a foreign language.

With a pained turn, he dropped the medal on the floor and dried his hands on his discarded pants. He pulled the folded papers from the jacket pocket. It was a tattered envelope with a letter inside. He took out the letter. He could not read the foreign text, but the single sheet signed off with the obvious lipstick imprint of lips.

"Love," he muttered. He looked at the envelope. It was addressed in English with both a foreign stamp and a Washington, D.C., postmark dated just before last Christmas. The return address was for an Anna Gordinonovich of Moscow, Russia.

"Russia!" He tossed the papers on the tiled floor. He looked again at the inscription on the medal. "Russian!" Suddenly, the conclusion that these men were simple hijackers seemed all wrong. Gunther recalled the War Department briefing and words of Captain Perryweather: the warning of Russian interest in Afghanistan and the "Great Game," as he called it. Gunther bolted upright in the tub, splashing water everywhere.

"Damn!" He reached for a towel, ignoring the growing aches and pains from the deck fight. Within moments he was dressed in Levis, shirt, and boots. He tossed on another long black jacket and this time passed on the Luger and shoved the more powerful Browning .45 in his belt line. Halfway to the door, he stopped, returned to the luggage, and picked up his Colt revolver, and shoved it into his belt as well. He carefully settled his Stetson on his head as to avoid the scalp wound.

Gunther ran down the hall and pounded on Kelly Homestead's door.

"Kelly!" he barked with urgency. No answer. He manhandled the doorknob in frustration. Locked.

He ran to Silas Verne's door and the reverend responded quickly.

"Yes?"

"Come to Lydia Latissimo room as fast as you can," Gunther bolted for her suite.

"Mrs. Latissimo!" he hammered on the door.

"What?" It was Marilyn's voice.

"It's Gunther." At this point Verne, still in a sleeping robe, had caught up with him.

Marilyn opened the door and the men rushed through. Both she and Lydia were in their sleeping gowns.

"What is the meaning of this?" Lydia demanded.

"I was just attacked on deck," Gunther explained, "by two men. They damn near tossed me overboard."

"Wha..." Marilyn declared and now in better light he saw their eyes study the abrasions obvious on his face.

"I returned the favor instead. But not before I recovered a letter from one of them while he lay dead."

"You threw them overboard?" Silas asked.

"Yes. One at a time. The letter was in Russian. And it is a strong possibility that these men were Russian agents."

"Russian agents," Lydia repeated softly and wandered to the liquor cabinet. She poured herself a small shot of brandy. "Mr. Gunther, would you like a glass?"

He nodded and Lydia poured him one as well and brought it to him. Then she returned to the cabinet.

"Recall what Perryweather said about the Russians back in D.C.?" Gunther asked them.

Lydia gulped the whole shot. She poured another.

"Well, I have seen these skunks before, all three of them. Several times on the ship."

"Three?" Silas asked.

"Three of them. And I just killed two." Gunther downed his drink in Lydia-like fashion and set the glass on a nearby table. "The third one is still out there, and I believe all our lives are in danger."

Marilyn paced the room, wringing her hands.

"Oh, sit down Marilyn," Lydia ordered. She didn't.

"It is very possible that Russia has sent men along to stop us from reaching Afghanistan, or reaching your husband," Gunther said to Lydia.

"Why?" Silas asked.

"I don't know why. I…" Gunther said, but his eyelids fluttered and his knees buckled. He caught himself with a hand on the back of a chair.

Marilyn rushed to his side. "Are you all right?"

"It's my head. They hit me…hit me with something from behind. I couldn't find what it was, but it knocked me cold." He allowed her to guide him to sit in a chair. "I woke up just in time, just a second before I was tossed overboard." She took off his Stetson and parted his wet hair.

"Good God, Mr. Gunther I can see your skull!" Marilyn dashed to a suitcase and pulled out a leather bag.

"We will have to tap Washington," Verne said. "The ship has a radio Morse Code device! We…we need to tell the captain!"

"No…" both Lydia and Gunther said simultaneously.

"We shouldn't telegraph D.C.," Gunther continued, "not with a message that could be clearly intercepted. Not until we get a handle on what is going on here. We can't tell the captain either. These Russians wanted to stop us, and surely the captain will just turn this ship around and head back to Virginia."

"We must go on," Lydia added.

"These men boarded this ship to bushwhack us. That means they have inside information from inside the War Department and maybe the White House. This is obviously bigger than I…we…can figure out just yet," Gunther continued. But, it would be safe to say that interest in your husband just doubled. Tripled. I think… ohhh…" Gunther moaned as Marilyn poured some medical alcohol on his head wound.

"I am going to have to stitch this up," Marilyn said. She now used a comb to carefully spread his long blond hair away from the wound.

"Can you?" Gunther asked.

"Mr. Gunther," she said matter-of-factly as she pulled surgical needles and thread from her kit, "I am a professional nurse. I am a graduate of the Florence Nightingale School of Nursing in London, England. Hold still. In fact, if I weren't a woman, I would probably be a doctor."

Lydia grimaced and shook her head at the doctor remark, "Not now, Marilyn. Please!"

"Stitch away," Gunther said, leaning slightly forward to accommodate her care. A nurse might come in handy where they were headed, he decided. "We need to hunker down. Watch each other until I can find the third man, the third Russian. And I worry about Homestead. I can't get a response from Kelly's room. He may be a heavy sleeper."

"Hold still," Marilyn ordered between clenched teeth. The room fell still and silent until the threadwork was done, each lost in the personal ramifications of this news.

"Got it," Marilyn said. "It's hard to bandage something like this, so I put a special Vaseline over it. Here, take this jar. Use this ointment when it feels dry. Wrap your head in a towel tonight when you sleep. I'll look at it tomorrow." With both hands, she gripped his face in her palms to examine his eyes and other bruises.

"Do you think the photographers are in danger?" Silas asked.

"I don't think so. They have been seen all day shooting every corner of ship. No doubt they are nothing but picture takers. At some point we'll have to explain what's going on. I'll do that." Gunther stood feeling slightly woozy and turned to Silas.

"Reverend, I want you to stay close to these ladies," Gunther pulled the .45 revolver from his waistline.

"Dear God," Verne declared.

Gunther took the reverend's hand and forced the pistol handle into it. "Onward Christian soldiers," Gunther looked him dead in the eye.

"I've already got one of those," Lydia announced, knocking down her fourth shot of brandy. "You don't think I am going to this godforsaken no-man's-land without some protection." She motioned toward her purse.

"Good," Gunther glanced at Marilyn. She shook her head, as much as to suggest that Lady Latissimo was drunk and to ignore her.

"She has a pistol, sir, as do I," Marilyn said.

Gunther let out a deep burst of air, retrieved his .45 from the speechless reverend, and shoved it back into his belt. "I am going to try Homestead's door again." He walked to the dining table and took two butter knives from the table settings.

"Kind of dull, aren't they?" Lydia asked.

Gunther ignored her. "Make plans to protect each other. Reverend, stay by their side. I suggest you stay here tonight." The women nodded.

"My husband is up to no good," Lydia whispered as she stared at the carpet.

He walked out the door and down the hall to Homestead's

room. He knocked and called out to the soldier. No answer. He stuck the butter knife between the door and doorframe. He rotated the knife, and the bolt moved. Using two knives with pressure and rotation, he inched the bolt clear from the frame and opened the door. As he expected, the room was empty and the bed still made.

Gunther sat in the chair and covered his face with his hands. His hat fell off his head to the floor. His eyes welled up. This was not good. Not good. He stood, spotted a spare room key, and took it from the dresser, but not before noticing the Homestead family portrait in a silver frame Kelly had set up when he unpacked. His eyes lingered over the faces. As was the fashion of the day, man, woman, and children stood tall with stoic, unsmiling faces. Would they be so stoic when they learned that their father, and her husband, was brutally killed on this icy night in the middle of nowhere? Why hadn't he walked back with Kelly to their rooms? He picked up the Stetson and settled it back on his head.

He left the room in a fervor, his right hand surrounding the .45 in his jacket pocket. He walked every interior hall of the ship on the hunt. He peered into every corner. He burst though the double doors of the hall and out into the snowy Atlantic night on a hunt for Homestead, a hunt for the third Russian. He only saw a few busy janitors.

Exhausted, Gunther stood on the top deck as an Atlantic gray dawn brought with it no respite. A maroon dot of a sun, filtered by the thick clouds, peeked over the far eastern horizon. It rose from a savage place, far, far east, a place where they were all bound. That place had already reached out and brought them death. The mix of the salty sea air, the melting snow on his face, and water in his eyes blended together like that of a wounded, wild animal, confusing pain with sorrow, revenge with hate.

◇

The Marconi radio room stewards did much more than send Morse code dispatches from newlyweds and businessmen from ship to shore and back. Each night they translated streams of

Morse code and created a two-sheet newspaper of American and British stock market figures along with basic bits of international news. These handouts were published in the ship's printing room and distributed throughout the two restaurants—first class and common.

This morning, the second morning since Kelly Homestead vanished, Gunther nursed an Egyptian coffee and held his news brief before his face, his eyes peering like daggers over the top of the sheet to study every face and figure that entered the common restaurant for breakfast. Silas Verne, Lydia, Marilyn, and the photographers stayed together or in touch, conducting their own search. His Russian prey was not eating in first class, but would rather have to dine in the commons restaurant. So there Gunther sat, waiting. Three meals a day with his Luger in his armpit. Waiting.

Breakfast passed. No Russian. Gunther strolled the decks.

Lunch vigil passed. More walking. No Russian.

Dinner passed. More walking, this time through many of the interior hallways. No Russian.

Food was served in the ship's clubs and bars at night. There were six clubs open until 2 A.M., as well as a gambling casino. Gunther prowled between them. Nothing.

Day three. No Russian.

Day four. No Russian.

Each night he went to Homestead's room, entered with the spare key he found the first night. He roughed up the bed, moved around the glasses and toiletries. Each morning a steward dutifully swept and straighten up. Gunther's ruse worked. If the ship's crew found Kelly missing, all kinds of complications and questioning might follow, preventing Gunther from conducting his own investigation. After he finished, Gunther collapsed into his own bed, but not before pushing the edge of the room's chest of drawers across the door. He read *War of the Worlds* until he passed out, his .45 inches from his hand.

Gunther deduced room service was keeping this brigand alive, as they were feeding John Smith the black photographer in the same manner. He watched the tens of stewards delivering hundreds of meals from the kitchen of the commons restaurant, feeding meals to six decks of passengers in twenty-five rooms per deck. He could not bribe or question all of them. But he tried a few…

"Excuse me. I am trying to find a business associate. He must have taken sick. He has a swarthy complexion. Black hair. He…he must be taking all of his meals in his room. Does he sound familiar?" he would ask.

"Ahhh, what is his name, sir?" they would answer.

"Well, I have only just met him on this trip. We met accidentally. We discovered we were in the same business…and well, made some plans to meet, and now I fail to see him anywhere."

"This man is not familiar to me, sir. Sorry," came their answer.

On the evening of the sixth day, Gunther decided he would have to knock on every door, with no guarantee the secreted man would even answer. But he would soon run out of time and options. Cairo was just two days away.

Late that evening while making his door-knocking rounds and offering dozens of excuses to disturbed patrons, he was interrupted by a shout.

"Mr. Gunther!" cried a woman with a desperate voice.

He turned to see Marilyn Bloom rushing toward him, her jaw slack and her face pale.

"The man!" she gasped.

"What?" He grabbed her arms. "Where?"

"That man you are looking for…he is in my aunt's room. He's dead!"

"Dead?"

"She…shot him!"

"She? Have …have you told anyone else? Does anyone know?"

"No."

He looked around, "Okay, breathe," he whispered. "Catch your breath and calm down. We will walk to her room. Calmly. If we pass anyone? Smile politely at them."

She sucked in some air and nodded. He turned her around and hooked one of her trembling arms with his. They walked at a normal pace to the room.

"Anyone see you run to find me?"

"No. I don't think so."

A man came in the hall from a seaside door. They nodded and smiled as he passed.

"Aunt Lydia?" Marilyn announced knocking on her door. The door swung open and the scowling face of Lydia Latissimo greeted them. Gunther marched passed her and saw the body of the third Russian spread on the carpet. He rushed forward, knelt, and felt for a pulse. Nothing.

"What happened?" he asked.

"Someone knocked on the door. I thought it was Marilyn who maybe forgot her key, and I answered it. I opened the door just a few inches." She looked down at the warm corpse and continued with a cold meanness to her voice. "He shoved the door hard. With his shoulder. I fell back. He…he stood right there smiling, leering." She pointed to the floor by the door. "I asked him what he wanted. I stepped slowly back to the dresser, to my purse. He shook his head and smiled. I told him I had money in my purse. I reached into my bag. I pulled out my revolver and shot him."

"Right in the heart," Gunther murmured, opening the man's jacket. "Must have died quickly. Heart stopped. Not much blood." He looked up, "Marilyn! Go get Reverend Silas."

"This is no damn time for saying words!" Lydia complained.

"Get him. And Marilyn. Calmly," he reminded her as he stood and walked to the bathroom and grabbed a towel. "No words, Lydia. I need his help with the body. We can't report this to any-one, and we must drop the body overboard." He put the towel over the wound, and then stood.

He picked the pistol up from the dresser, opened the cylinder and inspected the rounds. One empty shell remained.

"You don't trust me?" Lydia asked.

"Most people do not remember how many shots they fired in a shoot-out."

"Well, I most certainly do!" she remanded him.

Gunther started to search the pockets of the man's clothes. From the outside pocket he pulled a folding knife. Its white pearl and silver handle had a distinct European design.

"This was meant for you," Gunther mumbled and tossed the weapon on the floor. He continued the body search. He found a room key and shoved it in his pocket.

"You do that like a veteran thief," Lydia said.

"Yeah, well…there's nothing to steal here." Then he digested her thief remark. "Lydia, you…are a thorn bush. You should—"

Just then Silas and Marilyn barged in. The reverend stiffened in shock at the sight of the body.

"Dead?" he gasped.

"Deader' n hell," Gunther answered.

"Are you all right Mrs. Latissimo?" Silas stepped to her and clutched her hands.

"I'm fine, Reverend," Lydia said sweetly.

"What are we going to do?" Silas asked.

Marilyn paced. Lydia folded her arms and grimaced as soon as Silas looked away.

Gunther looked at the clock on the wall. It was 10:20. "Well sir, we are going to bury him in Davy Jones' Locker, at about 1 A.M. Grab an arm, Padre."

The two men hauled the body across the room and into the bathroom, and stretched him out in the tub.

Marilyn pulled a broom out of the closet and headed for the rug where the man once laid.

"Oh for God's sake Marilyn, put that thing away. There is nothing to sweep up," Lydia complained. The heart shot, the quick kill, and the man's layers of clothing had absorbed any blood loss. The carpet appeared pristine.

"I am going to search this Russian's room. I suggest you all stay here until I get back."

As Gunther made for the door, Lydia walked by him and right into the bathroom.

"What are you doing?" he asked her.

She had the door half-closed, turned, and stopped with an impatient expression, "I'm going to the bathroom, of course." Then she shut the door, to be alone with her toilet and her corpse.

Gunther stared at the door for a few seconds with a blank expression, then left the cabin.

Once inside the Russian's room, Gunther quietly closed the door behind him. He looked around to see the sparse coach accommodations. Three identical black suitcases were open on the floor and on a table. The maids, or the surviving suspect, had folded all the clothes into neat piles. Gunther began inspecting the clothes. In each suitcase, in each pile, the pants, shirts, even the underwear all bore the same Sears store brand.

Gunther searched the bathroom and saw on the sink three identical toothbrushes. Three straight razors of the same style were on the bathtub rim. These foreigners had completely outfitted themselves in American gear from a Sears store, ditching all overt suggestions of their foreign traces. Except for that piece of Russian jewelry and the love letter in the pocket of one killer, their national identities were secret.

Gunther groaned when he realized he would have to "toss" this cabin around too, like Homestead's, in a daily effort to fool the maids. Already, room service had made the two beds and picked up around the sleeper sofa. He ripped down the covers and moved the glasses off the service tray. Just two more days of "un-housekeeping," and this trip and job of deception would be finished.

At 1 A.M. Gunther returned to Latissimo's room. He fastened all four buttons on the corpse's jacket, which completely concealed the chest wound. He sat the body up, no small feat given rigor mortis had set in, but it was beginning to fade. Silas helped him drag it over to the door. They each took a side and slung a stiff arm over their respective shoulders.

"If we see anyone? Let me do the talking," Gunther said as they made for the door. Lydia opened it.

Gunther peered around the corner, spied no one, and the two hauled the body down the first-class cabin hall. Before they got too far, an elderly couple tottered toward them clad in night clothes, and the woman held a tray of milk and cookies.

Gunther started talking to the dead man, "…and we'll have the ship's doctor see you immediately. Imagine!" he declared. As the couple drew near then, Gunther said to them, "I wouldn't have the fish if I were you!" with raised eyebrows.

"Oh my!" the elderly woman blurted.

"Shouldn't make a wish?" The old man looked confused.

"A fish! Robert, don't eat the fish, you old deaf bastard!" the old woman shouted.

Gunther and Silas made it to a side door, and Gunther said, "I got 'em. Take a look outside and see if there's anyone about." He clutched the Russian alone, and Silas opened the double doors and stepped into the night air.

"No one."

"Did you look up too, to the upper deck?"

"Yes."

They resumed their precarious escort positions, stepped outside, stood by the rail, and looked in all directions once more. No one came or went. They faced the corpse toward open water. Then Gunther simply let the torso free. Head heavy, it bent in half, and then flopped over the side. They never heard the splash.

They both stood still and leaned on the rail for a moment, as if watching the ocean. Gunther casually looked around. No witnesses.

"What have I done, Lord Jesus? God forgive me. I have done these things with mine own two hands that you gave me, dear Lord," Silas whispered to the night sky.

Gunther was far more relieved than repentant. In fact, he sighed, smiled, and almost laughed right out loud.

"I think we got away with it. Rev, look, why doncha' say a few appropriate words and we'll go back inside," Gunther turned as if to rest his back on the rail and stare skyward, but really to look the ship over instead for witnesses.

"Heavenly Father," the reverend began and then whispered an eloquent speech about lost souls. Gunther knew it would make him feel better. It did. When he finished, Verne turned and straightened his black frock.

"Well now, you've done your duty well, sir," Gunther complimented.

"How is poor, sweet Mrs. Latissimo going to handle this?" Silas asked.

"Lady Latissimo? She's probably already reloaded her hog's leg by now. And she's ready to kill again."

The next morning after breakfast, Gunther walked to the cruise management offices, and into the ship's Marconi room, the portion open to the public. Inside, three stewards worked feverishly translating sent and received messages on the Marconi wireless radio. He stopped beside some giddy newlyweds preparing a message home, pulled a tablet of paper toward him on a high, slanted desk. The slip read the word *Messages*. A pencil rested in a lip of the wood shelf.

Gunther took up the pencil and stared blindly at the patterned wallpaper before him. He contemplated his words, trying not to reveal any secrets should they be intercepted by his newfound enemies, yet still briefly explain the situation.

He wrote:

"To Captain Marigold-STOP
United States War Department-STOP
Washington DC-STOP
Need address to send Homestead's damaged uniform home-
STOP"
Should I brush up on my Russian-STOP
Signed Johann Gunther-STOP

He handed the telegram to a young man in a crisp blue uniform who said, "That will be five cents, sir." Gunther handed him a coin.

"When will I receive a reply?"

"We will deliver a reply to your room sir, as soon as it comes in. Oh! Please write your room number on the bottom."

Gunther wrote down his suite number and left.

Sunset. At each of the meals that day, the ship's captain announced that the 6 P.M. passage through the Straits of Gibraltar was simply delightful. Few would want to miss the event. At half past five, the decks filled with sightseers, Gunther among them. As he watched the lovely scenery from the ship's bow, he spotted Harrigan and John Smith hustle around their camera tripod trying to capture the landscape. The huge, mountainous Rock of Gibraltar stood to the north, jutting into the midnight blue sky, the evening city lights glistened at its granite foot. Visible in the distant south, Gunther saw the lights of Ceuta, Morocco, the most northern tip of Africa.

Butlers passed through the crowd, handing out glasses of champagne from trays. Gunther accepted one, took a sip, and rested his arms on the railing. The ship's horn blasted like a baritone voice across the waterway, warning the smaller Spanish and British boats of its presence.

"Poor Homestead," he thought over and over to himself. He looked back at the Atlantic and knew the giant ocean would be his final cold grave. No engraved stone for his wife and children to visit. The image of Homestead's body flipping through the night air, then crashing upon the water, haunted him. What if he'd been conscious when he hit the water? What if he'd yelled for help, his cries blanketed by the towering ship's powerful engines as it chugged just out of his desperate reach? Doomed, alone and bobbing in the middle of the ocean! Gunther shook his head free of the nightmare. If only he hadn't insisted Kelly get a ticket, he'd be safe traveling with the others now, perhaps in less style, but at least he'd be alive. Gunther guzzled the champagne but it didn't give him the whiskey kick he wanted.

Of course, he reassured himself, Kelly was surely unconscious, probably knocked out first by that Russian rattlesnake, or rendered so by the long drop and concussion from the unforgiving water. A free-fall trip he himself almost made! If not for his mother? The ghost of his mother? A nightmare in his mind, warning him to wake up and shoot?

"Mr. Gunther!" said the Reverend Silas Verne with Lydia Latis-simo, her arm hooked though his as her escort. Marilyn trailed behind.

Gunther nodded at them, and Verne detected his morose mood. "Such a beautiful place, isn't it?" Verne said softly, looking over the coastal landscape. Gunther nodded again.

"Thinking of Sergeant Major Homestead?" Verne asked quietly.

"Yup," Gunther acknowledged, "I am. A navy burial for an Army man."

"Oh yes, but his soul is not in that cold water, Johann. He was a good man, and he is in that warm sky above," Verne added. Even Lydia seemed to gaze sympathetically on Gunther.

"Hmmm," Gunther muttered. There was a distinct, new warm breeze touching them as the ship slowly moved into the Mediterranean.

Silas stared solemnly at Gunther with a subtle smile so peaceful it was unnerving. After an awkward silence, Verne said, "Enjoy the view," and he and Lydia strolled off in the direction of the photography team. Gunther left in the opposite direction. He was off for his nightly task of tossing around Homestead's and the Russians' rooms, to keep their disappearances a secret. Soon he would pack their belongings and the porters would stack them on the dock, for no one to pick up, and the mystery for the cruise line would begin as he made for the Afghan mountains. Gunther knew the belongings of four men would remain on the dock.

In two days they'd see Suez, Egypt, then down the Red Sea, and across the Arabian Sea: in four days, British India's Karachi. Then, off they'd march into a land strange and new, and an enemy wild and unknown. Gunther stopped and studied the small fishing boat off the starboard side. Dark-skinned, barefoot men in turbans and beards worked fishing nets. One stood and stared back up at him. No hand waves. No smiles he could see. Even from this distance, Gunther discerned a sneer. Was it because he represented rich success on a giant boat of capitalists, bigger and better than the city where they live? Was he the wrong religion? The wrong skin color? Was he an ugly monster from another world? As alien as the Martians in H.G. Wells' book? Gunther's fingers closed around a crumpled, five-word-only, telegraph message in his pocket from Captain Marigold, that read:

"Learn Russian for your trip- STOP"

Teddy had somehow done it to him again! He'd thrust him into a foreign land, dodging bullets and killing the enemy. Gunther knew one thing for sure: a bullet to the head dropped the largest man and a knife to the gut doubled him over quick. No matter how bad it got in Afghanistan with traitors, rogues, religious tyrants, raiders, and Russian agents, these two truths he held to be self-evident. Somewhere along the way he hoped to avenge Homestead's death.

◇

Gunther and John Smith entered the first-class dining room for the last lunch before docking in Karachi, British India.

"Oh, oh…" the host moved to them at the door. "I am so sorry sir, but we do not serve foreigners in this establishment." He never once looked at John as he said it.

"Son!" Gunther drawled in his best Texican growl. "We are in Africa now. And you are the foreigner." Gunther motioned to John, and they walked to an open table by the window. The host signaled to the manager. He strutted up with a stern smile, interrupting their path.

"Sir, excuse me but you…ah…he cannot eat here."

"Listen," Gunther leaned toward the manager's ear. "My friend and I have a little business to discuss and we are gonna' sit right over there. You don't want a big-ass, ugly, table-busting scene in here now, do ya? The last day of this fine cruise?"

The manager's face went pale and he started to gasp in little breaths, trying to formulate an answer.

Gunther continued, "Now, it's all real simple. Just run on back there and get us some fucking soup."

Page 105

Gunther and John took seats at the table and began to talk about photography as if there were no problems.

Soup, sandwiches, and coffee were duly served to the...foreigners.

9
Riding Up Front

"Allo, allo, allo," The large man said, ensconced at his desk reading an old London Times. A placard before him read,

Captain Reginold B. Alt, British Royal Marines
Commander, Karachi Lodging

This Captain Alt barely looked up at the new group of arrivals fresh from the ship, consisting of Gunther, Lydia, Marilyn, Silas, and the photographers.

"Palatime? Palatime! We have customers!" he sang out almost in a melody.

An Indian in a turban emerged through a back door of beaded strands and began organizing housing.

"The group from the United States," Captain Alt said. "Here overnight."

Gunther lingered near the front window as the rest were issued housing. The military lodging office stood just inside the walled headquarters maintained by the British army. Outside, the hot, muggy street was awash with Indians and Brits in uniform and civilian clothes. The Brits were overdressed for the heat in suits, while the locals were in loose-fitting whites or very sheer, colorful cloth.

A prehistoric roar filled the air! Three elephants lumbered down the dirt avenue, guided by a single Indian soldier with a long switch stick. On their backs were giant saddles, and each beast carried a cannon and wooden supply boxes. Marilyn rushed to the window, her blue eyes lit in amazement.

Young teens and boys in tan uniforms scurried in and out of the office hauling away the luggage of each travel member. Gunther came last.

"Johann Gunther," he announced himself.

"We will post you in a fine house, sir. You are with…where is a…." the Hindi searched his list, "…Sergeant Major Homestead?"

"He didn't make the trip," Gunther's throat tightened with unexpected emotion.

"Okay," and he drew a very deliberate line across the name. "Let's go. Let's go!" the man declared, violently snapping his fingers. Several Indian youths grabbed the trunks and bags and hauled them out the front door.

"Have a very fine day, sah!" the lodgings officer sang out, barely looking up. "You'll be there in half a mo."

"Thank you," Gunther replied, as he followed the boys out the door and through the heavy pedestrian, mule, and horse traffic to a narrow avenue of small stone and clay homes that smelled of animal sweat and dust.

Once inside his temporary quarters, Gunther tossed his hat on the dining table and took a look around the sparsely furnished small abode. The house was likely once that of a local resident before the military seized it. It contained lovely hardwood furnishings upholstered in deep reds and gold that had seen better days. All the porters left but one, a lad obviously assigned as a servant, a thin stick of a boy with giant eyes.

"Tea, sir?" the youth asked with an impeccable English accent.

"Well, son, that would be just fine. Yes."

Then came a knock at the door. Gunther answered.

"Major Gunther," Lieutenant Kerry stood at attention on the small porch, hardly a surprise to see. This admin meeting was inevitable. What did surprise Gunther was the seven U.S. soldiers with him, all sergeants.

"Gentleman," Gunther said. "Come on in." The men, all dressed in their Army brown uniforms with pistol belts equipped with service revolvers inside flap holsters and campaign hats, marched solemnly inside. "Good to see you all made it."

"Yes, we did and it was a lousy trip," said one. Gunther scanned the name embroidered on his shirt.

"That's too bad, Sergeant Grimsley."

"We don't have Teddy by the balls and couldn't go first class like you did, sir," commented a Sergeant Parker, and the men erupted in laughter. Gunther shook his head.

"You know the president well, sir?" Sergeant Allen asked as the men grabbed chairs and stools around the small house to gather around the table. Two had to stand.

"Yes I do, sergeant. Rough Riders. Cuba. I hunt with the president about every two years," Gunther said. "Well, what are the plans, lieutenant? Where is Captain Boston?"

"Captain Boston is dead, sir," Lieutenant Kerry said.

"Dead?" an astonished Gunther replied. "How? What the hell happened?"

"Perryweather, sir. Captain Perryweather shot him."

"Perryweather shot him?"

"In a duel, sir."

"A duel?"

"They argued on the ship, almost daily, about everything," Kerry explained. "At the heart of the matter, we all really knew. Who was in charge of the expedition? Perryweather kept pushing and pushing him. Once they almost came to blows in front of all of us in the ship's mess. Captain Boston cursed him like a sea dog. Called his mother a shipyard whore."

Sergeant Grimsley chimed in, "Perryweather, that prissy bastard, took his dainty gloves out from his belt and slapped Boston across the face with them. Challenged him to a gentleman's duel. Them gloves didn't hurt nothin'. They were soft white gloves, but Boston got plenty mad and accepted."

"Perryweather went below…" Kerry continued, "and came up with two flintlock pistols in a wooden box."

"Flintlocks," Gunther repeated.

"It was like out of a storybook, sir," Grimsley said. "Then

Perryweather asked the captain if'n he wanted a second. A second!"

"That is dueling rules, Grimsley," Gunther added. "Each duelist can have a second, meaning another sir—"

Grimsley interrupted," Capn' Boston said–'I don't need a second more to kill your ass!'"

The men laughed, but this time not so heartily, more fondly.

"They stood sideways on the deck so's not to accidentally shoot nobody." Grimsley stood up and put his hand to his chest with a pointed finger skyward. "They stood just like this. Gun barrels to heaven. They turned and counted off ten steps." Grimsley demonstrated the movement. "Then on ten, they spun around and dropped hammer on them ol' cannonball pistols. Crack. Swish! Flash. Boom! I swear it took a minute for them pistols to fire off! Off went the bullets. But Capn' Boston didn't wait for all that old-timey, flintlock action to work all its steps, and he musta' moved the gun. Clean missed the limey. But Perryweather didn't jerk his smoke wagon and shot the captain right in the throat. Killed him dead."

"Killed him dead, sir," Kerry repeated.

Gunther sat there bewildered. He blew an exasperated sigh.

"The men have been talking," Kerry spoke up, "and well, I am next in command and well…new. I just don't think I can run a company this size in a place like this. We all think it best if you would fill in for Boston. You have seen a lot of action—"

"—And the president hisself has his respects for ya," Sergeant Allen interrupted.

"There are a lot of old-timers and vets in this contingent, Lieutenant Kerry," Gunther suggested.

"And none of us wants to ride up front," Sergeant Parker declared.

"Ain't none of us company commanders," Sergeant Allen advised.

"I can tell you they are all good men," Kerry continued. "I am half their age. It is my command decision to make, in the end, to surrender command. I think it wise, sir."

"Well, what say ye', gentleman?" Gunther asked the NCOs that huddled about him.

"We agree, Mr. Gunther and we put the laddy here up to it!" a Sergeant Callahan said with a deep, Irish accent. The others nodded and Callahan continued, "I think this Perryweather is a wee batty, and he won't care a saint's lick about us Yanks when the arrows start a flyin'. You're a West Pointer, and you've worked with the Brits in Africa before. Fought the Insurrectos in the Philippines. You're an old Indian fighter. It stands to reason you'd be a good choice to ride up front, sah."

Gunther stared at the floor for a moment. He grimaced and rubbed his nose, finally speaking with a tone of reluctance. "I guess I could. But I would like to do so quietly. Let's let Perryweather actually ride all the way up front and lead the expedition. And Lieutenant Kerry here can handle most of the daily command matters, but I am sure he could use the advice of some seasoned NCOs."

Kerry nodded. The men nodded.

"I tell you this," Gunther added, "I know my way in and around a good fight. You have my word, I will think of your safety. I am not reckless. Anytime you don't like what I'm doing, let Lieutenant Kerry take full command."

The men nodded in agreement.

"Where's Kelly Homestead?" Sergeant Grimsley asked.

Gunther looked down at the servant boy standing in the kitchen doorway, "Sonny! Get home. Get out of here. Go on!" The surprised boy shuffled out of the house. Gunther turned back to the group. "The sergeant major? Well boys, I too have bad news. And this is bad news for all of us. Homestead was killed on the ship... by Russian agents."

"What happened?" Callahan asked.

Before the astonished men, Gunther recounted the sad tale of Homestead's demise and the ugly affair of the three Russian agents. He reminded them of the territorial war between the Brits and Russia over Afghanistan. "As senior NCOs of this mission, I want you to know that there is more at stake here than trying to find a missing colonel or some giant horses. We have been thrust into some kind of international power struggle. Tell your men all this, as I do not wish it to be a secret among you. Keep your eyes and ears open as other agents may attack us."

With that, Gunther stood, and the others followed.

"We'll pass the word, sir," Lieutenant Kerry informed Gunther. Then he finished up with the business of travel. "We're leaving at 11 A.M. tomorrow, on a special military train to Kabul. From there we march out to the Khyber Pass and points north. Perryweather is in Kabul now with his men, an escort detachment from the Ninth Bengal Lancers and one unit of the Second Punjab Infantry. He is organizing the caravan. They will have horses, camels, and supply wagons at the ready."

"Tonight our men have an encampment on the west side of this base, near the railroad lines, sir," Sergeant Grimsley said. "We'll load up in the morning."

"The machine guns get here?"

"Yes, sir, ten gun teams and the ten wagons," Kerry answered.

"These machine guns will no doubt save our lives in a battle-field defense," Gunther said. "I want those guns mounted in the wagons, but with quick releases so we can remove them at a moment's notice."

"Yes, sir," Kerry said. "We'll come to collect you all for the train at 11 A.M., sir."

"Fine, Lieutenant," Gunther acknowledged as he stood and opened one of his steamers. He produced a tablet of paper and a pen and while writing continued, "One more thing Lieutenant. Find the nearest Bank of England branch in the morning. Take this letter and withdraw two thousand dollars in British pounds. Coins if they have them."

"Coins, sir?" Kerry said.

"Gold and silver coins always work better when you bribe officials and pay off cutthroats. Next, you will find some merchants by the train station. Buy five hundred dollars of additional food and water supplies to pack in on this trip. I have never been on a military expedition of any length where the quartermaster was smart enough to have enough food and water.”

The men exchanged glances, telegraphing their approval of their new commander.

“I will work on it at the break of dawn, sir.”

“Sergeant Grimsley, accompany the lieutenant,” Gunther said.

“Yes,” Grimsley said. “What shall we be callin’ ya, sir? Major?”

“I prefer you call me Gunth, or Gunther…”

“We prefer to call you major, sir,” Sergeant Parker said.

The men started filing out of the front door, but Callahan turned and said, “My way of thinking, sir? You take up for Capn’ Boston? In Perryweather’s eyes, you’re next for a duel, or a bullet.”

“If that happens? I’ll pick you for my second, Sergeant, if he gets me? You kill that son of a bitch in one second,” Gunther said with a smile and a pat on his shoulder. The men chuckled and filed out.

Gunther inspected the bedroom, finding a lantern, a military cot, and thatch chair. He grabbed up his cup of tea, walked to the front door, and leaned against the frame of the open doorway. India! Another place he’d never dreamed he’d see, yet here he stood. Even the very air smelled different. He detected the faint scent of some exotic flowers mixed with the smell of reed woven baskets and cattle dung. Then he spotted the servant boy he’d just dismissed sitting on a small wall across the dirt street.

“Hey there, young feller,” Gunther shouted with a half-smile, “I told you to take the day off. Go home! Go see your momma!”

The boy slid off the wall and walked toward Gunther. He looked about ten years old, clad only in ragged pants with a rag wrapped around his head to protect it from the heat. “I have no home.”

“Where are your parents?” Gunther asked.

“I don’t know,” the boy answered.

“Where do you sleep?”

The boy’s thin arm raised and pointed back inside the house, “In there, sir, on the floor.

“Do most of the boys…live here in these houses, too?”

“Yes.”

Gunther studied him. Long black hair. Dark skin. "Well then son, come on back in…and…and make some more tea." The boy marched past him and back into the house.

Not much to like about India so far, Gunther thought as the orphan walked by him. Hot. Dirty. Stinky. Lazy officers. Homeless children. News of a murderous duel. And now, a new job he did not want, commanding hundreds of men.

His ears detected a high-pitched yell down the street. He looked several houses down south to see Lydia Latissimo scolding some porters, something to do with them not following her orders. But, beside her stood two local men, dressed in bright-colored outfits and turbans. One carried a satchel and handed her some papers. She studied the papers, nodding her head. Gunther could not distinguish the conversation. He sipped his tea and daydreamed briefly of a duel between Perryweather and Lydia. Neither would survive.

Early the next afternoon, the travelers piled their luggage on the roadside and gathered on schedule for their escort to the military train station.

"Did you have some guests last night, Lydia?" Gunther asked point-blank.

"Yes," she admitted reluctantly. "They are local travel guides. I sent for them."

"You did? And…are you thinking of some extra travel, on top of the travel we have already mapped out?" Gunther asked.

"Possibly so," was all she offered.

"Hmmm, I hope you will keep us informed as to your travel plans," Gunther said in a sarcastic tone, just as Lieutenant Kerry, Sergeant Grimsley, and an Indian sepoy soldier arrived on the street with two large military coaches. All three men wore their Krag bolt-action duty rifles slung routinely across their backs.

Gunther admired the ornamental British coaches, not unlike the stagecoaches that ran in the United States but these were larger and more refined, with metallic trim and thick, glossy, black enamel paint. Each coach had two stout horses upfront driven by two smiling Indians dressed in green velvet suits.

Gunther ran a hand down the hot, slightly sweaty neck of one gelding in the team, "Hey, howdy, fellah," he turned to Silas Verne. "Amazing how horses the world over look the same, huh?"

"God's plan," Silas said with a smile.

Kerry slipped off his campaign hat, scratched his head, and studied the enormous pile of luggage. "Let's take all this luggage in the second coach, which has the team of four horses, and the passengers in the first since it has a team of two.

"Okay, Lieutenant," Gunther said, anxious to go. "Then let's get aboard." The drivers helped Lydia and Marilyn inside. Harrigan and Smith followed. Gunther peered into the tight quarters, gauging their size. He stepped to the rear of the vehicle, where the back of the coach had a two-foot wide running board, bordered by brass handrails—a place for servants to ride.

"I believe I'll ride on the back," Gunther announced to the drivers.

Reverend Verne stepped up to join him, "I believe I will as well."

"We will have to circle the outside of the fort to get to the train station," the Indian soldier advised. "The avenues in the middle of the fort are tied up with a parade. It will take us about ten extra minutes to get there. No problem."

Kerry, the two soldiers, and two drivers started loading up the luggage into the second coach. "You folks go on ahead. We'll catch up with you at the train station."

The coach lurched off down the street, past the Lodgings office, through the main fort gates, and off the military post. With an increase of traffic and noise, the wagon turned onto the Karachi streets. The roads held some automobiles, but mostly small horse-drawn buggies, coaches, large commercial wagons, and the occasional elephant. They were lined with trees, interspersed with houses and buildings of unique architecture followed by sections of abject poverty. Dirt roads. Brick roads. Cobblestone roads. The sacred cows wandered everywhere, hundreds of them, sharing sidewalks, blocking traffic, sleeping and grazing where they liked.

At one point, they rode near what seemed to be a game of polo, heavily attended by the British community, but upon closer inspection, Gunther saw the Englishmen were not knocking about a sports polo ball, but rather spearing wild pigs with long lances.

"Popular sport here!" Silas shouted to him over the din.

Gunther and Silas were commenting on these and other sights and sounds when their coach suddenly stopped short, jolting everyone forward. Gunther reached for the topside handrail and climbed another ledge up the back to peer over the top. Ahead, all the wagons and coaches on the wide street, some twenty of them, had halted in both directions. The street was large and bordered by well-kept businesses and large stone edifices.

Horses anxiously shifted about in their harnesses. One reared up on its hind legs. There was even an elephant saddled with a bamboo stand full of people on its back. Otherwise, an ominous silence fell. The cause of this gridlock seemed centered around the intersection just ahead.

"What's the problem?" Gunther yelled to his two drivers, but before he got an answer, he heard a roar of human shouts from around the corner of the intersection beyond his vision. The wave of sound grew louder. Not screaming, not shrieks, just a steady yell from seemingly a hundred or more angry men. The sound billowed down from the street on the right, but large marble buildings obscured the source of the outcry.

Forward and to his left some twenty-five yards away, just below an enormous marble building, a large group of Indians amassed on a stone plaza. More poured out from the doorways of this exotic palace. Tens, then a hundred, maybe more, filled the plaza. Before Gunther's shocked gaze, all these men on the plaza pulled weapons from their billowing white and tan robes. Some were bare chested and drew swords from sheaths on their beltline. These men remained quiet and craned their necks to glare up the street at the source of the onrushing roar. Gunther reflexively lunged for his Luger but didn't draw the pistol, as he was not the subject of their attention.

Then this cacophony erupted in echoes around the intersection. The Indians stood ready on the plaza, the stairs, and around the palace, shuffling and steeling themselves for a fight.

Verne climbed up to Gunther's height and they exchanged glances. Then, the raging, hollering madmen suddenly appeared in one massive human wave in the intersection with clubs, sticks, and curved swords held high. The charging group crashed headlong into the men on the plaza in a human tidal wave of flashing swords and spurting blood.

The horses pulling the wagons on the street went wild, yanking the coaches left and right as the drivers wrestled to gain control. The elephant trumpeted and lumbered back and forth with no route for escape.

"The Muslims and the Hindus," Reverend Verne shouted. "They frequently fight like this."

"Over what?" Gunther yelled.

"Over…God," Verne answered.

Their two drivers dropped from their seats to the ground and grabbed the reins of their horses. They pulled back on the horses' tack and tried to back the coach for a possible sharp turn to the left. Gunther saw the sheer fear in the drivers' eyes.

"We are going another way!" A driver screamed.

Gunther watched, mesmerized by the violence. The men, once engaged, were dressed and bearded in such a similar manner they were virtually indistinguishable from each other. The flashing swords glinted in the sun and their sticks and clubs rose and fell and rose and fell until the conflict became little more than a rubble of wounded and dead men. The blood from at least a hundred dead men drained down the steps. Survivors missing limbs bellowed in pain, and some crawled away from the debauchery.

A dozen of the surviving, enraged men on the border of this combat zone turned their attention to the wagons, carts, and pedestrians in the street. One of the lunatics raised his bloody sword in the air, let out a savage shriek, and charged the wagons. In a second a splinter group, caught in the wolf-pack frenzy of murder, joined him. Gunther heard Marilyn scream from inside the wagon and thought longingly of his rifle, packed so tightly away in his trunk in the second coach.

The drivers worked feverishly to turn their coach in among the stopped traffic. The elephant had enough! It lowered its head and butted the wagon of vegetables in front, while the creature's driver scolded the elephant to halt with a fierce paddle slap across the forehead. The wagon slid sideways, wheels broke, and it then flipped completely over, pitching the farmer and his produce through the air. With a triumphant roar, the beast ran off through the opening, its head shoving lesser wagons and carts aside like matchsticks. Carts flipped through the air.

A splinter group, still thirsty for any blood, began hacking at people in the wagons, carts, and coaches nearest them. Amid hideous screams limbs fell to the cobblestones within gushes of blood. A head toppled and bounced under a cart. Drivers and passengers leaped from their vehicles to dodge the onslaught. Gunther climbed to the top of the coach and drew his pistol. These killers were still out of range, but they carved a path closer and closer to Gunther and his wagon.

Suddenly, one appeared from between two nearby wagons. With his machete held high he bore down upon one of their drivers, tugging and turning on the reins of the horse team. From the top of the coach, Gunther fired and caught the killer on the top back half of the head. The small explosion on the skull crippled the body, and the killer fell back, dropping his steel weapon. The driver collapsed to his knees, cowering in fear.

"Let's go! Let's go!" Gunther shouted. The two drivers finally positioned the coach sideways on the street and jumped aboard. They whipped the horses into a narrow space between other stalled wagons and took off back in the direction they had come, weaving in and around the vehicles also jockeying to escape.

Two wild-eyed men with clubs, screeching like banshees, gave chase. The one in the lead drew dangerously close to Reverend Verne, still standing on the rear ledge. The killer swung a club at Verne's head and it passed within inches of the reverend. Gunther, now lying flat on top of the coach, fired two rounds down into the runner's bare belly. The runner dropped instantly and face first, as if tripped. The coach increased speed and outran the second runner.

Gunther holstered his pistol. "Which ones were the Muslims and which were the Hindus?" he asked Verne in exasperation as he climbed down to stand on the rear running boards again.

"I don't know. I can't tell," Verne answered, clutching the side rail with both arms in a bear hug.

"Thank you!" The Indian driver who had escaped the machete shouted over his shoulder, "Thank you, Mr. American."

Not even one minute's ride away from the riot, the streets appeared perfectly normal, even serene. They passed the pig-sticking contest again, the officers and attendees completely happy, clapping and oblivious to the small, vicious war unfolding just eight blocks away.

The second coach appeared on the road, with Lieutenant Kerry seated beside the driver. They were surprised to see Gunther's group. When abreast, both wagons stopped in the street. The drivers yelled to each other, "Turn around! Turn around. Muslim Riot! We will go around the other way."

Verne took this opportunity to slip off the back. "I'm…going to sit…inside." He opened the coach door and climbed in.

"Lieutenant!" Gunther called out. "Toss me your lever action."

Kerry had a Colt pistol and two more soldiers aboard had rifles. He slipped the rifle off his shoulder and pitched it into Gunther's eager hands.

"You'll get 'er back at the station," Gunther jumped down into the front seat between the two drivers. He cycled the lever, ramming a round into the chamber, and then rested the butt of the stock on his thigh. "If I'm gonna have to ride up front on this crate, I may as well do it up right."

10
The Highwaymen of Toomba

The rest of the trip to the military train depot was as uneventful as a ride in a city park. The two wagons pulled within the rear railroad cars, and from on top of the coach Gunther could see the locals along with the soldiers of the mission loading the boxes of supplies, weapons, and ammo onto the twenty-car train. Horses and camels were led up wooden ramps and onto open cars with fenced sides. Gunther saw two machine gun teams, one on a forward car roof, the other aft, setting up positions and stacking short walls of sandbags around each of them.

Lieutenant Kerry met Gunther inspecting these topside automatic firing posts. "Standard procedure they say, sir, for an Afghan run." Then Kerry ordered a few of the U.S. soldiers to break from the train and unload the coach luggage.

As Gunther dropped from the coach he saw the same two Indian men in colorful garb that Lydia had spoken with on the street the previous night. This time, the pair stood in the company of several natives clad in dirty white linens. Two colorful and ornate wagons were parked near them, one open and the other an enclosed coach. Six stout horses grazed near the men and wagons. A fat Indian woman busied herself about a wagon and a small monkey in a red velvet coat scampered the ground near them all. They appeared fully kitted out for their own extensive trip with a small trailer full of gear.

"No, no," Lydia began ordering the cavalry soldiers. "These suitcases are to go over there with those men. On that wagon, there!" She culled her and Marilyn's luggage from the rest.

Harrigan and Smith hustled up to the smiling men and Lydia talked and gestured with excitement.

Gunther returned the rifle back to Lieutenant Kerry as he walked toward Lydia. "What's going on?"

"Mr. Gunther, I am taking a side trip."

"A side trip?"

"Yes, there are some wonderful, health-restoring hot springs on a mountain near here. At Toomba. They are world famous. These guides are going to take us there."

Gunther was taken aback.

"Oh, we will be back here at the station in two days and on the next train to Kabul. You know you'll be up there for a week fussing about. We will catch up with you in Kabul before you leave. Well, don't look at me like that!" Lydia demanded.

Harrigan approached them before Gunther could speak and offered, "I believe John and I will join them. These men assure us that the scenery in and about the springs is savage and beautiful. We must photograph it for the society!"

The two guides wandered up and nodded their heads as Gunther eyed them from the tips of their curled pink slippers to the tops of their swirling headdresses.

"…and we may be able to get some fantastic pictures," John Smith said.

Lydia ignored Gunther and strutted off to supervise the soldiers loading her valuables into the Indian's garish wagons.

Gunther turned to Silas Verne, "You in on this, too?" The reverend raised both his hands and shook his head to the negative.

"So," Gunther said loud enough for them all to hear," this little bloodbath we just saw wasn't enough to scare the hell out of you?"

Lydia carried a satchel past him and stopped inches from him, "Maybe now you think you're in charge of this little toy soldier parade, but I will come and go as I damn well please."

Harrigan and John Smith sheepishly began hauling their photography footlockers to the guides' wagon. "We'll be fine Mr. Gunther. They said, people vacation there frequently," Harrigan assured. "It's a resort."

Verne stepped beside Gunther, "Maybe they will be safe with this group," he observed. "They look very professional."

"Safe!" Gunther said. "Look at 'em! They look like a pack of goddamn pirates from a fairytale book."

"Are you going to stop them?" Verne asked as the woman boarded the open wagon. One of these "pirates" handed them both frilly pink umbrellas, which they popped open against the hot sun. Marilyn gaily twirled hers, spinning the lace fringe. Harrigan and Smith, brandishing big smiles, jumped in the back beside their gear.

"I guess they will be all right. I am not officially responsible for the safety of any of them. And, you know, honestly, Reverend, I'd like to be rid of the whole lot of them." Gunther took off his hat, bowed slightly at the waist, and shouted to them, "Good-bye, me ladies!" and then muttered lowly for only Verne to hear, "and good riddance."

Lieutenant Kerry walked up, "Wha–where the hell are they going?"

"To a watering hole in Toombalalala." Gunther turned and headed toward the train.

"Toomba," Verne corrected, and he too made for the train as well.

The tour wagon and group started off for Toomba, but not before Marilyn smiled, waved and shouted in a grandiose, songlike manner, "Good-bye, Lieutenant!" all within a flurry of long blonde hair and a spinning umbrella, which seemed to freeze the young officer like a statue for a full minute. She looked back again coyly, smiled, and waved as he stood there gaping.

"Lieutenant!" Gunther barked just an inch from the man's ear. "Pick up your jaw. We're leaving now."

<>

None of the commanders on the train ride to Kabul spotted the peg-legged, hunched, soiled beggar that tried to board the last car of the train. The native railroad men seemed to know this poor soul and shooed him off like a pest, despite his insistent pleas. But minutes later, as the train pulled slowly away from the station, the rail men busied themselves with chores, and the disfigured man hooked a caboose rail with the handle of his cane and managed to leap and roll onto the back balcony with surprising agility. He had a life or death message he simply had to deliver to the man in the cowboy hat with the long blond hair.

Inside a railcar, Gunther, Kerry, Sergeant Grimsley and a sepoy Indian lieutenant named Satin sat around a scattered mess of maps piled on the serving table in their cabin. The men scoured over the planned route of the caravan and some combat strategies should they run across any of the many hostile tribes of the region.

"I know not what the British will do, but my concern is being hit by snipers in these mountain passes. We have to develop a troop formation that best protects us from tribal sharpshooters." Gunther drummed a pencil on the map. "Then in the open areas, they may sweep in on horseback and hit parts of our lines, usually the weakest parts. I think the worst event was the British retreat from Kabul in the 1840s," Gunther continued. "Some five thousand people fled for Jalalabad, in the dead of winter. The revolting tribes sniped and raided until the caravan—men, women and children—were decimated, starving and freezing to death. In just a few days! Days! This is my fear, gentlemen," Gunther looked at each face in the room.

"You know much of our problems, Sahib Major," Lieutenant Satin complimented.

"Learned it at the Point?" Grimsley asked.

"Sergeant, honestly, I think I was drunk most of the time at West Point," Gunther said, and the men laughed. "But, I do recall in that alcoholic haze, some lessons on the Afghan Wars. Plus, I have just been reading up on the battles of the last century here from a British history book. The mountains we face here are taller, steeper, quite jagged. The passes are very narrow in places. The tribes attack in massive waves or build encampments on the thinnest of ledges and snipe down into the passes. That's why I wanted the machine guns, to kill the massive wave attacks, and I have requested Army archers and dynamite. We'll shoot dynamite arrow sticks up at their perches, if need be."

"The archers left one day after we did, major," Kerry said. "They'll catch up with us in Kabul."

"That is odd," Lieutenant Satin said. "No one here has thought of this before."

"It is odd," said Gunther. "The bow is not new to this region. Alexander the Great came through here with legions of archers, and the British used the longbow and crossbow for centuries. Many of our American Indians tied dynamite to the arrows and fired them at us. Very portable cannons!"

Porters brought in coffee and tea on two trays and looked to set them somewhere, but the table was covered in charts.

"Put them there on Russia," Kerry pointed, and then added, "Well, surely Captain Perryweather is schooled in all these problems?"

"I don't know, Lieutenant," Gunther answered. "I have learned that the British officer can be as bad as our American ones can be. Once, an Englishman's family would buy his colors; essentially purchase his officer's rank. A favored son could often be thrust into a command with very little training. Buying colors has since been outlawed, but much tomfoolery like this still goes on. I tell ya men, I look out for rich officers, men from wealthy and important families. They often get their ranks from fame, connections and…and their wealth…and I don't trust such a man at first. They have to prove themselves to me. Time will tell with this peacock Perryweather."

"Time will tell," Grimsley repeated softly. "He sure knew how to push Capn' Boston into a fight and shoot him down, under his rules."

Gunther looked at Grimsley's profile, sitting in a chair beside him that should have been Homestead's. Grimsley was now the senior NCO.

"Can we treat with any of these hostiles?" Lieutenant Kerry asked Lieutenant Satin.

As versed as Satin was in English, he couldn't understand the question. Gunther recognized his quizzical look and translated, "Treat is a U.S. Cavalry word for make treaty or bargain."

Satin nodded. "We have made many appointments with tribes to keep the passes open. And we pay them a fee, a toll, or a monthly stipend. It constitutes an ugly business, but we have to." He pointed to three passes on the map. "These three are under the protection of the British government. They are run by mercenaries who are friendly to us…as long as we pay. One group is run by the Star of Africa, a black woman from Northern Africa. A former slave." Satin smiled. "She is famous for her cruelty, legendary for her exquisite beauty and for one gold tooth with an African diamond in it."

"The Star of Africa…is a tooth?" Gunther asked.

"Yes, Sahib Major. She is named after her tooth. She is paid to protect a pass. But there are just as many other passes that are wide open to any tribe tough enough to control them. The tribes fight each other for control. There is much money to be made running a pass."

Suddenly there came a vicious rapping on the cabin's glass window. The men turned, and the visage in the hall startled them. A hunched, filthy figure with wild hair babbled, "You! You! Blondie!" in English and pointed at Gunther. Two train porters appeared and grabbed the man's arms.

Gunther saw the look of either desperation or insanity flash upon the man's face. He stood and opened the door, "What do you want?"

"I must tell ya, tell ya of the bloody danger!" he said as the porters tugged his arms to haul him away.

"What danger?" Gunther asked.

"Ya friends, laddie boy. They are doomed!" He waved a filthy finger at Gunther.

Gunther indicated to the porters to release the man. The man limped into the cabin and a strong smell of dead animals, dried urine and bad alcohol filled the room.

"Who are you?" Gunther asked. Lieutenant Kerry lit a cigar to beat back the stench.

"Sergeant Adam Dollop, Sah. Ha! British Royal Marines. Retired." Unable to stand, the man dropped into Gunther's empty seat. "Wounded and tortured by the sharp swords of a pack of darkie scoundrels, ten yar ago, Sah! My pittance from Her Majesty is like a short piss in the dry wind, but goes a bit further in this savage land here than it would in ol' Britannia. So I stays here, I have." He snatched a cookie off a tray and shoved it whole into his toothless mouth. It disappeared without a chew.

"Have ya heard of the Stranglers, Laddie?" the man said. "The Thuggees, the murderous bloody cult of Kali?"

"No," Gunther crossed his arms over his chest.

"The Thuggees…" Lieutenant Satin added. "They are an ancient band of killers and robbers. A religious cult."

"Aye! Ha! Highwaymen!" the man shouted and pounded his cane tip on the wooden floor. "They each carry them a scarf with knots tied in it, the better ta wrap about ya neck and pull till ya eyes pop outta ya head."

Satin nodded. "Yes. These criminals were a terrible plight upon our land. They are all but gone, thanks to the English."

"Ha! All but gone, but not gone," the foul man corrected. "They are still at their secret work, robbing strangers on the trails."

"And this is your warning?" Gunther asked, ready to toss the foul creature from the cabin. He'd already wasted enough of his time.

"Yer lady friends?" The man slapped at a flea on his face. "I saw ya talkin' to 'em. And yer two men friends? They got in a wagon back at the station? I saw ya! Half those men were Thuggees!"

"Are you sure?" Lieutenant Kerry demanded.

"Sure as bloody rain. I knows the scoundrels."

"The men of Kali do this, Sahib Kerry," Lieutenant Satin advised. "They often escort travelers or meet with them on the road. At the night's campsite they dine and drink, then strangle every member in the party. They steal their possessions and give half to their church."

"Three to one!" the foul man added. "A Thuggee grabs a right arm. A Thuggee grabs a left arm. The third Thuggee hooks the neck with his knotted scarf and—ggagaagggghhh!" He imitated the process with his hands, and then stuck his gray tongue out the side of his cracked mouth.

Kerry bolted upright, "We must do something!"

"Are you hungry, Mr. Dollap?" Gunther asked.

"Why, I'm starving to the bone," the man answered in a child-like tone. "Tis very nice of ya to ask me, Sah."

Gunther opened the door and said to the porters, "Feed Mr. Dollap here a fine meal, will you gentlemen?" and the two porters reluctantly escorted the limping man away.

Grimsley opened all the cabin windows and inspected a bit for fleas. He took up a map and fanned the air.

"Is there really a famous hot spring in Toombala?" Gunther asked Satin.

"Yes, Sahib."

"We are just going to have to go after them. Damn!" Gunther said with a sigh. "Grimsley, get me two of your best scouts and three men. Lieutenant Satin, can you assign me your best scout and three men?"

"Yes, Sahib Major. I shall accompany you."

"I request permission to go, sir!" Lieutenant Kerry asked.

"If something happens to me, this whole shindig falls back on you, Lieutenant. You are too valuable. I know that you are busting at the seams to go."

"I request that you reconsider."

It was obvious to Gunther that the thought of a knotted scarf pulled taunt around the beautiful neck of Marilyn was more than Kerry could stand, least of which the murders of the other three.

"I have reconsidered. You can come," Gunther said impulsively. Then he looked to Grimsley, "And you sir, are in command in our absence. If all goes as planned, we will rescue the group and get on the next train to Kabul and meet you all there. Lieutenant Kerry? Get up to the conductor and stop this train!"

Kerry left for the engine compartment, Satin and Grimsley for the passenger cars to organize the rescue party. Gunther walked to the open window to watch the strange and unfamiliar landscape flash by. He pulled his pocket watch from his pocket. The train left the station one hour ago and this meant a lot of back tracking. "And I may do some wringing myself on the neck of Lydia Latissimo, if I can find her first."

There is hardly a group more desperate for news and gossip than an army—big or small—especially one operating in the field. When the Kabul train screeched to a halt from an engineer's sudden yank on the emergency brake, the soldiers aboard jolted forward, twitched and jumped about like turkeys in the barnyard after a sneeze.

Already in fear of an ambush, they scampered to windows and doors and dashed down the halls. Guns at the ready, men leapt from the forward and rear cars not to find an alien enemy, but rather to see the rescue party of eleven men pull horses from the open flatbeds down ramps. Gunther heard the general conversations through the onlookers.

"Where they goin'?"

"To rescue the women folk?" said the closest ones that knew.

"The womenfolk? From what?"

"The Indians."

"They got Indians over here, too?" said one.

"They got India Indians, ye goddamn dimwit."

Sergeant Grimsley pointed out two lean men in their late thirties, already on horseback, to Gunther. "That's Rosie… er, Sergeant Rosenthal and that is Private Gildenbeck. Gildy was a sergeant once too, until he got real drunk one night and cut off the right leg of a talking parrot—mouthy little bastard, the parrot, ahhh—that's a long story sir, but it was a captain's parrot in Kansas and, when all was said and done, Gildy was demoted to private."

"I see," Gunther checked his guns for ammunition.

"The parrot…well…insulted him, sir. But these two boys have served all over and are the finest scouts you'll ever find. Both of them are from New York City, but they read the ground like a Southwest Apache."

Gunther jumped into the saddle of a horse held for him.

"Whose horse is this?" he asked.

"Mine, sir," declared a man on the flatbed.

"What's his name sergeant?" Gunther asked.

"Ol' Bachelor," the trooper shouted. "He's named after me." The men laughed.

"Well, I promise to take good care of him, and you'll get 'im back the day after tomorrow."

"Thank you, sir."

Gunther patted the pockets of his field outfit–tan pants, shirt and boots to check their contents for knife, matches and other survival tools. He pulled his Western gun belt up another notch to better support the weight of his gun and holster. He tugged his tan Stetson tighter on his head. Then he slung a lever-action shotgun across his shoulder and slid his Mauser rifle into a leather rifle sheath latched to the saddle.

A troop tossed saddlebags of supplies across the back of each horse as the other ten members prepped their own horses and gear.

A private in a crowd of onlookers stared at the brown leather engraved Western gun belt Gunther wore. Gunther heard him say, "What kind of hog's leg is that?" He pointed at the pistol on Gunther's hip.

Gunther pulled the gun and looked at it. "This?"

"That," a nearby sergeant answered, "is a point forty-five caliber automatic pistol. The bullets come in a square box that ya shove up into the handle. Soon, the whole of the U.S. Army will be wearing them. You, too."

"What's that thing in yer armpit?" he asked, as Gunther positioned the Luger weapon for the ride, "above that Bowie knife on his left side, there. Up there."

"German Luger," the sergeant again answered for Gunther between spits of tobacco. "The Army tried that one and didn't like it. No punch. Don't like 'em myself. The Germans like 'em though."

"And he's a Kraut?"

"His first name is Johann. He's a Kraut."

"I'm American." Gunther tapped his hat and kicked his horse into a gallop.

"The British and Indian engineers carved this dirt service road that runs along the track for at least that far up the line," Lieutenant Satin told Gunther, "We can take it back to the train station.

The engineer blew the steam whistle, and the men hurried back aboard.

"Good luck, boys! May the Lord be with ya!" Grimsley shouted.

The posse galloped back down the trail to Karachi, in a race to beat a bloody sunset.

When the busy train station of the British compound fell into view, Gunther ordered his men to rein their horses to a slow trot. He craned his neck and stood in the saddle to discern the exact location where he first learned of Lydia Latissimo's surprise vacation to the hot springs and witnessed their farewell.

"There!" Gunther shouted, and heeled Ol' Bachelor into another run. The men followed. Near the dirt and flat rock trail where the group had departed, he stepped from the horse just before the gelding stopped.

"Here!" he pointed. The group reined their animals in before trampling the scene. Rosenthal and Gildenbeck slipped off their saddles and knelt before the wagon tracks, to read the imprints in the ground. The two were such a veteran scout team; they tied the reins of their horses together and left them standing. They walked up the trail a bit to follow the path.

"Lieutenant Satin!" Gunther barked as he peeled off his hat to wipe his brow.

"Yes Major!" the Indian responded.

"Can we get these horses some food and water? Quickly?"

"Yes, Sahib Major," the Indian said. Then he shouted orders to some Pushtan soldiers at the station building.

"Holding up well?" Gunther quizzed the remaining men.

"Yes, sir," they all answered nearly at once.

"We'll dismount and give our animals a break. We'll be here for about thirty minutes," he advised. The men stepped down and walked their horses about to cool them off.

Sergeant Rosenthal walked up to Gunther and reported, "We've got a bite on the wagon wheels. But there are other wheel tracks on that road. A lot of them. But look here." He guided Gunther to the tracks. Lieutenant Kerry anxiously joined them. The three knelt by the impressions.

"Course now…we are looking for a wagon, like you said. There are a lot of horse track all over here. This rear wheel here—the right one—has a wobble. We've got two horses, but only one of them is shod up to any damn good. It could be slow going at times as we try to pick the wobble and the horse track from the cluster." Rosenthal stood, then Gunther and Kerry.

As they spoke, two British couples with picnic baskets strolled by bound for the dirt road.

"That there's the source of our confusion," Gildy said. Three horses and riders apparently out for an afternoon ride, blissfully trotted by.

"Damn!" muttered Gunther. He turned and watched. Some Indian soldiers, under Satin's direction, carried buckets of water and feed to the horses. Another coach, pulled by two horses and, carting a laughing British man and woman, turned onto the dirt road, further crushing and confusing their plans. Then an Indian family appeared around the first bend of road walking in from the country. A few lone Hindu, with big backpacks of produce, followed.

Gunther raked his hand through his hair. "Damn!" he muttered once more. "Where are they all going, Satin?"

"The road goes out to the country. Then out to the hot springs. Many Hindu and British visit the springs. There are many stops along the way to Toomba, Sahib Major, and cutaway roads to other villages."

"I'll ride just ahead, sir," Gildenbeck said, leaping gracefully into the saddle. "See if I can't get a head start."

"Okay, Private. Hmm…" Gunther studied the road. "I guess, if these bandits were to camp on the way to the springs and commit murder…" he stared at the tall still trees for a few seconds—their long leaves seeming to bend more each minute under the muggy air and oppressive heat. "They would go off the road some."

"Not always," the officer corrected. "Thuggees construct a luxurious camp beside the road, attracting even more travelers that pass by to eat and stay with them. They feed them strong wine. They play sitars, sing and laugh. While they drink the Thuggees position themselves around each victim to garrote them, all at once on a signal from their master. As the hunchback spoke, they each have a scarf with three knots. One knot in the center goes for the Adam's apple, to crush it. Two knots on each end, so the back of each fist is supported and the scarf will not slip through their hands as they pull it tight. It is quick. It is their way."

"My Good God!" declared Lieutenant Kerry, overhearing the description.

"Make sure the horses take it easy on that water and feed, Lieutenant." Gunther raised his hat in the direction of the Indians catering to the horses. He hoped the busy work would keep Kerry from fretting about Marilyn.

"So this choke session won't start right at sunset? But maybe a little after when they're good and drunk?" Gunther asked.

"Yes, Sahib Major."

"Then we've got maybe five hours left to find them. You, your scouts, and our scouts take the lead, Lieutenant. You know the road. Be thinking about campsites."

"Yes, Sahib Major."

Rosenthal listened as he filled the inside of his overturned hat with feed and offered it to his horse. He spit a chaw of tobacco out into the dry dirt. "Never heard of such a thing."

The going was very slow, as the scouts dismounted at every intersection of the road to lie on the ground to put their eyes inches off the surface. They passed as many as twenty people in groups coming and going. Sacred cattle roamed the path freely and grazed on the roadside vegetation and on the fields of farm produce to the right and left. Spoiled and unresponsive, the cattle refused to budge when underfoot. The horses shoved on, and the occasional boot from a cavalryman spurred one or two cows aside.

"Major Sahib," Lieutenant Satin asked, woefully, at one point, "please advise your men to avoid causing the cows any discomfort,

as they are highly regarded. And Major Sahib, please do not in-
dulge in eating their flesh because it is the flesh of our ancestors."

"Yup," Gunther responded half-listening, his eyes on the road
ahead. "Let the stock be, boys, let it be," he commanded loudly
without looking at the men, knowing full well each American envisioned a week of well-done steaks with each passing religious
icon.

The tent party was just starting. The tour band spread colorful
sheets from long painted posts and dropped multistriped pillows on
the ground, on which Lydia and Marilyn happily settled. An Indian
quickly handed them silver chalices of red wine. Harrigan and
Smith wrestled with one of their footlockers to pull out a camera
and light stand.

The enormous tour guide, introduced to all as Ebeban, studied
the photographers at work, "My, my gentlemen, you must show me
how all of this works!" he declared with a glint in his eye. "Perhaps I will have such gear to photograph my children someday."
But he quickly bored of the setup process and ordered one of his
men to observe and carefully record the work with pen and paper.

Ebeban dropped a pillow near Lydia and sat contently, the small
bells on the tips of his curved-toed red slippers ringing out.

"Oh, sir," she told him, "this is as you promised. Wonderful
sightseeing and now a nice, cool evening falls upon us."

"And we shall have some wine and a fine dish of cooked vegetables and rice, and more wine and…" he pointed to his man
pulling from the wagon what appeared to Lydia a huge, odd-
shaped guitar.

The musician nodded as he set the stringed instrument on a
thatched mat. "It is the sitar, ma'am," he reported with a smile, re-
vealing but one yellowed tooth in his mouth.

Marilyn was already feeling the effects of just a few mouthfuls
of local wine, and she clapped with glee. Her head fell back, and
Ebeban glanced lustfully at her neck.

"Private Gildenbeck," Gunther called out as he watched the

trees grow long shadows across their path and felt a cool breeze touch the sweat on his face. The screech of wild birds and the hum and crackle of jungle insects began to fill the air. The scout rode up beside him. "Take a man and ride ahead at a good gallop. Damn the small tracks. Just look for roadside camps on the way to the springs."

"Good idea, sir." He turned off for the task, just as a sudden, menacing growl erupted from the thick woods on their left.

"What the hell was that?" a wide-eyed Gildenbeck spoke out in surprise.

"It is the tiger," Lieutenant Satin answered. "It is near their time now to fill their bellies."

The old scout spit again and blew a blast of air from his lungs. "Never heard of such a thing."

Now, almost completely dark, Gunther felt desperate. They had even caught sight of Gildenbeck on the road ahead, who had slowed several times to investigate hunches. It was at the moment of Gunther's lowest despair, a brilliant white light flashed, way ahead and to left. All the vets in the posse thought of a distant battle and the flash of canons on the horizon. That is, all but the naïve Lieutenant Kerry, who blurted out, "Lightning?" But Gunther realized it was too white to be a reddish cannon blast and too low for lightning.

"Charge!" Gunther instinctively yelled, the old cavalry commander in him bursting forth. He spurred his horse, and all the startled men followed.

"To the light, Gildenbeck. To the light!" Gunther commanded the two scouts way ahead. "Harrigan and Smith taking pictures, Kerry," Gunther shouted to the lieutenant as their mounts reached top speed. "They're taking pictures!"

"This will make a fabulous tintype!" Harrigan proclaimed from behind the camera. He flipped the Kodak's curtain off his head. Before him, perfectly posed and carefully staged, the travelers and their caretakers surrounded an evening campfire, framed by striped tents and banners. Each smiled and hoisted a cup of wine, but a keen eye would have noted the two men easing beside John Smith, seated in the grouping. The flash of the photo revealed their harsh glance at the large, muscular black man.

As the group crowded together to squeeze into another frame, the killers fell into perfect position for their plans. Ebeban glanced at the men seated beside Smith and nodded his head. Ebeban stood, yanked a pistol from his robes and fired straight at Harrigan. A knotted scarf flipped over Smith's head as two men grabbed his arms. Smith reflexively managed a hand grasp on the silk garrote. As he wrestled for his life, a similar scarf dropped about Marilyn's neck, and two men clutched Lydia's arms. Ebeban yanked his scarf from his belt and lunged for her head.

Ahead was an opening on the roadside, alight from a large campfire. As fast as Gunther, Kerry and his troupe galloped, Rosenthal's trained mount blasted past them, with the scout hunched low over its neck. He fell in line some ten feet behind Gildenbeck. As Gildenbeck and Rosenthal closed in, they slid their Springfield rifles from their saddle sheaths. Both now held their weapons upright and, with both hands, their torsos on their racing mounts as smooth as if they were one with their weapons.

Then came the crack of a gunshot from the roadside. A distant man fell back into Gunther's view onto the road. The glow of a campfire danced across the downed man and on the road before them, and Gunther knew the scouts were close when Gildenbeck, too, turned red from this flame. At a dead run, Gildenbeck fired three times to his left, followed closely behind by Rosenthal who blasted three more bullets into the camp as he passed. Gunther drew his .45 and was already preparing his horse for a wide left turn and then straight into the opening. The two scouts completely passed the site, reared their horses to stop, and turned, as Gunther rode straight into the circus tent campsite chaos.

The shocked Thuggees ceased their strangling. Four of them were already dead from the amazing marksmanship of the ride-by scouts. Two others, backing away from a convulsing and twitching Smith, were right in Gunther's path. Gunther fired at one twice, and the man flipped back into a stack of pots and pans. The other Thuggee barely turned to scramble before Gunther pumped two rounds into the killer's side. He fell in howling agony, clutching his side. The rest of the rescue party trampled into the camp, shooting and dismounting to chase down the killers. Rosenthal and Gildenbeck trotted into the site, their rifles at the ready.

Harrigan lay on the road, astonished and stunned. He touched his face, neck and chest searching for the bullet from Ebeban's gun. He was not hit, yet his expensive camera—his metallic comrade—lay blasted open beside him, its long, spindling legs askew on the ground. The bullet had struck the camera box and flung it down. He turned to it and cupped the box in his hands. With this motion, some internal spring released and the multilayer shutter lens snapped shut.

Two Indian scouts wrestled the Thuggee ringleader from a tent and onto his feet. Ebeban screamed and stumbled about in their arms. "Please no…No!" he screamed in a child's voice. "I am not a bad man. I have much money in the wagons. Much money! You can have it. Take it! Take it all. And the wagons." Lydia Latissimo stood. Holding her throat with her left hand, she marched over to Ebeban and slapped him sharply with her right hand and spit into his face. "You cretin!" she said with exasperation. "Cretin!" Gunther knew Lydia was all right.

Kerry dashed for Marilyn at first sight of her, and she collapsed into his embrace, sobbing with tears, her throat a bright red from the near-death clench of the religious scarf.

Gunther surveyed the carnage. Eight Thuggees dead. Lieutenant Satin attended to one of his Indian soldiers who lay dead. None of the travel party perished, but Smith, down on all fours, gagged and clawed at his throat. He was struggling for his every breath. Arm in arm, Kerry and Marilyn ran to Smith.

"I …can't …breathe…" Smith could barely whisper. His face cringed with each painful word.

"You've got to relax. Relax," Marilyn commanded and pushed free from Kerry. The trained nurse in her took rein of her emotions. Harrigan scrambled to his feet and joined them. Marilyn and Kerry laid Smith on his back. It seemed he was but one shallow gasp away from death. She pulled his jaw forward, tilting his head back and he shook from pain and squirmed much like a drowning man on dry land. "Get me that blanket," she ordered of Harrigan. Once retrieved, she rolled a makeshift pillow under his neck. "You must get control of yourself. Breathe slowly, John." She stood and gathered more blankets. Passing beside Gunther she stopped long enough to say in low voice, "His windpipe is crushed in. I don't know if he will make it. I am going to try to position his head to open the windpipe up. I may have to cut his throat open in a minute, to make an airway. Do you have a small knife?"

Gunther took his folding sailor's knife from a pocket and handed it to her, then he turned and strode up to the murderous tour guide, the last survivor.

Lieutenant Satin walked up also, pointing a finger at the ringleader. "He shot my soldier with his pistol!" Satin indicted.

"You don't understand Sahib…Sahib!" Ebeban pleaded with him. Gunther, sick of his voice, punched him in the face, and the bulbous man dropped further back into the grasp of his two guards. Then Gunther moved to his horse and yanked the rolled lasso from the saddle. With gritted teeth he looked into the trees above. Finding a stout limb to his suiting, he flung the rope over a branch and commenced to tie a hangman's noose on one end.

"Wha…" Harrigan muttered as he charged up to them. "You, you can't do this!" He stood at Gunther's side. "You can't hang a man like this!"

"Bring him here!" Gunther growled to the two Indians, and pointed a deliberate finger to a spot on the ground.

"You can't!" Harrigan protested. "He…he needs a…a fair trial. My God, man!"

"A trial!" Gunther roared. "Harrigan, have you looked at your compass lately? Do you know where the hell we are?" Gunther got face-to-face with the photographer and snarled, "We're off the fucking map. We're off your map and damn sure off my map. We are so far from home…they changed Gods on us." He dropped the noose around the babbling man's neck. "And I don't much like the

Gods around these parts."

"Sahib!" Ebeban screamed.

Gunther grabbed the halter of Gildenbeck's horse and ran the loose end of his rope around the saddle horn. With a weave and a pull the last knot was forged.

"Sahib!"

Gunther smacked the rear end of the horse.

"Sa…"

The startled animal dashed the length of the rope. The man bolted skyward. If the strangulation didn't kill him, the severe blow of his head on the tree limb above did. He kicked, gagged, and then twitched. The growing urine stain on the leg of his pants told the tale.

"Welcome to Texas, you skunk son of a bitch," Gunther growled.

Within two hours, the soldiers converted the campsite into a small military compound. Three Pushtan soldiers wrestled the limp bodies of the dead Thuggees into a pile near the road. The scouts stood or walked a perimeter, the horses were staked and fed, and Ebeban's tent became a medical bay. Gunther stood in the opening of the tent and watched Smith's progress under Marilyn's care.

"He has finally caught his breath," Marilyn reported with relief. She handed him back his unused folding knife. "But, it pains him greatly to speak." From over her shoulder, Smith smiled at Gunther. He attempted to sip some water from a cup that Harrigan offered him.

"Well, we have two wagons and a trailer now," Gunther said. "We can get him back to the British fort, and he can stretch out in the back on all these pillows."

In fact, the rescue party had quite a few new items now: beds, carpets, more horses, two large, sturdy wagons, one completely enclosed like a large passenger stagecoach that held most of the gear, the other half enclosed, half-open with a removable canvas canopy top. They now possessed three tents, cooking gear, various supplies and …a sitar. Gunther turned and walked by the instrument, grazing his knuckles across the sitar strings, plotting a way to keep it all. After all, to the victors…

On the road, Rosenthal and Gildenbeck started a scrub fire of their own. Surrounded by their saddles and gear, both kneeled with their rifles across their thighs, stirred a can of beans in a beaten pan, and brewed coffee. Gunther joined them.

"That was mighty fine shooting today, men. Riding and shootin'," Gunther complimented. The men accepted the words humbly.

"Coffee, sir? Beans?"

"Don't mind if I do have some coffee." He sat cross-legged beside them. "You don't have to call me sir, you know," he told them. "I'm out! I'm just a civilian."

"That was not a civilian that yelled, 'charge!' awhile back. Charged into the cutthroat's camp pistol first. No sir, no civilian," Rosenthal said as he carefully handed Gunther a hot metal cup. Several fat cows wandered into sight. All three men could picture a fine meal.

"What is the mystery of these cows, sir?" Gildenbeck asked, almost licking his lips.

"Well, Gildy," Gunther started, as he rested against a saddle behind him, "the stock here are religious icons. Like Gods, if you will. I am not a religious man by any measure, though forced to be a Catholic when born and raised…New York City, by the way!" he added.

"So's we!" Rosenthal declared. "Brooklyn."

"Brooklyn! So's I," Gunther answered with a smile. Rosenthal slapped Gunther on the leg.

"Imagine that, "Gildenbeck declared, "three cowboy Yankees in India."

With this acknowledgement, all three men clanked their metal coffee cups together.

Gildy spoke up, "My recruiter in Manhattan—and he'd seen the elephant many times—told me jern the Army, sonny! Travel to exotic lands. Meet exotic people…and kill them!'" All three broke up in laughter. It was a subdued laughter because nine of these exotic people lay in a pile some forty feet north of them.

"On this cow question," Gunther cleared his throat, "there was a revolution here in the 1850s. They called it the Great Indian Mutiny, and it was a course of study I had at West Point. The Brits have run this land now for several hundred years. But some Indians wanted their independence. To cook up this revolt, the rebels spread two vicious rumors that turned the local soldiers against the British. There are two kinds of soldiers here, Hindu and Muslim. To incite the sepoys—the Indian Hindu soldiers—the rebel trouble-makers started rumors that the government-issued rifle bullets were smeared with cow fat."

"Nahhh!" Rosie said.

"Yeah! Now to the Muslims," Gunther continued, "they spread the lie that the cartridges were smeared with pig's fat. I do know that to the Muslim, a pig is an unclean beast. If he eats a pig or fools with a pig in any fashion he will die and go to Muslim hell— that'll be a place called Gehenna—and he will suffer torments for eternity."

"Over a damn piggy?" Gildy cried out.

"Hell's got another name, other than hell," Rosie noted aloud.

"Hell's a life without pork chops to me," Gildy said tongue-in-cheek.

"…and New York Strip steaks!" Gunther added. All eyes watched the cow as it shuffled by.

"Go on by," Rosie ordered to the cow, "ya troublemaking tasty temptress, you!"

"Ahhh, she's a temptress, ain't she?" Gildy said. "Make for good company with these lonely beans."

Behind them, Lydia emerged from her tent and walked to a leather knapsack by the main, campfire.

"She okay?" Gildy asked.

"Probably. She's a mean-spirited thing," Gunther said as he turned.

He stood and walked over to her. As she reached for her bag, Gunther spotted her hands tremble. She looked at Gunther as he stepped near. "Why ever did you come back for us?"

"A hunchback beggar, an old retired Brit soldier, saw you all leave and knew the men you left with were all cutthroats. High-waymen. Lydia? Are you okay? Need a drink?"

"I am afraid I can't have a drink right now,", Lydia admitted. "I should not be drinking anymore. Mr. Gunther, I believe I owe you an explanation. An apology." With this she sat on a pillow by the fire. Gunther tipped his hat back on his head and sat on a pillow beside her.

"I …am dying," she admitted.

Gunther stared at her speechless.

"I have a cancer and it is killing me. Slowly. Marilyn is my niece, and…she is also my nurse. She is along with me to help me on this journey."

"I am very sorry," Gunther said. "Where is the cancer?"

"In my breast."

Without hesitation and much to his surprise, Lydia immediately unbuttoned the tight collar of her blouse down to mid-chest and peeled it back to reveal a stack of gauze bandages inside her corset. Without shame or hesitation, she pulled this back to expose her left breast. It looked gray with dead veins as thick as a marble pattern. In the center was an open wound about the size of a quarter.

She repositioned the gauze and fastened the blouse, saying, "Oddly, sir, it does not hurt too much. But the sore is getting worse, and I am feeling worse, all over. Weaker. Weaker every day. It is slowly eating me alive as it goes deeper into my chest." She suddenly sobbed with this admission. "Last week I could drink. I wanted to drink, but now I shouldn't, and I can't." She pulled a leather knapsack to her and opened the top and leaned it toward Gunther.

"I drink this now," she said, showing him four bottles of medi-cine. "It is beginning now to burn my esophagus like, like an acid, as they warned me it would. It is like drinking kerosene." She re-placed the top of the bag.

"I thought that this side trip to the hot springs might…might help me in some way. And, I need to see something beautiful be-fore I go into those dry mountains. One last time to see something green and beautiful, something like …like the green pastures of

Mississippi or the weeping willows of Louisiana."

Gunther could see her eyes well up and did not want to stare at her despair. He looked into his coffee as she struggled with her words and dried her welling eyes.

"I fear I will not live to see the end of this," she continued.

"Why make this trip, Lydia?"

"My husband and I were living in New Orleans, where he was stationed. I am from the South originally," she added and simply by saying this, it restored some of her spirit. "After I was diagnosed with this cancer, I left for a treatment at a doctor's center in Atlanta. It took four weeks of treatment. But, it was just a very expensive waste of time. Upon my return to New Orleans, I learned my loving, rascal, Yankee husband was gone. Gone. He volunteered in Washington for this horse hunt in Afghanistan. Not a good-bye. Not a note. He just left. Maybe he couldn't stand to see me die this way. I don't know. But, he would not help me. Or stay by my side. When I needed him the most."

They both looked into the fire for a moment. Gunther took up a stick and stirred the ashes.

"My husband is a good man…at times. He does come from a family of thieves in Boston, but they were more like Robin Hood thieves." She smiled affectionately. "They took care of their neighbors. Vito can be charming and quite the con artist. He was the one brother among six who simply loved school! He loved reading about history and war…well, he was accepted to West Point! The other brothers are all criminals now. Vito could never stay out of trouble. He stole…"

"…the West Point Polo Trophy and sold it to Indians. It is a famous story at the Point," Gunther finished her sentence for her.

They both laughed.

"So the story goes," Gunther continued, "Cadet Latissimo had to steal it back from a warrior's wicki-up. It was full of urine when he found it beside the bed. The brave used it as an …indoor bathroom. Any truth to that?"

"Yes," she said fondly, "he told me it was full of Indian pee, watermelon seeds and duck bones when he found it."

"And so it sits now in a glass showcase in the winner's dorm, no worse for wear," he said. "Where did you meet him?"

"In Washington. In D.C., at a ball full of politicians and military men. He was a dashing bruiser in his black uniform, and his black hair forced back against its natural will to be wild." She motioned with her two hands as if to push a mane of hair back. "He was a charmer, and he was sure a looker."

She reached into her dress pocket and pulled a half-empty bottle of medicine and took a swig.

"Somehow, he graduated. But no matter where we were stationed there was some kind of mischief afoot. He was always working some con. Making money somehow. In New Orleans he was selling furniture from the Carolinas and cigars and sugar from Cuba. Stolen, no doubt. My friend Margaret Mitchell is a writer, and she swears there is a book to be written about him."

"As you know, I did about three months with him as my captain at Fort Sill, Oklahoma, right before he transferred to Washington in the nineties," Gunther said. "He was selling canned goods to the wagon trains coming through. All the labels were steamed from the cans, and no one quite knew where they came from, or what was in them. But at suppertime, we soldiers always seemed to be down on green peas and beans at the mess hall."

They sat quietly for a moment. A slight chill passed through the forestlike jungle as the night settled in.

"I don't know what else to do but find him. Where else to go? Where do I go, Mr. Gunther?"

"To your family?" he asked.

"That is not the answer for me. To him is the answer. When I see him, when I look him in the eye, that is if the royal, two-timing, deserting, son of a bitch is still alive, I guess I'll know what to do. I might just fall into his arms and die right there, or…I might just strangle him."

She got to her knees, and then stood slowly, one leg at a time. Gunther tried to sit up to help her, but she put up a wagging finger and whispered with pursed lips, "Oh, no." She grabbed her knapsack handle, looked at Gunther, and said, "You see, Mr.

Gunther, I am not myself. From this medicine, and this pain, I am either cranky or…what was that you called me back on the ship, prickly or thorny…a thornbush? I was either drunk, drugged or a thornbush." She turned and walked toward her tent, then stopped at the canvas door and said, "And that is my sad story, Mr. Gunther. I hope you will not repeat it. Thank you for coming back for us. You are a better man than I first guessed." She stepped inside and closed the flap.

Gunther studied the fire and sipped the last of his coffee. Suddenly, Lydia Latissimo was transformed into a completely different person in his mind. He noticed out on the road Marilyn and Lieutenant Kerry met to speak. Now, there was an understanding between them. They held hands and shared expressions in the fervor of concern and love. In one brief day of shortened life, cheap death, and close calls, they had bonded as if they had courted for a whole year. Maybe more.

Lieutenant Satin and the Thuggee female servant walked up beside Gunther. The monkey followed her in a nervous, circular pattern. The lieutenant kneeled by him.

"What shall we do with these bodies, Major Sahib?" Satin asked.

"Well, what do you do here in India…with your dead, lieutenant?"

"We do know what the Thuggee God, Kali, wishes for her people. Sutti."

"Sutti?" Gunther repeated.

"Sutti is their practice. At the funeral, the man's body is burned, along with all his wives and all…of his slaves."

Astonished, Gunther looked to the female servant. She was wide-eyed and her breath came heavy and fast with a gasp. He guessed she knew a death sentence hung over her head.

"Are the wives and slaves captured and thrown in?"

"No Major Sahib. Not thrown in. It is their godly duty to march into the flame. They go willingly."

"Willingly!" Gunther uttered. "Well, my God man, this is the 20th century, and we are not burning anyone alive. You can…you can burn those dead sons of bitches over there, but that'll be that. I don't much care if their souls wander homeless, up and down this dirt road for all eternity, Lieutenant," Gunther finished in a quiet voice.

"I will, Major Sahib," the officer said as he stood. He further explained Gunther's orders in Hindustani to the woman.

With this reprieve, she smiled broadly and began chattering to her monkey. It screeched. She took Gunther's hat right off his head and began to fan him with it. Annoyed, he reached up and snatched his hat back.

Satin asked, "The woman says that she was a slave to Ebeban, and now since she has been spared Sutti, she has nowhere to go."

"Tell her to go home," he said.

"I hab…no home. Coach is my home," the plump woman in her forties interrupted, obviously with some knowledge of English. "Jou, Shahib leader. I will stay ju."

"Nooooo! No 'ju' don't. You don't stay me. Go, go see your mother," Gunther groaned. He'd had this conversation before to no avail. The monkey glared at Gunther's expression and screamed at the negative response.

"You!" Gunther pointed at her. "Can be his slave," and he pointed to Lieutenant Satin. The monkey jumped to the woman's foot and clutched her ankle.

"I have no need for a slave, Major Sahib."

"Neither do I. Nor do I need a gotdamn monkey."

Satin spoke to her in Hindustani. She argued back, and then broke out in huge tears. This really upset the monkey. It frowned and clutched its head in a monkey panic.

"Now I've got all the women crying," Gunther muttered, shaking his head.

"She wishes to cook and clean for you. She claims to be an excellent cook."

"Okay, okay, Lieutenant. Tell her to cook for all of us here tonight. After that, I will decide if she is a good cook."

She understood this, smiled, and left for the task at hand.

"And tell her to take that little jacket off that monkey. I'll not have a damn monkey running around with a better-looking jacket than I have," Gunther growled.

The woman heard this, stopped, and said seriously, "But he will become cold!"

"Good God!" Gunther exclaimed and waved her off.

"You don't suppose she'll poison us, do ya," Gunther asked Satin.

Satin laughed. "I do not think so. You have saved her life, and she is forever yours."

"Well that's just my luck. First woman that is forever mine… and she looks like a fucking buffalo."

"Yes, Major Sahib," Satin said.

"You play the sitar, Satin?" Gunther asked, his eyes back on the fire.

"A little, sir," he answered.

"Good. Good. Maybe you'll play a bit for us tonight, if I survive this dinner," Gunther said, wishing he himself could play. If he could, he would play a few quiet Southern tunes tonight, outside Lydia's tent.

11
Empire's Edge

A British district officer was little more than a clerk or a magistrate, someone who handled all small government problems, like licensing, taxes and a host of other mundane duties on a ground level in an assigned area. Some district agents scored regal abodes in the Caribbean or plush offices in African capitals. Some had hundreds of clerks and workers on their staffs. But, poor old George Hall had no real idea why he was assigned, all alone, to his empire's edge, near the Himalayas at a vanishing point where snowy heaven meets rocky hell. George thought his distant position might have something to do with his father's recent disbarment from a prestigious London law firm.

Hall was officially the first district officer in the underdeveloped region of Tasheebo. To call this a third-world location would be a compliment. Most district officers south of him in British India did a little paperwork and tried to socialize and play sports like pig-sticking, hunting and cricket, but Hall wasn't too athletic. In fact, unknown to many, he had a slightly gimpy left arm, which he concealed quite well under regular clothing. Hall leaned toward bookish endeavors as a brilliant student at Cambridge University, passing on sports whenever possible to master his courses in languages, a precursor for foreign government work.

A tall, skinny man in his mid-thirties with a shock of blond hair, Hall had little he could or would do each day but sit in his dirty shack of an office on the village main street and dread the coming of his first wicked winter.

Things were atrociously boring, as he wrote in letters to his sister in Scotland, but things certainly picked up when the Great

Red, White and Blue Sword and his henchmen galloped into their valley and slaughtered virtually every British Military policeman and soldier. Only ten days ago, this was a serene British military police outpost; the furthest post known to civilized man, in a place before the world turned in upon itself and became the far side of China and then seemingly started over again. It was a no-man's-land, and now this sector belonged to this raging icon of Red, White and Blue. The camp followers—the European and Indian women of these men—were tossed into the harem. Hall—weapon-less, dressed in white khakis, and wearing a pith helmet—had nothing to do with the Army, thus the American invader who intro-duced himself as Vito Latissimo spared his life. His close Ameri-can friends still called him colonel in their conversations, as Hall was often privy to.

George was now a prisoner, a captive in the classical Middle Eastern and Central Asian sense. He had free reign of the fort and village like the natives. Where would he go? How would he cross this treacherous land? Hidden in his office was a service revolver holding a mere six rounds! He was a frequent dinner guest of the Red, White and Blue Sword, joining him and his American com-rades in drink and the opium pipe, even granted permission to visit the harem. This big, loud American took an odd liking to Hall, slapping him on the back often, teasing him by calling him Mad Georgie and Limey with a boisterous laughter, and grilling him with detailed questions about England and world politics.

There were many foreign comrades charging about with this American. Ten foreboding men in dark, Cossack-like clothes that Hall was positive spoke Russian. And, despite their rustic, common clothing, they acted like military men. One of the Cossacks was a military leader of some sort as the others responded and treated him with such due respect. Hall nicknamed their apparent com-mander in his village the Czar. George knew the Russians had quested for Afghanistan and India for decades, and after being re-pelled in 1897 and 1903 invasion attempts, the Russians seemed defeated, disinterested and disjointed. Also, they were preoccupied with Japan, but Hall knew well that somewhere in Moscow, there was a side office in a military headquarters with assigned commanders obsessed with running the British out of India.

Despite the jesting, the dining, and the binges with all these foreign men, Hall knew, if he tried to escape, he would be slaughtered in the worst fashion. In fact, he felt the colonel would have him maimed for fun at any given second, as crazy as his cold, steel blue eyes would flash for no reason. But, he was worth more alive, no doubt, as he would be held for ransom. Where could he go without a horse, anyway? Without a military escort? Into the violent hell they called this Afghan pass?

George Hall was much more concerned with the colonel's second in command, Akbar Rasp Mohammad Dunkar, Seer of the Fourth Moon, Son of the Eternal Well, Vizeer of Clanestan. Akbar now possessed a new title as spiritual advisor and military general to the great American Vito Latissimo. It was Akbar that dreamed up the title Red, White and Blue Sword, to strike fear and inspiration in the hearts of the peoples of the Northwest Frontier.

Akbar did not binge drink or smoke, but prayed five times a day on a small carpet. His eyes were like black stones, and it seemed a dozen metal weapons clanged about, concealed inside the multilayers of his long robes when he walked.

So, George Hall quaked at the knees the afternoon a messenger from Akbar summoned him to the fort's main towering turret—cannon room—a high lookout place they used as their headquarters. Inside the war room, he found Akbar shifting about. Latissimo faced the large open bay window, temple leaning against the frame. Rick Valentino, one of Latissimo's friends, sat astride one of the three cannons. The Czar stood mid-room with arms folded, his stern face outlined by a thick black moustache.

George Hall walked up beside the colonel to pay his respects. The man turned and mumbled, "Hello, Limey," with a smile. Latissimo's face had rested against the stone window frame for so long, its porous texture buried a deep red mark design on his skin. Hall could tell the man was so intoxicated he could feel no pain. The colonel reeked of pungent opium smoke.

The window offered the panoramic view of the snow-crested

Hindu Kush Mountains to the southeast and the village of Tasheebo in the valley below and the tent city of his tribal soldiers on the field to the right.

"The man who would be king?" Latissimo said. "Or, the king who would be man?"

"You are both king and man," Akbar Rasp told Latissimo. "King of what you have won, and just a mere man in the eyes of Allah."

The colonel's custom-built, curved sword, with those three colors of his moniker baked into the enamel, lay on a marble table right beside the opium pipes and Russian vodka bottles. A silver star was inlaid in the middle of this abstract American flag in the form of an edged weapon.

Valentino ran a hand down a canon and took a bottle from the table. He walked beside Vito and set the bottle on the wide, stone sill, almost hard enough to shatter it.

"Paisan," Valentino said with a grin.

Latissimo lifted the bottle up to his thick, olive-colored lips and gulped the clear alcohol. "Ha! You hear that, Paisan? The eyes of Allah are upon me," Latissimo sang. "All the livelong days!" He was in tune with the old song, "I've been working on the railroad."

"Give poor Georgie Hall a drink!" he told Valentino.

Hall grabbed a chalice from the table and accepted the Russian vodka.

Akbar walked to the window and rested his arms on the ledge. The strong evening wind blew into his long beard and swirled his long gowns. Hall sensed the sheer evil in his presence as he passed.

Then Hall heard growling animals and approached the window to look into the courtyard below. Just inside the walls of the fort, two Mongolian guards stood fast, wrestling six enormous mastiffs on their leashes. Some thirty feet away from the dogs, eleven remaining British military policemen and some Indians gathered in a small fearful clutch by the wall, held at bay by these dogs. They were the survivors of the battle for the godforsaken place, the last of some two hundred men stationed there, most of which still lay maimed, stripped, dead and stinking on the grounds, in swirling fogs of buzzing flies on the parapets and by the gates. The gold teeth were chiseled from their mouths, every strip of metal on their uniform removed, and every quid in their pocket, pilfered.

Farther out, Hall could see the criminal Army patrol the small city of Tasheebo, its maze of filthy streets and alleys outside the fort's gates. Occasional gunshots rang out and echoed across the valley, as squads executed inhabitants when they saw fit. Villagers were coerced to drag the dead into large stacks, where another mass funeral pyre would soon commence.

"I tell ya," Latissimo said with a slur, "if they don't burn these bodies faster, we are gonna' have all manner of diseases here."

Akbar turned the colonel's attention to the men cowered by the dogs below. "Let one go. Let a British scoundrel go," he suggested to Latissimo. "Let him tell the bastards in India of what has hap-pened here."

"Yeah," Latissimo replied. "He can spread the news."

"I will write a letter of passage for him, an order that he shall not be bothered by anyone on his way, or they shall feel the wrath of the Red, White and Blue Sword," Akbar said. "Pick one, my king."

Latissimo pointed to a soldier at the far right of the group. "You!" he shouted across the courtyard. "You old fucker! Come up here! Bring him up here!" The men culled the elder Brit from the group and guided him to the stairs.

"I could carry such a message, Vizeer," George Hall offered.

Everyone else laughed, everyone but the Czar, turning Hall's stomach into a knot.

"You are here for another reason, District Officer Hall," Akbar said, as he busied himself with pen and parchment at the table.

"Nooo, Georgie," Latissimo said as he put his arm around Hall's shoulder. "Thanks for your kind offer, but you are gonna stay here with us. We are gonna find out if you're worth some-thing. If you're not…well?" the colonel shrugged his shoulders.

Hall's palms instantly started to sweat.

"How much are ya worth, Georgie? One hundred pounds? Two?"

"Ahhh…" Hall looked at their faces, feigning surprise, but he knew well this was coming.

"Come on, Georgie," Valentino goaded. "Tell us true."

"Two hundred pounds," Hall answered, hoping his life would be worth that much. Probably not, but a high price would keep him alive.

In a moment, the door slammed open, and the disheveled prisoner was shoved inside.

"Feeling fit to travel?" Latissimo asked with a large sneer, while looking the exhausted troop over. He was a man near sixty, a gray-haired, military police officer in a torn uniform, bruised and caked with dried blood. The man refused to answer. Instead, he stood at attention.

"What is your name, soldier?" Latissimo asked, sipping from the vodka bottle.

"Sergeant Michael McGillacutty, Sixty-seventh Regiment."

Latissimo offered the man the vodka bottle. The sergeant stared at the bottle, then looked away.

"It doesn't matter to me, Sergeant McGillacutty if you drink or don't drink. Either way, you are a fine soldier for your country. You will not live or die here today if you have a drink from my bottle," Latissimo explained. "Take a drink. You deserve it."

The sergeant took the bottle and took a mighty gulp.

"You will report to your superiors in India, Sergeant McGillacutty," Akbar advised him and handed him the letter. "You will tell them what has happened here. Tell them we are holding prisoners for ransom. Some are listed in the letter and here are our terms for their release. Tell them there is a new leader in the northwest."

"Yeah, tell them a new American Caesar now owns this high ground," Valentino said. When Hall looked to the Caesar, he noticed Latissimo's eyes started to flutter and his body wavered, but he suddenly snapped alert with Akbar's next announcement.

"You are blessed today, Sergeant," Akbar said as he shoved the sergeant to the window. "The eyes of my God are upon you. Your God is just a false curiosity in your London museum. Your churches are testimonies to your stupidity. I warn you, Allah will only wait for your soul for so long."

Latissimo stumbled back to the ledge and put his right hand on the sergeant's shoulder, more for balance than an act of friendship. The dogs below were coughing and gagging wildly.

George Hall peered over the window ledge as Latissimo stuck his left hand out the window in a fist reminiscent of Roman emperors deciding the fate of gladiators. He turned his thumb down.

With this signal, the guards below released the six mastiffs. The dogs leapt upon the quivering men and, in one minute of mayhem, tore into them, tooth and claw. There was no escaping this bloodbath.

Aghast, Sergeant McGillacutty stepped back from the hideous view, his face pale. For lack of any other option, he stepped back and returned to the position of military attention.

George Hall, feeling faint but not wishing to show weakness, looked higher to the mountains ranges boarding the valley.

"Get the sergeant a mount," Akbar ordered a guard at the door. The guard grabbed the old sergeant by the collar and yanked him out of the room. Akbar whispered to another guard. Hall overheard the word "harem." Then Akbar joined Latissimo back at the window. Vito seemed hypnotized by the violence below.

"Look at their strength!" Vito marveled, shaking his head as two mastiffs ripped the last intact man apart in a tug of war.

"Ahhhhh, ladies!" Akbar declared, when two women arrived in the room. He pushed the blonde-headed, pale-skinned one to Latissimo. He knew her American looks would be more to his liking.

"Great one," Akbar told the American, "it is time to retire to the harem."

Latissimo took the blonde's arm and left the room, with Valentino and the second woman in tow.

Akbar spread charts and papers across the marble table. The Czar approached the table and snapped his fingers. A Cossack cohort entered the room. From under a map, he pulled a handwritten letter to his man.

The men spoke in Russian. George Hall tried to make himself small and unnoticed at the corner of the window. He couldn't translate the conversation, but he did discern the words "haste," "Americans," "Trans Caspian Russian Railway," "attack Zanrala" soon or next week.

"Good afternoon, Mr. George Hall," came an icy, deep voice behind Hall's back. It was time for him to leave.

"Oh, yes, well…good afternoon, Vizeer," Hall said, pretending to be startled, as if he had not been listening. Hall pretended not to know that Akbar and the Czar were plotting against the colonel and sending a message up the great railway five hundred miles west of them, on a train that ran straight to Moscow, a train Hall knew could deliver thirty-thousand soldiers a month to the northwest region. He pretended not to know the next village to be attacked and slaughtered. He pretended not to see the solemn stare of the Vizeer as he left the room.

In an empty corridor, District Officer George Hall rested against a wall, aware that to exit this fortress he would have to pass the monster dogs and piles of bone and flesh. Surely, Zanrala, with soldiers and citizens, would soon become another pile of bone and flesh, too. What insidious plot was afoot? What conspiracies? His chest heaved and he burst into sobs at the world gone insane before his very eyes, the dogs of war slipped in a nightmare of brutality, slavery, rape, distrust, power, lies and murder. Insane.

<h1 style="text-align:center">12
The Final Intoxication</h1>

What passed through the India railway station only yesterday as a lean, mean posse, now returned slowly as a sloppy caravan of soldiers, with two colorful tourist wagons of supplies, two teams of stout work horses, a singing cook and an overactive monkey—all with Gunther in the reluctant lead. They dismounted, and Lieutenant Satin shouted for the stationmaster as he jogged away to make travel arrangements. Lydia Latissimo and Marilyn made their way toward the comforts of the British-based railway restaurant off the main platform.

Gunther opened his pocket watch, checking the time before he wandered near one of his new wagons to peer inside at Smith. John Smith had improved slightly in the last twelve hours and sat up in a bed of pillows. Smith could breathe easier, but still could not utter a word. He gave Gunther a thumbs-up sign and a half-smile, but Harrigan seated beside him, avoided the Texan's eyes. It seemed the photographer could not overcome the brutal visage of quick hangman justice.

Someone dangled a metal canteen into Gunther's view, and he reflexively grabbed it and downed a swallow. He handed it back in the direction from which it came and turned to see the face of his new cook with a giant gap-tooth smile. He reluctantly grunted a thanks, as she walked around the side of the wagon, wearing the monkey on her leg like a red velvet anklet.

Kerry joined him. "Let's hope we can get to Kabul by morning. Perryweather is quite likely to leave without us."

"Yup," Gunther said.

After his brief meeting with the station supervisors, Lieutenant

Satin returned.

"Major Sahib, the next train is in one hour. We have two flatbeds for our use. We will be able to take the wagons and everything we need. I have telegraphed ahead that we are coming."

"Good work, Satin," Gunther said with a wink and smile.

"Captain Boston? Lieutenant Kerry?" a voice beckoned from the platform. Two young men, Americans, dressed in U.S. Army browns, polished boots and campaign hats, stood among the stacks of luggage, waving for attention. They jumped off the platform, crossed the tracks and greeted the group.

"Lieutenant Daniel Day," said one, shaking Kerry and then Gunther's hands.

"Lieutenant Marvin O'Conner," said the other.

"Yes, I am Lieutenant Kerry, and this is Major…well, Johann Gunther, but he is acting as major."

"Confusing…" O'Conner grinned, shaking Gunther's hand.

"Yeah. Confusing to me, too," Gunther said.

"Captain Boston…is deceased," Kerry advised.

"You…you don't say?" Lieutenant O'Conner said. "How may I ask, sir?"

"Shot in a duel aboard ship sailing over," Kerry answered. "We'll have time to explain the details en route."

"Glad we caught up with you. We really have no idea where we are going, or why. Just following orders," Lieutenant Day said.

"You boys miss the ship back in Virginia?" Gunther asked.

"Well sir, we were dispatched from Washington the day after you left. On sudden orders," O'Conner answered. "We…we don't usually…we aren't usually…"

"…deployed," Day finished. "We are not sent off. Anywhere this sudden and to a place like this, I mean. We are on the U.S. Army Archery team, and we just travel to compete and perform in shows."

"The archers!" Gunther declared. "Man, I am glad to see you boys. Did you bring your bows? Your gear?"

"Yes, sir," Day answered.

"Did you bring crossbows, too?" he asked.

"As requested, sir."

"Great," Gunther said enthusiastically. "Let's get your gear over to this side of the tracks. We load from here in one hour."

The four men made for the platform. O'Conner spoke up. "What will we be shooting, sir?"

"With dynamite, mostly, Lieutenant," Gunther said, grabbing a suitcase, "and at…the occasional, local tribesman."

"We've…ah…never shot at anyone before, sir. Just targets and things…for shows," O'Conner said.

"That's gonna' change, lieutenant," Gunther added with a smile.

Gunther and Satin sat on the row of sandbags by the machine gun teams as the train slowly rolled into the outskirts of Kabul. It was a city of expansive stone and rock.

"Peshawar, of Pakistan, is to the east and is really the business capital of these lands of the northwest," Satin told Gunther as the train slowed to a chugging crawl for the safety of the pedestrians and animals ahead. "Not Kabul or Kandahar. There really is no border. Peshawar is where many of the Afghan rulers winter. It is a place of great commerce. Merchants come from Persia, Turkestan, and China. Peshawar has the Indus River to ship out to the Arabian Sea and the oceans beyond. Here in Kabul it's more savage and distant and without such a great river."

"And the key of India is not Herot or Kandahar, the key of India is London," Gunther recited.

"Disraeli," Satin said, supplying the author of Gunther's musing.

Gunther slapped Satin's shoulder and smiled broadly at him. "Yes!"

"I have been attending college in London," Satin said proudly, and Gunther realized he'd traveled across the world and met a kindred spirit.

The conductor cranked his horn to clear the track.

Satin pointed to the south, to a series of cramped streets. "The streets here are fashioned after Peshawar. There, over there is Rug Street. And there, the Street of Jewelers." The men blinked and winced in the sudden glare from the Street of Armorers, from where the sun's rays ricocheted off thousands of curved-steel scimitar blades and knives displayed on great rug-draped tables for sale. "Over there. The almond growers from the Hindu Kush Mountains. I don't know if you are aware Major Sahib, that Hindu Kush means Hindu killer, for all the Hindu people who have died in the extreme weather and harsh life…and the many wars of mountains."

"Who are they?" Gunther pointing to a group of some forty or fifty tall, gaunt men with hawkish noses under turbans and white robes, all carrying long rifles.

"They are the Pathans from the hills, but look over there, the Afridis." Satin pointed to another group of oily faced men, their skin and robes caked in dirt and their full beards so filthy they looked like dead buffalo hides to Gunther.

"Afridis. I have heard of them," Gunther recalled from his recent British history readings about the region.

"They try to own the Khyber Pass and try to control as many of the valleys and passes as they can. I fear we will do battle with their kind. Over there is the Street of Money Changers. You may find coins there from ancient Greece or Rome, with the faces of men like Caesar or gods of the worlds."

"I'd like to have such coins," Gunther commented, hypnotized by the throng of mixed races, tall, short, fat, or gaunt, in layered tapestries trimmed with baubles or in sheer rags, in delicate slippers, leather boots or bare feet. Women in ankle-length veils somehow contrived to glide through the masses like agile athletes.

"Satin, does this railroad track go farther to the northeast?" Gunther asked as a turn in the line ahead offered him a view of the distance.

"It goes many miles northeast, Sahib, but only in broken pieces. The Afridis, the Koklanare, or whatever band wishing to make war will destroy the track or blow up the trains. The train company will not go beyond Kabul right now. It is too afraid."

The train continued on at a camel's pace with jolts and bumps, testing Lieutenant Kerry's balance as he paced the flatbed, anxious over the timetable. He noticed that being late was not a worry for his new Texas commander. Gunther sat chatting beside Satin, as relaxed as if on a sightseeing tour. The engine finally trimmed its steam and rolled to a stop at the Kabul military station.

At that moment, Kerry smelled the odorous air, a mix of garbage, dead dogs, cats and horses. Kerry spotted a contingent of British officers mulling about the platform, toe-tapping and fidgeting with impatience. As Gunther and his group dropped off the flatbeds, the Brits spied Lieutenant Kerry and approached.

"Lieutenant Kerry?"

"Yes," Kerry answered.

"Captain Perryweather requires your immediate appearance in his office," one officer said, framed with a salute. "We are leaving in two hours for the frontier and time is of the essence."

Overhearing the demand, Gunther hauled a saddlebag off the train and told them, "Sounds like just the meeting for you, Lieutenant."

But, the British officer turned smartly to Gunther, "And he demands your appearance also."

"Demands," Gunther repeated with a grimace.

"We will handle your possessions, Sahib Major," Lieutenant Satin offered, ordering his men to raise the ramps to offload the wagons.

Gunther nodded, following Kerry and the Brits to a nearby coach. Kerry turned and waved to Marilyn as she and Lydia emerged from a passenger car. With the crack of an English leather horsewhip, Gunther and Kerry were whisked off for this overdue and no doubt somewhat hostile meeting.

Within minutes, the wagon passed through a security gate and stopped at a stone and wooden single-story building. The escorts, Kerry and Gunther entered the waiting room, and Gunther caught a glimpse of Perryweather in the next room sitting behind an ornate desk. The commander issued verbal and written orders, last minute in nature, to attentive men. He wore a Class A dress uniform of plumes, decorations and medals. Gunther took a seat in the lobby, stretched his legs, and tipped his cowboy hat over his brow. Kerry sat in a more reserved posture, with his cavalry hat in hand, and knew well he was caught in the classic leadership waiting game—a mental chess match to establish a pecking order—and there was no better way to do this than in an office with a desk, a flag and a boring waiting room. Gunther wasn't playing this mind game. He leaned back in his chair, propped his feet up on a nearby table, and nodded off. "Captain Perryweather will see you now," an aide advised, his voice rousting Gunther from his light sleep.

He rose, groaned and, with a finger, flicked his hat back on his head. He made a gracious gesture allowing Kerry first entrance into the office. As he guessed, Perryweather was too busy to even look up at them and ignored their entrance. When he did, Kerry saluted. A Siamese cat prowled the room. It leapt upon the desk and plopped down on some papers, proceeding to lick its outstretched hind leg.

"Sit," Perryweather growled. They did. He eyed Gunther's tooled Western gun belt, clothes and boots with disdain.

"We are making ready for a departure in an hour. Since you are here, I shall not ask what delayed you from the rest of your regiment."

Kerry caught some movement from Gunther and turned to spot him removing some wax from his ear with his finger.

"It has come to my attention, that the United States forces here, Lieutenant Kerry included, have elected that you, Mr. Gunther, take makeshift command over their company."

Gunther just stared at him. Kerry nodded.

Perryweather continued, "The military does not function on democratic election, and I find this succession of power illegal, dangerous, and foolhardy."

"I find," Gunther said calmly, "your accession to power, via assassination, illegal as all hell, too. Promotion by duel. Yeah. Neither of our militaries, our countries, allow for that."

Perryweather leaned forward. "A duel, such a matter of honor on the high and open seas, and on a merchant ship registered out of Denmark, Mr. Gunther…is not illegal."

They traded cold stares. Kerry sat to the side watching the mental showdown and remained uncomfortably quiet. Gunther could tell he recalled the shocking deck-side duel that laid his Captain Boston low, but he also relived how Gunther slipped a hangman's noose around the neck of the crying Indian guide and ran the Hindu clear up a tree so fast his head split open like a cantaloupe. Gunther was more than a match for this conspiring Lancer commander. Kerry looked first at one, then the other of these two stubborn men and appeared truly uneasy for the first time.

Perryweather continued, "You make no mistake, I am the ranking, active-duty officer on this mission. You, Lieutenant Kerry, answer to me," Perryweather declared with a finger at the lieutenant. "You, Mr. Gunther, you, sir… I do not know what the devil you are, but I know where you will be, and that will be under my scrutiny and out of my bloody way!"

Gunther smiled and stood, "You know," he pointed to a shoulder epaulette on Perryweather's uniform and said calmly with a smile, "the last time I saw a shocking red plume like that? It was on a whore's dress in Abilene, Texas. God, she was a sight. Fucked twenty cattle drovers in three short hours."

Perryweather was speechless.

Kerry stood and made for the door.

"Let's go, Lieutenant," Gunther said. "We've got packin' to do."

Kerry saluted. Perryweather didn't. The two left the office, then the building. The aides gathered the coach and team for the return trip to the rail station. While Kerry remained quiet, his mouth contorted with each minute as though he painfully considered every thought, expressions not unnoticed by Gunther.

"Looking for a handle on the moment?" Gunther asked, as they both stared ahead at the foreign streets and strange peoples.

"Eh, you might say so, sir," Kerry answered in an exasperated tone.

"So was that whore in Abilene," Gunther said with a serious face.

Kerry turned to Gunther and they both broke out in laughter and climbed aboard the wagon.

The train carried them north to the last working depot in the rail line, where they unloaded and settled in with the rest of their expedition, staked and tented out for their last night before morning's march. The crew organized the two wagons around a fire and the Hindu cook set about preparing a fine meal for Gunther's small troupe.

Gunther, Kerry and Grimsley prepared for the departure, then readied to bed down for night. Gunther rolled up some blankets to use as a pillow by the fire. The camels caterwauled and snorted so loudly that Gunther poked medical cotton into his ears to muffle the wails.

At 10 A.M. Gunther put a boot in a cavalry stirrup and swung a leg over his new U.S. Army mount, a fine gelding named Acorn. He prowled his American contingent as they prepared to leave, first gazing on all the salty, over-the-hill soldiers, interspersed with the younger troops as they packed up their supplies on camels, horses and wagons. As requested, he spotted the ten additional machine gun wagons. Then he saw the two young Army archers beside the dynamite wagon, their new assigned responsibility.

The men looked back at him with friendly curiosity when he passed, unsure of the tenor of leadership he possessed. He would have to do much work to gain their confidence. He knew how. Treat them with respect. Keep them fed. Keep them alive without taking foolish or unnecessary risks.

After the round, he returned to his wagons. Young Lieutenant Kerry tied his horse to a rail attached to one of the multicolored, half-open civilian coaches. Hardly a coincidence, it was the one carting the young nurse, Marilyn. She sat beside Lydia. Gunther wondered if Lydia might finish his murderous mission for him, if she got her hands on her husband's throat first.

Beside Lydia sat the Baptist preacher, again out to convert the Muslim world into Christianity one soul at a time, even though he'd lost both his wife and daughter the last time he tried. In this passenger wagon sat the photographers; one could no longer speak, and the other, from all indications, considered Gunther a killing savage.

Holding the reins in the second painted wagon was the Hindu

female cook and former slave. Her monkey scampered across her lap. She smiled broadly at Gunther as he passed.

"You want anything? You tell me," the woman reminded him as she thumped her chest.

In the silver pots and pans hanging off the side of the wagon, he saw a distorted mirror image of himself, a soldier/civilian, somehow in charge of this misfit outfit, seemingly on a hunt for giant workhorses, but really on a search and destroy mission for a lost Army colonel.

Up front, hundreds of Her Majesty's finest soldiers and Indian sepoy soldiers mounted on camels or horses, or lined up for their foot march, awaited a command from Captain Perryweather, who was waiting off in the distance mounted on a stout black horse.

A horn sounded with a British melody, and the caravan began its trek north. It slogged its way through the last rocky and muddy streets of Kabul's outskirts. Each man and woman likely realized this was the end of the civilized world as they knew it, and a savage world of twisted men and mountains lay ahead.

Gunther rode to the left of the staggered parade and Lieutenant Satin. A platoon rode beside him on his lancer charger.

"We made it, Major Sahib," Satin said.

"Yes, sir, that we did," Gunther returned with a smile.

Lieutenant Kerry handed the reins of his wagon to Reverend Verne and deftly dropped astride his moving horse beside the wagon, to the obvious delight of Marilyn. Kerry caught up with Gunther and Satin.

"See you got the womenfolk properly off," Gunther said.

"Yes, sir," Kerry replied.

"With a minimum of bravado, I hope, Lieutenant?"

"A minimum, sir."

As the British pierced the open, flat plain, Gunther heard the distant hollering, whistles, and catcalls of men with accents, all coming from the last building on the last street just up ahead from the Americans. With a raised eyebrow, he studied this very last stone building as they rode near. The men stood on a stone patio outside the establishment, some raising pints of beers and glasses of alcohol. A man played a bagpipe and another a flute.

Captain Perryweather maintained a stiff neck, a sneer and an aloof chin. When he did, the men jeered even more.

"Scottish Highlanders," Gunther noted. Some were indeed wearing kilts. "Wish to hell some of them were coming with us. They are a tough breed."

"This is a tradition," Satin commented. "They often send off the poor souls bound for the mountains like this."

"Saints be praised," declared Verne from his wagon's perch. "They're all drunk as Cooter Brown!"

More Scots poured from the bar doors and crowded the open patio of tables and chairs of this very British looking pub. It could have been in Trafalgar Square itself, with its painted outdoor brick, a canvas canopy, and an ornate black sign with gold letters. Gunther read the sign above the door at the same instant that Kerry read it out loud…

"The Final Intoxication?" The lieutenant recited with a confused tone.

"Yeah," said Gunther, "It's the British way of saying, 'Last Chance Saloon.'" He shook his head and smiled. "And it is, Lieutenant! It's the last building, on the last street, in the last city, at the end of the world. It must have a great view sitting there on the veranda, on a clear night."

"Yes Sahib Major," Satan said. "It does, as I have sat there myself."

Gunther tipped his hat to the boys and shouted, "Save me a pint, boys! I'll be right back!" With this, the men laughed and cheered at a higher pitch. Gunther closed his eyes for a second and envisioned himself right there among them at mission's end. Then he opened his eyes to the giant mountain range before them, one that looked like inverted, whitecapped, jagged knife blades on the savage horizon.

<h1 style="text-align:center">13</h1>
<h2 style="text-align:center">The Khyber Pass Drop</h2>

In the first afternoon afield, Perryweather made a general inspection of the troops in transit. Before long he passed the Indian Lancers and his men, then rode upon the American contingent holding up the rear.

"What in hell are these two party wagons doing here?" Perryweather demanded, pointing at the bright, gaudy tour coaches. His horse bucked and snorted along with his outrage as he circled the two rolling Hindu wagons. Lydia Latissimo steered one and the cook piloted the other. The monkey traversed the top rim of the cook's wagon, screeching back at the captain and waving a hand at him.

"Get me that goddamn cowboy!" Perryweather ordered to his aide-de-camp, and the young man stood in his stirrups, craning to spot Gunther's Stetson in a sea of bobbing helmets, cavalry hats and turbans. Once spotted, off he galloped.

Within minutes, Gunther, Kerry and Marilyn rode up against the flow of the caravan.

"There are no camp followers on this mission. You can't bring your whore along!" Perryweather shouted and aimed an accusatory horsewhip at the cook.

"This is transport for the ladies, sir," Kerry broke in. "The Hindu is a cook and caretaker for the ladies."

Lydia spoke up. "Captain, these two wagons are for our comfort on this journey. My niece, Marilyn's, and mine. Nothing more. I am responsible for them, not Major Gunther." Her voice was pleasant, but serious. "And, that poor woman you refer to as a whore, is nothing of the kind."

The monkey also chastised Perryweather. Thwarted, Perryweather tugged his left rein and peeled off from the scene. Lydia and Gunther exchanged smiles.

"Oh, how I hate military men, Mr. Gunther," she said with a wry smile, shaking her head.

"I know, Lydia," Gunther said softly with a nod. He and Kerry left for the head of the American line.

Hot in the day. Cold at night.

Boring days passed, enlivened for Gunther only in philosophical discussions with Eaton graduate Lieutenant Satin and sessions with launching dynamite sticks on arrows. The first night, Gunther drew up extensive plans with Kerry and the sergeants about how to travel the chasms and yet remain in tactical formations. He met with the snipers and briefed them about their enemy's method of operation, picking and sniping away at them from the highest crags their rifles would reach from.

The next night was an explosive archery night. He worked with archers on target practice with sticks of burning dynamite tied to their arrows. Their job was also to counter enemy snipers and tribesmen perched in the mountains. The rehearsals drew many spectators from the group, as the two bow experts inched their laden arrows closer and closer to their targets and dabbled with fuse lengths.

After supper each night, Kerry and Marilyn took long walks, arm in arm, about the encampment. The older U.S. soldiers sat around their camel-dung campfires resisting catcalls to the young couple as they passed, the duo seemingly oblivious to the alien world around them.

Gunther and Satin would make random "tours" of the British and Indian units by riding ahead of the Americans and weaving among the other armies. The lieutenant would explain the gear and methods of these troops. Gunther felt relieved to see the Brits had three Maxim Machine gun teams. The big monsters could really lay down firepower.

Five days of boring, rugged travel brought them into a narrow pass bordered by mountains as vertical as thorny spikes. They thinned the lines out considerably, to a point where even a single wagon would not fit through. Just as Gunther was about to reach for the dynamite to blow open a larger hole, the horses somehow managed to pull the wagon through.

The Brits and Lancers dropped down to two lines of men and horses. At another point, Gunther became concerned with the sharp turns ahead. The other sides were completely invisible from view. But, he saw Perryweather dispatch Indian scouts ahead to reconnoiter the turns. Finally, after several of these harsh turns, they marched into a wide valley.

The valley was enormous and breathtaking. The sides gradually sloped upward to thick patches of forests and beyond. But the ability to see for miles constituted greater risk than turning sharp corners!

As the last of the Americans came through, a large band of wild brigands descended from the trees into view about three hundred yards ahead of them. A hasty retreat, or worse, a chaotic one, was not possible due to the narrow passes and turns behind them. The men could not escape back through that tiny crack of the mountain pass. A perfect ambush.

Gunther shouted commands. "Split the machine gun wagons," he directed. "Keep the wagon covers on. One team faces the right, one team to the left. I want you way up that slope." He pointed to a safe, high spot that offered a wide view. "Snipers! Dismount. Split into two groups and do the same. Watch the heights. They can't rush us right now, so they must have rifleman in the crags and ridge tops up there. Where are my archers?" he questioned aloud.

"Here, sir," the two lieutenants rode up.

"You know what to do." The men dismounted and assembled their gear.

"Lieutenant," Gunther said to Kerry, "order the men off their horses and camels. Guns at the ready."

These wily tribesmen on horseback, at least one hundred fifty of them to Gunther's estimate, approached the sides of the group and began slowly infiltrating the lines, scanning the goods and wagons.

Their faces looked arrogant. The Americans raised their weapons, assumed war faces and made ready to take action on command.

One tribesman in a group, with a rifle slung on his shoulder, dismounted and walked to a machine gun wagon, reaching up to a canvas cover to peer inside. But Gunther was near.

"Get back!" Gunther roared as he trotted up to him, working the breast of his horse to force him stumbling backward. Gunther realized the man probably didn't understand a word. He forcefully pointed to move back. The tribesman sneered and grabbed the stock of the rifle slung on his shoulder.

"No!" Gunther barked. He drew his .45 and shot the man in the face. His cheek erupted in a blast of red, and his body lurched back. The turban flung from his head, and the man collapsed on the ground. His group was shocked, their horses rearing and sidestepping with the explosion. Gunther raised his pistol threateningly at all of them. His countenance expressed a single message of death that transcended all languages. He muttered with an evil sneer, "Sergeant, you kill any man who comes close." And his soldiers each took aim at the Afghans.

Gunther holstered his weapon and galloped to the front of the caravan. The surprise of this invasion and Gunther's single gunshot were lost in the overall confusion of the moment. At the head, Gunther could see Perryweather, his aides, Reverend Verne, Marilyn and a handful of other allies all on their horses before eight robed men. Four tribesmen remained on horseback. Four afoot.

Gunther trotted past the British troops and Lancers, all still in their parade formations. Only his American forces had received combat orders. He stopped short of the meeting, dismounted, handed his reins to a soldier and walked near enough to the group to hear the conversation.

"The Sheik Allah Baliwa wishes to inform you that you must pay a tariff before making your way through the pass," the bearded man said with a smile, in perfect English with a British accent. "I am his caliph, Insastan Mukbar, Servant to the Sons of Baliwa "

"And what is the tariff?" Perryweather asked.

"Oh, not much, sir. Only one-third of everything that you

carry," the man said quietly, "as a tax and tariff…and a tribute to the local sheik."

Perryweather remained silent. Gunther walked closer.

"We will also take the customary hostages," the caliph added.

"Hostages?" Perryweather repeated.

"Yes," he answered with a smile. "You will receive them back upon your return from your mission. Just a few of your officers and …and that lady." He pointed to Marilyn, but his eyes caught Gunther walking up to them. He eyed his boots, outfit, and hat.

"I am Caliph Makbor," he said with a smile. "You! You are an American cowboy? Your men look as though they are ready to fight a war. I know a little bit about you American cowboys."

Gunther stepped slowly up to the caliph with the broadest, friendliest smile he could muster. He stuck out his right hand as a way of an introduction. The caliph's men behind him remained motionless at this Western sign of friendship they all had seen countless times among the British. The caliph took the hand and shook it with an amused face as though Gunther was a simple-minded, country fool.

"I may be from a faraway land, Mr. Caliph," Gunther lowered his voice, "but I know a skunk when I smell one. I know a little bit about skunks, and all skunks are the same." Gunther spoke with that same wide smile, hoping the toothless, robed men behind the caliph could not speak English. With his left hand, Gunther slid his Bowie knife out from his under his jacket. He pressed the tip against the belly of the Afghani.

"There is a rifle aimed at your head as we speak, Mr. American cowboy." The caliph said calmly with a smirk.

"And there's a Bowie knife at your gut, Mr. Caliph. And I know a little bit about you already, too. You're real quick to send your people to their death. But, not so quick to die yourself. Think about your white and red guts spilling out on your feet. Can ya picture it?" Gunther maintained that big smile.

The very air in this chasm changed. The caliph's men sensed it. They and their horses fidgeted, but their caliph waved a hand to stop them. Perryweather now spied the glint of the Bowie at the caliph's stomach. Verne did, too, and he gasped and stepped his horse back.

"What if I told you that no matter how many of your people died today, you…would be the first? Because I will shove this knife up your fucking gut and out yer throat…with a twist."

The caliph remained silent. Gunther's smile evaporated into a malicious sneer.

"Captain Perryweather!" Gunther barked over his shoulder. "Prepare your men for combat."

As if hypnotized by these events, Perryweather startled awake with the call of his name, turned his horse, and galloped off, shouting orders.

"What's it gonna be, Mr. Caliph?" Gunther asked.

Behind them, the Lancers quickly took battle formations and spread out, readying their weapons.

"Well?" Gunther continued, "are we gonna finish this pig-sticker's dance, or are you gonna back the fuck off, you bush-whacking son of a bitch?"

The caliph didn't seem to understand every word, but plainly understood raw emotion and saw the readiness of the troops.

Gunther let the handshake drop, and with this newly freed hand yanked out his .45. He backed away, lifting the outstretched gun to his eye level and aimed at the caliph, whose eyes showed real animal fear. Someone gasped. The caliph backed away to his horse.

"The sheik," the caliph said as he mounted his stead, "will still not grant you passport through this pass."

"You tell your sheik," Gunther added, while raising the weapon to his caliph's head, "my gun is my passport."

With a smug look, the caliph and his entourage turned and rode back up the pass, and all the other scoundrels evaporated from the caravan and galloped off with him. This time not back into the tree line of the slope, but rather straight ahead.

"Rosenthal! Gildenbeck!" Gunther shouted, as he watched the tribesman gallop away. Like an echo, the men behind him passed the call down the line. He flipped the Bowie knife in his hand from a saber grip to a reverse grip and shoved it back into its sheath.

Reverend Verne swept off his hat and wiped his brow of sweat with a handkerchief. He muttered, "Oh sweet Jesus, master of all heaven and earth…come among us now."

Gunther watched the group ride away. "I shoulda shot that son of a bitch right between the eyes while I had the chance. I hope I don't see that face again," was the prayer he muttered while holstering his handgun.

"That was quite a bit of dangerous grandstanding," Verne added.

Marilyn remained as still as a statue. "If not for that grandstanding, I might well have been riding off with them as a kidnapped hostage."

"We would not have let that happen, my lady," a nearby British officer said.

"Sir!" yelled Gildenbeck, as he and Rosenthal rode near him and then stopped in a cloud of rock dust, which Gunther fanned away with his hand.

"Follow them," Gunther said, "carefully. Follow them, just far enough to tell if they have a large contingent, or where the hell they are going. Then get back and report."

"Sir!" the scouts yelled and made their way up the valley.

Perryweather rode up, with his eyes on the distant caliph and the two cavalry scouts in pursuit. He stopped beside Gunther. The soldier walked Gunther's horse back to him, handing him the reins.

"If you pull a stunt like that again," Perryweather growled, "I will…"

But Gunther mounted his horse, ignored the Brit, and spoke loudly to Lieutenant Kerry. "Have the men advance in the ready formation. Eyes, ears and guns. We may have bought some time here today."

"Yes, sir," the lieutenant said and turned off to alert the troops.

"Gunther turned to Perryweather. "You are more than welcome to join us in a combat formation, Captain, or you may continue with your…horse parade." Gunther rode off to the rear.

"I have never quite seen anything like that, Major," the

lieutenant said. "I have never read or heard of such a thing, at West Point or anywhere." The men rode side-by-side as the caravan proceeded north.

"You mean, a general sticking a blade up to an Indian chief's gizzard? That isn't in a textbook at the Citadel?" Gunther said with a smile.

"Yes, sir, well, not quite like that…anything that tricky I mean."

"Yeah," Gunther nodded. "War, Lieutenant, is all about the trick. It is all about the 'drop.' Getting the drop on the enemy, be it man-to-man, or army-to-army, it's all about the drop. As a deputy sheriff, I learned this the hard way. When real close up with a scoundrel, face-to-face, it is important you have a few tricks up your sleeve to capture your opponent. A handshake, like the one you just saw? That is one of my favorites. You tie up his gun hand and pull yours with your left hand. A Frenchman taught me many of these tricks. He was a lawman in Oklahoma. Born in Paris. Taught me the idea of cheating to win."

"A Frenchman?" wondered Kerry aloud.

"Yup. Sheriff Joc DePiere. Hell, he even cheated me out of five thousand dollars. That's a long time ago and a long story." He pointed up front and changed the subject. "Perryweather over there? He is a duelist. That is how he killed your Captain Boston. Fair play. Marque De Queensberry rules. He doesn't think like a savage. He thinks he's better than a savage, but it's all pomp and circumstance to him. To me? Fighting is a knife, in the back, in the dark. Everything else is less than perfect."

"Why did you shoot that Afghan like that, so fast? Weren't you afraid it would start a …a war?"

"Yup. But when I saw those tribesmen ride up, I thought the war had already started. It was just time to shoot. When it's time, it's time."

"How do you know when it's time?" Kerry asked.

"Cause it's time," Gunther answered.

14
The Red, White and Blue

At dusk, the men began to make camp for the night. Guards were posted, rotations set and meals prepared. Gunther lay upon a bed of Marrakesh pillows beside his wagon. The cook handed him a cup of hot tea. He worried about his two scouts and… .

All heads turned to the sight and sound of six riders shouting and waving from the north. Gunther jumped up from his rest, threw a halter on his horse and galloped bareback to the front line.

The incoming men were British soldiers, all of them bleeding and filthy. They fell off their horses and into the arms of the men who rushed to greet them. Perryweather also was soon upon them.

"The Walsi police headquarters," an exhausted sergeant babbled. "The Fort Vic compound…and the village…"

"Well, what is it, man!" demanded Perryweather, motioning his medics to hurry and help them.

"Rebels…many tribes attacked us, sir. We, we could not hold them off. Me and the boys made a break for it, as all was bloody lost. Poor Captain Finley, sir…there be canons, sir…and he was blown to pieces!"

The medics inspected the men's wounds and gave them water. The British company's surgeon arrived with a large satchel of medical supplies. One of the exhausted horses collapsed suddenly, its hide a foamy white froth. Its breath labored and pained.

"Through it all, they sent in messengers to get the last of us to surrender. These scoundrels said it was the work of the…the Red, White and Blue Sword. And that he would be merciful to us, if we'd just raise the white flag."

Both Gunther and Perryweather exchanged quizzical glances.

"Did you see this man?" Perryweather asked.

"Not close, sir, but the leader was a giant of a man, with a head of curly hair. Pacing, he was, the whole time on a hillside and directing the waves of attacks. The savages!"

Another soldier spoke up. "Did ya hear of us, Captain? Was ya comin' to reinforce us?"

"No, Corporal. We did not know. We are here on other business."

"Well there is surely no one to rescue now, sir. No one." Gunther took a close look at this man's right arm. It was ripped to shreds and turning dark green colors. Worse, Gunther could smell death about him.

More soldiers, ever curious, congregated to hear any news. Reverend Verne and Marilyn arrived, both bending at the knee to help the wounded.

"Where is this place, this Walsi?" Perrryweather asked an Indian scout beside him.

"Thirty-five kilometers from here, Sahib Captain. North and west. At the end of this pass and then a left toward the Himalayas."

A British officer stepped slowly over to the downed horse, charged his rifle and shot the horse in the head.

"Get these men some food and water. Care for the horses," Perryweather said, with his arms folded across his chest. "Then find out the details. Every detail." He wandered a bit over to Gunther as the onlookers dispersed to spread the word through the camp.

"Is this our man?" Perryweather asked, quietly.

"It could be. The Red, White and Blue Sword," Gunther said.

"Are your scouts back yet?"

"Not yet, and I'm getting worried. But, they are very good men."

"Let me know when they get back and what they saw?"

"I will," Gunther said and, with the first civil words spoken between them, the men parted. Gunther leapt on his horse, and at a slow gallop returned to his wagons.

"What happened?" Lydia asked.

"I think we have received the first report on your husband,

Lydia."

She'd been tying a tent cover over her wagon. She dropped the lines and stepped down from the coach as Gunther relayed the story of the Walsi attack.

"Pacing the hillside…like General Grant in the Civil War. His hero," she commented. "But what does this mean?" Lydia asked.

"It means that your husband has become a king of sorts. A Kipling king. He has gathered an Afghan army. With it, he's taking territory," Gunther assumed.

"We will go to Walsi, of course?"

"I think we have to," Gunther answered, and he turned to Harrigan and Smith, as they returned from seeing the wounded soldiers. "And, you gentlemen will get some war pictures when we do."

Smith tried to speak, but clutched his throat from a sharp pain.

Harrigan paused by Gunther, as Smith walked past him to the fire. "He can't utter a sound, Mr. Gunther. I shudder to think that he…he may never speak again. That his voice box has been forever damaged."

Gunther shook his head. "That would be a shame. He is such a conversationalist. Such a smart man."

Gunther dropped back onto his pillows and stared at the open sky. An American some distance off quietly played a soft tune on a harmonica. The stars looked the same as in Montana, or Texas, the same stars he had steered many a high plains and desert night by, like a captain of a ship in the mid-Atlantic. But what a strange world this was under these heavens. But, not too strange, he thought. The enemy was still savage, and had only changed clothes, as they were still breaching into forts, and tearing into the heart and soul of each other. He itched to jump on his horse and hunt down Rosenthal and Gildenbeck, but he knew he shouldn't leave his command position.

Lydia slipped into her covered wagon to sleep, and the photographers settled on the ground. Verne and Marilyn remained with the wounded in the surgeon's tent. The cook and her monkey slept in the other wagon and Gunther winced at her loud snoring. Finally, sheer exhaustion took over, and he too was off to sleep, interrupted only by the piercing sound of a screaming, begging man having his right arm sawed off.

In the morning, the caravan assembled, Brits to the front, Indians in the middle and the Americans to the rear. Upon Perryweather's command, they all headed forward into a series of wide and thin passes. Still no Rosenthal and Gildenbeck.

They entered another large valley, this one devoid of any green forests or grasses, just rock and more rock on either side gradually leading up to sheer cliffs. This landscape reminded Gunther of lands he had seen in Nevada, Oklahoma or even southern California. Since Caliph Mukbar's surprise approach yesterday, he now feared these valleys between the mountains more than the narrow gulches. In such broad valleys, formidable armies could amass for maneuver and attack.

The Indian scouts wandered ahead, but still within view, as they explored the walls and rims and turns. Gunther knew what these trackers were looking for. Whether searching in Nevada or Afghanistan, they would search for rocks that seemed to be displaced. No easy task, since rain, floods and rockslides had already moved rocks into irregular patterns. It took an experienced eye to determine changes made by nature and those made by man.

Humans disrupted these natural patterns as they passed through. They searched for imprints in the ground or the careless droppings of clothing or gear. A thread. Horse or camel dung, even dried up whispers of it. A tracker and scout could not find the unusual without first mastering the usual. Good trackers studied the habits of men and their transport, how they walked, limped crawled, ran, rolled and jumped, and how these tracks looked a day, a week, even a month later. But more so, a good tracker used his instinct.

"Like an animal in its run," Gunther's old French Sheriff De-Piere taught him. "He follows the path of the least resistance." The path of the hunted is also not hard to deduce, especially when you have been the hunted.

Bam! Bam! Two gunshots rang out across the plain, snapping everyone's attention to the north. Gunther stood in his stirrups to see Rosenthal and Gildenbeck off in the distance, but charging into view, their horses at a full and desperate gallop. Rosie's pistol was pointed in the air. He fired yet again, and they could barely discern Rosie's voice, "They's a comin'!" he yelled. "They's a comin'!" It looked like a chase with Rosie and Gildy fleeing for their lives.

"Lieutenant!" Gunther shouted to Kerry, "make the men ready."

As the machine gun wagons fanned out wide to the east and west, the snipers rode out even further. The Brits and Indians also spread out, following the commands of their leaders, but the Americans, holding up the rear could take advantage of some higher ground and superior firepower. Gunther knew they would be key to surviving this raid.

About one hundred yards behind, the cavalry scouts appeared, several hundred tribesmen on horseback, maybe more. They brandished rifles and waved swords and started a cacophony of warlike, savage shouts that could chill a man to the bone. It was a hypnotizing sight to behold. Was this the great Red, White and Blue Sword of the west? Was this Colonel Latissimo charging them like an insane madman?

"Lieutenant Kerry, give the command to fire at will, when they come into range," Gunther ordered.

"Yes, sir!" Gunther lifted his binoculars and saw not Colonel Latissimo, but rather the Caliph Mukbar leading the invaders.

"Yup! I shoulda shot that soma-bitch when I had the chance," Gunther murmured.

From a distance, Gunther watched Rosenthal and Gildenbeck enter into the front lines alongside the Brits, spin their horses, pull them down on their sides and hang over the top of their mounts with drawn rifles.

"Now that is some fine soldering," Gunther couldn't help but whisper as he smiled from this skillful display, or maybe he smiled just from the sheer electricity in the air. This enemy was getting close.

"Let's kill all these sons a bitches!" he declared to all who could hear and, with one gigantic, pulsating roar, the machine gun teams opened fire. The bullets pelted indiscriminately into the tribe. Men and horses shredded and tumbled. Some disintegrated beyond recognition. Next, the Brits poured rifle rounds into the charge. Within a minute, Gunther spotted Perryweather waving a hand for his attention. Perryweather made a half circle movement with his hand to the west, and then Gunther saw the Lancers mount and make ready for a cavalry charge. Gunther gave Perryweather a thumbs-up.

"Lieutenant Kerry, advise the men there will be a Lancer charge from the west."

"Yes, sir!" Kerry responded, and told his riders to pass the word.

"Now," Gunther said quietly, "If only he'll wait until the right moment. It's like a shooting gallery right now." He worried that the Lancers would intermingle with the enemy too soon, forcing the machine guns—currently chopping the enemy to bloody ribbons—to shut down. The enemy frontline still remained some distance from the Brits, and their own fallen tribesmen, and milling horses became obstacles for the nearing Afghans.

The Lancers rode west, turned and, with a wave of the command flag from Perryweather's party, the unit pulled swords and pistols and charged down the slope and into the enemy's side. Soon the cavalry was intermingling with the tribe, shooting where possible, but also dueling on horseback.

"No! No!" yelled Gunther. "No!" This was too soon. The allied machine guns shut down as the Lancers crashed into the invading force as the shooters feared hitting their own. "Kerry! Tell the machine guns to shoot the east flank, away from the Lancers. Damn! Damn! Keep shooting!"

Afghan sniper fire began plinking all around them. It kicked up pebbles and dust and gouged into the ground, and their rifleman took positions on the cliffs to their right. But Gunther's archers were on cue. Archers sent sizzling, smoking arrows airborne. The archers walked a few blasts up the mountainside to get their bearings until the projectile explosives were detonating above, near, or right on the snipers.

One of these arrows fell short and exploded below a pack of

enemy snipers, but the force destroyed and dislodged the rock wall right under them, causing the entire ledge to break free in a rock-slide. Some ten riflemen plunged, screaming to their deaths. Americans witnessing this plummet war whooped. And Gunther just smiled. But his attention returned to the close-quarters battle below.

The Lancers were deep inside the enemy charge, and the Brits were ordered in to help. The American and English machine guns were virtually silent, taking occasional shots at snipers they could spot.

The Americans were in reserve, due to their rear position. "Shoot at who you can!" Gunther ordered with a sense of desperation, and the soldiers took careful aim at the enemy for clear shots. Gunther galloped his horse around the hillside observing from different views. He decided that a retreat would be smart, and then once the men were free and untangled from the enemy, the machine guns could go back to their best work, but he was not in a position to order such a move. Even if he could, the lines of communication were chaotic. The British trumpeters themselves were now shooting and sword fighting for their lives. The Americans had to help. They couldn't shoot in among the men.

"Fix bayonets!" Gunther ordered, reluctantly, and his men knew the inevitable was coming. The hardest work of the foot soldier was the bayonet fight, fixed upon the rifle or in the hand—the goriest, unforgettable up-close gutting of a human being. Gunther rode up to Kerry, who was affixing his knife to the end of his rifle, "You stay here… ."

"BUT—"

"Lieutenant!" Gunther barked, "You will stay here. Keep the machine gun wagons in position. Keep the snipers in position. They will continue to shoot at targets when clear to do so. This hillside will be our position of retreat. You will make it a safe haven and cover a retreat if we need one."

Gunther galloped to his wagon, where his nervous cook stood in the front perch watching. "My rifle!" he yelled as he approached.

The cook knew instantly and jumped into the open back of the wagon, shuffling through the gear and produced his Mauser. She handed him the weapon.

"Thanks," he said with a nod, "What is your name anyway?"

"Mesha," she answered.

He turned and spotted Reverend Verne, Lydia and Marilyn in the second wagon, nervously watching the butchery below. He trotted to them as he hooked the sling of his rifle on the saddle horn and peeled off his lever-action shotgun from across his back.

"Here." He handed Marilyn the shotgun. "If it gets bad, go down fighting. You won't like the alternative. Crank the lever and pull the trigger. Lydia, get your brace of pistols out."

Lydia lifted her vest and displayed two revolvers already tucked in her belt.

"Thatta girl," he said, but with a distracted smile, and he dashed back to the men. Those already on horseback made ready. They dropped the supply haversacks and saddlebags to the ground. The men riding camels chose to stay mounted on the towering beasts, as they had months of camel charges in practice maneuvers from years prior in the great Oklahoma Camel Experiment. The ride was rough, but these camel men sat higher than on horseback. The camels also were more powerful beasts than rammed and frightened horses, and this gave them an advantage.

Gunther skirted the group and, once up front, he drew his .45 and yelled, "We are going to cut right through the middle of them. Kill the enemy as we go. Then we'll run right out the other side, turn around, and do it again." With this, he spurred his horse straight to battle below, gathered speed with the war whoop, "Charge!"

An Army trumpeter roared the American assault and the rumble of one hundred men, horses and camels followed. Lieutenant Satin was not the only combatant who heard the sound and the fury of the approaching army. He dueled viciously with an Afghan, his military cutlass saber versus curved scimitar, each man on horseback. For all the travel, preparation and buildup, it had come to this for Satin, these two men, face-to-face, till death do them part. Satin maneuvered his trained warhorse with only his clenched knees. His enemy turned to the hill, as if watching for the relief forces to come bounding from the north. Satin used that distraction to slash and cut at the man until he tumbled backward off his mount.

In fact, all around him, Satin could see the tribesmen were affected by the sound and sight of the relief charge. The sheer presence of the fresh men, bayonets fixed, caused a panic in the weakened enemy. Several horses reared to escape even before their riders could respond. Others followed their example. Within minutes of the hillside charge, the tribe fled from the fight, the men and horses stumbling and leaping over the dead and dying.

Satin galloped to the charge and waited for Gunther to draw near. With the tribesmen in full run, Gunther and his men slowed to a trot.

"Do we chase them?" he shouted to the cowboy soldier.

Gunther surveyed the bloody mess around him. Rosie and Gildy were still up front shooting the enemy in the back as the force fled. The pair jogged forward while firing. Bodies flew from horseback with each round.

"No. No, we won't chase them," Gunther answered. "We have a mess here, and I don't know what's around that first bend. Might be an ambush."

Perryweather, afoot, disheveled, a bent sword in hand and covered in blood, ran up to them, "Good timing, Gunther!" he commended. Gunther leered down at the man until Satin interrupted with, "My horse, Captain Sahib!" Satin offered, and Perryweather leapt onto Satin's horse to ride double behind him. Satin could read the American's anger and had obviously cut off a severe tongue-lashing on the poor timing of the Bengal Lancer charge.

"Grimsley!" Gunther called out, and Sergeant Grimsley, astride his snorting camel, rode forward. "Get the snipers and machine gun wagons down the hill and in range to cover us here. We've got a helluva' clean-up action here. Get all the doctors and medics."

Grimsley dispatched the commands as Satin carried Perryweather over to a lone horse, its former master among the dead and battered on the ground. Satin knew it was evident by the scattered and exploded remains that the American and British machine guns were responsible for most of the enemy dead. Had his Lancers waited just another few minutes, the machine guns would have rendered the tribe useless.

Satin jumped at the sound of pistol fire. He turned to see Gunther, still on his horse, stepping slowly in around the mess. On occasion, Gunther fired his .45. Satin could not see who or what he was shooting, but after seeing Gunther's quick hanging of the Thugee, he could guess.

Then suddenly, they all heard another rumble of distant horses and a chorus of yells. All heads turned to the south. Another group, a small army on horseback, raced down the west side of the valley far ahead and stabbed right into the side of the fleeing Afghan tribe, blasting away with rifles and pistols as they went.

"What the deuce?" said Perryweather, positioning his horse for a better view.

"The Star of Africa!" Satin declared.

"The Star of—" Gunther yanked his binoculars from his saddle pouch and examined the surprise attack.

"The Star of Africa, yes Sahib?" Satin asked. "Is there a dark-haired woman leading them?"

"Yes, there is a woman, Satin!" Gunther noted, "She has a helmet on, a knight's helmet like one from the Crusades! But, I can see the long hair from underneath."

"Then she is the Star of Africa. The British government pays her to patrol this pass and keep it open and safe."

"She's a damn-sight late," Gunther mumbled, "but…better late than never."

Gunther and the men watched the Star of Africa and her ragtag group make short work of the remaining scattered bandits. Satin saw them off in the distance as they searched among the dead, and then they slowly mounted up and headed toward them for a meeting. In the last twenty minutes, some five hundred tribesmen were likely killed.

Satin returned to his Lancer captain for orders. The commands were the same as Gunther's orders. Head count. Medical attention. Kill wounded horses. Bury the dead. Satin searched the faces of the men as they gathered for assignments. Were his best friends still alive? One friend waved a feeble hand his way, and Satin smiled back.

"Namir?" he asked a few others. "Have you seen Namir?"

The answer was not good, and Satin looked as if all the energy had drained from his chest. He fell to one knee. His eyes welled up. He dropped his sweaty forehead into the palms of dirty hands. The moans and screams of animal and man echoed all around him. When he looked up again, just ahead of him, at Gunther, his face was the essence of a living nightmare. Mounted on his black horse, Gunther looked like an executioner from hell. His mount stepped gingerly in and around the pounded flesh below, as he fired his pistol down into each unfortunate man and beast alike.

15
The Star of Africa

A Hindu medic shouted out.

"Thirty-seven," repeated a sergeant down the line. The small team of officers surrounding Captain Perryweather waved their hands in acknowledgment. Lieutenant Satin walked his horse over to Gunther, who sat motionless astride his, watching the approach of the Star of Africa group.

"Thirty-seven Lancers dead," Satin told Gunther.

Hot wind in the valley whistled by them, moving Gunther's hair, bringing with it the smell of fired gunpowder.

"I heard," Gunther said, not looking at him. "All Indian?"

"No," Satin said. "There are both British and Indians in the Lancers.

Gunther's horse stutter-stepped and snorted.

"I know he made us charge too soon," Satin added.

"Too soon!" Gunther barked, then looked down at his friend. "If at all! There was no reason to charge the Lancers," he snarled through thin lips. "Some of these Brits are 'charge happy,' always have been." He looked back across the valley. "Every three years something new is invented that moves the cavalry closer to extinction. Those machine guns up the hill? One such invention. This is a horrible waste," Gunther added with a quiver in his voice.

"Yes."

"Lose anybody close?" Gunther added.

"Yes, Sahib. Very close."

"Well…I am very sorry for you, Satin," he said, then sighed.

A lead horse sped forward from the group carrying a bearded male rider in a black turban and white robe. He galloped toward them and waved a long white sheer cloth.

"Here ye!" The Afghani rider shouted in broken English. "Here ye! Comes the Star of Africa, friend and ally to the Queen Victoria of England!"

Rosie and Gildy mounted their horses and flanked Gunther, the stocks of their hot rifles resting on their thighs.

"We follered them, sir," Rosie spoke up. "Dark fell. Then we's got bogged down and couldn't leave. Whenever we saw them pack up for the attack, we broke our cover and rode on."

"We figured a moment's warning was better than none," Gildenbeck finished.

Gunther nodded.

"Here ye, British, the Star of Africa is forthcoming!" The messenger continued his broadcast. And she, majestically leading half that salty pack, now spearheaded the group. The other half of her raiders remained, picking over the defeated tribe like buzzards. As she drew near, Gunther guessed she was at least six feet tall and muscular inside her tight gold pants and shirt, both outlined with inlaid sequins. Brown leather boots covered her calves, from which a leather boot knife handle protruded beside one knee. She still wore her knightly helmet with a jewel-encrusted frontal piece that covered her nose. Long black hair flowed from underneath the helmet. A sword in an ornate sheath crossed her back.

She guided her men in the direction of Perryweather and his English officers and sergeants, as they obviously appeared to be the uniformed leaders. Her men, in robes, turbans and tunics, looked no better than the caliph's men they had just bested. Gunther turned his horse and walked it slowly to the gathering. Satin followed.

They arrived at about the same time as the Star of Africa. Several of her men dismounted first and stood ready to assist her, but she lithely slipped one leg over the mount's head and gracefully dropped to the ground without assistance. Standing tall, she peeled off the helmet, tucked it under her arm, and addressed the Brits.

"You are the commander?" she asked of Perryweather.

"Thank you for your assistance," Perryweather said, studying her from head to toe as she looked away from him to scan his group.

"Think nothing of it," she said. "It is my profession to help the British. You will of course, tell your superiors of this? In particular, a General Raymond?"

"Most certainly, Madame. Captain Perryweather at your service." He bowed slightly. "What is the name of this valley?" Perryweather called out to no one in particular.

"Ishghan," a nearby Indian scout replied.

"Ishghan," Perryweather repeated, nodding his head. "I shall submit a report to the general's high command. This shall be called the Charge at Ishghan! Madame, your help will be surely noted and," he turned to the men about him and shouted, "and you shall all receive medals for winning this brave day!"

"Winning this day?" came Gunther's laconic voice from the left as he approached, and all turned their heads.

"Thirty-seven men are dead in five minutes," he said, as he stepped off his horse and walked in among them, "because you called for a cavalry charge minutes too soon." Gunther strode right up to Perryweather. "Minutes."

"Are you second-guessing my orders?" Perryweather asked.

"The heavy guns were winning the day. I don't call a horse charge into friendly fire a win. I call that stupidity and a bloodbath."

"How dare you, sir!" Perryweather barked. He dropped his hand and clutched at his leather glove draped over his beltline.

"Oh, another duel, Perryweather?" Gunther interrupted. "You try to hit me with that fucking glove, and I'll kill you where you stand."

Perryweather froze. The two were almost nose-to-nose, and Perryweather's hand dropped away from the glove. In fact, the entire group stood motionless and silent. They had all witnessed Gunther's impulsive nature.

"Kam on heh," an old Scottish sergeant interrupted with a calm voice. "Let's noo' fight aboot it. We jus' fought enouf for one day." This somehow eased the tension, as several of the officers and NCOs shuffled their feet and mumbled in agreement with the Scot.

"I'll have you up on charges for threatening an officer," the Brit said menacingly.

"You forget, Captain," Gunther added as he turned from him and headed back to his horse, "I am not in your little toy soldier Army. For which I am more than happy." Gunther grabbed his horse's reins, started to leave when he was called from behind.

"And you? You are the commander of this other foreign army?" the Star of Africa asked. She walked over to him. Three of her men followed, one leading her horse.

"Yes," Gunther answered and he looked at her to see the single, most beautiful face he'd ever seen. It instantly captivated him. Her skin was dark, but not as dark as a common Indian, rather lighter, as if from some racial mix. Her features were symmetrical and her eyes a deep blue. Her hair was inches thick and wavy. Her nostrils flared slightly with exertion but did nothing to spoil her overall aquiline features. Gunther could only assume they flared in excitement at the sight of his confrontation with Perryweather. It was not in his nature to stand and stare at a woman, regardless of how overwhelming her beauty and presence, so he reluctantly looked away, but all too soon for his liking. He continued to head toward the battlefield.

"You are not dressed like a soldier," she commented as she walked beside him.

"I am a former soldier, but I have been asked. Well, I am being paid such as yourself—" he nodded her way "—to be here. Captain Perryweather back there, killed the first American Army leader in a duel. And somehow, I am now in command."

"Ohhh, I see," she said. "This is your remark about the glove and the duel."

He nodded. They continued walking the field for a few seconds more, and she added, "But, as I see it, you are completely correct. What is your name?"

He stopped and turned to her, trying to ignore those eyes, "Johann Gunther. I was once a major in the United States Army. Now, not unlike you, I am paid for my services."

"Ohhh, I see," she said again. "Well, former Major Gunther, as I understand you are completely correct. Your machine guns would have killed these infidels, and the horseback charge was a fool's folly. That is why I was late and was unprepared to help as quickly as I would have wished. I saw you start a charge down the hill to save the lot of them."

"He is interested in medals on his chest, and distant machine guns don't win medals. Charges win medals," Gunther observed. They walked on again in silence.

"You have another name, you know?" she added with a wry smile. The smile revealed her gold tooth with the inlay diamond—the star for which she was named. She smiled even broader when she noted the jewel caught his eye.

"I do?" he asked.

"Yes. By placing your large American dagger up to the soft rib of the band chieftain yesterday, and because you are wearing a cowboy hat of the Americas, they are calling you…how shall I say this in English? Big American Knife."

Gunther smirked, and they continued to walk on. Her language was schoolbook English, but her accent changed with certain words—French? Hindu? Dutch African? Her exact nationality remained elusive.

"Yesterday!" he observed.

"Yes. There are many travelers and mule teams and merchants that work between the tribes. They are already speaking of you from only yesterday, Johann."

Gunther felt pleased that she used his first name. He felt there was something musical in the way she said it.

"You shall make camp at my compound. All of you," she blurted. She snapped her fingers, and one of her men following them ran up. "You will tell the duelist Perryweather since he is at my service, to advance his Army to our camp this evening." She turned to Gunther. "It is only two kilometers down a pass to the left." She looked back at her guard. "Tell him we have the safety of many men, munitions, walled fortifications and medical supplies. Cots. Tents. Nurses."

"Big American Knife!" she said with a half-smile, walked up to him, and shook his hand like a Westerner. Her grip was as stout as any broad swordsman. "Will your Army come also?"

"I believe it shall. As it is at my service…Miss Star? What is your name?"

"I shall inform you of this tonight. But, I must go. I will prepare the medicines. But first, I must strip that tribe of all their valuables. I will leave three men to guide you. We shall treat your wounded, and then feast in honor of the brave men who must charge when they need not charge, who die, when they need not die." She leapt onto her horse, pulling the reins to the right to gallop off before she scarcely touched the saddle.

Gunther watched her dash off with impeccable horsemanship as her men reacted to her sudden departure and tried to mount fast enough to keep up. How in the world, Gunther wondered, did such a mixed-race woman become the respected leader of wild mountain men, in this man's world of abused, mistreated and cowering women? And how could she be so damned beautiful? But he quickly tried to shake his head free of this most unusual woman. He needed to return to the problems at hand. A man moaned at his feet.

"We've got one awake here!" Gunther shouted. Reverend Verne, some Brits and Marilyn jogged his way. Gunther peeled off his hat and held it in the air to shade the man's head. He knelt beside the bloodied troop.

"Am, am I alive?" The Lancer mumbled.

"You, sir, are very much alive," Gunther answered. "You have a cut or two, and I believe the docs can stitch you up better than a torn blanket."

"Do I have me legs and arms?"

"That you do, sir. And all fingers." Gunther stepped back and let the rescuers do their work. He spotted Perryweather talking among some of his aides, but glaring at him from a distance.

"Peacock bastard," Gunther muttered.

The Star of Africa's three guides could not utter a single word of English and barely any Hindu, but Lieutenant Satin was able to communicate with them in monosyllables. The four rode ahead and guided the caravan past the bodies of the dead tribe, already ravaged furiously by wild dogs and buzzards. Gunther, surrounded by Lieutenant Kerry, Reverend Verne Rosie and Gildy, all on horseback led the American contingent down the long slope past the carnage.

"Buzzards look the same everywhere," Rosie commented.

"So they do," Gunther replied, watching about a hundred circle and descend in a tornado-like military formation upon their warm meals. The dogs barked and jumped at them in a battle for flesh.

"Least ways they ain't smelling rank yet," Rosie said.

"Give 'em till noon tomorrow. What's left of 'em," Gildy added.

"I lost my daughter in a pass like this, by men like them," Reverend Verne spoke up. "We were coming through the famous Khyber Pass and a gang of corsairs stopped us, just like these did yesterday. They wanted some of our goods. Then they wanted hostages, too. They wanted my sweet daughter, Amy."

Oh Lordy," Rosie said. "How old was she?"

"Fourteen. The guards we hired were Indians. They were like the thieves we stopped, really, and they weren't very brave and well, they gave her up and one-fourth of our goods for passage, for toll. They took a boy and the wife of another reverend. My little Amy slipped right off her horse without a peep and walked right over to them. One of them put his arm over her shoulder and smiled. Smiled a big ol' toothless smile. She never peeped. My God, I wonder what I have done."

"Sure she's gone?" Rosie inquired. "How long ago was this?"

"Ten years ago. We never saw them again. The expedition was a failure, and when we returned through the Khyber, well, we never saw the tribe again. By this point, my wife died of sickness. I was a sheer, empty hull of a man that the Lord had to refill. I think maybe that is why I volunteered to come back here when the War Department asked me, maybe to…maybe see if my Amy is…."

"Why'd ja come here in the first place?" Rosie interrupted, punctuated by a spit of tobacco.

"The Lord's work spreading his word, Corporal. It was, is, my mission in this pitiful life. I am but a servant. We dreamed of creating an outpost out here, a church on the rock, a place of truth, against all their heathen Gods."

"At some point over the Atlantic, they changed Gods on us fer sure," Gildy added. "I could feel it. The change. A cold change, and I still don't like the feel of this air here. It ain't right."

"That is why what you did yesterday, Mr. Gunther, was so righteous," Verne said. "These vermin needed to be run off at gun and knife point. There is no bartering with them. None. And let their heathen souls be picked apart by the buzzards and dogs of hell," he finished with a growl, staring straight ahead.

Gildy raised an eyebrow and twisted his lips, looking askance at Rosie and Gunther, as such was mighty bold talk for a man of the Lord.

Three hours after a hard, left turn through a chasm, then across a valley, they approached the encampment of the Star of Africa. It looked expansive and spread across a green slope that buttressed up against some cliffs, some of which were gradual, some sheer. These cliffs contained caves at various heights with an intricate design of man-made stairs and ladders to them. Below the caves, the small city of tents was intermixed with clay and rock huts and houses. Surrounding it all, a poorly designed rock wall, but Gunther saw teams of men constructing a part of it. Armed guards with rifles patrolled the perimeter. Inside the wall, women worked and children played. Cattle, chickens and sheep, some penned, some grazing, dotted the landscape. It reminded Gunther of some American Indian caves and rock cities he'd seen in the Southwest.

The three Afghan guides punched their horses from a trot to a gallop as they neared the main gate of this wall, whooping and hollering. Gunther scanned the caves and spotted the Star of Africa—whatever her name was—at the mouth of one, with her hands on her hips surveying their arrival. Within an hour, the whole procession filtered into the compound to the left of the buildings and dismounted. Orders were made to make camp.

Women, covered from head to toe in robes except for slits around the eyes, jogged up to them. Some walked horses with litters attached. They were there for the wounded. The injured, soaked with whiskey, opium and cocaine-laced medicine to mask the pain, hobbled off with their help or were carted off to the center of the compound, the military doctors, Marilyn, Lydia and the reverend in tow. Once again, Harrigan and Smith busied themselves with photographs the instant their feet touched ground.

Mesha also fell into her routine. She started a fire by the wagon and, in minutes, was handing Gunther a cup of English tea. Rosie and Gildy had to fetch their own, shooing off the monkey that wanted to climb up their legs as they went.

"Thank you, ma'am." Gunther accepted the drink. As he sipped, he noticed a man in silk-colored clothes jogging across the field, heading his way.

"Are you Major Gunther, the Big American Knife?" he asked.

"Yes."

"You are invited to a special dinner tonight by the Star of Africa, at her cave, Sahib," he said.

"Her…cave?"

"Yes, Sahib," he answered. He pointed to an outbreak of rocks on the cliff. "It will be just before sunset. I will come to guide you there."

Gunther looked up to the cave on the cliff where he'd spotted her earlier. She was indeed standing up there watching him. Gunther swept his hat off in a grandiose gesture toward her and bowed. She immediately spun and disappeared into the entrance.

"Tell the Star I shall be there. And what should I wear for this occasion?"

"Wear?" said the messenger, "eh, eh, eh, eh…it does not matter what you wear, Sahib." Smiling, he turned for the city.

Rosie stirred his tea and murmured, "That'll spin yer spurs."

"The Big American Knife!" The guide shouted into the cave.

"Enter, please," the voice of a woman followed the announcement, but it was not that of the Star's.

The mouth of the cave was huge, as was the cave itself, the ceiling some thirty feet high in places. Several smaller chambers appeared to adjoin the larger one, with their entrances partially draped by attractive tapestries. There were several fires crackling, and they bathed the walls with a golden reddish light.

Gunther removed his hat as the female who answered approached. She was short and heavyset, and her face and body were wrapped in what resembled one giant scarf carefully woven round her and invisibly fastened. There was a slit for her eyes, her nose was covered and, with a thin slit for her mouth, she grasped a huge cigar, an odd sight that made Gunther smile. The guide disappeared back down the side of the cliff. The woman with the cigar handed him a chalice of red liquid. He smiled as she turned, he smelled of it first, then sipped. It was red wine.

There were animal skins and large, colorful tapestries draped on the walls. Gunther stepped over to them to study the art, all embroideries of war action and hunting in what appeared to contain African, Indian and European settings and people. He considered them suitable for an art museum display.

Then he noticed several cut tree trunks, each about six feet tall, braced vertically and secured by the far wall. These posts had stout, smaller branches tied horizontally to them with ropes. Resting haphazardly against the wall and on the floor were swords and daggers, in piles of wood shavings and bark. War posts. Shaped like humans. Gunther realized, this was how the Star maintained her athletic conditioning and muscular strength, by hacking, stabbing and slashing at these pells—a medieval training system for edged weaponry.

"You see my pastime?" The voice came from behind him. Gunther turned in time to see her emerge from a smaller opening in the cave wall. She was barefoot and dressed in a sheer white outfit with a golden belt tied at her waist. Her cascading hair hung down on her shoulders and over her breasts.

"Yes."

"You do such a thing as this?" she asked.

"Well, yes I do. I have a friend from the Philippines, and we train with bamboo sticks and wooden knives. A system he calls Kali. We also hit trees and wooden posts. We train knife fighting on them too, but not swords. You have some very big swords here."

"I need two hands to handle these swords. You will have to show me Kali," she said.

"Whatever is your name?" Gunther asked.

Her woman with the cigar handed her a goblet of wine. Star motioned for them to sit among some oversized pillows arranged in a semicircle, "My African name was Zuella Tilwanabon. As a slave it was Pasha Ziarre. As a wife it was Pasha Bin Mohammad Sular Hemgabib. Now, I am a diamond in this coal bin, on a mountain in the midst of nowhere. The Star of Africa. A nickname from the jewel I wear. In my tooth. I lost my real tooth in a fight in Zanzabar. I replaced it with this golden one, holding the jewel. But please call me Pasha. Everyone here forgets that I am Pasha."

Gunther stared at her, fascinated, "That, my dear lady, could be a song."

She smiled, "You like my diamond?" She leaned very near for his inspection. He could smell lotions from her hair and body.

"Yes, it is very beautiful."

"It is the Star of Rhodesia. I was the daughter of tribal princess and an Indian merchant who lived there. My parents were killed, and my tribe was sold into slavery."

"By whom?"

"Tippu Tal of Arabia."

"Good God! I know of him. I tried to capture him in North Africa," Gunther said.

"True? This is true?"

"Yes. In 1894, I was dispatched by the Army to work with the British. He was sending slaves to the Americas, after it was against the law. He is a slippery bastard and always escaped."

"A bastard, he is, Johann. I will not tell you all he has done to me and to my people that he ensnared. I was sold to Indians in Bombay. They schooled me as a prostitute," she admitted matter-of-factly. "I was very young. Sold again. Sold again. The last time to Hemgabib, the keeper of this pass and other passes. He was a pirate first, then a mercenary here in the northwest. But, he was a learned man. He lived in England for years. He played professional cricket in Lord's Stadium. He once held a fleet of ships. To the Horn of Africa, a pirate is like a businessman, like an English shopkeeper."

Gunther listened intently.

"He liked me. Then he loved me. He sent me to Paris for a while to school, then England. To school again. He came and went on his ships. I loved him and could not wait for him to return. He set me free to live in London. He asked me to follow him back here."

"And you did."

"I did and learned to ride at his side to work the passes for the British army. I also studied fencing in France and England. I can… maneuver the sword, and I can shoot the head of a crow out of the sky."

Gunther smiled. He now understood her unusual accent—tribal Africa, Indian, French and British mix.

"And he is dead?" Gunther asked.

"He is dead. He was killed protecting this valley. When he died, I took over. It was only natural because I have protected this pass beside him, as his second in command."

She stood. "Come with me." She walked through another cave entrance in the wall. As Gunther approached, he could hear bubbling liquid. Not knowing where they were going, Gunther snatched up his hat. Once inside, he saw her standing before a steaming, hot springs pool, maybe ten feet wide. Clear water gushed in from a spring to the right, and the waters overflowed down into other, lower pools in the cave. A small fire burned nearby, as did numerous candles. More artwork decorated these walls, and the floor, and hassocks and pillows surrounded the pool. Steam rose from the water, and there was a strong smell of salt in the air.

She stared at him with a smile. Then, she untied her belt and dropped it to the ground. She slipped off her satin suit. Once naked, she coyly looked over her shoulder at Gunther, who tried to hide his obvious compulsion to gape at every beautiful inch of her.

She stepped into the steaming pool. Gunther took the cue. He flipped his hat onto his head, rested his goblet on the pool's edge, and then sat on the hassock. Possessed with a new and certain urgency, he quickly unhooked his gun belt, peeled off his boots and continued to undress. As unshyly as she was a moment before, he soon stood naked before her, but for the white hat resting on the back of his head, smiled, and was about to step into the water.

"Wait Johann!" Pasha said with a smile and an open palm in the air. "Shequantgh-gahhh!" she shouted in the direction of the big cave. Then she asked him, "You have not bathed in many days?"

"No, I haven't. Not a good bath." Much to his surprise, the woman with the cigar marched in, hauling two buckets. "Douseyanmon. Douseyanmon," the woman said, directing him to a smaller pool a few steps away. As she walked by, he saw into the buckets. One was empty, the other full of soapy water and a large brush.

"Ha!" Gunther laughed, as did Pasha who said, "Go on. Go on with her."

"Douseyanmon," she continued.

He did as commanded. "Yeoow!" he yelled as he slowly dropped in the water. It was about three feet deep.

"It is hot!" Pasha said with a smile. "I am quite use to it. Don't worry, I do not wish to turn you into soup."

Gunther settled in, determined to survive the hot shock and the obvious, upcoming bath with dignity. It was after all, not the first time he was bathed by a woman.

The woman, still fully clothed in her scarf sat in the pool next to him, her legs in the water. She ran her hand across his face.

"Not much chance for a bath, but I did shave."

She took his hat and flung it on a pillow. She removed her cigar and stuck her nose into his long blond hair. Her face wrinkled in discontent and looked disapprovingly at Pasha. She filled the empty bucket three times and poured it over his head.

"We both have many scars," Pasha noted.

"Yours are perfect," he said. "They are right where they should be. Like art."

"Johann, you say that to…to influence me. You lie."

But Gunther was not lying. The cigar woman brought out a rather stiff, soapy brush and began scrubbing off his outer skin. He managed to utter, "My scars are ugly and scattered without reason."

"You have been shot?" she asked.

"Eleven times. Fortunately, most of them when I was a young deputy…a policeman…in the Oklahoma Territory. They have healed well. I am not sure how well I would handle these wounds today."

"Shoogoti. Shoogoti! Loy!" the cigar woman demanded while motioning upward. He got the message and stood. She proceeded to brush his torso and legs. She lifted up his genitals with one hand and buffed all underneath with the brush.

"I believe I will have a few more scars after this," he mumbled, trying to stand still as the woman brushed his backside with fervor. Pasha appeared to find all this very entertaining as she rested her arms on the ledge of the big pool.

"How old are you?" Pasha asked.

"Forty-three."

"Do you have a wife and children?"

"No," he lied, but it didn't feel like a lie, just another lifetime of another person who was a young fool.

"I am forty. No children. I was taught as a child, how not to have children. Do you hurt anywhere?" she asked.

"Well, this hand," and he lifted his left hand, "the lower two fingers are often numb. I can barely move the pinky. They cut a part out of my right leg here, and my right arm here…" he raised his leg and pointed to the missing hunks.

"A man of value. A man of a rich life should bear the scars of living."

"Beats dying, I guess," he mumbled.

The woman finally completed his bath to her satisfaction. She climbed out of the water.

"I feel like the prize bull at a county fair," he mumbled as he stood.

The cigar woman picked up all of Gunther's clothes and waddled away into the main cave.

"She will wash them. Do you…," Pasha said and turned to the cave entrance, "Shequantgh!" The woman re-appeared in the entrance.

"Do you want your boots and gun belt polished? Your pistols cleaned?" Pasha asked.

"Can she do this?"

"Oh yes. She cleans my guns and leather like no other."

"Okay! Such an elaborate scheme just to disarm me," he said. The woman picked up his gear and left again.

"She is very good. You should see her with my horses," Pasha added.

"Yeees…I'll bet they're all very…clean," he said, noting his stinging skin. He walked to the large pool, was about to step in, but stopped first, "May I, ma'am?" he asked.

"Oh yes, sir, you may, now," Pasha invited. "And I wouldn't worry about being totally disarmed," she added, watching him closely as he eased into the water.

He asked, "And what of the men here with you? You do not have a new husband? You must have many men to choose from."

"The men here in the mountains? They are more interested in themselves, their hands and their hind quarters," she said. "And little boys."

Gunther raised an eyebrow.

"Some nights they dress up like women, putting on powdered makeup and stick-lip—"

"Lipstick," Gunther corrected.

"And they have parties of sex. Some say these ways are an inherited line left from Alexander's armies from all the Greek men back then who loved men. Alexander the Great loved men. And women. It is in the blood for some here," she finished. "It is not like Africa. India. Or France. But, not all the men are like this. There are men here that have wives, too, but women are like cattle. They hide their faces and their ankles, and the men can act as they wish, like fools. Their religions make women like slaves."

"I did not know this," Gunther said, sipping his wine.

"There are some real men here, too. We have some from the Tripoli. Pirates. And men from India and Africa. I do not find them interesting. The pirates, once. A little."

"A little," Gunther repeated. He hung his arms outstretched on the pool's edge.

"Johann," she said softy and walked across the pool to stand between his legs, chest to chest with him, "do you find me exotic, interesting? Attractive?"

He took in her face just inches away. Her hair smelled like exotic flowers. He wondered what type. He managed to answer calmly, "Ooooh, yes." He held her shoulders and ran his hands down and up her arms.

"I find you exotic. And interesting. And attractive," she said and kissed him, deep but fast, leaving his chin jutting out for more as she backed away. She reached for his wine goblet, sipped from it, and then pressed her lips against his. With a whisper of energy, she slowly let the wine leave her mouth and trickle into his. The wine gone, she plunged her tongue into his mouth. He moaned and was lost in the fire of her mouth, the heat of her body, and swirling flow of the hot springs. It all melted into one.

16
The Next Day

"Major Gunther!" A call echoed some time later through the caverns.

Gunther, naked and intertwined with Pasha upon her bed of animal furs, stirred.

"Wha…?" he growled until he realized where he was. "Yeah. Yeah!" He snatched a long fur from the bed and wrapped it around his naked shoulders. Pasha sat up slowly.

"My men are calling me," he told her.

When Gunther cleared the small cave and walked into the main one, he saw both Lieutenant Satin and Lieutenant Kerry standing at the entrance, silhouetted by a clear blue morning sky.

"Gentlemen," he said.

"Major, we have news," Kerry reported. Both men were all business, ignoring Gunther's nakedness, but for the long animal fur. "A British military police sergeant wandered in last night. The man was in terrible shape. He said they'd lost a battle at a police outpost. He'd been released by an American madman to tell the British that the fort at Tasheebo was now lost to the queen by the hands of the… Red, White and Blue Sword."

"He has many horror stories of torture and murder," Lieutenant Satin added. "The sergeant said his life was spared from a pack of killing dogs so he could bring us this message."

Pasha, wrapped in her own fur, appeared beside Gunther.

"Ma'am," Kerry said with a nod, pulling off his hat. Satin followed suit.

"Captain Perryweather announced we march for Tasheebo this

afternoon, at noon, sir," Kerry added.

"What time is it now?" Gunther asked.

"Seven-twenty-two A.M., sir," Satin informed after a look at his pocket watch.

Very well then," Gunther said. "Prepare the men. I'll see you in the column at noon. Bring my horse to the foothill at eleven-thirty. Thanks for the news."

The two officers turned to leave, but Gunther stopped them, "This British sergeant. Keep him around until I talk to him. Don't let them ship him off to India just yet."

"Yes, sir," Kerry said, and they left for the encampment below. As Gunther and Pasha returned to her bed, she said, "I have not asked you, Johann, for it is your business, but you are after the American Colonel Latissimo? He is the Red, White and Blue Sword."

Gunther sank onto the bed, "Yes, I am. He first came here on an expedition to find…"

"Horses. Giant workhorses. These horses are just legends of these mountains." Pasha sat beside him and then eased her torso across his chest. He immediately began stroking her hair.

"You know of Latissimo?" Gunther asked.

"Oh, yes. He met many of the tribes here. Up and down the passes. He first came with Western armies. Then he turned on them. Killed them."

"Killed them?"

"Yes. I do not know all of this treasonous tale," she continued. "He allied with some Muslims. Russians helped him. Latissimo ambushed his own friends and the British in the Khyber."

"Russians killed Americans and British?"

"Johann, everyone kills everyone here. Latissimo slowly started to dress like the people here. Learn their languages. The traders say that one morning Allah sent a sunbeam to shine on his face when all else around him was cloudy and dark. They say it was a sign that he was to be a king by Allah's decree. A leader of tribes. Latissimo is being guided and helped by an evil man, Akbar Rasp Mohammad Dunkar, Seer of the Fourth Moon, Son of the Eternal

Well, Vizeer of Clanestan."

"How do they get all these titles?"

"It is tradition. What you do becomes part of your name. Like a history book. You are Johann Gunther, Big American Knife. The more you do? The longer your name shall become."

"And Akbar?" he asked.

"He is a jihadist," she answered.

"What is that?"

"The Jihad. It's what makes these people crazy," she said distastefully. "It's the great struggle. Any struggle against anything that is not Muslim, anyone that does not believe in Mohammad. Jihad is, is…death."

"Russians?" Gunther mumbled out loud, lost in thoughts of the days past aboard the ocean liner.

"Yes, we have Russian soldiers that travel through our passes. I let them come and go, as they trade with our people. They have never caused a problem with us. I report their passings to the British. I know the Russians want to own all of Afghanistan. They want to own the Khyber Pass and all the trade that passes through, all the way to the sea. They do not want the British. The Muslims here do not want either of them. They will help one kill the other. Then they will kill who is left. It is Jihad.

"If the Russians take over?" Gunther asked.

"If they do? I will leave here, as they will not pay me to guard this pass. I will return to London or Africa. Perhaps I will visit… Texas," she said running a finger over his lips.

"I need to…meet Latissimo," Gunther said, not wishing to reveal his true mission.

"You need…to kill him," Pasha concluded. "He is a maniac, and the Russians are no good. Their government is no good, and it is soon to be in chaos. The revolutionaries who seek power are like foolish dogs and madmen. Their dream will come to no good. Since this sunbeam fell upon Latissimo's face, Latissimo has allied with many tribes who believe the story. He has killed many Americans, Afghans and now the British, too, who do nothing to us except try to keep the peace."

"So…he wants to be king? Like Rudyard Kipling's *The Man Who Would Be King?*" Gunther surmised.

"The Kipling tale is a hundred years old, when these lands were as far away as the moon. Now they are mapped and coveted by international powers. Does America want this land, too?"

"No," he said. "As beautiful as this land can be? We have land just as beautiful. Mountains just as beautiful. Rivers just as lovely."

"You do?" she asked, as she slipped a leg over him and lay completely over him.

"But," Gunther added with a smile, "they do not have something as special, and as beautiful as you. Nowhere in the world. Not even in the stars."

They kissed. "I am not through mapping and coveting you yet," he added in a whisper.

17
The Mountaintop

Gunther found his clothes hung on the back of a chair, cleaned and immaculately pressed. His gun belt shown with effort, his pistol cleaned, even his knife appeared oiled and spotless, and his boots looked new. His hat was brushed and as clean as when he first bought it in downtown Fort Worth. Pasha emerged from behind a partition, buttoning the neck of a white shirt.

"Hurry," she said. "I want to show you something before you leave."

"You are!" He eyed her state of half-dress, her long and muscular, naked legs. She smirked and yanked some pants hanging over the partition top. "The work of God is superior than my legs." She stepped out and buckled on a leather belt equipped with a British pistol and an Indian knife, taut around her waist.

"We must take a ride up to the mountaintop," she said. "I try to go there every day. It is my special place. The place that I go and think about…everything."

Once dressed, they left on foot. From the mouth of her cave they walked some thirty yards to a ledge, then on up the path to a broad clearing. In this clearing, Pasha led him to a wooden stable made of thick tree trunks, tended by several Afghans. Two men at the livery saddled two horses for them. They mounted and, with Pasha in the lead, both trotted their horses to the top of the clearing and slipped into a passage in the rocks. This passage snaked to higher elevations.

The path on the mountain ridge widened, and the horses seemed to know their way. Pasha continued on ahead

Page 204

of Gunther, who followed as her guest. She pointed out this or that flower, a bird, or the occasional tree. Names bounced right off of Gunther's head like raindrops off a hat. But they were interesting. A mountain ram leapt from a tall rock before them. The horses climbed steep paths in places, and they lunged and slipped on the loose stones. They passed through a thick patch of fog in one place. How high could they go, Gunther wondered. Time passed. Were they indeed to run out of space? Out of sky?

Then the elevated land leveled and they passed through fog, or was it low hanging clouds? An intense stillness, a vacuum ensued. Trees and rolling hills somehow existed at this great height, just as though they were in a forest on flat ground below and for a moment he felt confused and disoriented. The mountaintop forest extended for miles. There were snow-capped mountains off in the distance, still twice as high as their own location. The air remained mystically still.

She led them to a jutting edge, where they dismounted and tucked the reins of the horses into a tree branch. She took Gunther's hand as they walked to a precipice covered with green moss. They looked out over a misty, blurry gray of clouds and blue, an azure that seemed to blend heaven and earth together seamlessly. To Gunther, they almost floated, where the sky of humanity met the space of the stars, where man lost his boundaries, where all things were possible, where all human trial and endeavor seemed meaningless. It was dead silence. He found it difficult to breathe. The work of God, as she'd advised.

"It is…beautiful," he told her, fighting back a sense of speechlessness to continue. "And really Pasha, it…is a lot like you. You are intangible. Indefinable. Borderless. You have brought me to Heaven, or as close to Heaven as I will ever be. You…you give me a peace…that I never…."

She kissed him, and they held each other in this no-man's-land, this Shangri-la, where no other thing seemed to exist. No past. No future. Just this moment. In their time. And he held her close. Tight. Even desperate. For he was wise enough to know there would be no other moment like this again, no other chances. None.

Never in his life would there be a richer moment with magic seconds of pure perfection, they rested on this precipice of God.

They took this moment from the madness of what waited below, a purgatory of pain, of conflict, of power, of politics, of ego and sheer madness. Life and death. So fast. So fleeting. So frail. They took their moment. Seized and savored it.

18
After the Mountain

Astride their horses, Lieutenant Kerry and Gunther wandered about the grounds, inspecting the readiness of the men as they broke camp.

"How many horses did they put down?" Gunther asked about the wounded British animals from the previous day's combat.

"Eleven, sir. All butchered for steaks," Kerry answered.

"You can bet Perryweather won't be eating those horse-flesh steaks. There are few things worse than a wounded horse, Kerry." Gunther advised. "They don't handle pain well. I've seen them hit by cannons, shot in the flanks by guns and arrows. They…they try to run from the pain. It's really a pathetic sight." Gunther changed the subject and flicked his gaze toward the hospital tent, "The wounded men will stay here?"

"Yes, sir. And…" Kerry's words trailed off.

"What, Lieutenant?"

"The wounded will not be the only ones to stay." Kerry pointed off to their right.

Gunther saw the Reverend Silas Verne in heavy conversation with several of the Afghans. Verne also spotted Gunther, and he waved one of his long gray hands at him. He started jogging toward Gunther.

With a pull on the right of his reins, Gunther trotted his horse part way to meet him.

"Major Gunther," Verne started. "I—I wanted to ask you. Will you be needing my services any longer?" The man seemed euphoric.

"Well, why, Reverend?" Gunther asked, looking down at him and the several families that followed and surrounded him.

"I held a service for the men last night, and we sang some hymns, and these good Afghan and Indian people heard us and joined us."

"Yes…?" Gunther commented.

"Yes and well…apparently Major, they are Christians, or part Christian and, and they are very interested in worshipping the Lord."

How many?"

"Eighteen? Twenty or so." He stepped close to Gunther, re-moved his huge black hat, and placed a hand up on Gunther's knee. "That's ten more souls than I even spoken to on my last trip here. This is a…a solid place, here. An established place. Good Lord, I might be able to do something here. Build something here."

The men just stared at each other. Gunther shifted in his saddle.

"Lieutenant Satin is with you," Verne continued. "He speaks the languages. And his men speak the languages…and…and, Major Gunther, the direction you are now going? I have not gone before. I cannot help you."

Gunther looked up the valley ahead, then back down to the hag-gard faces of the men and women around them. "Yes, well, this is all true. And we need someone here to help tend to our wounded. Sure enough we do. I think, sir, I can release you of your duties."

Silas clapped his hands and smiled broadly. His eyes filled.

"Though I do worry for my spiritual guidance on the rest of the journey," Gunther added.

"Oh, oh, and I worry about this, too!" Silas declared, trying to hide his glee with a sudden serious face. Then he realized Gunther was being somewhat facetious.

"Well, Reverend, when I pass through again, I expect to see a nice church with a big, rugged cross pointing to the sky," Gunther said.

"And you shall, sir! For there's wood here aplenty. And there are hands here aplenty! And I shall see you again my solid friend when you pass back through."

"Good day to you all," Gunther said to Silas and the group with a nod and started off.

"May the Good Lord bless and keep you!" Gunther heard Silas say over his shoulder.

Gunther and Kerry led their horses toward the British headquarters tent, a splendid rig, surrounded by Iron Jack flags waving in warming, morning winds. Some aides were lowering the flags, dismantling sections of the tent, and packing the mules.

"I guess we really don't need him," Kerry said, almost to himself.

"No, not really," Gunther added. "Religion sure is a funny thing. Makes war. Makes peace. And always needs money either way. The Brits have a chaplain. This is where Verne's wife died. Where his daughter died. He's a born missionary, and a place like this is just where he needs to be."

"What will the Star of Africa say?" Kerry asked, as much as to prod a little intel about Gunther's naked night in a cave with a wild woman as to get the answer.

"Well, she's liable to take my head!" Gunther said with a smile.

"Major Gunther!" a British commander bellowed from the tent porch when he saw the cowboy. "Your presence is demanded forthwith in Captain Perryweather's tent. Now!"

"That is if I still have a head after the Brits are through with me," Gunther commented.

◇

"You're always so busy," Gunther picked at Perryweather as he watched him scour over notes and direct his men in their packing duties.

"You would be, too, if you were a proper military leader. Not some discharged scoundrel consorting with the local savages."

"Yeah well, those savages looked pretty damned good charging down the hill and saving your ass yesterday."

"Take your hat off in my command tent!" Perryweather ordered. But just as his last word ended, two men ripped the canvas roof right off the tent.

Gunther tugged his hat further down on his head, "Might chilly in here, suddenly."

Perryweather shook his head, pursed his lips, and for a moment Gunther thought the Brit actually caught the humor of the situation. "I presume Lieutenant Kerry has done his duties and kept you abreast of the latest?"

"Yes he has," Gunther said.

"Sergeant McGillacutty," Perryweather rested a fist on his table, paused, and looked Gunther in the eyes, "tells a singular and wicked tale. I…I think that Latissimo has gone quite mad."

"The Star of Africa tells me he wants to be king of these mountains," Gunther added. "So much so, he turned on and ambushed his own army unit to get rid of them."

"Good God! Of all the ruthlessness…" Perryweather sighed.

"And…he has made a series of allegiances with local tribes. And he is cavorting with your old friends, the Russians."

"Russians!"

"She said that she sees Russians up and down these passes all the time."

"They are at work here to own the bloody continent! Sergeant McGillacutty estimates Latissimo has amassed some one thousand tribesmen," the officer said.

"One thousand!" Gunther exclaimed. "Are we sending for re-enforcements?"

" No. We shan't need them."

"Oh…shan't we?" Gunther answered back.

"Mr. Gunther, the British army has been overcoming these Afghanis and these Indians with superior military discipline and strategy for hundreds of years. Often at odds of their ten to our one, as in against the Khalsa." He picked up some papers from his table just before two aides, removed it to the wagon. "I don't suppose you are familiar with Khalsa or, for that matter, any British stratagem."

"Nor do I want to be real familiar with looking down the barrels of one thousand Khyber rifles," Gunther added.

"I suggest you leave the military planning…to the military." Perryweather studied his papers for a second and then peered up at Gunther. "Or do you suggest a wild run on foot up a hill such as your best day at San Juan? With everyone pretending to have horses and all?"

Gunther shook his head and let the remark pass. "I guess I'd better speak with this Sergeant McGillacutty," Gunther suggested.

"Yes, of course, by all means…Breakstone!" Perryweather summoned an aide. "Take these men to Sergeant McGillacutty."

Leading their horses behind them, Gunther and Kerry followed Breakstone to McGillacutty's tent, leaving Perryweather to return to his packing. Inside, the Irishman sat on a bunk. He appeared disoriented, but the old trooper gathered himself at the first sight of Kerry's uniform.

"Sergeant McGillacutty!" Gunther said. "My name is Johann Gunther, the leader of the American expedition here. This here is Lieutenant Kerry. How are you today Sergeant?"

"I…don't know." He ran a knobby hand through his greasy gray hair and stood.

"I am a feelin' that I should be donnin' me boots and me guns and moving out with the brigade."

"I think you need some sick call time, Sergeant. You have been through a lot, and you look cut to hell. Look at you! Look at your arms," Gunther said.

"Aye. I have been through the barbs, sah."

"Tell us of the battle, Sergeant," Kerry asked as he and Gunther sat on nearby stools and listened attentively. The sergeant repeated the tale for the pair. Some one thousand men from several tribes, all flying under the flag of the Great Red, White and Blue Sword, appeared at the mountain pass before the village of Tasheebo early one morning.

"They set up cannons on us."

"How many cannons?" Gunther interrupted.

"Ten me thinks, sah! Ten or…or maybe fourteen? Before we knew it, there be cannon balls! Loping over the wall and hitting our positions."

"What kind of walls?"

"Stone and mortar, sah."

"How tall?"

"Twenty-five feet in parts, sah. With parapets. When the cannons breached some holes in the walls? In a giant sweeping assault, they all galloped down the slope, broke through the village streets below us like…like flood water…and hit our walls…like a sea of roaches to eat us alive. Once through the village, they poured through the breaches."

"Where is Fort Tartan in relation to the village of Tasheebo?" Gunther asked.

"The village sets on the east side of them main gates, almost right up to the walls of Tartan. The fort is on a higher slope from the village, sah. All rock and hard ground."

"Lieutenant Kerry, hand him a pencil and some paper," Gunther ordered. Kerry reached into his belt kit bag and passed a sheet and a pen to McGillacutty. The sergeant started sketching.

"Draw the breaches in the fort walls, too, Sergeant," Gunther said. "You had machine guns?"

"No, sah, not out there yet. Promised to come from India," the man answered while drawing, "But we have three cannons mounted in the top of a turret. Right up here." He drew in the large window of cannonry. "The boys fired volleys down their damn craws, but to no bloody avail. They just surprised us and overwhelmed us. They spread out sa far, even twenty cannons couldn't a slow them."

"Did they have machine guns?"

"Nooo, sah."

McGillacutty handed Gunther his crude drawing, and the Texan pushed his hat back, leaned forward on his stool, and scrutinized it. "This pass in the mountains, can the cannons of Fort Tartan reach that pass?"

"No, sah. You'd be safe all around the mouth of that pass as the cannons, even the big ones in the main turret, cannot be reaching that fah."

"Did you make a map like this for Perryweather? Or any of his men?"

"No, sah," the soldier replied.

Gunther groaned then continued. "The enemy released you as a messenger?"

"Ta report in on the loss of the fort," McGillacutty said as he reached into a knapsack beside the bed. "A bastard named Akbar wrote a lettah of passage, called it a passport, fa me to make me way."

Gunther read the English version of the announcement, which was also written in Afghani and Hindu. He read the signature section aloud, "Akbar Rasp Mohammad Dunkar, Seer of the Fourth Moon, Son of the Eternal Well, Vizeer of Clanestan. Conqueror of Tasheebo. He wasted no time adding that last title." He handed the parchment to Kerry.

"Sergeant…I believe that your Captain Perryweather is about to march on that fort. I think he will run the Light Brigade straight into a stone wall, if it'll make for a good oil painting on the wall of your House of Commons."

"Sah?"

"You do need to ride out today, but back to your headquarters and report all this. Exactly as Akbar asked."

"Sah?"

"McGillacutty, we need re-enforcements, hundreds of them up here, and right away. Pass the message. Plead my case. We've got a Russian-Muslim conspiracy; together they are on the warpath with an American as their leader. Who is your general?"

"General Woolstitch, sah."

"Get to Woolstitch and tell him everything."

"Shall I report first to Capn' Perryweather?" McGillacutty asked.

"Has Perryweather given you any orders?"

"Just to get well, sah."

"Then you have no orders but to get well. Get well in India! Perryweather will be gone in forty minutes as we will soon embark on Fort Tartan," Gunther advised. "I ask you for the good of your comrades, dead and alive, wait until we leave. Then don your boots and your guns and ride like the wind to Woolstitch."

"Sah!"

"I will arrange an escort for you of American and Indian scouts."

Gunther and Kerry stood, and McGillacutty bolted up also in respect.

"I shall not be leavin' ya to those dogs, sah," McGillacutty said with a salute. Gunther returned with a short, half-salute to quickly shake his hand. "Good luck to you, Sergeant. I fear we will need rescuing."

Gunther, then Kerry exited the tent. They collected their horses from where they were tethered nearby and prepared to mount. "Kerry, get two of our scouts for this escort."

"Rosie and Gildy, sir?"

"No. I have another job for them. Two others. Get a hold of Lieutenant Satin and get two sepoy scouts, too, for his trip back."

"Yes, sir."

"And Kerry?" Gunther, in deep thought, shuffled the dirt about with his boot, then stared at the hundreds of men around him prepping to leave. "The scouts you and Satin pick? The youngest. Married men with the youngest kids. Let's help get somebody the hell out of here."

"That'll be hard to find among these old-timers, sir." Kerry commented.

"Yeah," Gunther said with a chuckle, "but…try. Ask Grimsley. He'll know. Satin has some real young men we can save."

"Save? Not too optimistic, sir?" Kerry asked.

"Not at all, Kerry. You and me? We're stuck here, amigo. I've got a real bad feeling about this Fort Tartan."

The caravan was prepared to move: hundreds of men, horses and camels, with tens of support wagons. The horses, all in anticipation of a march, snorted and stutter-stepped about in loose, makeshift lines. The camels stood still like statues with bored expressions, their lips and jaws shifting about like old men with teeth problems. Gunther trotted his horse to the front, settling beside Rosie and Gildy, and sized up the men, the valley and mountains ahead.

"What's up boys?" Gunther asked.

"Nothin' much major," Gildy answered. He spat tobacco juice. "The Brits sent their scouts ahead an hour ago. None too fast either. They walked off like they's half asleep."

"I sat with some Brits and sepoys here on their last night," Rosie reported. "They think they are up here to put down another small tribal uprising. Like it was just another easy mission. Sunday in the park. Just a short run. Like we'd do with the Comanch' whenever they'd get feisty."

"Hmmm," said Gunther.

"There's a smidgeon of talk about you," Rosie added in a tease, with a long look up the valley.

Gunther stared at his profile. Finally Rosie continued, "Seems the story of you killin' that savage for just looking over our wagons is a popular tale."

"And," Gildy added, "no less, putting the tip of your pig-sticker up beside that sheik's rib cage and running him off. That there is no small campfire yarn either."

Gunther ignored the comments and gave new orders, "I want you boys to take some men and run ahead. Far ahead." He pulled McGillacutty's map from his jacket pocket and opened it for them to see. The two deftly eased their horses about and craned to study the drawing. "Set up runners and keep me constantly posted. Spy on this place, boys. I want to know everything. Troop size. Movement. Routines. Everything."

"Reckon it'll take ya'll two, maybe three days to get there," Rosie guessed. "We'll be there in a day. We'll keep ya posted, major." The pair galloped to the rear to organize their team.

Gunther watched Perryweather mount his horse and trot to the head of the line. He commanded his trumpeter to sound off. A flag bearer lifted his staff, and the unit flag came alive in the mountain gusts. The whole human mass slowly stumbled forward in an erratic gate, bound for the wilder north. As before, the Brits were in the front, the Indian sepoys in the middle, and the Americans brought up the rear.

Gunther rode back toward the Americans. While he passed some of the British on the right column, those both afoot and on horseback, some called out to him with smiles and nods.

"Govnah'!"

"Major!"

"Remember the Alamo!" This caused a small cheer and scattered laughter.

"Why, there's Machine Gun Gunther!" another horseman shouted.

"Show us that bloody Bowie knife!" one cried out.

Gunther stopped his horse. "This little ol' thing?" he asked and extracted the fourteen-inch weapon from its sheath and held it high. This instigated a small disturbance of cheers, war whoops, and laughter. It was indeed obvious that Gunther's exploits had spread through the men. Not to mention the obvious: his machine gun teams so expertly whittling down the attacking tribe two days earlier. Gunther re-sheathed his blade.

"Stick it to him, Major!" another cajoled, but Gunther wasn't sure, by the sound of it, if he was to stick it to the enemy, or to their pompous leader, Perryweather.

Once back by the American expeditionary force, Gunther scanned the group for his small, colorful dual-wagon train of civilians. He wanted to warn them against continuing and ask them to stay at this safer encampment. Battle was surely ahead. Lydia, Harrigan, Smith and Marilyn were in one open coach, with Harrigan at the reins. Gunther's new lifelong Hindu servant and her spastic monkey rode in the other coach. Gunther turned his horse about and now walked with the wagon's slow movement.

"Mr. Smith!" he shouted to the photographer in the wagon. "How is your voice this morning?"

Smith could only wince and shake his head to the negative.

"Did you have a pleasant evening last night?" Lydia Latissimo chided from her coach seat beside Smith.

"Yes ma'am," he said.

She stood in the wagon to talk to him more, but her torso lurched as if a violent revulsion rumbled through her insides. Her mouth filled and in a second, projectile vomit flung from her face. Without additional warning, she tumbled right out of the wagon! Head first! A good eight-foot drop! Gunther leapt from his horse, as Harrigan halted the coach. Some of the American troops stopped, others veered around them to continue with the procession.

"Lydia! Lydia!" Gunther bellowed, kneeling beside her, turning her over and cradling her head.

Marilyn dropped from the wagon with a medical bag. "It is her medicine," she advised. "She needs more and more each day." Marilyn produced an ammonia capsule from her satchel, crushed the ampule, and waved it under Lydia's nose. The sharp ammonia smell hit the air and jolted Gunther's head back. Lydia's head shifted in Gunther's arms. She was bleeding from her forehead and nose.

"Lydia! Lydia," Gunther pleaded and tapped her cheek.

Her eyes opened. "My Lord. My Lord, well…I…what…"

"You've fallen, Aunt Lydia," Marilyn reported as she dabbed at the wounds with a cotton towel.

"Fallen?"

"Yes, fallen."

"Out of the wagon!" Gunther said. "Lydia, would you please consider staying here at this camp?"

"Oh no," she mumbled as she pushed up from his arm. "No, sir."

She got to one knee, determined to rise. Gunther and Marilyn exchanged futile glances as each took an arm to stand her up.

"I will see my husband," she declared, much like a drunk. "I will see him."

Harrigan and Smith opened the back coach gate, as Gunther and Marilyn guided her over, up, and in.

"I am going to ask all of you to stay here. I do not like the prospects ahead," Gunther said.

Smith and Harrigan blankly stared at Gunther. Smith returned to his seat and Harrigan turned and picked up the reins. Marilyn guided Lydia to her seat.

"You know my answer, sir!" Lydia stopped and growled at Gunther. "You know why!"

Indeed, Gunther did know. There was no turning back for any of them. The wagons followed the troops. Gunther leaned forward on his saddle horn and watched his caravan waddle off in the ruts and rocks of the hard ground. He grimaced, lifted his Stetson to run a hand through his hair, and then heeled his horse into the flow of soldiers.

Within a moment he heard, "Are you ready for a better view for an hour or so?" It was a gruff voice from his right. He turned and saw Sergeant Grimsley, astride a camel loping along beside him.

"Well I reckon so!" Gunther declared. He pulled a rein to the right and left the procession. Grimsley and camel followed.

The sergeant tapped the shoulder of his beast with his stick and emitted a series of clucking and shushing sounds. The beast groaned and fell to its knees, forelegs first, then rested its belly on the ground. Grimsley slipped a leg over the unusual saddle and slid to the ground. Gunther dismounted and approached the camel, passing his reins to Grimsley. He took the camel stick, looped a leg on the humped saddle, and tapped the neck. The great creature bolted up, hindquarters first flinging Gunther viciously forward. Then tossed back. It brayed like a donkey. Gunther smiled and nodded at Grimsley and he mounted his horse. The trade complete, Gunther tapped the rear flank with his cane, and this ship of the desert cruised on. There was only one thing stranger than seeing a camel walking by, and that was actually being on one while it walked. Gunther settled in for the experience.

He looked to the mouth of the cave up on the hillside. There she stood, the beautiful Star of Africa, her arms akimbo. A woman unlike any other! She seemed to be watching him, but one could not be sure at such a height and distance. Still, he took off his hat and waved it. She responded, immediately. He'd told her he'd be back. He'd promised. Hell, he might even stay awhile.

19
Getting There

"They are about forty kilometers away," The Pakistani tribesman reported to Latissimo and Akbar.

"Maybe four or five days."

Latissimo wandered about the stone room with his hands behind his back. Akbar swept aside the bulk of his black robes and sat upon a slate tabletop.

The man continued, "Five hundred men. Six hundred men, maybe? They are flying three flags. The British Union Jack."

Akbar nodded.

"The India flag," he added.

And Akbar nodded again.

"And the American Stars and Stripes."

Latissimo swung about with wide eyes, "Americans? Here?"

Akbar stood. "Of this flag, you are sure?"

"Yes," the tribesman answered. "Maybe two hundred of them with this flag. They all ride camels and horses and bring machine guns."

Akbar turned to Latissimo. "We expected the Americans, they have reached us sooner than we planned. They are looking for you. You are an officer of the United States Army, and you are missing."

"Found alive, I am absent without leave! A traitor," Latissimo corrected, but then took a deep breath.

"You are the leader here of almost two thousand men, many of whom are camped at the basin of the fort. You are far from the United States." With this, Akbar turned to his soldier. "Watch them and tell us every move."

"Praise Allah," the man said as he left.

"Praise Allah," Akbar replied with a bowed head.

"Praise Roosevelt!" Latissimo declared with a sneer. "This is all his doing. His curiosity. He'd be here looking for me himself if he could."

"Your cowboy president will not be president for long," Akbar said. "Some pale, fat businessman will take over your country, and they will forget about you and forget about Afghanistan. Forget about Pakistan. Forget about India. And we will sharpen the sword of Islam."

Latissimo sat on the table next to him.

"You will have ships of money. You will own this and many passes, collecting tools and tributes. And, because you help us, you will be respected in Russia and the east. A man of international power. Above any one country. Above the United States of Distant America."

"I didn't think the Army would come this far after me. And where in the hell are the machine guns the Russians promised us?"

"They will be here soon. But, we will see what the cowboy president wants when the Americans come."

"That we will."

"When they arrive, we will invite them to dinner," Akbar decided.

"Fucking dinner?"

"Dinner. We have had many dinner meetings with the British in the last two hundred years. A common truce dinner. The British love to have such meetings and negotiate. They love to make the peace and sign papers in their King's English. We know what the British want. They think this has been another skirmish on the Northwest Frontier they have to quell with a treaty. The British always pay us for our peace."

"The Americans just want to see if I'm alive. They will report back they found me."

"We will kill them all first," Akbar said. "Let Washington live in confusion for another year or two."

"You don't know my cowboy president," Latissimo muttered. "He keeps an ace up his sleeve."

"An ace? Is this like a snake?" the Afghan asked.

"Ahhh, yeah…yeah. Like a fucking snake. These are no ordinary soldiers he sent."

"Allah fears no snake."

Latissimo found this funny and laughed. He slipped off the table and paced. "Yeah, a dinner sounds nice. Nice. But an American-style dinner. With a fucking big table and chairs. None of this pillow shit on the floor. And inside this fort. Downstairs in the main chamber. No tents outside. Lots of food. Get your boys out hunting. We'll have us a nice dinner and we'll chat, chat, chat.

"We shall have such a dinner," Akbar said. "Take their money, and then we will slay them all."

"A horn!" shouted hundreds of men in unison. A voluminous, brassy horn, man-made and powerful, echoed through the wide pass and the rocky hillsides. Then, while one blared, a second horn, one of a differing tone and tenor, resounded. Was this some kind of attack signal?

The source emanated from the wide pass ahead. Gunther, with Kerry and Satin, now mounted on horses, followed him at a gallop toward the left hillside to take a look. In the distance, they spied a small group of men, some on foot and others on camels, headed their way. Gunther and Kerry exchanged curious glances and took off to find the head of the expedition and the Brit's front line, where the horn blowers would first make contact.

Two dark-skinned hairy tribesmen with ivory-colored horns were afoot and in the lead. They took turns sounding off. Behind them were two more, each holding cords with metallic balls of smoking incense. The balls swayed side-to-side with each step. The rest were five men each mounted on a camel. Some waved colored flags on long poles. As they grew near, Gunther heard them chanting.

Captain Perryweather drew the entire expedition to a halt with a raised hand and waited for the horn blowers, chanters and camels to approach. Some twenty feet ahead, this foreign parade also stopped and fell still and silent, but for the flapping flags as wind whipped bits of rock and sand between them all.

The man on the lead camel started singing. He looked old, pale and bald and was wrapped in a white robe. The horns blasted, startling some of the British horses, which neighed and stepped about.

The man began to sing out in English, "The great Red, White and Blue Sword, Scourge of Tartan and all to be seen and heard from Khyber…exalted ruler of the Great Northwest…hereby does invite the leaders of this caravan, the brave commanders of England, India and the United States, to attend a dinner in their honor at Fort Tartan. Foods of many nations will be served in this evening of peace."

Perryweather looked surprised and confounded, unable to find an answer at first. Eventually, he said, "It would be an honor to—"

"The dinner will commence at sunset tomorrow," the strange man interrupted with a whole second chorus about the food, drink and proper attire. He never once looked at anyone, just stared ahead. He was blind. He clapped his hands when finished, and two men behind him dismounted and took from their saddlebags two decorated clay urns. They carried the urns before Perryweather, placed them on the ground and removed the lids. They contained colorful fruit.

"Medicine of the desert, of the Muslim," Satin leaned over to Gunther and whispered. "A good gift. This was once the gift of Saladin to Richard the Lion-Hearted."

"Tell the Red, White and Blue Sword, the commanders of this expedition will be at Fort Tartan at sunset tomorrow," Perryweather said to the bobbing head of the blind singer. "And thank him for his generosity."

Silence.

Lieutenant Satin trotted his horse near Perryweather. "Captain, they await a gift in return."

"Yes, oh yes, yes…Atterly," Perryweather called an aide. "Atterly, get the man… ah, ah, what do you think, Satin?"

"Wine, sir, would be fine," Satin replied.

"You heard the man, get him a case of my wine."

Atterly went to Perryweather's mess wagon and returned about five uncomfortable minutes later with the wine. He passed the wine to one of the gift bearers. At the moment the transaction was complete, the blind man started singing in a foreign tongue. The horns blew again, and the whole parade turned and marched away at a slow pace.

Satin returned beside Gunther and Kerry.

"This a trap?" Gunther asked.

"It is of course possible, but meetings and dinners such as this have gone on here for centuries. Also, it is the way of the Middle East Islam Muslim. Peace and treaties are drawn in such meetings. Or two warriors meet from respect. They talk. Wars are avoided. Or not, and they kill each other the next day."

Suddenly, the two horn blowers and incense swingers climbed aboard camels, and their whole procession dashed off as fast as the animals could carry them.

"They will announce our acceptance and prepare for our arrival," Satin advised.

"Smells fishy to me," Lieutenant Kerry said. "Like an ambush. Would they poison the food?" Kerry asked.

"It's happened before, but not often," Satin answered.

Perryweather's aides dismounted and started inspecting the urns of fruit like a bunch of curious monkeys. The captain spotted Gunther off to his side, "You, of course, will be in attendance," he said.

"Of course," Gunther replied.

"Good luck," Kerry said.

"Oh, you're coming with me. You're my food tester," Gunther advised.

"Thank you, ma'am," Gunther said as Mesha handed him a hot cup of tea and a plate of food. He carefully sat on the rocky ground, resting his back against a wheel of his wagon. The sun was setting, and a night chill seeped across the open pass and narrow valley. Harrigan and Smith carried their food from the fire and sat beside him.

"Do you think there will an ambush at this dinner?" Harrigan asked, as he juggled his chow and drink down into a cross-legged, seated position. Smith did the same.

"It appears unlikely," Gunther said." It sounds as if such dinners and meetings go on here quite a bit between the English and the locals. We use to powwow with the Indians once in awhile in Oklahoma and Kansas.

"Wear…your guns," Smith painfully rasped with his injured throat.

"That is the first thing I have heard you say in weeks!" Gunther declared. "And, I will wear a brace of pistols and a knife."

Smith smiled.

"He has been whispering a few things of late," Harrigan added. "Can we come along to this dinner tomorrow? Just to take pictures?"

The idea of capturing a photo of Latissimo in whatever state he currently was in, be it a wild-bearded mountain man, a turbaned sheik or in a three-piece suit, was appealing.

"Hmmm. I will ask Lieutenant Satin if that would be rude. No doubt, Perryweather would love a handshake photo of himself if they strike a treaty."

"No doubt," Lydia sat in a chair near them.

"You have to eat something." Marilyn rounded the wagon.

"I am all right," a pale Lydia replied.

Lieutenant Kerry handed Marilyn a plate of food, and they both sat on a large rock.

"What will you do, Johann? When you see Colonel Latissimo?" Harrigan asked. "He has become a brigand and a traitor. Will you arrest him?"

"I'm not sure what I'll do, but nothing tomorrow night. Tomorrow night is like a truce night," Gunther said, spearing a vegetable on his fork.

"I am going," Lydia announced.

"What will you do when you see him, Mrs. Latissimo?" Lieutenant Kerry asked.

"I…I don't know. We have been married for twenty-three years.

He didn't leave me for any ordinary woman, a socialite or even a squaw. He didn't leave me for some distant Army post in Colorado. He left me for…a kingdom. What do you do with a man who leaves you for a whole…kingdom? Is one woman worth a kingdom? Imagine a soldier boy's sandbox, a playground of war making, and boozing and debauchery? He's in charge here, like a president. A general. A king!" she said and sipped from her medicine bottle. "Oh, I won't be drinking this past midnight," she reported in Gunther's direction, holding up the laudanum. "I will have my wits about me, painful as they are." She shifted uncomfortably in her chair.

The camp fell quiet as they ate dinner, except for Lydia, who waved off food that Mesha offered. Mesha handed Lydia some tea instead, and she accepted. She sipped it and asked for more sugar. Gunther flipped the monkey snippets of bread, and it leapt into the air to catch them.

"You left your wife, didn't you, Mr. Gunther?" she asked sardonically.

He didn't answer, and Marilyn shook her head at her aunt's lack of tact.

"Did you leave your wife—your children—for a kingdom somewhere? Or some trollop you thought you had to have? Then you left her, too?"

Still no answer.

"You left her for the Army. Then you left the Army?" she added.

Gunther cocked his eyebrow at her, but did not see the face of a woman trying to torture, but rather a tortured woman. He looked back to his plate and continued eating. Between bites he said, "Lydia, I was very young. I honestly do not remember exactly why. But the idea of the Army had something to do with it."

"Well, yes, you were young and foolish. Vito is not young," she said. "The idea of the Army and the actual Army, are two different things."

"That they are ma'am," Lieutenant Kerry said.

"Helen of Troy was a woman worth a kingdom," Harrigan spoke up. "The face that launched a thousand ships."

Gunther winced at the remark.

"Well, I guess I am no Helen," Lydia said, as Gunther had anticipated.

"Lydia," Smith said with a low, gravel whisper, "your husband is a weak man. A fickle man…who gives in to himself." He gulped painfully, and this was all he could utter, but it was enough.

She stared at the black man for a moment and nodded. "I do believe you are the smartest man here, Mr. Smith. And unfortunately among us here tonight, you are rendered the quietest."

"Well, on that note," Gunther said as he stood with an empty plate. "I need to go see a certain British captain about a Trojan horse."

"Hello in the camp!" Gunther shouted as he approached the group of British officers sitting around their campfire, one such crackling fire in among many as the troops bedded down for the evening in small groups. Perryweather stretched out, his back propped against a saddle, sipping brandy.

"Entrez!" a voice declared.

Gunther stepped into the inner circle and squatted down. "Nice fire," he commented. "I see the fruit was not poison." All around the men were the pits and skins of the fruit and the upturned urns.

"Nay, mate," an officer remarked. "Proper fruit."

"Mr. Gunther," Perryweather declared, as he sat up a bit more. "Brandy?"

"Well, I don't mind if I do."

One of the officers poured him a drink in a thick, expensive glass and handed it over to the cowboy. Gunther turned the fine crystal in his hand, catching the red and yellow rays of the flame passing through the craftsmanship and the golden liquid it held. He smelled and sipped the aged brandy.

"Mighty good," he said.

"What brings you to our humble campfire?" Perryweather asked.

"I reckon that we will be near Fort Tartan tomorrow."

"Yes, you reckon correctly," the Brit said.

Gunther sat beside Perryweather and reached into his jacket pocket, producing a paper. "By chance, did Sergeant McGillacutty draw for you…a map of the valley? Of the town below the fort?" Gunther handed him the paper.

"No. No, he didn't," the officer said and took the map.

"I asked him about the ranges," Gunther continued. "The distances between the pass, the mountains, the town and the fort. Tomorrow, when we enter the valley through this pass--I have an idea. I think we should spread out along the edge of the mountains."

"Spread out…" Perryweather repeated in a mumble, as he looked the paper over.

"The sergeant said the fort has three cannons in a top turret. The cannons will not reach three-quarters of the way to the mountain's edge. Nor will any rifle fire reach from the fort. Nor would any machine gun fire, presuming they have machine guns."

"Yes…" Perryweather agreed.

"This leaves us only to worry about the tribe camped out beside the village. If we camp along the rim and set up our guns quick enough, far enough apart, we could defend against them should they try anything," Gunther said.

"Well, we certainly cannot all remain just inside the pass in a long line. We will have to enter the valley. And we'll have to camp. And we shouldn't just camp next to those tribes of cutthroat animals. Hmmm. Damn splendid idea, Gunther. We'll spread out in a half circle and organize our defenses," Perryweather said and sipped his drink.

The other officers nodded and repeated, "cheers," in various volumes.

"I believe I will also post snipers at various heights along the cliffs," Gunther added.

"I certainly hope they will come to their blasted senses and surrender the fort in a treaty," the Brit said, staring at the fire as if hypnotized.

"It wouldn't be the first time, sir," an aide said.

"They've got us outnumbered two, maybe three to one,"

Gunther reminded them.

"Yes, but the bastards always have," Perryweather implored. "They like to trifle with us and then make a deal. They make out all right—the brigands—but in the end, they know the queen's revenge."

"Hear! Hear!" came the group.

Gunther swigged the brandy and stood. "Hope so."

"Jolly good work," Perryweather said as Gunther started to leave.

"He needs to drink more often," Gunther said with a smile to the men, pointing a thumb back toward Perryweather. They laughed. "Thanks for the brandy, boys."

A drunken Perryweather was far more amicable, almost normal, Gunther thought. He walked back to his two wagons, through the night camps of quiet men, through the smoke and the smell of tea and coffee brewing, cigars, pipes and cigarettes, the aromas of cooking spits of scavenged or saved meals from the mess wagons.

Scattered across the ground on a chilly night, whether British, Indian or American, they all looked the same. The dog soldier. Dreading war, but loving it. Cussing it, but lost without it. All looking for one last, little, simple pleasure before the next day's sacrifice befell, be it a hard march, a boring post, a rugged walk, an open wound, a lost limb. Death. All drawn in part to do some duty for their queen, their king, their country, their president, their God. Duty.

Yes, duty called, but in part. That other part wanted out on the next train. Off, to be in the arms of a good woman somewhere, someplace where rifles were but ornaments hung above the fireplace. Off. Gunther, too, was drawn to the urge of leaping onto a camel and kicking its sides beet red all the way back to the coast. Away from this madness! This sandbox! Where is his Helen of Troy? Was it a Star of Africa? True, the thought of all those U.S. dollars being automatically deposited in his bank account gave him some solace.

In the distance, Lieutenant Satin lightly strummed the sitar in a soft, slow song.

"Good night, Major," an American troop said as Gunther walked past some men on the cold ground, already wrapped in their blankets for sleep, but he couldn't tell from whom.

"Good night, soldier," Gunther replied softly.

20
Scorpions, Leopards and Rams

The sun was bearing overhead, allowing no shade for the scouts on their wide, high mountain ledge. Gildy, Rosie and six Army scouts, prone, dirty, hot and hungry, kept a vigilant study of Fort Tartan and the small village almost a mile below and beyond them. The ninth scout tended to the horses and gear on the other side of the icicle thin mountain, safe from view.

Gildy rubbed his eyes and rolled over on his back with a long exhale.

"Wake me when the war's over, boys," he sighed. But, before he could shut his weary, dry eyes, he caught a sudden movement on a mountain to east. He sat up.

"I hear tell," a scout said while he watched the guards walk the parapets, "that when one of them Muslims die, they get 'em a passel of saloon girls in heaven!"

"Only if they die while killing people," another scout answered.

"That's none too neighborly," said another.

"The things we do fer women," Rosie noted.

"Somebody's a falling off that mountain!" Gildy declared, scrambling to look through his spyglasses.

All others sat up to see. In the far distance it seemed not one, but two people were plummeting off the mount, ricocheting off steep ledges and bouncing off the rock sides.

"Wait a plum minute!" Rosie said, his binoculars catching up with the fall. "They ain't people, Gildy. That's a…that's a ram!"

"Yeah," joined in another scout, "and he ain't falling. He's jumping…he's running away from something, jumping after 'em."

"A dad-blame leopard," another said, his glasses a bit higher. "That there snow leopard is a chasin' that ram!"

"Boy, howdy! Look 'em go!"

Gildy, unable to follow the amazing descent, dropped the glasses from his eyes. Now that he knew the falling objects were actual animals he tracked their amazing descent unaided.

"Look at them jump up on those teeny ledges!" Rosie said. "How can they do that!" The ram was jumping fifteen or twenty feet at a time and landing on what appeared to be mere inches of rock outcroppings, the mountain leopard right behind him. At some points, the rocks gave way under their hooves and paws, and still the creatures danced down the mountainside.

"I tell ya that ain't right! It ain't natural," a scout said.

"Well, whattya mean? Ain't natural? Yer lookin' right at it!" another chastised.

"These critters must have to hunt like this all the time, damn near straight up and down," Rosie said.

The leopard seized the back of the ram and both lost their balance, the leopard first—with his teeth clenched deep into the ram—then the ram as it seemed to peel off the wall to follow. They plummeted, the giant, spotted cat squirming in the air to naturally land feet first, wherever that was. They both hit stone some feet down. The leopard never once lost the death grip. There, there was space to kill. The snow leopard tore viciously into the ram as it froze, in the shock of near death.

The men watched for a moment.

"Bet he's delicious. Whatcha bet?" Rosie wondered aloud.

The action over, all the men laid back down on the ledge, carefully propped their hatless heads over the lip of the edge, and continued spying on the fort below. Even Gildy decided to look some more and pass on his nap. He spotted more action, this time much closer…

"Don't move!" Gildy whispered to Rosie.

The other scouts scrambled away from Rosie.

"Wha?" Rosie said.

"You gotta …a…damn thing on your back!" a scout answered.

"A what?"

"Some kinda' scorpion-looking thing." Gildy said, crawling a bit closer.

"It's about as big as a frog," another scout whispered. "I ain't ever seen anything like it…"

"Like a big seashell."

"Like a tarantula, but a scorpion."

"It's as bright green as a piece of jewelry."

"Can ya' dust it off?" Rosie pleaded.

"I ain't touching that thing!" Gildy said.

"Well can ya shoot it?" Rosie implored.

"We'd give away our hidey-hole!" a scout reminded.

"I tell you what, if that big ol' dang thing stings you, we'll just shoot you and save you the damn agony!" a scout offered.

"It's a real big green scorpion," Gildy advised his friend.

"Bigger than the ones in New Mex?" Rosie asked.

"Bigger than Fort Marcy scorps, Rosie," Gildy replied with reluctance.

"Ohhh, Lord."

"Well, be still, and maybe it'll crawl off," Gildy ordered.

The men moaned and shifted in an uneven choir as the beast dragged itself along by its pinpoint pincers right up Rosie's back.

"Maybe it'll crawl off," a scout repeated, his voice aquiver.

The creature stopped, its head surveyed the men, and it then tiptoed to Rosie's shoulder.

"I still can't feel it," Rosie whispered.

"Shut up, man!" a scout ordered.

The scorpion started a march down Rosie's right arm. When it passed his elbow, it stepped into Rosie's line of vision. Sergeant William Tuttle Rosenthal had once faced down ten charging Comanche, fought courageously in numerous battles, even drummed up the courage to ask General Swenson's beautiful daughter to dance a jig at open ball at Fort Leavenworth. But as brave as he was, he took one look at that crab-shelled, hideous monster and lost all control. He shrieked and yanked his arm back. The scorpion clung precariously to the jacket sleeve. Enraged, it reared its huge stinger and slammed the needle into the back of Rosie's hand before flipping onto the ledge.

The scouts groaned and cursed. One flung a dagger square and deep into the beast's back, pinning it to the dirt. The stinger struck the dagger repeatedly, its legs thrashing, body railing.

Rosie gripped the stung hand in shock. Gildy crouched over his friend, drawing his knife. Another scout grabbed Rosie's good hand away. Gildy and yet another scout seized the wounded limb. Gildy cut a half an inch slash above the sting, which was already rising into a lump. Then he cut the lump open. A scout cupped a hand over Rosie's mouth to prevent him from hollering across the valley. Gildy carved at the wound and at the risk of poisoning himself, put his mouth full on the wound and sucked all the moisture out he could. He spat blood and venom. A scout handed him a canteen. He sat back, washed his mouth with a gulp and spat again. Then again.

With tears in his eyes, Gildy knelt back up and examined the wound.

"Did it get me bad?" Rosie asked, his face pale.

"It gotcha, amigo. How bad? Don't know."

"Look at the size of it!" Rosie said as he stared at the impaled, struggling scorpion. The men powdered his wound with a secret compound of baking soda and herbs from their kit and wrapped it in strips torn from a clean undershirt. "It's as a big as a small dog."

"It ain't that big," one said, securing the bandage.

"Easy fer you to say, it wasn't nesting on your back," Rosie complained. "Whatcha so sad fer," he asked looking at Gildy. "Whatcha all lookin' so sad fer?"

"Well, dammit, Rosie, it ain't every day a feller has to damn near cut his best friend's hand off!" Gildy replied.

"Hell, I'll be all right! It's just a…." and Rosie passed out cold.

21
Ghost Riders and Vultures

The crack of a gunshot rattled through the dawn air. Lieutenant Kerry's body spasmed. His legs kicked out, and he sat up, gasping for breath, heart racing. He kicked off his blanket, as did hundreds of groggy men around him. They all staggered and stumbled to their feet, scrambling for their weapons. Indian guards posted at the rear passage behind them galloped full speed back to camp, revolvers pointed straight to the heavens, all yelling strings of Hindustani words in desperate tones. Kerry strapped on his gun belt and grabbed his Winchester rifle from the ground beside him.

"What?" he mumbled to no one near as he jogged to the rear. "What?" he shouted, jogging toward the riders. He passed Lydia and Marilyn emerging from their wagon. Lieutenant Satin appeared, jogging beside him.

"What?" he asked Satin.

"An army's coming," Satin translated.

Gunther caught up with Kerry, armed with his Mauser rifle. "What is going on?" the Texan asked.

""Satin said an army's coming. One of the rear pickets sounded the alarm," Kerry answered.

They both looked back toward their cavalry. Each troop rushed to his respective assignment, some half-dressed and looking half witted from the sudden alarm. The machine gun teams climbed into the wagons.

The frightened sepoy guards bolted past the American contingent, as if they just escaped hell itself, and maybe they had. An army of men on horseback appeared like a hellish apparition from

Page 234

around the rear passage rock wall. This army, some eight hundred to one thousand men, riding gray horses, looked like ghost riders from hell. Kerry could see they were another tribe of Khyber mountain men, with gray, long narrow faces and black beards. They all wore the same sheepskin Cossack hats and thick, filthy jackets.

At this distance, their clothes and horses looked soiled and muddy, and they appeared as if they'd ridden all night. Kerry lifted his binoculars to study the tribe. As they drew near, the mud stains looked more like bloodstains. Most of them carried the Jeizhar, the infamous Afghan long rifle, backpacks and saddlebags of mesh netting on their horse flanks. A hundred or so vultures followed them.

"Sweet Jesus," Kerry said as he handed the binoculars to Gunther. "They look like a haunted army. Ghosts, with vultures trailing the dead."

"Charge the guns!" Gunther roared to the rear. The order was relayed all the way to machine gun wagons. Gunther knelt and raised his rifle.

Sergeant Grimsley stepped up and said, "Now, major, don't go troubling trouble, cause then trouble will trouble you."

But, as the riders came within two hundred yards, the entire tribe acted as though the Americans, Indians and British weren't even camped in the valley. Instead of a violent charge, these ghost riders traced the far wall of the pass, riding about fifteen to twenty deep, trailed by vultures as though the scavengers were pets. Neither man nor bird even looked their way. Their sheer indifference added to their ghostliness.

"Koklanare," Satin said, his one eye behind an expanded telescope.

Kerry and Gunther turned to the sepoy officer waiting for more information.

"Koklanare. Vicious people from the northeast. Men for hire. Bandit warriors."

Suddenly one sole rider broke from the trotting waves of the tribe. He alone whipped his horse with long reins and charged the

Americans at a full gallop. Abruptly he yanked back on the reins to stop the horse, causing it to rear and neigh in pain and surprise. Once stopped, he began to yell at the Americans with a goading and angry voice. Still, none of his passing fellow tribesmen so much as looked his way.

"What in the hell is he yelling?" Gunther asked Satin.

Kerry could discern the one word he heard so much—"Jihad"—inside the madman's tirade.

"He is yelling about Jihad," Satin explained. "He is yelling that Allah will chop off the feet of our wives and children, and they will walk on bloody stomps for an eternity trying to find a false heaven."

"Feet!" Kerry interjected from behind his binoculars. "Look at their saddle bags…it looks like…feet inside them."

Satin zeroed his binoculars onto the flanks of the horses. Sure enough, it appeared the mesh bags contained…feet. Feet cut off at the ankles. Some were bare, some in boots and others in shoes.

"Feet!" Gunther repeated.

"They have cut off the feet of some poor tribe!" Satin declared. "It is the curse of Fateh Khan, the fate of a traitor." Soldiers around them gasped and mumbled. This observation was passed on in whispers behind them. Soon hundreds would know, from the Americans through the Indians, up to the Brits. The tribesman screamed on with his shrill words of fanatic hate and Jihad.

"Why do they keep the feet?" Kerry asked.

"They will be paid a bounty for each foot," Satin said.

"By whom?" Gunther questioned.

"By whomever…has the money. Whoever sent them," Satin answered.

"The vultures are picking up the dropped feet," Kerry observed through his binoculars. Kerry didn't notice Gunther step back behind, but jumped when he felt a piece of metal rest upon the top of his right shoulder. Eight inches of Gunther's Mauser rifle, extending beyond his shoulder blade.

"Jesus, Major!" the startled lieutenant said. The Texan was about to make a shot. He reached down to his belt and pulled a bullet from a loop. He stuck the primer end of the shell in his right ear. He knew what was coming. "Do you…"

"Don't move," was Gunther's calm, whispered response. "Satin, what else is our crazy guest saying?" he asked. Kerry knew the remark was meant to distract him. It didn't work. Kerry winced.

As Satin tried to translate, Gunther squeezed the trigger. The weapon blasted, bouncing on Kerry's shoulder.

"My sweet Jesus!" Kerry declared, leaping out from under the barrel. The bullet dropped out of his ear. But he looked intently at the screaming rider.

The rifle bullet split the air and struck the tribesman at his left ankle in a puff of red. His left leg was thrown back and up over the saddle, the wounded foot remained attached to his calf by a few muscle sinews. The round also creased the left flank of the horse and cut open the saddlebag. While the man was tossed airborne his words turned into a scream of surprise. The horse, fired up from the slice on its side, bolted forward. The rider lost his seat, but his right foot still remained in the right stirrup. The tribesman hit the ground hard, and on first contact was hauled off by his caught foot behind the crazed, galloping horse. Numerous severed feet tumbled from the various canvas bags strapped to each saddle. If the bullet traveled on to the Koklanare beyond, Kerry could see no sign. Hungry vultures swooped down.

"You missed him," Kerry said, believing Gunther had wanted a heart or headshot.

"Naaaah," Gunther answered staring at his work.

Some of the Americans whooped at the shot, as all readied for a sudden attack. The tribesmen continued their hypnotic trot up the valley and past them, despite the wounded, screaming tribesmen now banging across the rocky grounds of the valley. While Kerry watched, the horse with his rider, whose foot was hung in the saddle stirrup, ran right straight at him!

Gunther seemed delighted at this prospect. He set the rifle down, slapped Kerry on the arm and jogged forward with a motion for some of the nearby troops, "Come on!" he shouted. "Stop the horse!"

Several fanned out, waving their arms to corner and calm the frightened horse. The animal dodged several times, dragging the rider bouncing and spinning over the rough ground. Eventually, they managed to encircle the horse, and it trotted to a nervous halt.

"It's feet all right, major," a sergeant confirmed the booty left in bloody canvas bags. "People's feet!"

Kerry and Gunther walked up to the man to find his jacket quite ripped, but still thick enough to spare his flesh from the rock ride. He'd lost his Cossack hat, and his hair was matted with blood. His right leg was still hung up in the twisted stirrup.

"Well, pretty rough ride there, huh, Stumpy?" Gunther said with a growl, leering over him. He took out his Bowie and sliced the right leather strap of the saddle stirrup. The man's good foot dropped to the ground. Gunther stood up studied both the feet, turned to Satin, and ordered, "Translate." Satin did.

"That foot's okay! But brother! That other un? That's about to come clean off of ya! Hanging on by two skinny muscles." The Texan said with a crazed smile.

Satin translated.

"Hear tell you boys were real busy with your Jihad business last night," Gunther continued in a low growl while looking over the horse. The man could barely babble. "Jihadden' around and all." He stood by the man and bent at one knee.

Satin translated. Gunther waited.

"Well, we have a little ol' religious saying, too, back from where I come from."

Satin translated.

"And it goes a little something like this…what ye shall sow? Ye shall reap…" Gunther said as he stepped back and with a chop of his Bowie, completely severed the last sinews of the man's left foot. Gunther finished in a growl, "You sorry sack of shit."

Satin was speechless. The man howled.

"Tell 'em that last thing now, Lieutenant," Gunther chided.

Satin translated as the man squirmed and shrieked.

"Get him back up on his horse, boys." The Texan ordered. He picked up the man's foot, still in the leather shoe.

The soldiers lifted the tribesman and threw the chopped foot up over the saddle. The Koklanare screamed and collapsed forward over the neck of the horse.

Gunther walked around to his left side and tugged on the torn net saddlebag. "Seems like you lost some of your load here." He had the man's severed foot in his hand. "Here. Here ya' go. Go on and take this one back with ya." He crammed the foot into the saddle against the man's stomach. "You know, so your trip's not a total loss. You can sell 'em your own damn foot."

Satin, Kerry and the soldiers stood in silent shock.

"Translate there now, Satin. This feller has to know what to do with his foot." Gunther said, and Satin translated.

"Git outta here!" Gunther shouted as he turned the horse and slapped its rump. The animal galloped off toward the tribe.

Gunther and Kerry walked back beside the troops, with Gunther snatching up his rifle from the ground. Lydia, Marilyn, Smith and Harrigan watched the cowboy closely.

Captain Perryweather and some of his staff galloped up on horseback. He stood in his stirrups and looked over the scene. "Shooting up the locals again, Mr. Gunther?"

"Why won't they attack?" Sergeant Grimsley wondered out loud, watching the tribe trot by, still hugging the valley edge. "We just shot up one of their own."

"Could be," Gunther guessed, "that ol' boy was a bit nutty, and they didn't care much for him. Could be this is a day of treaty. A cease-fire. Either way, Lieutenant Kerry? Keep a full watch on them until they're gone." Gunther pivoted and made for his wagon.

"You heard the major," Kerry told Grimsley. He followed Gunther, passing Lydia, Marilyn, Harrigan and Smith.

"I do declare," Lydia commented, "sometimes, Mr. Gunther… sometimes, you frighten the hell out of me."

"Sometimes when you frighten the enemy, you can't help but frighten your friends," Gunther stopped to say, then continued to stroll back to his campfire, with the rifle barrel propped over a shoulder.

"He shot and cut that man's foot clean off," Harrigan said to

Kerry as they watched Gunther. "He's just as bad as they are."

"No sir," Kerry said." He didn't start that little war party. He was just doing a little sowing and reaping, like he said. Still…I must admit to you, that was about the most crazy-assed thing I have ever seen," he declared.

The men split to wander back to pack their beds. The sun had grown visible over the horizon. The treaty day had begun and, if they lived through today, what would happen tomorrow—when all deals were off?

22
The Last Supper

The scout had much to report! Sergeant Gildenbeck rode into the joint forces camp at an intense pace, scanning for the American contingent and, in particular, Major Gunther.

He spotted Gunther, Kerry and Satin inspecting the machine gun wagons in the rear and cut his way through the busy billet activities to reach them.

"Gildy!" shouted Gunther, waving his hand as he saw the dusty scout approach.

"Major! Major!" Gildy slid off his horse as he approached. "There is another whole damn army with them now, sir. You must have seen them come through."

"Yes, Sergeant," Gunther replied. "They marched right past us early this morning. Hung to the far wall over there," Gunther pointed out. "Barely looked at us."

"They have set up tents to the southwest of the other tribe that's already camped by the fort. I figure there are eight hundred of them. As soon as they cleared the pass, I worked my way back here."

"This almost doubles the size of the enemy," Lieutenant Satin noted.

Gildy briefed them on the miniscule details, rather impatiently, because he seemed preoccupied with another problem. "Major… Rosie…has been stung pretty bad."

"By what? A bug?"

"No, sir. Up in the mountains, the place is crawling with these…these green scorpions. They are gigantic. Rosie got hit by one. Right here on his hand. He has been near dead since yesterday."

"Damn," Gunther sighed. "Well, let's get the doc and see—"

"Major," Satin interrupted. "Enquire of the British doctor. He is more familiar with the sting of the green scorpion. It is sickening. Wretched and sickening."

"He looks to me like he is dying by the hour," Gildy added. He reached into his saddlebag and pulled out a package wrapped in a tan uniform shirt. He whipped open the shirt. A huge green scorpion hit the ground. The men jumped back. Then they carefully leaned in for a closer look.

"That's the monster what got 'em," Gildy said.

"Good God!" Kerry declared.

The beast's crablike arm twitched, and the men jumped further back. Gunther even grabbed at the handle of his .45.

"It's alive!" Kerry shouted.

"Naah, it ain't, sir. Winston stabbed it with a bayonet clear through. It just keeps twitching like that. The fucker."

"Well, let's head over there. Satin, you lead the way," Gunther said. "Need a fresh mount?"

"Wouldn't hurt."

"Lieutenant, trade out mounts for the private," Gunther ordered Kerry. Kerry took the reins and led the tired horse away.

Gunther, Gildy and Satin made their way to the British army medical tent on the north side of the camp.

"It don't look good, Major. They are dug in, and now they are reinforced. The numbers just ain't with us," Gildy said.

"I know. I know." Gunther sighed. "But, I don't run this circus, and if we cut and run now? Surely all these poor Brits and Indians will stay and die. I will have to think of something. Hey, listen. In some kind of peace parlay, Latissimo has invited our officers to a dinner at the Fort tomorrow night."

"Nahhh! Are ya' goin'? They'll sure as shit kill ya'll, sir!" Gildy said, astonished.

"According to Satin and the Brits, this kind of thing is common. The tribes here usually do some marauding, raise a little hell, then take a big cash payment from the Brits in a treaty to stay quiet for a while. They get the money and most of what they plundered. But, hell or high water. I'm down for the dinner. At least I'll see the insides of the place."

The men walked in silence for a moment, and Gildy weighed the consequences. He was bewildered by what might happen.

Then Gunther continued, "Anyway, come tonight, you'll see a bunch of us all duded up and riding in for the dinner. If they slaughter us for dinner, your orders are to get the hell out of here. Get back to India. No revenge. No hesitation."

Gildy remained silent, shaking his head.

"I am bringing both my guns and my Bowie knife. If they pick a fight? I'll kill one for every bullet, and as many as I can fit on this knife," Gunther said with a smile.

"I reckon that'll be one full skewer of a knife, sir."

"Reckon so," Gunther said.

Gunther's bravado seemed to break Gildy's glum feelings. Near the British medical tent, Satin dashed ahead. When Gunther and Gildy entered, Satin had already located the doctor and was explaining the problem while guiding him by the arm to the front.

"Good day, gentlemen," the doctor announced himself. He was in his late fifties but fit and strong of stature. "Doctor Christian Leavingworth at your service," he said as he shook Gunther's hand. "Haven't formally met you yet, sir, but I have seen you in action, and I do so admire your fortitude from afar."

"Thank you, Doctor," Gunther said.

"And you are Private Gilden…"

"Doc, Gildenbeck. Looky, my friend was stung bad and —"

"Yes, yes of course. Come with me, my good fellow. I have applications for you. Oral medicine and salve. The sting of the green scorpion is not a death sentence in most cases."

The doctor walked Gildy deeper into the tent for these supplies, as Lieutenant Kerry galloped up on Gildy's fresh mount.

"Here is a powder for the skin. It will burn the old chap, but you must apply it six times a day. Here are some tablets. Give him three every two hours-"

"Six times a day fer the powder. Three every two hours fer the pills," Gildy mumbled.

"That's correct. For his fever and his stomach. One for the poison." The doctor shoved the medicine, along with bandages in a small canvas sack.

Gildy bounded to the front, medical sack under his arm. "Anything else, sir?"

"No. Go on, Gildy, and get some of that into Rosie. Anything changes, come tell us," Gunther ordered.

"Yes, sir," he saluted, then gracefully launched himself onto the fresh horse. Kerry opened the saddlebag, and Gildy shoved the medicine inside. Gunther lifted the flap door open on the tent and shouted in, "Thanks, Doc!" He didn't wait for an answer, but, after a brief hesitation, the doctor stepped out.

"Private! He mustn't be stung again. Two stings will surely kill him in his weakened state. Take all precautions," the doctor warned.

"Much obliged to you!"

The physician withdrew into the tent, and Gunther, Satin and Kerry turned south. Gildy trotted his horse to the outskirts of the camp, then hit a full gallop to the Northwest Frontier.

Gildy soon came to an area of large scattered rocks and was forced to slow and let his horse pick and choose a hoof-safe path. As he spoke soft words of encouragement to his mount, urging him to step carefully, the consummate scout in his soul couldn't resist fixating on the natural and disturbed patterns of the rocks on ground. He read the signs. He was amidst the wide trail of the ghost army that rambled through earlier. He memorized the different overturned, split, and pulverized rocks of all sizes, to record in his mind a picture of what eight hundred horses do to this type of terrain.

At one point, he glanced over his shoulder. Off in the distance he could see Gunther and, for a moment, he thought the major looked his way. Gildy waved, and Gunther waved back.

"Good luck to you, Major Gunther," Gildy whispered.

Lieutenant Kerry was taken aback as he approached his

commander's wagons. In just a few hours they would be off for their dinner at Fort Tartan, and he wished to check in for any last minute plans and orders. He found Gunther sitting perfectly still on a stool beside the enclosed wagon, a towel wrapped around his shoulders. Mesha, armed with a hairbrush and a pair of shears, carefully chopped off his long blond hair. Her monkey cautiously climbed up Gunther's leg and crouched on his lap, watching every snippet of hair fall. When a significant batch fell forward, the monkey grabbed it, studied it, smelled it, and shoved it into a side pocket of his velvet suit.

"What's the monkey's name?" Gunther asked, barely peeking down at it.

"Manuke," she answered.

"Man-u-ke," Gunther repeated. "What's he gonna do with my hair?"

"He will stuff it in his bed. He must like you very much."

"Cleaning up for tonight, major?" Kerry interrupted as he walked up.

"Actually, Lieutenant, I am cutting my hair so no som-bitch can grab it if we get in a fight tonight. Hair's a damn, silly, vain thing, anyway."

"A home for bugs," Kerry added.

"A home for bugs," Gunther repeated.

Gunther peeked down from his rigid pose to see if the monkey was actually picking anything off his hair and eating it. Mesha clipped on until he had but an inch of hair left. Next, she lathered up Gunther's face and flipped open a straight razor. The monkey fled.

"I came by to see if anything had changed for tonight, sir."

"You mean do I still need you to come with me?"

"Yes, sir. That, too!"

"Yes, Lieutenant, I do."

"Any final orders for the men?"

"Sergeant Grimsley will be in charge. If they do not hear from us, or should we fail to emerge from the fort by midnight tonight, he is to conduct an orderly retreat back to the Star of Africa's village. If the Brits and Indians are smart, they'll all go with him. They must maintain the best rear guard and beware of snipers. Travel all night and day until they reach her village."

"I will convey that message to Sergeant Grimsley, sir."

Mesha buried two fingers right into Gunther's nostrils and pulled back as far as she could stretch, exposing his throat.

"He cannot say words now," Mesha warned Kerry as she skinned the hair from his neck. "His Madam's Apple must not move."

Gunther was not about to correct her as to whether he was Madam or Adam.

"This hullabaloo is about to begin," a scout from the mountain-top ledge reported. "They's amassing at the mouth of the pass." With the remaining light from the sunset, he could see invited guests gathering below.

Under a nearby rock outcropping, Gildy checked Rosie's temperature with his hand on the sick man's forehead.

"I'm cold," Rosie complained. "When ya see me shivering like a tail of a rattle snake, you can guess I am cold."

"Frankly, yer face is beet red and yer forehead is hot," Gildy said as he crawled to the ledge, picked up his binoculars and looked below. He saw Captain Perryweather and two of his lieutenants in their Army blue uniforms in one open wagon.

"Reckon Gunther's gussied up like a Texican?" Rosie asked.

"Yup, that he is," Gildy answered as he saw Gunther, Lydia, Marilyn and Kerry in another wagon. "He looks like a cowboy at the O.K. Corral."

"Gildy, you remember when ol' Sergeant Shaunessy stepped into that field shower, opened the barrel and, when the cold water hit him he dropped clean dead?" Rosie asked. "They said the cold water stopped his heart. Fell right down and died right there. The shock of it!"

"He was sixty years old. He had no business getting naked in the Oklahoma winter and taken an ice-cold shower like that."

"Yeah, yeah," Rosie said with a shiver. "I am sure cold."

"Don't shower," Gildy mumbled, eyeing the progression below. Several of the Indian commanders climbed into a third wagon. Then, the three wagons started down the trail to the village main street.

Gildy sized up Captain Perryweather and four British officers as they sat in their wagon. They were all in their Class A uniforms, with oversized hats and cavalry swords. Several Indian commanders and Lieutenant Satin, equally flourished in red outfits, sat in their coach. Eight British and Indian soldiers, fully armed, walked beside two slow-moving wagons, four men per wagon. Three U.S. soldiers pulled this escort duty for Gunther's wagon.

Gildy scanned the road ahead of them. The main avenue of the village was lined with ten-foot tall poles of roaring fire torches, all the way to the open main gate. The Koklanare to the east and the tribes to the west, ensconced in their tent cities, busied themselves with dinner and chores and seemed to pay no attention to the slow caravan.

Gunther leaned back in his wagon seat, legs sprawled and a hand placed casually near the handle of his pistol. With enemy tribes on either side of him, despite his relaxed demeanor, he felt exposed and nervous. The tribe to the west reminded him of a large American Indian encampment. The tents were more elaborate and personalized with artwork. There were some women walking about. Some children. To the right, however, was the ghostly Koklanare. No sign of individual personality. No women. Certainly no children. Quick camp. Small fires. Small meals. Simple tools. Sparse tents. Mercenaries on assignment. A traveling war party.

The roadway was made of open dirt patches and broken and crushed stones, fashioned more from time and weather than any design, and its rugged surface gently rocked their wagon, and the occupants side-to-side. He studied Lydia's profile. Her anticipation, her breathlessness was evident. She stared ahead at the hamlet's main road and to the open gates of the fort that held her husband.

"Whatever is the word," Lydia said softly, her head bobbing

slightly from the hard wheels on the rugged road, "for a man who left you, without a warning, not a note, not a good-bye, at your worst time? He leaves. Then he is lost. He is presumed dead. Then, he is alive. Alive and just inside those doors."

Marilyn put a hand on her knee. Gunther had a few words but chose not to offer them.

"I guess I am such a fool to come this far," Lydia added. "He left me to die in a hospital. He doesn't care."

"Aunt Lydia," Marilyn offered in a sympathetic tone, "there may be a reason. Look at all this. He may be on a secret mission."

"Oh Marilyn, the president would know of any such secret mission."

As the small caravan rolled into Tasheebo, Gunther noted it was like many rustic towns in the Wild Wild West, only a bit more gray and white. It had a wide main avenue with primitive stores and markets on each side. Streets and alleys led off like tributaries. On these streets, Afghan horsemen mingled with Mongol camel drivers. They wore pistol belts and carried rifles. This could have been Abilene, Texas or Tulsa, Oklahoma, but for the fact the men wore dress-like robes. Men and women walked the streets with satchels of goods. Men hammered away on metal in primitive blacksmith shops. Both crude and sophisticated wagons traversed the road.

To Gunther's surprise, a tall white man with blond hair stepped from the doorway of one the buildings. He wore a black suit and, as he placed a bowler hat on his head, his eyes caught Gunther's stare.

"There's an Englishman," Marilyn said.

Gunther touched the tip of his hat in acknowledgement, and the man nodded. He walked north on the broken wood and clay sidewalks also headed to the fort. The wagons moved at a slow pace to allow the foot guards to keep pace beside them.

This main street ran about a hundred yards then turned into a slightly angled road that led up to the main gate of the fort. The fort was more like a castle and appeared taller to Gunther at ground level than his prior view from across the valley. The two main gates stood wide open, and servants dressed in red robes awaited them. As they drew closer, he could hear exotic music from within, odd melodies from instruments he did not recognize. Woman wailed songs he could not identify.

The wagons entered the courtyard as the servants guided the horses by the steps of the main building's front doors. There was a pungent smell hanging in the air, unlike the odor in India and Karachi. One mostly of odd foods, the flavors of which he could not predict, nor would he care to eat. Colorful pennants swirled in the warm sunset winds. While everyone dismounted, the Englishman wandered near Gunther and the ladies.

"Good evening," he said in an educated British accent, stopping by them to help Lydia descend.

"Good evening," Gunther replied.

"It looks lovely here," Marilyn said, taking in the scenery.

"Yes indeed, my lady, doesn't it?" the man said with a sarcastic smirk. "Why just two weeks past, fourteen men were eaten alive by rabid dogs right over there. Amazing what a few flags, a rake—some nasty bones, you know—and pretty torch light can do."

They all stood still, shocked, and stared at him. Gunther broke the silence and offered a handshake, "Johann Gunther, I'm with the Americans."

"George Hall. I'm with the kidnapped." With that, George Hall shook his hand, and then ascended the steps leading into the castle.

Perryweather and his lieutenants approached the group, all gawking at the blond man in a bowler hat.

"Who the bloody hell is that?" Perryweather asked.

"George Hall," said Gunther as Lydia wrapped an arm around his elbow.

"He's been kidnapped," Lydia added over her shoulder as they climbed the stairs.

"George Hall," repeated a lieutenant. "He's on the books as the district officer here, sir."

"Yes, yes," Perryweather recalled. "Assumed the poor bloke would be skinned alive by now. He hardly looks kidnapped. Brushed bowler and all."

As they entered the stone building, servants approached and

volunteered to take any jackets and hats and lay them on a carpet by the door. Gunther left his hat and fringe jacket there, fully exposing his Western gun belt, two guns, and the Bowie knife. The ladies left their jackets, but the officers remained in full uniform.

Lydia grasped Gunther's arm as they walked down the hallway, guided by the smiling tribesmen. "Hold onto me, Johann. Tight. I'm dizzy," she whispered. "I don't know if it is from the pain in my chest or from what I am about to see." Gunther squeezed her arm as they moved up the stairs.

Once inside the dining room, Gunther felt he was thrust not into a Middle Eastern fortress, but rather into a chapter of The Legend of Robin Hood. The defeated British forces had adorned the place with wooden mantels and furnishings. It was a kingly dinner in a regal hall. An enormous, long wooden table, chandeliers holding thick, burning candles the size of chair legs. The musicians he'd heard earlier played in a stone alcove. There were some thirty people in this hall, all local tribesmen as far as Gunther could estimate. In addition, he spotted three obviously Russian officers in their black uniforms. Then, he saw a familiar group in the far north corner: U.S. Army soldiers some feet away.

In the dress blues of an American Army officer stood a grinning Colonel Vito Latissimo, his black and gray hair slicked back, balancing a drink in one hand and a cigar in the other. He joked with several other Americans, also in their dress blues of various ranks from corporal through sergeant to lieutenant.

Lydia drew upright. She released Gunther's arm and marched toward her husband.

My God, what if she's got her brace of pistols hidden in that dress, Gunther belatedly thought to himself, she'll shoot him down dead, and all hell will break loose in here.

Instead, Gunther saw Latissimo's face break into an astonished and happy expression. "Lydia?" he bellowed. "Lydia! Ha-ha!"

Gunther could not see her face as her pace virtually became a skipping waltz to the colonel. He put his hand near a pistol but, to Gunther's shock, she completely embraced Latissimo with a clutch equal to his own! He lifted her off her feet and spun her once in the air.

"Absence makes the heart grow fonder?" Kerry said over Gunther's shoulder. They walked toward the couple, followed by Perryweather and his troupe.

"Oh, oh my God," Latissimo said, appearing to dry a corner of his eye.

"I thought you were dead, Vito," she announced.

"I almost was. I…I couldn't get a word out to you. You see how far away I am."

"And you couldn't get a single word out to me even when you were closer? Say in India? When you started out on this…thing?"

"Mission, darling. It is a mission. Not a thing," he said melodiously. "I so wish I could have, my darling, but I was told to keep the mission very secret. Very. From the president himself, actually."

She curled her lips when she looked to the man at Vito's right, "Hello, Sergeant Valentino."

The man nodded with a raise of his glass.

"Of course, you are here too, his perennial partner in crime," she said with an air of jealousy. "And I see, so are Anthony and Spezio."

These men also nodded with respect.

"Hello, Mrs. Latissimo," Spezio added.

"And who are all these others?" she asked.

Latissimo made the introductions. Curiously enough to Gunther, all six of them had Italian surnames.

Perryweather interrupted them and, in a formal and proper manner, announced himself and his top officers.

"It is like we are in…in an Atlanta ballroom and not on this godforsaken rock pile," Kerry whispered to Gunther as they remained nearby to oversee, but not too close.

Lydia, this time clutching Latissimo's arm in a vice, urged him over toward Gunther. "And this Texas gentleman," she said, "has seen me safe throughout this long journey. He has saved my life from inescapable death."

"Inescapable death!" Latissimo repeated with a half-smile, eyeing Gunther. "And a Texan! Way up here." He took a long look, raised an eyebrow at the Western gun belt, and the two .45s…and the knife.

"Colonel Latissimo, I presume?" Gunther shook his hand. He looked down at Vito's face, as he was quite a bit taller. Latissimo's head was broad and enormous, and his white teeth huge. His brown eyes glinted with mischief.

"I do, or don't know you?" Latissimo half-asked, half-stated with a confused expression.

"Actually Colonel, you do know me, I was a private at Fort Sill, Oklahoma, while you were in command. Johann Gunther. Under Ragland's group. Company B."

"Johann! Johann the German!" Latissimo said. "How in hell did you wind up here? What are you doing here?"

"That is a long story—"

"I hired him to protect me," Lydia interrupted. "I knew finding you would be most dangerous, and I needed a…smart man good with a gun."

"Good…with a gun," Vito repeated in a low hum, still smiling. "Good enough, say, to shoot a man's foot off at one hundred yards? Ah? Huh? As I heard that happened down in the valley just yesterday."

"The American Army is worried about you Colonel," Gunther said, ignoring the remark. "They said you needed rescuing. The official commander, a Captain Boston, was assigned this task but he was…killed last month and somehow, as a former veteran officer, I wound up in charge."

"Johann, your German private, was also Johann, a major, once," Lydia added.

"Major?"

"Yes, sir, West Point, Class of 1895," Gunther said.

"Damn, son, I wished I'd warned you about that first," he said chuckling and looked to his friends for approval.

"I wish you had, too." The men stared at each other, sharing an uncomfortable bond forced between their obvious counterpoints.

"So do you, Colonel?" Gunther asked bluntly.

"Do I, son?"

"Do you need rescuing?"

"Not tonight, Major Johann Gunther," Latissimo said in delight. "Oh, tonight, consider me ever so rescued." He looked at Lydia and smiled broadly. She seemed refreshed to see him, even radiant, and returned a genuine smile.

"Your two pistols," Latissimo said. "They look like square… boxes?"

"Semiautomatic, Colonel. They are prototypes by a John Browning. We believe that very soon all of the U.S. Army will carry them."

"Ohhh," Vito said, getting a good look at the holstered weapons. "Perhaps later we might get a demonstration of these weapons?" He leaned forward near Gunther's ear. "Johann, I am on a mission here that I cannot reveal. One that perhaps even Washington does not fully know about. One that the people that sent this Captain Boston to find me didn't even know about. I'll explain some of it to you, but not now."

The Colonel leaned back and studied Gunther's face waiting for some acknowledgment, a smile, a clue, something, but the cowboy remained expressionless. It was, of course, the perfect and imperfect lie. The classic secret mission, so secret the White House hadn't known of it. Not even the president? Perfect because it seemed improvable. Imperfect, because it was preposterous.

"What is all that?" Latissimo asked, glaring over Gunther's shoulder. Gunther turned to see Harrigan and Smith busily at work setting up their camera stands.

"Whoa! Whoa! Boys!" Latissimo said as he and Valentino approached them.

"No pictorials tonight, gentleman. No. Sorry. Some of my friends here will think you are stealing their very souls."

Sergeant Valentino began dismantling the tripods before the photographers could react or move. The two men, intimidated, relinquished the chance without comment and packed their gear.

Then, Latissimo passed by Gunther and commented, "I hate to see my bad side in the National Geographic." He steered Lydia away across the room. It seemed to Gunther that Latissimo's speech was almost a growl, yet almost a low song. Coupled with his mischievous expressions his voice was both intoxicating and even whimsical.

"Uncle Vito!" came a feminine cry. Latissimo spun toward the voice.

"Marilyn!" He grinned as she rushed up to him. He seemed truly speechless. "My god, you are even more beautiful." He held her arms and looked at her. "Well…what? I..." he stammered. "Have you finished your medical schooling?"

"Yes, sir, I have," she beamed.

Latissimo guided Lydia and Marilyn to the far side of the table, talking all the way. Kerry looked at Gunther in astonishment, shaking his head. It appeared to them that in five short minutes Vito Latissimo had charmed the last five years of woes, lies and trouble right out of the women.

"He's a complete scoundrel, isn't he?" Perryweather said to them from nearby. "And before the night is over, he will charm my country out of thousands of pounds in a king's ransom." The captain and his entourage wandered after the colonel, no doubt to impress and engage him.

George Hall, a glass tumbler in one hand, approached Gunther and said softly, "He's a complete and utter madman. He'll gut you in a second. Listen ol' chap, should you get out of here alive? Zanrala is to be next. You must warn them."

"Zanrala?"

"It's an outpost. A fort and a village not unlike this one, but more toward Russia's way." George Hall smiled broadly as if pretending to be talking about something else. "He will slaughter everyone, man, woman, child, that he can't bugger or sell."

"And he is selling you?" Kerry asked.

"Yes. I shan't be alive if not."

"Attention! Attention," An Afghan declared through the chamber in Afghani, Hindustani and English. All eyes turned to this man on the main stairway. "I present to you, Akbar Rasp Mohammad Dunkar, Seer of the Fourth Moon, Son of the Eternal Well, Vizeer of Clanestan, Caliph of Tasheebo."

A bell clanged from somewhere. The odd music stopped. The servants froze in position and bowed their heads. From a hallway upstairs, the announced man emerged. From the surrounding hush flowed a few mumblings—all religious sounding to Gunther—as this robed man descended the stairs with an air of floating majesty. His dark-skinned fat face was arrogant and condescending. He wore a curved sword on a golden cloth belt.

"That," whispered George Hall, "is the menace. The bat in this belfry. He is called a great man. And for here, that also means he is a great murderer."

Afghans bowed even further and kissed his fingers as he approached them. Some swooned. He walked to Gunther and Hall. Hall bowed, took his hand, and kissed the backs of his fingers.

"Master," George Hall said obediently.

Akbar turned to Gunther, slightly raising his hand for a similar royal treatment. Gunther smiled, rested his hand on the hilt of his Bowie knife, and canted his hip in a casual manner. Casual, yet the message was clear. There would be no finger kissing. There would be finger cutting off before there would be finger kissing.

"I see that you are not a man of faith," Akbar spoke.

"Not much."

"And not of the white Christian God?"

"Nope."

"Pity, as a man of Jesus is at the very least half a man of Allah."

Gunther stared silently at him. The man's eyes were black pits. Mad eyes.

"Is this the knife you used to scare the tribe away in the South Khyber Pass? You are, of course, the Long Knife they speak of now in the valleys below?" Akbar asked.

"This is the knife."

"May I see this long knife?"

Gunther smiled and pondered it for a second, as he didn't favor handing over his edged weapon to the belfry bat. "Only if I may see your sword."

Akbar laughed and looked at those about him. Only then, these others nearby laughed, too. Except, George Hall. George started sweating. For some reason this cultural exchange caught the attention of everyone in the room. It was one thing for this renowned Afghani Muslim cleric to meet with foreign soldiers; it was another for him to meet an American cowboy. Even Latissimo watched bemused.

Both men drew their blades and exchanged them. Gunther had only a passing interest in the tribal weapon, as he had seen many. This one was jewel encrusted and heavily engraved. Akbar rotated the Bowie with some fascination. He felt of the yellow and brown stag handle. He touched the tip, ran a finger down the edges.

"Who makes such a knife for you?" Akbar asked.

"A man in Fort Worth, Texas."

"Fort Worth," Akbar repeated. "A military fort?"

"Just a city, named after a fort."

"I see. A city. I must ask you this, Long Knife. Will you please consider becoming a Muslim, a child of Allah?" Akbar turned, raised his hands and said loud enough for all the Indian and British soldiers to hear, "Would all of my new friends here tonight become the children of Allah and praise him? As his way is the only way. The only light."

This really disturbed George Hall. His face flushed red.

"Will you, my new friend?" Akbar asked Gunther directly.

"Have to pass on that one," Gunther said as they returned each other's edged weapons.

"A pity," Akbar said with a frown, but with little emotion. "Tell me, Long Knife, do the Americans care about my country?" He was presented with a small glass of red wine. The servant handed Gunther the same. The room's occupants gradually ignored them and returned to their conversations.

"Not really. Most Americans do not know it even exists."

"I am so glad to hear this. The British and the Russians and the Indians, and even the Pakistanis care very much about my poor country. They are always squeezing us and pulling and pushing us."

"Seems like you have made friends with Colonel Latissimo, who is an American and you do have your Russian friends right over there."

"They are here now as my friends. Yes. We have a few things in common."

"But not Allah."

"No, sadly, not Allah. But they are working for Allah's peace. And I need them."

"I can see no reason why America will ever care to push or pull your people. You are very far away from us. Leave us alone, we will leave you alone," Gunther said.

"Yes! How can we bother you! We are so far away. I am glad to hear this. But your country is very, very much like the cowboy. Your President Roosevelt is a cowboy, yes?"

"You could say so, yes."

"And you are a cowboy?"

"I consider myself more of an old horse soldier than a cowboy."

"Horse soldier. Hmmm. But, why else would you ride all the way over here? I worry. It will be better when your country dismounts their horses and becomes big and fat. When they all become white businessmen in suits, counting their money inside the tall metal buildings that your people like to build." He gracefully raised his hand in the air while looking at the ceiling. "Like now, in England." He sipped his wine and continued, "Great Britain once owned most of the world. Now they only tiptoe in and out of it, obeying their white, fat businessmen in London. They are not at all like your Roosevelt, or like you or I, Long Knife. Men! Out here on the battlefield. Men with beliefs. Men with swords and knives. With purpose."

Gunther stared at him after his militant speech. Akbar looked white, soft and fat under those robes to Gunther.

"Dinner is served!" a man declared in three languages.

Akbar smiled and left Gunther to take his place at the head of the table.

Lieutenant Satin slid alongside Gunther and said, "Akbar expected you to give him your knife as a gift. Now he has been snubbed."

"Yeah, well…fuck him," Gunther growled. "I don't much like

the idea of having my own knife stuck in my back next week."

"Shit," George Hall whispered. "Not next week. Not good him asking you and everyone else to convert, and by tonight! Not good at all."

"Why?"

"It is the Muslim way to first offer a peaceful conversion. They must offer. If you refuse, only then may they kill you. Your public request is fulfilling this rule. You've had your bloody chance."

"I see," Gunther said.

"Conversion by the sword, ol' chap. And not next week. I'd rather say tonight or tomorrow!"

"Well George, have Latissimo and that Russian converted?" Gunther asked.

"Oh, bloody hell, no! Akbar is just using them to run the British and the Indians out of here. Once they are gone? Akbar will turn his sword of Allah on them."

"They know this?" Kerry asked.

"I think they do. Really! But the self-confident bastards believe they will win out in the end and beat each other. International poker. The great game. Sticky wicket, eh?"

"Very sticky," Gunther said with disgust as the servants guided them to their chairs. Gunther and Perryweather were taken down to the far end of the table near Akbar, Latissimo, and the increasingly more comfortable and happy Lydia. She'd obviously had a few glasses of wine. But Gunther knew that once left in private with the Colonel, Lydia would touch off a severe marital spat!

The food and drink were served. Kerry found himself positioned on the far end and none too pleased with the leering Sergeant Valentino propped beside Marilyn and chatting happily.

Opening pleasantries aside, the conversation quickly turned to diplomacy and business.

"Captain Perryweather, let's mix some business with pleasure," Latissimo suggested while dipping some bread into a goblet of red wine and nibbling upon it. Perryweather dropped his napkin on his lap and folded his hands on the table.

"We now own this fort, this pass—a key pass on the northwest side of the Khyber," the colonel noted. "Everything that comes down and through, or up and out, must hump through here. Now, I propose that we supervise it for your government. Manage it. Protect it for you. Oversee the commerce. Police the area."

"I think we were doing quite fine policing it before you came along, sir," Perryweather said.

"You were," Latissimo said with a nod and wry smile. "You were. But there is one point you must re-emphasize. You said it yourself. We…came along."

Gunther passed on his wine to keep the clearest of heads, carved his dinner, which appeared to be some kind of poultry, and watched the negotiation unfold.

"You came along in quite a scurrilous way, sir. You invaded, killed, and tortured."

"Love the way the Brits talk, huh?" Latissimo commented as he looked to his American officers. "Scurrilous. Sergeant Valentino, now when was the last time you heard anyone use the term, scurrilous?"

Valentino shrugged. Latissimo dipped his bread again. Wine dribbled on his chin from the oversaturated bread. He chased it with his tongue and wiped it with a finger. "War for profit, Captain Perryweather. War for profit. I am not sure that all war isn't for a profit in the end, you know? The dreamers and the fools fight them and the smart ones get paid."

"And now you ransom the queen for money for your crimes?"

"Ahhhhh, yeah! As we sit here and break bread tonight, I will tell you that you can buy our cooperation and services and frankly, gentlemen, even more so? Also, buy back your lives…" he said with a deadpan expression.

"You forget," Perryweather interrupted, "we have a huge force with us…"

"That we will destroy. You are outnumbered, Captain. With no hope for re-enforcements." Latissimo said calmly. "Turn away to escape? We will snipe and cull, clip and kill and chase your ass all the way back to India. Remember your history lessons. Look, I do not, do not, want such…such wanton bloodshed, commander, but I will so order it. You, sir, have nothing to bargain with, but one thing. Everything you've got."

Perryweather's eyes cut toward Gunther, an act not unnoticed by Latissimo.

The colonel looked curiously at the Texan, cocked his head, and pursed his lips.

"You, sir, have you any money from our Uncle Sam?" he asked.

"Not a slim dime, Colonel," Gunther said while chewing. "I have no interest in this godforsaken land, this pile of rocks you call a fort, and this saw-tooth trench you call a key pass. I, for one, simply cannot imagine what goods would come to and fro here that would be worth a small war over."

"But you do have some interest in your own life, Mister Major Johann Gunther? And the lives of the men that Captain Boston's death has caused you to shepherd over?"

"That, sir, I most plainly do," Gunther replied. "But, I don't have a dime from a queen or a king …or an uncle, to offer you. The Army was sent here to check on your welfare and see if you have found any special workhorses in these mountains. You are alive and well, and you have no such horses. I am concerned with the health and welfare of your wife. If you will take that responsibility over, I'm ready to leave right after this fine supper."

Lieutenant Kerry squirmed a bit in his seat. Gunther was clearly dropping down to his drawled, simple Texas accented talk, and that growlish tone had thus far preceded many episodes of sudden violence.

"Now, as far as all our lives are concerned?" Gunther stopped eating, wiped his mouth with his napkin, and continued, "In that fact, all that I can offer you is the promise of one bloody, bloody, fucking Sunday afternoon that will tear the size of your tribal army down by perhaps…oh say, half. 'Bout half. Maybe more? All I have to offer you, sir, is not killing half your men. Half your army gets to live. And there won't be no running away and chasing, clipping, and all those things you just mentioned. It'll all be head to head."

"Ohhhhhhh!" Latissimo moaned at Gunther's words with raised

eyebrows. "Point taken, Johann, and strong words from a free man who is, shall we say, all but unencumbered by military rules and regulations. Point taken. I think Mr. Gunther here has sat in on one too many of my parlays with the Cherokee back in Oklahoma," the colonel commented, and they all continued eating for the next few minutes.

"How much you got?" Latissimo suddenly and bluntly asked Perryweather.

"Twenty thousand pounds."

"Gold coin? Because you know, Captain Perryweather, paper money isn't worth shit up here among these people. I mean they wipe their ass with it, and even then they complain it's too rough. Worthless. A coin now, a solid coin, they bite with what blackened teeth they have left. A coin is…is pretty and shiny and has somebody's face on it."

"Coin of the realm."

"They don't care whose face is on it. They think it must be a god or a king to have their face cast on gold. I will take it. The queen's face? Her face is beautiful on gold, and I will take it. With this queen's fee, we will contract ourselves and establish a commercial base. We will allow for transport of goods through here, and we will charge a tariff as we see fit. To operate. You will be allowed to return home and announce yet another treaty in the history of the great Northwest Frontier. Another feather in your warrior's pith helmet. However feeble the feather, my fine-feathered friend."

All eyes fell upon Perryweather, a man without a choice, who had to agree to a choice. "This is acceptable," he reluctantly agreed.

The group ate in silence, until one voice on the far end of the table spoke up.

"Does this…does this mean I am to go free now, colonel?"

Everyone in the hall now looked to see George Hall, his neck extended awaiting an answer.

Latissimo glared at him, then returned to scooping the food from his plate. Without looking back up he added, "George Hall is an additional five hundred pounds."

Next, all eyes shifted back to Captain Perryweather, who appeared a bit surprised. "I…I am afraid I am…flush out for you, sir."

"Flush…out?" George Hall repeated solemnly.

"Then the diplomat stays with us," Latissimo concluded with his mouth full.

Hall became speechless as the very life seemed to drain from his face.

"I'll pay for him," Gunther said while eating. He too did not look up.

"You will?" Latissimo barked. "I thought you said you had no money?"

"I have my own money. Not the government's money."

"How much money do you have?" he asked.

Gunther looked him dead in the eye. "Damned if I'll tell you," he said in almost a growl, but then he smiled. "You drive too hard a bargain." Then he added a wink and a smile to defuse the confrontation.

Everyone knew what this meant in the ransom poker game. What was thought to be a financial raping of the expedition's money may have been a bluff. But, Latissimo let the game pass when he smiled back at his old Army private.

"Okay. Okay. You both deliver this money. Here. Tonight. And you have a deal. And you, Johann, one more thing for your deal. You also need to demonstrate those box pistols you are wearing. Then you'll have yourself a treaty and a British district agent."

"Sounds like an excellent plan!" Sergeant Valentino declared, apparently interested in Gunther's experimental pistols.

Gunther glanced at Lydia. It was obvious her husband was not here on a secret mission, but instead fancied himself a pirate king.

Gunther hand signaled Lieutenant Kerry over. He whispered into Kerry's ear, and the officer left the building for the camp to retrieve five hundred pounds from Gunther's stash. Inspired by this, Perryweather conducted his own hand signaling and dispatched two lieutenants for their part of the bargain.

The rest of the mealtime consisted of much small talk. People spoke among themselves unless Latissimo interrupted them, but he continued to be entertaining, engaging and an attentive host. He seemed to disengage himself instantly from being a ransom warlord and appeared very interested in learning what his guests had to say. He and Perryweather discussed the Crimean War, and Perryweather seemed to actually forget where he was and whom he chatted with. At one point they both laughed out loud.

"Aaghhhhh!" gasped a Brit at the table, who stood and clutched his throat with both hands. He thrashed about, and his chair fell back. Everyone stood at this scene.

"He's choking!" Marilyn declared.

Indeed the man's face went from purplish red to ghastly white. Two Afghanis beside him rushed to his aid. They bent him over the table and pounded his back as he gasped and groveled. Marilyn ran to their assistance as the three worked on the man. She thrust one fist with great force into his gut under his ribs and with her other arm bent him forward over her arm.

With a ragged cough, a small fruit pit tumbled out of the man's mouth and rolled onto the table. A sense of relief filled the room. The man moaned, raised his head, and studied the pit.

"I'm okay," he reported with a weak voice, trying to wave his help off. The two Afghans smiled at him, brought the chair upright, and sat the weakened man into it. One of the Afghans handed him a glass of water.

Gunther looked at Latissimo as he stood watching the life-saving event with curiosity, his huge white bib tucked in his shirt collar. They suddenly exchanged glances. The irony of the moment was not lost to either. Tomorrow these men would kill each other, but tonight they responded as simple humans helping humans. This, Gunther was learning, was the dichotomy of the Afghan people.

As Marilyn rounded the table and passed Latissimo, the colonel reached out and grabbed her arm and kissed her on the cheek. "My little niece…da' nurse," he said softly and with great pride. She blushed and reacted like a child.

When the last dishes were whisked from the table, Akbar stood and announced, "Will everyone please meet in the courtyard as our servants will clean the room and prepare for the entertainment."

"This means brandy and cigars!" Latissimo shouted.

Everyone filtered out, passing masked women who balanced trays full of drinks and cigars. The sun was setting, the sky a deep red, and the air held a dry chill.

"That is what we call in the States, giving away the farm," Gunther told Perryweather when they regrouped outside.

"Bloody hell," the British commander cursed, but to himself. "He got the better of me."

"Cheer up, old man. I can't say I could have done better," Gunther sympathized.

"I think he does not wish to work with us and would sooner slit our throats," the captain concluded.

"I agree, we—"

"Mr. Gunther!" Latissimo yelled from the fort steps, "How about that promised demonstration?" His words and mouth wrestled around a thick cigar.

In an instant, Gunther tossed his glass high into the air, drew a pistol, and blasted the goblet into smithereens. Then he opened fire on a flaming torch on a towering post in the yard. Jerking his right hand aside, he yanked out his left pistol and smoothly fed rounds from both guns in a rapid-fire succession. Fifteen bullets plowed into the lamplight. It shattered the clay oil carrier and burning wood and fire exploded until nothing but crackling embers remained on the ground below.

"Whhhoooo-we!" Latissimo hollered.

"Yeah!" his soldiers shouted in rousing approval.

Gunther shoved his left pistol under his right armpit and with his now empty left hand reloaded the right-hand gun with a new magazine from his gun belt. Then he repeated the process for the second pistol, ramming the right gun under his left armpit and reloading that one. He holstered both weapons.

Lydia and Marilyn started to clap and then so did all the Americans. The British and Indians applauded politely. Akbar just stared at him, expressionless.

"A square gun! Bullets in a box!" Latissimo declared, shaking his head.

"The hall is ready, Master," a servant announced to Akbar. Inside, the musicians began playing their exotic tunes. The group mounted the stone stairs and re-entered the great room. Gone were the dining room tables and chairs. The hall had been converted from an English castle into a tribal lounge of many colored pillows, sweeping drapes. Half-masked dancing girls in sheer clothing floated about the room. Men, leaping like acrobats, bounded across the floor, juggling balls and spinning poles.

"George Hall! Johann!" Latissimo called out. "Come here. Come over here and sit by me. This is our last night together you know, George Hall. Come on! Lydia, if you will excuse me for a moment, I need to talk some turkey with these boys."

Hall and Gunther sat in an arrangement of chair-like pillows as the gypsies and acrobats juggled a series of colored pins, poles and balls.

"Leaving us for jolly ol' England, George Hall?"

"I hope to, sir," Hall answered.

"You will be missed here!" Latissimo noted. "Really. You were good company."

The men watched the performers as they leapt through large hoops and somersaulted from each other's shoulders.

"Curious thing, these acrobats," Latissimo leaned over to Gunther. "Imagine, not a thing to worry about in the world, except making that triple flip. Nothing else to strive for. To work for. Just the next triple flip."

Gunther nodded.

"I see these acrobats sometimes…you know…working out around our camps. Practicing. They work out and exercise, just like the Ringling Brothers Circus back home. They strive so hard to…to juggle a fifth pin. We go to war. We kill. We come back to the camp…and these guys are working out in yellow tights."

They sat in silence.

"I seem to recall our last meeting now, Johann." Latissimo

continued, "It was the standard, re-enlistment meeting right before you mustered out. Fifteen years ago? Sixteen? You told me there was not enough money in the Army. You wanted out to make some money. Me? I have always made money with the Army. Extra money, but I was sympathetic with your plight, kid. Now, we meet again, and you are a West Point graduate, and even some kind of gun for hire."

Gunther stared ahead at the entertainers.

Latissimo continued, "Are you ready for one more recruitment speech? Pick up where we left off? We could use a legionnaire like you up here on this frontier. Someone…unencumbered by the usual rules of polite society. Somebody with the ambitions of a ringleader and a keen, cannibal eye for money. Somebody I know that can back that up with a fist and a bullet. I've seen you kill at Cache Creek and Duncan Canyon in the old days, and today I've seen you shoot the hell out of those box guns."

"Legionnaire? That's an odd choice of words, Colonel. But, what kind of money is there to be made up here?" Gunther asked. "A little extortion money? Ransom money?"

"Oh, oh, the big Double-Os, my boy! Oil and opium. The world is about to become addicted to them both. Very soon, all the military machines of the world will run on oil. Every battleship. Every nation. Right now the Russians are rebuilding their entire fleet to run on oil. The infantries will make metal cars with canons on them! They'll operate on oil. And, people—after a good, hard day's work in the oil business—can't turn down a good euphoria from opium. You can smoke it, rub it in your nose and on your gums. You can drink it and inject it. And much of it will all come through here.

"Johann, I need agents and representatives. I need guards, soldiers, captains, but like the conquering leaders of Rome, Johann, not those hillbillies, cowpunchers with rifles we worked with back at Sill. The ones you and I were smart enough to leave behind.

"Ahhhh, great Rome! Italians once owned the world, even owned Great Britain. We can handle the Brits and Indians again. The Afghanis? Them, too. You know what I mean. Indians are

Indians. Dumb." Latissimo rapped his fingers on Gunther's upper arm, "You and I know about real Indians, Johann. Oh, we've seen them. The brutality. Their tribal wars. The torture among themselves. There was once a time when a woman on a ranch couldn't step out her back door for fear an Indian might slit her throat or rape her. Savages. Savages! We fixed that. You and me and, and the likes of Kit Carson and…Hell, the Army, man!"

Gunther and Hall watched the colonel's performance intently.

"You know what they"—he leaned near Gunther's ear—"do you know what they are starting to say in New York and Boston, and Richmond and Washington?" he asked with disdain. "That the American Indian is a peaceful, noble savage. That they all lived in a…a Garden of Eden!" His arms went wide as his face twisted. "That we, we, taught the Indian to scalp and kill. I've got news for those intellectual, fancy boys who take their caviar shits on porcelain toilets! The American Indian has been killing since they learned to swing a club and scratch out an edge on a piece of slate. They were scalping and maiming before the Pilgrims sailed in. Brutes! A brute with no sense between his eyes but to eat and fuck. And kill. That's what!" Latissimo's knee bounced nervously.

"Remember Sergeant Louis Lorimar, Johann?"

"Yes, I do."

"Jesus, they skinned ol' Louie alive with a dull, thin rock. Do you remember that! The fuck, we taught them to do that! They invented that little game all by themselves. Took him three hours to die," he said, as he sat back in his pillow. "Hours! Noble, my ass. Garden of Eden. Well, we ain't noble here either, mister. These greasy goddamn nomads only understand a split skull or a rotting corpse!"

A woman slid up in front of them and belly danced. Latissimo looked sheepishly at Lydia across the room. She grimaced and shook her head.

"You boys ever read *The Prince*, by the great Italian Niccolo Machiavelli?"

George Hall had. Gunther indicated no.

"Hundreds of years ago, this…this genius, Machiavelli said it is better to be feared than loved since you cannot have both. He said that, and I quote here gentlemen, 'there is nothing more difficult to carry out than to initiate a new order of things. For the reformer has enemies in all those who profit by the old order. The leader must inflict the most injuries possible all at once, and not have to renew them every day.' He created an Italian empire."

"Which failed," George Hall added.

"Eventually. All fail when they get soft. The Romans, Johann," the colonel continued as the siren glided off to vibrate her bejeweled belly button elsewhere. "The Romans, now the Italians. We are still the master race. It is in our blood. We lost the world when we became decadent and…and fat. When we lost the will to conquer and destroy our enemies in one day, we lost the empire. We became what the British did right here today. You saw it. We paid our enemies like the Huns to leave us alone. We paid the Khans to leave us alone! Now the Brits are paying me to leave them alone."

He took a gulp from his wine goblet. "Hey, Johann!" He shook Gunther's shoulder. "You Huns ain't so bad. The Kaiser is busy whipping Europe up into a lather. A German like you would still make fine legionaries of my little Roman kingdom. You Hun bastard! Haaa!"

"Colonel, I am not too sure I like it out here."

"Well, if you travel a pass or two away, these mountains open up into the greenest, paradises, valleys and lakes. Breathtaking. It's just breathtaking."

"It has its moments."

"Well, think about it, Gunther. And try to decide fast, because I can't predict how the next few days are going to fall around here," Latissimo whispered and lightly raised a finger to point toward Akbar. "He's a nervous bastard, and he's got religion on his mind all the time. Five times a day he drops to his knees, faces Mecca, and prays like a goddamn fool! He doesn't like a bunch of these Church of England types, or American Protestants parading around his rock garden out here. This is Allah country."

"Does he like Roman-American Caesars or Russian czars?" Gunther asked.

"Ha! Hell, no. But we play each other like an ol' Jew's harp. And I get more rich and powerful every day. I am the great Red, White and Blue Sword! Well, think about it, Johann. Think about it." He leaned back in chair. "I have big plans. And there are many extras with the job. That belly dancer with the ruby in her belly button? I have fucked her twenty different ways. Yup! Life in my Khyber Pass army here is not like Fort Sill, Oklahoma! Not at all."

Latissimo then purveyed the room again, his attention captured again by the acrobats. "Julius Caesar. Marco Polo. Alexander the Great. These are the men on my mind." With another gulp he stared hypnotically at the performers again. "Imagine…not a thing to worry about in the world, except making that triple flip. Nothing else to strive for. To work for. Just the next triple flip for tomorrow afternoon's matinee."

Gunther looked again at Lydia, who appeared just out of earshot. Her eyes stared blankly at the ground, her face contorted deep in thought.

Kerry appeared with a canvas satchel of George Hall's ransom. He walked to Gunther, and the Texan waved him over to Latissimo. The colonel snatched the bag, opened the leather drawstring and ran a hand through the heavy coins. Next, the British lieutenants carted in a black-lacquered chest, sat it down before the leader and cracked open the lid.

Latissimo leaned forward and laughed. "Another day. Another twenty-two thousand pounds," he said as his probing hands rolled the gold coins. Akbar walked up behind them and peered into the treasure box. He nodded in satisfaction. George Hall stood, set his drink down, and walked to the door, obviously leaving the entire building.

"Don't go away mad, Georgie!" Latissimo pretended to plead. "He's such an Englishman!" Latissimo proclaimed to Gunther. "He loves England. That is all he knows. He is not worldly or wise like you and I."

Gunther had a sudden, impulsive urge to shoot Vito Latissimo right in the head, just as fast as when he shot that goblet in the air an hour earlier, which would mean certain doom for all. But perhaps later? He studied the broad, sweaty forehead of this mad-man. Where would the bullet enter? Roosevelt was so right. Mur-der was truly the only option.

The dancer and acrobats went on, but with the extortion and ransom funds paid, the dinner party began to break up.

"I will need to return with the appropriate receipts and forms. The treaty itself," Captain Perryweather said.

"Of course. Sure, sure, sure, sure," Latissimo agreed. "Tomor-row. Come see us tomorrow morning."

Lydia walked up to Gunther, took both his hands in hers and raised them to her chest. "I will stay here," she said.

"No," he said, "no, you cannot."

"This is where I need to be, Mr. Gunther."

"Lydia, please."

"No," she finished solemnly.

"There will probably be a war tonight, Lydia. A fierce war."

"I know," she said, freeing his hands and gently pushing him away.

Marilyn saw this and approached. Lydia embraced her and whispered something in her ear. Gunther could tell by Lydia's de-termined expression nothing he could say would change her mind. With fear for her, and regret, he joined Kerry and Satin and to-gether they left the room and retrieved their jackets and hats by the door.

"Mr. Gunther," Akbar called to him.

Gunther stopped and turned to him. Satin and Kerry continued on.

"I have something for you, something as your people would say, like a souvenir for you." He tossed a small, bright object through the air, about the size of a nugget. Gunther reflexively snatched it, opened his palm, and what he saw in his hand utterly horrified him, and instantly made him feel faint. He felt his stomach and lungs burn. He forced his face, however, to remain perfectly placid. In his hand was undoubtedly the gold-encrusted tooth containing the Star of Africa jewel, obviously broken from the mouth of the woman herself. A bit of dried flesh still clung to the root.

"I thought perhaps you would like to have this memento of your conquest. You are a man of many women? Yes? I ordered an excursion by the Koklanare last week. It was just as you would say—business. They chopped many feet to strike fear in the local tribes. And then killed them all. And they took this tooth…for you."

"Well, thank you, Akbar," Gunther said with a smile. He shoved the tooth into his jean pocket. He kept his hand in there to conceal his twitching, "Say, there was another man that really got on my nerves. Tall, thin, religious American with a beard and big, black dress hat?"

"Yes, yes I am told of him, too," Akbar added. "He shall trouble you no more." He ran a finger across his throat to signify an execution. He grinned.

Gunther nodded and winked at Akbar. He tried his best to conjure a sinister smile. Then he left to catch up with the others as they boarded their wagons. He was speechless, deep in thought, imagining Pasha's torturous end a waking nightmare. The maiming. What were her last bloody, wet moments like? He grew sick to his stomach.

"Will she be all right?" Marilyn asked him, rousting him from these dire thoughts. "Will my aunt be safe?"

"No, Marilyn," he answered honestly. "This place is a madhouse."

She turned to Lieutenant Kerry, walking beside the wagon as they left the courtyard.

"Are you all right?" Lieutenant Kerry asked Gunther.

"No," Gunther mumbled.

"Whatever shall we do?" she asked.

"Come back and kill all of them," Gunther said softly, his eyes staring downward.

"This was their last supper."

Akbar and Latissimo stood by the front doors watching the group depart.

"The English officer is all spit and polish," Latissimo said. "I'll bet he can fight a bit, but he is not cautious. He's a real pip."

"And what of this cowboy?" Akbar asked.

"He is the ace up Roosevelt's sleeve I told you about," Latissimo replied.

"The snake?"

"Yes, the snake. I tried to convert him tonight. But he is just too damn independent to take advice and orders."

"What shall we do with your wife?" Akbar asked.

Latissimo looked over at Lydia as she spoke to a few of the Americans.

"Throw the bitch in the harem. Let her be fucked to death by the tribesmen. I cannot believe she came this far, and for what? What? To torture me again? Wait until no one can hear her scream for help, pick her up, and toss her worthless ass in with the party girls."

"I will arrange this."

"Good," Latissimo said. "Tomorrow morning, when all their soldiers are loaded up, fat, sassy, happy, and ready to go home, relieved that they dodged a big fight with this ransom, as they leave, we'll hit real hard in a rear assault."

"Allah will descend a wave of death upon them. And what of your niece?"

"Oh, spare her if you can. Let her live and return home safe. She was such a beautiful and special child. Now she is a nurse with her whole life ahead of her. Did you see her jump up to help that choking Englishman?"

"Yes. I did. I shall assign this task to some of the Tarak guards of the Koklanare. They will find her, isolate her, capture her, and deliver her to the arms of Northern India."

"She seems to fancy that young lieutenant. I wish we could save him, too, but we'll never find him when the killing starts. Nice dinner, huh?"

"Yes," Akbar agreed.

"It was their last," Latissimo said.

23
Only Cricket Is Cricket

Lydia felt abandoned. Her army of allies left for their camp by the mountain pass. Most of her husband's men wandered from the main room. At first, her husband was busy talking to his men in differing corners, but he left the chamber, suddenly. She could see him and Akbar standing midway down a long hallway. Whispering. She hung her purse on her shoulder expecting to leave for Vito's bedroom or someplace where they would have some privacy. She no longer had the strong arm of Gunther on her elbow to count on. Instead, she squeezed her bag between her arm and body and her elbow felt the weight and form of her trusty pistol. This was her new confidence. Her last confidence.

"Vito?" she called out in a charming tone. He looked at her and waved his hand.

"Vito!" she repeated, this time less patient. She was swept up off her feet, from behind! Each of her arms clutched by a foreigner in a turban and robe. She screamed out.

"Good night, Lydia!" Latissimo shouted out in a singsong voice from the hall." And good-bye!"

"Vito!" she declared.

The two men hauled her down another hall, lit by smelly torch-lights. They descended a short flight of steps. She lost a shoe. Her feet barely touched the cold stone floor.

"Where are you taking me!" she demanded.

Three men in similar garb stood guard by a large wooden door. They opened the entrance for Lydia and her two escorts. She was carted into a brightly lit spacious room full of women and colorful furniture. There were at least forty or fifty women, she first guessed. One of her escorts yelled something in a foreign tongue to an older tribal woman, who profusely argued back.

Lydia was tossed free so abruptly she hit the wall and then the floor. Her chest burned and hurt enough without this mistreatment. She fought back the pain, gasped for breath and climbed to one knee. This room looked like a college dormitory with dozens of beds, separated by sheer, colored curtains.

The tribal woman walked to her, muttering, grabbed an arm, and hoisted her to her feet.

"Where am I?" she demanded? "Is this where women sleep?"

About thirty women gathered around the commotion, dressed in various colored gowns and slippers. Some had their faces wrapped, some did not. One woman drew a cup of water from a barrel and handed it to her, which she reflexively took and drank. She said thank you, but knew a bow of the head would best communicate the message.

The elder woman shouted to the back of the room, "Ameee!"

And the women echoed the call throughout the basement, "Ameee!"

A tall, blond, thin woman in her early twenties wrapped in an orange silk robe appeared from the group.

"You speak English?" This young woman asked.

"Yes. Where am I?"

"You are in the harem, the brothel of the Great Red, White and Blue Sword."

"A…harem! Why in God's name am I here?"

"You are now in the harem. You are now a slave. A harem girl. Are you English?" The girl asked of her.

"No, I am an American. Vito Latissimo's wife! His real wife!" she reported.

"The Great Red, White and Blue Sword's wife! My name is Lydia Latissimo."

"We are all his wives," the blonde girl reported. I am an American, too. My name is Amy Verne," the girl offered.

"Amy….Verne?" Lydia repeated, incredulously. "The daughter

of a Silas Verne?"

"Yes, yes that is him. I was kidnapped years ago and taken into slavery. I have been bought and sold many times." The words she said were few and matter-of-fact, but her expression spoke volumes.

"Oh, oh my dear sweet child!"

As the wagons trekked back up the rocky road to the expedition's camp, a silent and solemn Gunther spied George Hall on the trail, struggling along his way with a large piece of plaid luggage. He had the desperate look of a man completely out of place and with no answers, bound for nowhere.

"Where you going, George?" Gunther said as their wagon drew close.

"Anywhere but here, and each step feels better than the last."

"Pick him up," Gunther ordered his driver.

The corporal stopped the transport, and George Hall threw his suitcase in.

"I am ever so grateful indeed for your generosity," Hall said with a grunt as he launched himself into the cart. "Not just about this ride, but about the ransom. But nonetheless my good fellow, I feel we shall all be dead by noon tomorrow."

"We are going to have a meeting on this subject as soon as we enter the pass. I would appreciate it if you would attend and offer any help or information."

"Certainly."

Within a short time all the English, American and Indian officers and their top-ranking NCOs gathered by a hastily lit fire just inside the pass wall, the proceedings invisible from the fort and tribes in the valley.

"Gentlemen, we have negotiated a treaty," Captain Perryweather reported. "The ransoms and extortions have been paid."

There seemed a sigh and sense of relief among the troops.

"However," Perryweather interrupted, "once paid, it became more than apparent that we will be attacked when we try to embark tomorrow morning."

As this was the first news from the hopeful dinner that most heard, it was not well received.

"I must agree," George Hall stood and said. "I am the British district political officer here and had been kidnapped. Held captive for ransom. These men here have rescued me. I have seen Latissimo's tribes and Sheik Akbar make war for weeks now. They are bloody, bloody killers. They will surely keep your money and attack you no later than tomorrow."

"Those of you familiar with your British history," Perryweather continued, "will recall the locals here are crack experts in this type of pursuit assault. They charge, then back off and pick away at you for twenty-four hours a day. Then they charge again and again. Then snipe again and again. They conduct small raids on our weakest caravan points. Five or more days of this is sheer torture. It is a most sticky wicket."

"With the Koklanare riding with them? They outnumber us two to one," a Hindu commander added.

"Maybe three to one," an American officer chimed in with a tone of frustration.

"We could stand and fight them," Sergeant Grimsley suggested, and others mumbled in agreement or disagreement.

"Or, make it back to the Star of Africa's camp," said an Indian sergeant.

Gunther stood up from his perch on top of a rock. "Akbar told me that the Star and all of her people…our Reverend Silas Verne also…have been killed. It was their feet in those fishnet sacks thrown over the backs of the Koklanare horses we saw yesterday. The Koklanare chopped off their feet, tortured, and killed them all."

The group fell silent. As had happened many times in the past in tense and desperate situations, Gunther scanned the faces of the men, counting the seconds of silence, awaiting the proper commanders to speak up and take control. None did. In this void, he spoke up.

"We can't stay here on the perimeter of the pass and hold off a contingent twice or more our size," Gunther said. "Though that choice is better than leaving and being brought down from behind like…sheep fleeing from a pack of mountain lions. Defending is dying. Leaving, running is dying. No. We attack."

"But major, you just said we couldn't make a stand. We certainly can't attack them," one said.

"One thing the Army did teach me, gentlemen, is that if you are in a fair fight, you just didn't prepare well enough. We do it with superior firepower, using our machine guns and explosives. And the element of surprise."

"How can we possibly surprise them?' Lieutenant Satin asked.

"We go in three hours."

"Three hours?" one repeated in astonishment.

"We surprise them by attacking in just three hours. At three A.M., when they are deepest asleep. We pelt their tents with heavy machine-gun fire and dynamite arrows. We do this first to the Koklanare camp on the east side. We kill their best fighters."

"In their sleep!" A British lieutenant interjected. "My goodness man. That isn't exactly cricket is it?"

"Lieutenant," Gunther replied solemnly, "only cricket…is cricket." This observation seemed to score with the group.

Gunther continued, "We divide up our machine guns. Half on the east side of the pass, half on the west. At three A.M. seventy percent of the guns open fire on the Koklanare side of the field, and their horses, too. We focus most of our dynamite first on the Koklanare, too. Meanwhile, the other thirty percent opens up on the Latissimo tribesmen on the west side.

"The Koklanare will be in disarray, scrambling to mount, load, and counterattack with no real plan. At the smartest tactical moment, when we seem to have them stymied, then we turn that seventy percent machine-gun fire and dynamite onto the Latissimo tribe on the west side."

"There are women and children in that tribe," one soldier said.

"I have no wish to kill horses, women or children," Gunther

said, pacing before the group. "But there is a price to pay for being with the wrong people, doing the wrong thing at the wrong time. This is especially true when my life is at stake, and the lives of my friends and comrades here." The men agreed, some reluctantly. There were head shakers.

Gunther continued, "After we hit the two tribes hard with machine guns and dynamite, our horse soldiers charge up the dirt road to the village. Then we send in our men on camels to sweep through the tent cities. The machine-gun teams will join these foot and camel troops and get closer in range of the fort.

"The west-side camel force moves up on the west side of the village. The east side does the same. The horse soldiers make a run up through the village to the fort. If, providing—" Gunther looked to George Hall, "—they do not have machine guns. George Hall, do you know if they have any machine guns?"

"I haven't seen any," he said.

"If we get within dynamite range of the fort, we can blow the gates or blow holes in the wall."

"That might work," an Indian commander said.

"Killing as many of them as possible in their sleep is imperative," Gunther said.

Perryweather propped a boot up on a bench and rubbed his face. "I…I have no other plan that would better ensure our survival. We are doomed if we just leave. Doomed if we just stay. After this assault, even if we are driven back, we will have wounded their numbers so…so dramatically, we have a damn solid chance of leaving safely."

"We could also set up some booby traps for a retreat, as the remaining stragglers will probably give us a good chase," a British officer added.

"Dynamite is also jim-dandy for that," Grimsley said.

"Horses and men while they sleep. Children, too. My God, sir, I hope the good Lord forgives us on Judgment Day," an Englishman muttered.

"Well, fellers, that's the point. If your superior officers review this plan someday and think we were too brutal, then just blame it all on me. Tell 'em, …tell 'em some renegade Yankee son of a bitch dreamed up the scheme and held a pistola to your head and said 'fire and charge.' The British army can't court-martial me."

"Neither can the American Army," a soldier called out.

"Speaking of which, sir," a British officer stood, "and where exactly, may I ask, will you be during this attack?" His tone was half-antagonistic, as if to suggest Gunther might remain in the rear and watch his deadly plan unfold.

"I will charge the fort, sergeant, where I fully intend to shoot and kill every son of a bitch in there, myself."

"Here, here!" and "Yeah!" the men shouted. There was laughter, albeit somewhat nervous, but laughter nonetheless.

"We have very little time to prepare. And preparation must be done in complete dark and in as much silence as possible," Gunther ordered. "One officer in charge of all machine guns, with two under him for the east and west. One in charge of the cavalry assault. Two under him for the east and west. One in charge of the dynamite assault and so on. One officer remaining here in charge of the orderly retreat, ambush, and booby-trap of anyone that follows us. Captain Perryweather will, of course, be making those assignments. Gentlemen, the combat clock is ticking. It's do or die. I pray for all that it's worth it, that I see every one of you again tomorrow morning for coffee."

"Make mine tea," a Brit said, "and inside that bloody fort!"

And the group laughed again. Some shook a fist in the air.

Perryweather set about tasking the assignments. It seems he got his wish, Gunther thought…a cavalry charge. Bengal Lancers in the lead.

Gunther leveled his Stetson on his head and left for his wagons, but was stopped at the edge of the pass by a clearly distressed George Hall.

"Say, you are really charging into all that?" Hall asked.

"Yes."

"This isn't any business of yours. You are an American. And, aren't you the least bit frightened for your own well-being?"

"Yeah, but I am more mad than I am frightened right now,

George."

"What should I do, Mr. Gunther?" Hall drew his Webley revolver out of his suitcase, and held it, barrel up, to the night sky. "Should I fight? Should I attempt an escape through the pass?"

"George, you are a civilian. A British civilian. This is indeed more of your business than mine, but you are not a soldier. You are a diplomat. Still, you may do anything you wish, I think. No one expects you pick up a lance and charge," Gunther said. "But for me? Latissimo is a crazed man with guns and power and full of greed. Evil! To me, there is only one thing worse than a crazy man with a gun. That's a good man with a gun who won't stop him."

"Won't stop him…" Hall mumbled, trying to digest this rule.

"Code of the West," Gunther added with a slight wink, and with that said, he walked away, leaving Hall with his gun still pointing at the sky. He looked at his pistol. Then he looked up at the brilliant night, but he wasn't searching for distant stars, he was looking for something else grounded far more within.

24
Gunfight at Fort Tartan

George Hall watched the procession make ready, with a pocket watch in his hand, appreciating every peaceful moment before 3 A.M. The cool midnight mountain air flowed briskly under the light of a half-moon. The Americans quietly mounted their horses and camels hidden inside the pass. Nearby them, the Brits and Indians climbed aboard their animals. The infantry readied their rifles and packs. All positioned their guns and swords for quick access to blast a path to the fort.

Hall knew that within minutes their machine-gun teams, positioned high on top the cliffs to their east and west, would rupture the valley. After a hail of thousands and thousands of bullets, Perryweather would shout "charge." A mob would flood toward the village and fort. It was a one way, do-or-die ride into the valley of death.

British commanders leaned around the rock walls in a study of the sleeping battlefield before them. Hall spotted Gunther atop his horse, pacing to and fro before the men. Gunther stopped and took a position before his troops.

"You are all men of the long tooth," Gunther said to these veteran American soldiers, but the Brits and Indians heard him also and heads in their ranks turned and craned to hear Gunther's words. "Long in your Army. Long in your ways. And, you could die toothless, old and decrepit. Widowers. Farmers. Or shopkeepers. Or...or you could be henpecked, disgrace living lost in a big city, lost on a dirt farm on an open plain, shoveling pig shit out of a pen.

Probably…probably some of those jobs sound pretty good to some of ya round about now. Sound pretty good to me."

All that listened smiled and some laughed.

"But instead? Instead, you chose this life. The soldier's life. The way of the gun and the way of the horse. And you kept to it. So your fangs could taste what you longed for. And…you could snarl and snap and bark back at what you hate."

He strolled his horse across the middle front of the U.S. and British troops. Hall noticed that even Perryweather now paid strict attention. Gunther continued.

"Your whole life. Your whole life you've lived in this man's Army. You know what it means. You know what we do. Tonight, you have marched to the ends of the earth. To the high ceiling of the earth and sky. An ol' boy from Kansas, or New York…"

"…or London, sir!" a Brit private called out. There were a few quiet chuckles.

"…or London…" Gunther added. "Places ol' boys like us would never otherwise have dreamed of seeing. Here it is, and here we are. Alone. Alone, but we still have each other. We will strike out today for all that is good. We will strike so that each of us will live tomorrow. And if we fall today…should we fall today, we shall fall for all that has been the meaning of our lives. The meaning of our life. Death to our enemies."

"Death to our enemies," the men repeated, lowly. Solemnly. Some also said, "The meaning of our lives." These phrases rippled through the group, even well through the Brits and Indians.

"For we are the men of the long tooth. Old. Wise. Still as fast as a damn snake. Poison is our bite, gentlemen. Death is our business. Death to our enemies."

And with that, Gunther turned his horse to face the mouth of the pass to await the onslaught. His hand rested over his gun holster. His fingers rippled across the brown leather in a drumbeat of anticipation. A fingertip touched the small, hard lump in a side pocket— the extracted, bloody tooth of the Star of Africa.

The rocky ridge perch jutted midway up the range and overlooked the pending battlefield. It was a precarious perch, but Harrigan and Smith knew any battle photographs they would capture would be received with the greatest fanfare and respect in the United States, possibly even around the world. They toiled with the camera settings and lenses to coax and finesse the nighttime light into lasting images on their film. They also anticipated great flares of explosions and soon, even breaking dawn light in a few hours hence, should this bloodbath last that long.

"If we lose the battle?" Smith whispered through his injured voice box.

"I don't know. We have no escape if we lose. Perhaps Latissimo would let us pass?"

"He seemed unwilling to be photographed tonight."

"Maybe he will appreciate the…the art of war. Let us preserve the night and his victory?"

Everything in place, the two men sat in silence and watched over the quiet valley.

Harrigan kept track of time on his watch and informed Smith at 2:55 A.M. The men stood beside their cameras.

At first, they could barely see the thin, burning fuse of a few arrows zip through the air. Several more than they detected launched because no less than eight explosions rocked the Koklanare camp. To their surprise, there was no immediate reaction. Five spots blew a fiery red. No real action yet.

Then, just down below them on the edges of the mountains, the machine gun teams opened fire. They guessed ten teams, but it was difficult to discern. Hundreds, if not thousands, of large-caliber bullets pelted, in sweeping forays, the several hundred Koklanare tents. Dynamite arrows followed. The concussions rocked the valley in sight and sound. Tents were mashed into blurry pieces. The very ground popped and rippled in waves from the lead rain.

Smith snapped photos, but Harrigan stood mesmerized. Then he took to his camera twisting it to the far left, where other machine guns took apart the Latissimo tribes. Lesser firepower allowed these groups to awaken and scramble from their tents in a half panic. They ran the field in search of safe haven or a leader with a battle plan. Many scampered naked or half-naked to the fort.

The screams began both in surprise and pain. The machines guns crisscrossed the encampment. One gun team too far right hit the makeshift horse corrals. Koklanare horses and camels exploded and melted into a pile of red, brown and black rubble. Missed and wounded horses fled the area, scattering across the valley.

They could barely hear some of the Koklanare tribesmen shouting orders in controlled voices, but much closer and right down below them was the one loud, commanding voice, Captain Perryweather who yelled charge. Horns of action blared.

The dynamite and lead missiles decimated the people, their tents, their temporarily erected structures, the rope corrals, supply sites, everything. The gun and dynamite teams sprayed the area in an organized crisscross fashion that spared little. Many were riddled from two directions almost simultaneously.

"I'd say more than half their horses are dead or killed," Harrigan noted.

Yet even under the most intense fire, a number of both lucky and smart tribesmen on both sides of the valley still survived, still scrambling and now even shooting back and finding horses to ride.

Harrigan and Smith now saw below them the expedition's cavalry at full gallop. Indian, British and American men on horses and camels, some six hundred of them, raced up the wide road to the village, bound for Fort Tartan. As they advanced, this Army fired to their right and left into the tribes, when targets became available. Small arms fire popped and sparkled and bordered their advance, as the men above snapped more action pictures.

"I see Perryweather," Harrigan announced while looking through his binoculars.

"And I see Gunther. Hard to miss with that hat and buckskin jacket," Smith said with a cough. He wiped the cold sweat from his brow.

"The fort's gates are still open!" Harrigan spied. "Can't they hear this? Don't they know we're coming?" He watched as tribesmen, now touting rifles, either afoot or mounted, poured into the fort seeking refuge. "They must be letting as many of them in the fort as they can. It'll be like a trap!"

On timed cue, the machine gun teams now evenly split their assault on the two east and west tribes. Their fire now seemed more aimed and calculating. They picked their targets, but many lived. They were weaving through the destruction and gunfire toward the center road and the cavalry charge.

"Come on, boys! Come on, boys!" Harrigan said desperately, spit coming from his mouth. There were tears in eyes. "My God, Jesus, can't you ride any faster, boys?"

Gunther felt as though he were flying on a thundercloud of horseback soldiers, cutting a path through the flashing flames and smoke of hell on either side of him. He saw no tribesmen worthy of trying a shot at and wasting a bullet, just men stumbling about in shock, bellowing to each other in a foreign tongue.

Cannons! Suddenly, all three cannons from the fort tower erupted, cracking the night open. The explosives launched not at the charge, but smartly at the wall of machine guns on the mountain range doing so much damage. Gunther worked his horse over to the edge of the charge and turned to see where the missiles would land.

Gildy and the scouts did a jig on their ledge.

"They're short, Rosie! The cannon rounds fell short of the machine guns!" Gildy declared, "That German boy can cipher them cannons!"

"Keep yer knickers on, you idiots," Rosie, once an old artillery loader, said while wrestling the cramp in his stomach. "They'll just adjust and shoot again."

The entire castle shook. The explosions shook walls and interrupted the whispered conversation between Lydia and Amy. Gray dust poured from the walls and ceilings.

"What was that?" Lydia asked.

"The cannons," Amy answered. "Someone is firing the three cannons up in the tower. They have tested them before."

The women in the harem shook off their sleep and rose from their beds. Several began lighting lamps and scampering about the rooms.

"They're coming," Lydia said with a vindictive sneer.

"Your friends are coming?" Amy asked. "They will be killed! There are not enough of them."

Lydia studied the nervous women. She stood, her large purse in hand. She reached into it and pulled out her large silver revolver. "Ladies!" she cried. Everyone looked at her. Gasps echoed in the open bay when they spied the handgun. "Ladies, you all stick with me. We're fixing to escape!"

Amy translated, but could not communicate the deliberation in Lydia's message.

Lydia marched to the main doors and banged on the wood. "Hey! Hey you!" she hollered. "Amy, tell that brute at the door we need help in here."

Amy stepped to the crack in the double doors and spoke. Then she jumped back.

The cannons above fired again, frightening the women even more. Many paced and some clutched each other in pairs. Finally, they could hear a series of metal contraptions slide, clang and un-lock on the other side of the door. Lydia placed her revolver behind her back. The double doors opened as a giant of a man in a turban and robe pulled them apart, his face twisted in anger. He roared his complaint.

"You, you monstrous brute," Lydia declared. "You've guarded your last harem." She revealed the gun in an outstretched arm and shot the man point blank in the head.

As the man tumbled back, his skull split like a hacked melon, Lydia stepped around him to the hallway, ready to kill again. No one followed her.

"Amy, tell these women to leave. Now!"

Amy spread this order and then turned back to the first Ameri-can woman she'd seen in twelve years. "Where are you going?" she asked.

"I am going to kill…" but she stopped her sentence as their eyes locked. She brought the pistol down to her side. "I…am going to get you out of here young lady, and back to the American camp. Your young life is a very important thing. It might be the real reason God brought me all the way here."

Amy ran to her side, and the two stepped carefully down the cold stone hallway. The cannons rumbled again! They shook the women's lungs, but not Lydia's resolve.

25
Machine Gun and Cannon

Just as the lead horses in the charge approached the south side of the village, prepped for the mad dash down the wide main street and right into the stone citadel, Gunther's hellish fear became a reality.

Machine guns! Probably no less than three opened fire from the castle's high main turret window, sharing space with the three cannons. The bullets ripped through the air and pounded into the earth at the feet of the invading force. Then the shooters raised their barrels, zeroing in on the meat of the charge. The barrage caught many of the lead horses and men as the rest of group instinctively peeled off at the sides to dodge the firestorm.

"Damn!" Gunther cursed aloud and cut his horse to the left. "They do have machine guns." When the guns stopped, their three cannons fired, now zoned down to the roadway and away from the frustrating failures of targeting the mountain range. After the three vicious blasts, the machine guns kicked in again. The guns were positioned in front of the cannons, and they had to take turns reloading. The horse soldiers galloped for cover behind the village buildings to their east and west, but not before the gunfire and the cannon balls tore into and apart some two dozen troops. Moans and screams of the flipped, cut, and seared men and horses filled the air. Going to help them was an open invitation to receive the same treatment.

From the cover of buildings, Gunther turned to study the mayhem still behind him. The soldiers further back in the charge blended into the tent cities on either side of the road and suddenly

Page 288

found themselves clashing with the sporadic tribesmen still among the tents and gathering their wits, weapons and resolve. Some of his men were in dire circumstances.

Gunther gazed up at the upper levels of nearby buildings. Some were two stories. He estimated the range of protection offered by this cover and spurred his horse straight into the tent campgrounds.

"Come with me!" he shouted to any of the troops who could hear him.

He swung his shotgun up at the ready. There were so many fights spread before him; he had difficulty choosing whom to help. A Koklanare solved that problem. Three tribesmen were slashing their swords at a sole British Lancer who yanked and torqued his horse away as best he could. One of the swordsmen heard Gunther and turned from this group to advance on his approaching horse. The man leapt from side-to-side to get a sword cut on Gunther's horse. Each second he darted in and out of Gunther's view, behind his horse's bobbing head and neck. The Texan had enough. He pulled a hard rein to the left and shot the man with a one-handed grip on his long gun. The shotgun punched into the man's neck and shoulder. With a gasping grunt he spun and fell back.

It was clear Gunther could not shotgun the other two swordsmen battling the Lancer as they all struggled too close. Instead, he galloped in, dropping the shotgun to sling length at his side and pulled his .45. A Koklanare turned just as Gunther pounded two rounds into his chest. The man stood and slapped his chest in disbelief.

"Well then…die, you son of a bitch!" Gunther barked and shot him again in the face. He fell as if kicked in the face by a horse.

The Lancer freed his revolver and shot his third attacker.

"Cheers!" the officer declared, and not waiting for a reply, he joined the others who had followed Gunther into the camp fray, trying to help untangle their troops from other small skirmishes.

Bullets cracked and whistled over Gunther's ducking head. The men back by the buildings set up fields of fire and were shooting at every visible tribesman they could spy darting through the tent city. The Koklanare and local tribesmen were scrambling wide of the far west side of the campground and around the far side of the buildings. They were flanking the far side of the village toward the fort.

Spotting this escape route, Gunther galloped after them, hollering for more help until his throat grew hoarse.

"Follow them! Follow them and shoot them down! Shoot them down," he called.

With this alert, scores of the men—British, American and English—took off in pursuit.

Gunther dropped the reins, took out both his pistols and began shooting the tribesmen down, most in the back. His Army followed suit. Pistols empty, he re-holstered them, scooped up his lever-action shotgun, and pounded the men down. It seemed like a heartless slaughter of some forty to fifty tribesmen, but Gunther knew if he left them, they would later regroup and kill them in an even worse manner.

But, Gunther reared his horse to a short stop and threw up a hand when he saw some of the Koklanare ahead. They turned and hunkered down, preparing to make a stand. Some of them ducked into alleyways to gather and shoot at their attackers.

"Cover fire from the rear! Front retreat! Retreat!" Gunther ordered, and he and the front men turned their horses and raced back to the main Army as the rear soldiers fired steadily upon the enemy.

This front and rear guard of the impromptu international unit met and together turned the corner toward the south side of the buildings. Once there, Gunther flew into a rage at the sight before him.

Lieutenant Kerry veered off the road to avoid the fort's machine-gun fire, then he galloped into a Koklanare emerging from a tent with a rifle in one hand. Kerry kept his horse at a mad dash and fired his revolver at the man. One bullet struck the long gun, splintering part of the stock and jarring the firearm from the tribesman's grip. This man charged at the horse, pulled a curved blade from his sheath, and screamed some unintelligible string of threats.

The Koklanare dodged and danced in front of Kerry's horse, an apparent veteran of many man-versus-rider takedowns. Kerry could not lay his gun sight again at this darting figure. Right. Left. Then right again before the horses head and neck. Kerry fired at a glimpse of the man's knee, but missed him. Before he could look left, the tribesman slashed at his thigh and lunged into the air grasping a handful of the soldier's tunic. Buttons popped free as he yanked Kerry right off the horse just as Kerry fired a shot so close that it blew the turban clear off the man's head, cutting open his scalp.

But, the pistol tumbled free when they both struck the ground hard. Kerry lost all his wind when his shoulder crunched into the turf. The horse stopped, reared on its hind legs, and bellowed. Kerry could tell the Koklanare had trouble seeing from the eye close to the gunshot wound and was still disoriented from the concussion of the blast. He scrapped up a handful of dirt and flung it at the Afghan's face as he struggled to one knee.

The Afghan cursed and swung his knife wildly at the lieutenant. Kerry hammer-fisted his knife arm as the slash missed and traveled by him.

"To me, Clapper!" Kerry called to his horse. Its eyes wide, it charged the two men, causing the Koklanare to leap back. After the horse dashed between them, the Afghan saw Lieutenant Kerry standing before him with a wicked, mean half-smile. His cavalry sword now unsheathed, its point aimed right at the face of his enemy.

Kerry rushed in slashing Xs in the air, and the Koklanare, brandishing a weapon half that of Kerry's army sword and with a distinct curve, did his best to fend off the attack. As the sky burned a yellow-red from dynamite, fire, cannons and bullets, as the roar of angry men rolled across the grounds, with the moans of dying souls, with the fatal bellows of doomed horses surrounding them, Kerry's and the foreign enemy parried, dodged and thrusted, dueling for life and death.

Then Kerry's sword struck the forearm of the Koklanare. Its edge cut a deep wound to the bone, yet the man still held his weapon! Kerry's return backhand slash ripped across the face and down to hit the weapon arm yet again. This time, the curved sword fell, and the Afghan stutter-stepped back. With an animal-like cry, Kerry stepped forward and drove the blade straight into the man's chest, twisted it, pumped it, and pulled it back. "To your hell with you!" he shouted. The man dropped to his knees in shock. Kerry dashed to his pistol, picked it up and shot the man in the head.

His rifle? Gasping for breath, Kerry searched around as he motioned for his horse, "Come Clapper. Come." There on the ground near the road lay his long gun. Somehow, he'd lost it when he first saw the Afghan, as if he'd tossed it away to draw his pistol, since he couldn't maneuver the rifle into position? He slung the weapon to his shoulder, swearing never to do such a damnable fool thing again!

"Oh boy," Kerry sighed. "Oh boy." Clapper had a single slash across his chest. Kerry placed a hand over it and felt for his horse, but there was nothing he could do in the middle of this battlefield. He mounted the magnificent gelding and prodded him northward with his pistol up and at the ready. He knew another crazed enemy could appear at close quarters from behind any tent along the way. Soon he spotted more Brits and Indians headed in the same direction. He called out and joined them. They traversed a jagged path toward the village under the protection of an expert line of fire killing any pursuers who dared follow them.

Lydia dared to peek out a hallway fort window. She was not prepared for the chaos before her. A nightmare of destruction on a hellish red landscape met her gaze. The smell of blood and burned human flesh assaulted her. She grabbed at the hem of her calico dress and held it over her nose and mouth. Below, the desperate tribesmen hauled guns and supplies as they poured into the courtyard gates on foot. Some found horses and camels to ride on. Sergeant Valentino was down among them barking orders. She guessed some two hundred were present awaiting his orders. Another American traitor stood commanding them to climb the stone stairs and take positions along the walkways at the top of the walls and by the windows cut into the walls.

Boom! Boom! Boom! The three cannons roared on the floor above, the sudden sharp smell of gunpowder filled the air as dust dropped on Lydia from the reverberations. Amy, who stood quivering next to her, shrieked and dropped to one knee, as though about to cry or faint.

"Child?" she asked Amy. "Child! Do you know of any other way out of here?"

"No I don't," she said. "Just through the main gate. "If there is a back door or gate, I have never seen it."

"Then I am afraid we are trapped here, and we must help clear the gate."

"Whatever can we do?"

"Whatever…." then the pounding sounds of the machine guns cut loose. She knelt near Amy's face. "We are going to have to stop those cannons and machine guns from above."

"That would take an army," the girl said.

"I am an Army wife, and that will have to do," Lydia said with steadfast resolve. "Do you know how to get up there?"

"Yes, I do, ma'am."

George Hall tumbled over in a cloud of dust and rocks. One moment he was standing on the road back at the pass and the next he was blown upside down, picked up and tossed in a blast of fire-hot air.

"What the bloody…" he mumbled and started feeling of himself. Wounded? All together? He had to spit out a small, dry pebble from his mouth! His pistol was still tucked in his pants. All together!

Another cannon round struck between him and the mountain wall. Hall scampered up the road. It was clear he'd chosen the worst place to watch the battle, right where the cannonballs were dropping short of the machine-gun teams. In a panicked moment, he found himself at the border of the tent city. Next, the loud reports of machine-gun fire peppered ahead, and he cut right into the burning tents.

"How can I get back?" he whispered, looking at the safety of the pass behind him, the security of men and the camel teams preparing their secondary charge.

"Mother of God!" came a man's inhuman cry behind him.

Hall turned and with trepidation, tiptoed to his left to see the source. It was horrible. A Koklanare stood over a downed Indian soldier. He had recovered the sepoy's lance and was sticking him with it. But not deeply. He was torturing the soldier. Prodding him. Poking him. Raking the spear across his chest and stomach.

"See here!" George Hall declared impulsively. "Stop that mess, now!"

The sepoy cried out again, being now so low, he was whining like a pitiful animal. The tribesman laughed and spun the spear tip, partially burying it in his stomach.

Now Hall was outraged and pitched forward at a dead run, yanking out his revolver.

"I say, stop that!" Hall roared. The Koklanare finally heard him and looked up. It was the smile on his face that really did Hall in. When he saw that smile, he shot him right in the chest. The man stepped back, his smile evaporating. Hall shot again, and the tribesman fell. The Brit ran to the sepoy, who struggled for breath and inspected the sobbing mess.

"Oh, my dear fellow," Hall said, his eyes welling up at the sight of the gutted Indian. "What? What shall I do with you?" The man was disemboweled, his intestines cut and splayed. An eye gone. Half his scalp carved back. Blood pumped and streamed from him like a punctured barrel with twenty holes.

"Aaagghhh!" howled a voice from behind.

Hall turned to see another attacker, brandishing a sword, closing in fast, his gown flapping and furling like a flag in slow motion. In fact, it seemed time slowed down for George Hall, almost stood still. In these timeless seconds, Hall's mind flashed the faces of his English friends killed when Latissimo first arrived, and he again saw the mad dogs let loose on the men in the courtyard. He felt all the anguish of the last two months.

Hall dropped to one knee and shot the charging man. The round caught him at the base of his throat, and he twisted away, dropping the edged weapon, clutching his neck. But, from sheer momentum or otherwise, this killer still stumbled forward.

Hall stood and instinctively fired again. The man, his face contorted, eyes like a hypnotized monster, still closed in. Hall thrust his left arm out straight, hand open, catching the man at his throat. Hall fired yet again. He felt the force of the pistol discharge hit the man and blow back on his chest, flapping his shirt and even blasting up his nose. The tribesman's feet left the ground. He fell back, writhing.

Hall's stomach was now afire, but from rage, not like the shredded stomach of his ally lying before him, whose very life increasingly abandoned his body with each painful heartbeat.

"Kill me," the sepoy groaned.

Hall looked down at the nametag on his uniform. It read, "Lieutenant Satin."

"May…may your God bless you, Mr. Satin." Without hesitation, Hall lifted the pistol and shot the eviscerated soldier in the head. Then he set about methodically gathering up the man's weapons and ammunition scattered on the grounds.

A hundred yards behind him the camel troops now made their charge. As Hall reloaded his revolver, he heard the camels first—their bleated howls and grunting—hundreds of them. What a powerful sight to see, these giant creatures rolling forward like fierce and alien monsters, these armed men atop them, gun barrels forward, with a countenance of anger, of revenge…of courage. Hall felt all those things.

Hall held the sepoy's rifle in one hand, raised it up high, and cheered the charge as they came, as they enveloped him, and as they passed. They blasted past him in a sweaty heat, almost as intense as the cannon blasts that rippled over him, rattling his lungs moments earlier. The machine gun wagons followed. And George Hall followed.

Mesha's toes clung to the small, stony ledge on the safe side of the pass rock wall. She lifted Gunther's binoculars to her eyes and searched the human madness for her master. How was he? Where was he? There! She saw Gunther safe behind the south side of the buildings. She could see his big white hat.

"He is still alive," she told her monkey, who cowered at her feet, shivering with fright from the explosions. Then she lost sight of Gunther, as it seemed he'd charged back into the tent city. Her gut instincts soured. She scaled down from the ledges, her furry sidekick close at her heels

"Come on," she told her monkey, as they ran to the wagons. She opened a steamer, grabbed one of Gunther's pistols and a box of bullets from his war chest. She grabbed a handful of white bandages and shoved them inside her blouse.

"Come here, coooommme here little one," she said to her pet, kneeling down. The monkey raced to her arm and clutched it.

"Good. It's good." She grabbed his red jacket by the back and set the creature into the wagon bed. With a quick snap, she clipped a leash to the monkey's collar. This caused the simian to go wild.

"I will be back. I will be back," she assured him. She knew the monkey would immediately start gnawing on the leather leash, but it would take at least three hours for him to gnash his way through it.

"Momma will come back, baby," she said with utter confidence. She started a slow run to the battlefield.

"What's goin' on?" Rosie asked Gildy.

Gildy and the scouts paced the ledge, swearing one second and cheering the next.

"They got 'em some machine guns, Rosie," a scout said. "They started a shootin' at us when we got near the village. And they walked the cannon fire in on the road, whenst' they figured they couldn't hit our machine gun teams. Our boys done split up and are on both sides of the main street now, protected by the buildings."

"And they's sittin' ducks if they don't pull a plan out they ass," another woeful scout said. "And yonder, some of the boys that jumped off the road? They's a fightin' fer their lives in among the tents with those camel cowboys. Gunther and some boys routed out some of them and chased 'em down."

"Look there," Gildy pointed nearby. "Our camel soldiers are moving through the tent campgrounds. The machine-gun teams are down and gettin' on the wagons to move in closer with them. I hope they hurry. They can't take the main road. They'll have to sneak through the tents.

"Lordy! Anybody we know dead yet?" Rosie asked.

"Don't know. Lots of 'em dead out there."

26
What the Hell?

"What in hell is going on?" Gunther shouted to a group of Brits as he vaulted off his horse.

"A charge, Major," one said.

"A bloody forlorn charge," added another solemnly.

"Forlorn?" Gunther mumbled. "Forlorn charge!" Gunther realized what was afoot. In a desperate moment in battle, a cadre will ask a young officer or sergeant to charge into hell itself. The officer is not from a privileged or pedigreed background, but rather one from the common ranks. If the man wished to advance in both rank and prestige, he volunteered himself and his men for a doomsday mission. If successful, his career was assured. The forlorn tradition was centuries old, and these forlorn were about to gallop right into the barrels of machine guns and cannons of Fort Tartan.

Gunther bolted through the milling infantry, pushing, bounding and bouncing off the backs and shoulders of the men to get his hands on the young British commander just ahead. But the lancer charge slowly began at a walk as the horses and riders filled in behind the leader.

Perryweather was not on horseback but rather wandered afoot, tailed by his aides, all of them jogging away from the front lines of British and Indian Lancers astride their horses. Perryweather and his lieutenants even saluted the riders. Gunther dashed right past them heading for the lead lieutenant.

"Nooo!" shouted Gunther. It was apparent the Lancers were about to spur on and gather speed.

"Into the breach!" the forlorn lieutenant shouted.

Gunther growled, "Breach?" Then declared angrily, "There is no breach you damn fool! Wait! Wait!"

The lead officers turned the corner, swords out and pointed forward. In an instant the machine guns would take their turn in the firing cycle, and they would surely drop their sights to the main street and eviscerate these young Lancers.

Gunther was at a full run now, closing in on the commander's horse. He lunged out and grabbed the halter. He was dragged a foot or two but dug his heels into the rock and dirt road and yanked the horse's bridle at the mouth hard to the side. The animal bucked and whinnied, its front feet clopping in giant steps to counteract the sudden turn.

No! You damn fool!" Gunther declared to the rider, now with both hands on the halter, wrestling the beast to a stop.

"What do you want, sir?" The lieutenant announced in anger. The entire lancer charge came to a confused, cluttered, bucking halt behind them.

"Get back. Get back!" Gunther ordered. "There is a better way to do this!"

"I do not take my orders—" and suddenly, heavy, thick, machine-gun fire tore up the road in front of them, the gun teams in the tower were walking their rounds upon them "—from you." But the commander lost his spunk for his last two words of complaint.

The lieutenant wheeled his horse in the direction Gunther pulled him, and the entire charge turned with them, dashing back for the cover of the buildings, seconds before the enemy fire would have drilled them down. Less forlorn, a sense of relief was obvious among the enlisted riders in the rear.

Aghast, Perryweather watched as Gunther jogged beside the returning riders.

"What in…." Perryweather started, but Gunther's rage interrupted him.

"You stupid, stupid son of bitch! Those men would all be killed!"

"Well…not all of them!" Perryweather answered impulsively,

immediately unhappy with his response, but he continued, "How else can we get to the fort?"

Gunther ignored him and passed him by. "Grimsley!" he shouted for his sergeant major. "The dynamite!" He approached the back wall, extracted his Bowie knife, dropped to a knee, and stabbed the building.

"He's gone bloody mad!" Perryweather declared.

Gunther drilled, chipped, and hacked into the clay and-stone masonry.

Sergeant Grimsley dismounted his camel with his canvas satchel in hand, as did twenty of his camel riders. Grimsley ran to Gunther and opened the satchel for him. The Texan removed four sticks of dynamite and shoved them into the new hole.

All the men afoot, all the men on horses and the men with camels retreated briskly as Gunther lit a long match and touched off the twisted fuse on the sticks. Lieutenant Kerry rode up, fresh from the skirmishes in the tent city, but his eyes widened, and he cut his horse to the left to avoid any blast.

"Sweet Butterball Jesus, look out!" an American cried out, ducking his head.

The blast shook the lungs of everyone nearby. Debris flew. An Indian horse reared, and a sepoy soldier toppled off. When the dust cleared, a giant hole appeared in the wall.

"We are gonna blow a hole through the center of all these buildings, all the way across town, and get within twenty feet of the fort wall, all under protective cover." The idea immediately caught hold.

"Start taking the walls down boys. All the foot soldiers will follow," Gunther ordered his demolition men to the task.

"How in bloody hell will we get into the fort?" A British soldier asked.

"When we get near the fort, we'll be close to the gates and try to blow them."

Gunther spotted Lieutenant Kerry and waved him over. "Kerry! You get this whole operation going across the street." He turned back to the men and continued, "As we get halfway, get some riflemen on the rooftops and turn them loose on the fort windows and the tower. Watch the alleyways down here. Watch out. These sons of bitches are already congregating in the alleys.

"You and you," Gunther said to several sergeants. "Take a line of men down the outside walls, and see what you can do. See how far you can go. You and your men go with Kerry. You all stay on this side."

Gunther studied the force. Hundreds of men, at least three hundred feet deep, tried to stay behind the cover of the buildings. "They may turn the cannons on the buildings," he advised, "when they figure out what we're doing. So we have to work fast. We need to get as many men safely up the street and by the fort as possible."

It was clear that Perryweather had lost complete control of this Army, as American, Brit and Indian hung on Gunther's every word.

Gunther looked through the crowd, "Now, where are my dynamite, bow and arrow boys?"

Lieutenant Kerry guided his camel team of explosives experts back deep into the tent city and turned it facing east, calling a halt at the roadway.

"Line up!" Kerry ordered, and the men and their animals, still out of easy sight of the tower, worked into position bordering the road.

"Prepare!" he warned.

Kerry's plan? In a break in enemy fire, they would charge across the open road all at once. When the machine-gun fire ceased, before the cannons again erupted the night air, Kerry raced his whole crew in a mad dash across the main road to get to the other side and into the other tribe's tent city and to the east side of the village buildings.

"Go! Come on. Come on," he shouted, lingering back as if to coax or even push the last men, camels and horses across the road.

A few men yelled with satisfaction and glee as they crossed, but some were instantly ambushed! Small bands of tribesmen, afoot and angry, rushed in on them, blasting away with their bolt-action rifles.

"Fire!" Kerry commanded. "Fire!" And his men raised their rifles and fired at the small ambush, but shooting from the back of a moving horse, even worse from a moving camel, offered little target control, and the first barrage completely missed. At the very least, this line of red-blasting gunfire caused the enemy to flinch. Some of them even dove headlong onto the ground.

British officers on the west side had shadowed the Americans' progress south and were well on their way to offer support. A British lancer unit virtually crashed into the flank of this tribal ambush, shooting and stabbing the Afghans down in a wave of destruction.

"Come on, Yanks! This way!" The British lieutenant said, when the raiders were dispatched or routed.

Kerry and his team followed the Lancers all the way to the cover of the buildings. He leaped from his horse and pointed at the south wall.

"Dismount and blow big holes in the walls, men!" Kerry ordered. "Come on, come on, come on, come on! We are tunneling our way to the fort!"

The tower door hung partially open, and Lydia peeked inside. Eight men feverishly worked three cannons, and another six men labored in front of the cannons, manhandling three machine guns. Lydia waved Amy to her side and, once she passed the door, pushed her into a hallway corner. Amy dropped to one knee and covered her ears as the three cannons fired, the concussions flinging the door open and back.

Lydia crept back to the doorway for another peek. The machine guns cycled through their turn as the cannons were reloaded. She saw three cannons, and she recognized that two fired by a trigger lever and one by fire and fuse. Once the cannons were charged, the cannoneers shouted to the machine gunners to clear out of the way. They dove and covered their ears. The fuse team touched off their fuse, and Lydia watched the red flame eat up the fuse. She raised her pistol, bracing the barrel against the door. The instant the cannons fired, Lydia fired her pistol. She shot the closest man in the back of the head. Her pistol report was completely buried inside the blast. She jerked back behind the door and held the pistol in two hands, intent on killing anyone who appeared to look into the hall. But it was apparent from the English and Afghan voices, the workers assumed a lucky enemy bullet drove into the tower and caught one of their men.

The firing resumed. A cycle of machine guns, of cannons and then of machine guns again. When the cannons blew again, Lydia ripped open the skull of another cannoneer with a revolver round.

"A sniper!" she heard an American declare. "There must be a sniper."

"Stay low!" another said.

"Allah mayer jo a hola!" an Afghan shouted, obviously cursing. Then in broken English he continued to the gunners, "Jo….find dis riflemans. Ju shoot 'em him!"

With the camels well past him, George Hall jogged among the machine-gun wagons as they weaved north through the encampments. When he arrived south of the village buildings, he saw a perimeter of men, rifles raised and at the ready, protecting the rear and the hundreds of soldiers and fresh camel troops.

Hall watched these soldiers, now afoot, pour into a huge gaping hole in a wall of the first building. It was obvious that the troops were making their way to the fort's walls through the inside of the village buildings, which shielded them from enemy fire. Explosions rocked across the road. Hall turned to see Lieutenant Kerry executing the same plan to the east side.

He spied the wagon gun team leaders conferring with a U.S. sergeant. Then they darted back to their wagons and jumped aboard. Hall ran for them, catching up to the nearest one.

"Where are you chaps going?" Hall asked as he closed in on a team.

"Some of the boys is' going across the road," the team sergeant said. "Some staying here on this side. Runnin' up the far side of the village. Clean out the far side of the village. Clean out the alley-ways. See what we can shoot at the fort up yonder. Major Gun-ther's orders. He wants us to draw a little gunfire, too, so's they can burrow up to the fort."

"Can I help?"

"You can climb aboard and get some bullet belts ready, or something. Ain't a preacher are ya, limey?" the sergeant asked as he sat behind the big gun.

"No."

"Saints be praised, we need one. Well, come on and climb aboard."

Hall threw a leg up and flipped into the back. The wagon took off as the gun team made the gun ready. Hall watched them feed in a belt of ammunition from an open, square metal can. He watched as the triggerman charged up the weapon.

"My name is Wilson Brendle Russell," the belt feeder said. "They's call me Pretentious, for reasons obvious once ya get to know me."

"George Hall. Nice to meet you, Mr. Pretentious," the Brit said, surprised he could actually find himself half-smiling.

The sergeant turned to Hall and said, "Mr. Hall, we'll take care of the front of this gun. We'd be much obliged if you will shoot anyone else right between the eyes that you see wearing bed-clothes, front, side or back, with that rifle of yours."

"Then…bedclothes-wearers be damned, sergeant!" Hall said with a nod and lifted his rifle. A round was in the chamber. The wagon, one of six, took off for the corner of the building. Hall did not feel the fear he thought he would. This was a different kind of fear, one mixed with a bizarre exhilaration. It was a fear that al-lowed him to shoot at people in "bedclothes." He wasn't keeping score, but he realized then he had already killed two of them.

Mesha lifted her long dress with her left hand and clutched the big revolver in her right. She passed several Afghans, alone and in groups, but none paid her any attention as she could have passed for any tribal camp follower. She'd lived a tough life, but had never seen the carnage of this nightmare.

Tents blazed. Bodies burned. Nothing equaled the smell of human flesh afire. Even the smoke appeared a reddish-pink. She remembered the smell and heat from times when her friends walked into the funeral fire of their dead masters, as was their ritualistic fate. Gunther saved her from the fate of a slave dog. Gunther was a stranger, then. A man from another world. A man in a white hat. He didn't know her. Yet, he looked at her face and saved her. This Gunther was a special man. A good man, delivered from across the world by her Hindi gods to save her. She would help him. She would go to him.

All about her, bodies rolled and writhed, or lay dead still. She leapt and tiptoed about them, even stepping on them if she had to. She fell to the ground as a cannonball exploded too close, rocking her brains as if she were punched. She started to crawl.

"They are all split up," Gildy informed. "Half of 'em are on the west side and half are on the east side. They are blowing holes in the walls and running in."

"Holes in the walls?" Rosie asked.

"Running in the holes and moving up the street to the fort under the cover of the buildings."

"That's Gunther's idea, huh? What's that other shootin'?"

"The machine-gun wagons are running up the far sides of the village. And foot soldiers are moving with them."

"And, they's still tribesmen in the campgrounds. We're shootin' at them as they pop up," a scout added.

"Well, hell man, whose winning?" Rosie wanted to know.

"I still see shitloads of Afghanis running through their campgrounds," Gildy said. "And even more pourin' into the fort. There are packs of them walking the village. Like hunters. And they have men shooting from walkways atop the fort and from windows in the walls. Rosie, I can't tell who's a winning yet. We've killed a slew of 'em, but there's still thousands of them left."

"As the Lord is my Shepherd," Rosie declared, "we is in a fine mess."

27
The Smoke Wagon

Hall raised his rifle to aim at an approaching alleyway and at any possible hidden enemies, but one of the two wagon drivers hollered, "Heeyah!" The pair of horses bolted into a gallop.

The wagon almost doubled its speed and with it a series of jarring bumps so severe the short, pine panel walls rattled. Hall's rifle pointed to heaven and he tumbled over from his kneeling position. Gunther slid a foot on his back, and the top of his head rammed the back of the wall. "Jumpen' Jehoshaphat!" Pretentious cried out to the driver. "This ain't the Kentucky Derby. We got men trying to shoot steady back here!" Hall looked up to see that Pretentious had been tossed from his short stool, but he still managed to lean forward and guide the bullet belt into the machine gun as the gunner fired bursts.

"They're shootin' at us." The driver shouted the complaint over his shoulder.

The gun team wagons were all at a full gallop now and cutting a wide berth around the west end of the village. Some foot soldiers followed as best they could, stopping to make rifle shots at the Koklanare and tribesmen they could see dashing about.

As they approached a large avenue about mid-village, they all spotted a small army aiming at them. Hall fired into the group as their machine gunner spun the big gun on its three-legged pivot their direction.

"There must be a hundred or more!" Pretentious cried out. A rifle shot cracked through the air and tore open his throat. Hall watched him gag and tumble over the side. There one second.

Gone forever.

"Hall, get up here," the gunner shouted.

George Hall crawled to the side of the machine. "Feed this belt. Feed it man, or we are deader than Pretentious."

More enemy rifle rounds zipped and hummed through the air. One cracked into the wood-framed top of the wagon. Their wagon, along with the others, tottered over the terrain, such easy targets, but any more speed would destroy their aim.

Hall mimicked what he saw Pretentious do. He grabbed the oily belt of bullets and hand fed the run into the side of the gun. Inches from the heavy weapon, the pressure and sound destroyed Hall's hearing, and his eyes streamed with tears. The gunner pounded the general area of the enemy, wrestling to hold the piece upright over every bump and crevice the wagon wheels hit. Hall felt he might soon bounce right off the transport.

The sides of the wagon took fire, beating the wood like pounding hammers. A round or two pierced and splintered the right wall and smacked into the left wall.

A bullet caught the kneecap of the gunner. White bone and blood splashed across Hall's shoulder and neck. Hall thought they were through for sure, but when he dared look up at the man, the gunner sat like a statue, face stern, eyes wide, fingers firing the machine gun as if the shot pained him less than a bee sting. His lips rolled in silent curses.

The other gun team wagons must have witnessed this plight. They swarmed in at angles to blast the side street cluttered with tribesmen. Then Hall saw American soldiers from the rooftop leaning over the edge to shoot down into the group. The entire enemy group fell in a rainstorm of bullets in less than a minute of superior firepower from multiple angles.

The wagon came to a stop flush beside a building wall. The two drivers raised their rifles, ready to shoot any tribesman who might come their way.

"Watch our backside!" The gunner called to a driver. One stood and faced the rear at rifle ready. The gunner turned to Hall. Hall flicked off a small piece of knee bone stuck to his cheek in a spot of blood.

"You did good, George Hall," he said, clutching his leg. He handed Hall his knife. Hall took the knife and knew immediately to cut a piece from the rolled wagon canvas in the bed. With a long strip of the canvas, he wrapped the piece around the gunner's leg and tied it off, just as the wagon jolted and its rear right side lifted off the ground.

"We got us a horse down!" The driver announced as Hall heard the animal bellow. The remaining horse also cried out and stutter-stepped to side, towing the off-balance wagon sideways.

"Cut him loose," the gunner ordered as Hall worked bandaging the leg. The gunner took out his pistol and looked south. He mumbled, "Lost a horse. Lost ol' Pretentious. Lost a knee. I'd say we are through fer the day."

"I'd say so, too, sir," Hall agreed, and he tugged the knot tight. "You need medical attention ol' chap."

"Feelin'…not so…" and the gunner fainted. The big revolver fell on Hall's back and dropped on the floorboards. Hall lunged forward to catch him and cushion the descent.

Bam! A driver shot the wounded horse with a rifle as the second driver unbuckled the reins.

"We need outta here!" one said.

"Either of you know how to work this machine gun?" Hall asked.

"Nope. We is just supply team drivers."

"Ain't never seen one of them monsters before…till this trip." The other said while climbing back into his front seat.

"Well then, can just one of you run the horse and one of you feed this ammo belt? In case we need to defend ourselves on the route back? It's not hard at all. I think I can shoot this thing if we need to. We need to get this brave man to the medical hospital at camp."

"Sho nuf!" one said, throwing a leg over the sideboard. "We've done our damn part today," he said as he sat on the gun feeder's stool.

"Maybe we can swing by and pick up poor ol' Pretentious?" the driver asked as he worked the reins on the remaining horse. "We surely don't want the enemy to find him out here and defecate 'im."

"Yes…desecrate him," Hall mumbled as he took the gunner's seat.

"Ah yeah, and that, too," the driver said.

28
Flaming Arrows

Gunther and a team of men low-crawled across the flat rooftop, their movement covered by the small wall around the building edge. These roofs were made for prayer. The eastern sides were holy spaces for storing blankets and religious icons. They stopped near the short wall.

"There's your target," Gunther told his two bowmen, Lieutenants Day and O'Conner. Their support teams and trained shooters crouched behind them. The Texan pointed at the large bay window cut in the stone fort tower from which the cannon and machine-gun fire originated. "Can you reach it from here?"

"With a few pulls of the bow, sir," O'Conner answered, "we can walk an arrow or two into it…eventually."

"E…ventually?" Gunther repeated.

Day looked at O'Conner as if his aspirations were crazy. Gunther did not find this encouraging. Just then, buildings connected under them shook as the demolition teams below blew their way further uptown. Just ahead of them, an entire roof collapsed with one big bang, taking two chimneys with it. Gunther did not find that encouraging either.

"While some of you fire at the tower, get some of your men to lob some dynamite arrows over the wall and into the courtyards." Gunther waved the dust and smoke from his face.

"Yes, sir," Day said.

"Don't stay here too long as they will surely spot you… eventually. Move up when you can. There will be some rooftops intact you can use as we progress. I hope."

"Yes, sir," O'Conner said as their team prepared the explosive arrows for launching.

Smoking arrows flew from the rooftops on the east side of the village.

"Looks like our brothers-in-arms across town are under way," Day said.

"After enough tribesmen get into the fort," Gunther continued, "they may shut the gates. When we get close, I want you to look for my signal and start firing on the gates."

"They are very thick, Major!" O'Conner said.

"I know," Gunther shouted over a roar. "All these men below are counting on you."

Gunther lingered to see the first missile airborne. Lieutenant Day picked up his bow and strung a notched arrow fitted with a stick of dynamite. A sergeant lit the fuse, and Day unleashed the aerial bomb. It flew far, hit the tower wall, and then dropped into the courtyard. They saw a flash of yellow, heard the muffled explosion, even some screams.

"Well," Gunther surmised," that got somebody."

O'Conner fired his arrow. This smoking arrow actually stuck in the clay mortar of the tower between the stone blocks. The blast showered rock and stone down into the courtyard, but did little damage to the structure.

"Get some inside that tower window!" Gunther demanded, and he low-crawled away to a roof hatch, opened it, and dropped inside.

To the east row of village buildings, Kerry supervised the advance as the explosives teams laid their work on interior wall after wall. With each lit fuse, the men ran back into the rubble and awaited the next blast.

"Damn British engineering!" A demo man cursed aloud.

"Hold thy tongue, you knave!" a Brit demolitions soldier said with a smile. He turned to Kerry. "Most of these Main Street edifices were designed by us forty years ago. Stout, sound and modern, I'd say. Given the day. Our lads cooked up the mortar and the locals, under our supervision, cut the stone from the hills by our camp."

A planted bomb sizzled off and rocked the air.

"Will we get through all of them?" Kerry asked.

"We never build anything we can't blow up in the end!"

"Even the fort?" Kerry asked.

"Now, mate, not too sure we have enough explosives to do that bloody fort in."

This time, the stone and mortar wall blew a clean, almost round breach, some ten feet high and fifteen feet wide. It was an outside wall that revealed a wide alleyway. The men let out a cheer with this progress, as Kerry waved the group onward.

"Secure the alley!" Kerry shouted.

Rifle fire! Ten or more Afghans jumped into view, howling for revenge and shooting wildly into the room. Kerry dropped to a knee and pulled his pistol, his other men lifted their rifles, firing at the enemy from hip high. The exchange took seconds, and men fell on both sides. But, as soon as a tribesman crumpled, three more appeared in the opening. The allies inched backward, shooting and feeling their way back to the hole in the wall behind them.

Kerry dove shoulder-first into a clutter of broken stone and wooden furniture, his revolver empty. He reached for the bullets in his belt loop, but a sepoy troop in the next room caught his eye. This Indian stared at a burning fuse on a red stick of dynamite, his mouth counting seconds.

"Get down!" the ordinance sergeant ordered, flipping the stick into the swarm of killers in the alley. One Koklanare dropped his rifle and, with both hands high, leapt to catch the twirling bomb, hoping to pitch it back to its igniter. Eyes wide, his jaw dropped with effort. He vaulted for a solid grab on the bomb, caught it, and tossed it back. But the fuse was not long enough to complete his plan. The blast ripped the man into a red and yellow mist and shreds right before Kerry's eyes. He simply…disappeared. It blew the others near him down like lifeless rag dolls. One Koklanare splashed and melted into the wall across the alley. The beam in the wall above the hole cracked, and the ceiling almost collapsed, crunching down about two feet into a very precarious support position.

The men left in the alley moaned. Some screamed. Kerry continued to reload. His soldiers, shell-shocked from the close blast, slowly stood, barrels raised, bayonets fixed. Then the welcome sound of Maxim machine-gun fire shook the ground. Ours! It broke the air, and automatic fire pounded across the alley, pelting rounds into the walls, the ground and the enemy. There were still more Afghans on either side of the hole. And then there were none. The gun wagon teams were doing their jobs of sweeping the alleyways of the enemy.

"The next wall!" Kerry ordered, as he closed the cylinder on his loaded Smith. He thought of the man diving to catch the dynamite. Such valor. Would one of his own do such a thing?

"They are moving north!" Gildy reported. "They are blowing the walls and shooting from the rooftops. Gunther's got our dynamite boys on the roof, on both sides of the street shooting arrows at the tower and into the fort. The gun wagons and foot troops are flanking both sides of the village, doing their best to clean out the rats."

"Anybody we know dead yet?" Rosie asked again.

"Not that I can tell. But there sure are a lot bodies out there."

"What are the Lancers doing?" Rosie asked.

"Getting ready to charge, I 'spect."

"Charge on what?"

"The fort," Gildy said. "Soon as they blow the guns in that tower, Perryweather will probably charge the Lancers."

"Well are the dang gates still open?"

"So far they is," another scout replied. "They's people be still running in. I reckon if they shut them gates, we is screwed like a checkmate."

"Either way, we best be thinkin' about breakin' down our position up here and getting down to the camp. We're going to need to escape this pass in a hurry." Gildy crouched by Rosie. "Fit to travel, mi amigo?"

"Nope."

"That ain't the right answer."

"You ain't gettin' the right answer. Ask again and see what ya get." Rosie moaned, turning his head away.

"Rosie, you are going to have to sit yer horse!"

"Gildy, I can't even strike a dry match."

The other scouts were packing their sparse camp supplies in haste.

"Leave me," Rosie said. "I was dead when that land crab monster stung me anyway. Leave me. Leave that whiskey."

"Ohhhhh hell," Gildy groaned.

29
The Tower

The fuse on the old canon fumed. It blew. Lydia killed her third man. The sound of her shot to the back of his head was buried inside the blast. She saw the Afghan's head flip forward as she pulled back away from the door. She could hear the men argue in English and broken English as she backed away to crouch beside Amy, her pistol aimed at the ready.

"You will shoot dis sniper," one roared.

"We do not see a sniper," an angry American voice shouted back. "Everyone is shooting at us."

"Someone of them is doing very good!" an Afghan declared in broken English.

A shadow fell on the wall across from the doorway. Lydia estimated where a man would appear if one should step into the hall from the room. She gritted her teeth and narrowed her eyes.

The shadow grew. A man appeared. He was one of Latissimo's sergeants. His arms were down, his hands weaponless, as he inspected the far side of the hall. When he looked behind the door, his eyes locked on Lydia's. They knew each other. His jaw dropped.

"Ly—"

Bang. She shot him dead center in the chest. The man's expression displayed his shock. He stumbled back and fell on his side. Lydia knew her ruse was over and others in the tower gun room would soon come to investigate this. She had two rounds left in her gun, twelve more in the pocket of her dress, and no time to reload.

Two more men appeared, this time armed with rifles. They looked down the hall at the moaning sergeant. They turned and saw Lydia. They raised their weapons…

Bullets banged into the wall before them and cracked through the air just over their heads. Lieutenant Day, prone on the rooftop, sucked in a deep breath, sat up, and pulled back on the great bow. A private leaned over and lit the fuse on the arrow, and Day released the bow. A stick of dynamite tied to an arrow shaft destroys the perfect path of a perfect arrow from a perfect bow fired from a perfect eye, and most of his life Day's aim was usually perfect. But these explosive arrows were like throwing dice. Bull's-eyes were as rare as lucky sevens.

"Come on," Day muttered watching his arrow spin and loose trajectory. "Come on. Come on...."

The arrow path widened in a small spiral and leaned slightly to the left. A line of tribesmen appeared on the fort, all with rifles seemingly aimed right at him.

"Duck!" Day shouted, and his cheek crushed against the pebble and stone roof. He only heard his dynamite boom, but this time it was more muffled than the others. And not the muffled sound of ones prior that fell into the courtyard.

"It went in, sir," a private said, daring to peek over the wall.

"In?" Day repeated.

"In the tower window, sir. She went in, and it blew."

Day peeked up. The cannons and the machine guns were silent. There was some faint smoke emanating from the window.

"Yerrsirree, Bob!" Day hollered.

The blast from inside the gunroom was horrendous, one hundred times more than a cannon being fired. It shot intense pain down Lydia's ear canals straight to her brain and reduced all sound around her to an unintelligibly muffled hum.

The blast lifted and slammed the two men with rifles into the hallway wall, where they seemed to melt into their shadows, disintegrate into a bath of red and yellow. It looked to Lydia as if a giant ocean wave had smashed into them. She saw one of their arms from the elbow down simply leave the upper arm. It flipped once, hit the wall, and tumbled away, the hand still opening and closing. The rifles spun like propellers and bashed against the wall.

Lydia slowly stood, then turned to help Amy.

"Are you okay?" she asked the girl.

Amy mumbled. Her mouth moved. Lydia felt as if she had handkerchiefs stuffed in her ears. "I can't hear you, Amy, but come on!"

30
The Gates

Dawn broke red over the valley. Gunther lay on the roof amid some thirty of his men firing rifle rounds at the tribesmen as they popped up on their balconies to shoot over the fort wall. He estimated a line of at least two hundred shooters. Some remained up until their Khyber rifles ran empty, others fired a shot or two and dropped behind the cover of the fort wall. He need only aim his Mexican rifle at a single space where one once stood and, in seconds, this enemy would quickly stand up to shoot again. Another fifty or so fired at them from open portals in the fort walls. Most of their fire was directed at the gun wagons and foot soldiers they could see on each side of the village, not at Gunther's small rooftop troupe.

Smoke continued to pour from the open gun turret of the tower. Day's brilliantly aimed dynamite arrow had set the interior on fire as well as killing the cannon and machine gun crews.

"Charge now, Perryweather," Gunther mumbled, "before they man those guns again." But, another problem unfolded before him. He first heard, then saw, the main wooden gates closing.

"Down there!" Gunther shouted pointing toward the gates. He scrambled to the northwest corner of the roof, his closest riflemen in tow. "They are shutting the gates!"

Gunther rained fire into the men he could barely see who tried to push the gates closed. His men followed at a low run and blasted away. The first barrage dropped at least eight tribesmen, but more dashed forward to take their place. The closed gates meant Afghans fighting on the streets would have no escape.

"Charge, Perryweather!" Gunther begged aloud to no one. But a charge would be futile as a dash up main street would never arrive in time to slip inside the closing gates. Tribesmen pushed and pulled courageously under the heavy fire until the gate doors met, set, and were locked from inside.

"They beat us, boys," Gunther said, admiring the men who braced the doors against their onslaught. He waved at his bowmen on a nearby rooftop. He caught their attention and pointed a pumping finger at the front gates. Day acknowledged with a thumbs up. The wooden doors were thick and full of iron beams. It would take a lot of dynamite arrows to tear that up.

Rifle fire beat across the roof! Their rooftop attack on the gate guards drew the attention of all the enemy shooters on the wall. Gunther and all his men fired back while low crawling for their short rooftop wall of cover.

A flaming arrow flew overhead and stuck on the front gate. Gunther peeked to watch as the dynamite blew, cutting out just a small, thin piece from the already pockmarked gate.

"Oh, damn," he said rolling on his back and shoving rounds into his long gun. "It is going to take a whole lot of that." But then, his eyes cast across the smoking gun tower. Movement. He squinted for a closer look. In the open bay window, with smoke billowing from behind, stood Lydia Latissimo, leaning over and surveying the landscape like a tourist at Buckingham Palace.

"Lydia?" Gunther whispered in astonishment with a half-smile. Then, a blonde-haired, young woman appeared next to her, timid in pose and expression, and looked out.

"Who in hell?" It was obvious that Lydia barked some commands at the scared girl.

"Get that man out of the way," Lydia told Amy.

Amy grabbed a leg and started tugging, but much too slowly. Lydia dashed to her side and together they both dragged the bleeding carcass away. Then Lydia hauled a machine gun to the left wall.

"Come here now and push." The two women then rolled a

cannon as far to the window's ledge as possible. Then Lydia got behind the rear, squatted and lifted the end, dropping the barrel aim down.

"Is it on the gate?" she asked, blowing a lock of her hair from her face.

"I think," Amy answered. "You think you can fire it off?"

"Young lady, I was stationed at Fort Sill, Oklahoma, for eight years. A cannon is a big gun with a big bullet." She spun a wheel, threw a lever and opened the back. With all ten fingers on a brass rim, she extracted an empty cartridge. It was still hot from the last blast but not hot enough to deter the lady.

"Get me one of those." She pointed to a wooden box of rounds.

Amy hauled out the large projectile, cradled it in her arms, and the two dropped the pointed end in the cannon. Lydia shut the back, ran the wheel tight and pulled back on a large, metal lever that clanked into place.

"Cover your ears."

She pulled a thick, short rope. The lever sprung and the cannon fired an explosive round that hit the front gates and shattered the whole right side.

"You did it!" Amy declared.

"Get me another. This time a little to the left."

Gunther watched the right half of the gates evaporate and let out a yell. He rolled to his feet and ran for the southeast corner of the roof, which offered cover from a room-sized structure. He craned his neck to see south, hoping to spot Perryweather and the Lancers.

"Goddammit, Perryweather!" He pounded both his fists in a fit on the ledge. "This is the moment!" He leaned over the ledge to look into the alley below. British, Indian and American men had gathered for the final building walls to fall.

"Hey! Hey!" he called below and caught their attention. "Will someone tell that stupid son of a bitch to charge?"

"Ahhh, who, sir?" a U.S. sergeant asked.

"Perryweather! Charge the Lancers. The gate is coming down!"

"Yes, sir," a sergeant said and bolted through a hole and back to the troops.

"Got...damn...it!" Gunther hollered, pounding his fist with each syllable. Behind him another cannon blast resounded and the round blew the second half of the gate doors wide open.

"It must be fucking tea time!" he roared in utter exasperation. Arrows zipped by him, lobbing explosives over the wall and into the courtyard.

"Captain Perryweather," the American sergeant interrupted the officer speaking to his lieutenants.

"Yes?" he said.

"Major Gunther said charge, sir."

"Charge?"

"He said charge. Said them gates are coming down."

Perryweather yanked on his gloves, strutted to the building's edge with the sergeant in tow, and leaned around the corner. Sure enough the gates were down, one half still flying in smoky smithereens.

"Mount!" he ordered. The call went out.

"Colors!" A lead horseman raised the staff that flew the British Union Jack flag. The captain leapt on his horse and took the lead position.

"Charge!" And in one moment, four hundred fifty horsemen, gun barrels forward, bolted up the main street in a group as wide as to cover the whole avenue, with Perryweather in the lead, holding a pointed sword forward, aimed right at the gateway.

The sergeant ran back into the hole and back to his last position.

He heard their thunder, unlike any other. Gunther stood up. Over and in between the rooftops and buildings he spied them coming. He smiled, then laughed. There he saw Perryweather in front, bent forward as if to stab the very heart of the fort itself with his sword.

"Go get 'em, you beautiful sons of bitches," he said, wiping a tear from his right eye.

He looked back to the tower window. It was dark and empty,

with thick gray smoke rolling out of the top. He shook his head in wonderment of Lydia Latissimo. He knew that top room would soon blow and blow big when all the ammo touched off. He prayed she and this mysterious blonde would somehow escape from it. He knew she was smart enough to leave. That room…had to go.

The bow-and-arrow squad roof-hopped closer and closer until they came to the alley and the building just across from Gunther.

"Blow the top off that tower before Perryweather gets there!" Gunther shouted to them. "Fast! Else their ammo will explode right on top of the Lancers."

His archers fired away. At close range, no fewer than four sticks of launched dynamite disappeared in the open bay window. Seconds ticked and Gunther watched as the Lancers were now halfway to the fort.

Come on…come on…" he prayed with a finger in each ear.

Then the explosives and all the ammunition went off in a senses-stunning shock wave. Gunther fell back. He watched the entire top of the tower blow out sideways in a million pieces. The round, cone-shaped roof shot straight up about twenty feet, fell apart, and rained down in the northwest courtyard. Stone shrapnel ripped across the inside balconies of the walls. Gunther assumed this had to tear and peel tribesmen from their sniper perches.

He leaned over the ledge with more commands to the men in the alley.

"Follow the Lancers into the fort. Leave reserves back on the south side to cover our retreat. Have some men work in and around these buildings. Clean out any Afghan nests. Kill everything. Everything! Get the machine-gun wagons back to the pass to secure our retreat."

"Do you want the men to…" a corporal started to ask.

"Just go about it smartly, man!" Gunther shouted. Then he made for the roof hatch and climbed down the ladder, just as the demo team blew the last exterior wall. Outside this wall was a wide road and the very fort itself. He dropped into the room full of anxious men, ready to charge. The blown walls, rooms and allies behind him were filled with soldiers at the ready.

"Wait fer the cavalry, boys," he calmly told the congregating troops. "When they pass and get through the gates, we will follow them in.

"Pick yer shots, men," Grimsley advised. "It'll be a mite crowded in there."

Gunther concentrated on loading his pistol magazines. He loaded his shotgun and bolt-action rifle, then let them drop sling-length to his sides. He positioned his Bowie knife at his waist. He had three more things to do. Get the Brits back their treasure chest of money. Then, he would find Colonel Latissimo and that fucking sheik son of a bitch, and kill them both.

31
Charge of the Perryweather Brigade

Captain Perryweather aimed the tip of his sword at the blasted, splintered and smoking main gates of Fort Tartan. With his Lancers behind him, his horse tore up the main village street so fast it seemed to fly. He crouched so low over the horse's neck, its mane flying back in the wind teased his nose. He shared the reins in his left hand with his Webley revolver. He was the first up the street, and would be the first to burst into the courtyard. The first. Forever the first in this battle. If he lived? He'd be a legend in the halls and pubs of Mother England. Huge paintings of this would adorn the walls of regiment headquarters and museums.

Halfway there, the main turret blew and, when it did, the top lifted off and disintegrated into a spray of a red-gray dust and huge rocks. He thought instantly of the fireworks he'd seen on the Thames River. This American renegade, he thought, this Gunther, had indeed delivered, with the timing of a stage play, each event of the battle. The blasted doors. The blasted turret. The enclosing men. His charge was all choreographed into a momentum that won battles and wars.

As his Lancers charged, he saw his other Brits, Americans and sepoys afoot and creeping up the sidewalks or crawling across the rooftops beside him. They cheered. He smiled. But as the fort approached, Perryweather homed in on the doors, shutting out all other sights and sounds.

"Into the breach!" he heard himself yell, and he felt invincible. Timeless. His men roared. The portal of war was upon him. He passed through it to find a sea of confused and angry men with startled faces turning to gape at him. He did not need to order open fire. Hot lead poured into the courtyard enemy.

Captain Perryweather did not stop at the gate. He and a contingent dashed for the main building, its powering, gaping roof now smoldering, up the gradual steps, and to its open doors and large archway.

Gunther saw Perryweather and the Lancers as they dashed passed the last avenue before the fort.

"Go! Go! Go! Go!" Gunther ordered, shoving on the backs of two men before him until the whole group left the last building and raced for the gate.

"Cover those windows!" he reminded the shooters assigned that task. Across the main avenue he could see Lieutenant Kerry ordering the same. Both groups of men shouted and cursed death upon the enemy.

Gunther took the lead and drew both his pistols and ran to the west corner of the main gates. He slid around the corner and witnessed bedlam. Hundreds fought before him, horses charged, all blasted, pushed, chopped, stabbed and fell into piles of rubble of twisted broken bodies and blood. Where to shoot first? Where? His infantry peeled around the gateposts.

"The balconies!" Gunther shouted. Each man dropped to a knee and picked off the enemy staged on the walkways of the interior wall.

Gunther shot at any piece of the enemy he could see. By now some of the Lancers had fallen, or their horses lay slaughtered or moaning among the infantry. At times the mass would move and openings would swell, then close in ferocious combat.

With each passing second more foot soldiers entered the compound and by sheer numbers, sharp blades and bullets, the tribesmen stumbled back and then further back, at first sporadically, then seemingly in a wave out of necessity. Soon, several sergeants found the open ground to establish some American and British firing lines.

"Push them!" Gunther shouted. "Pour it on!" Above the din and the irregular skirmish lines, he stepped forward, climbing and sometimes stumbling over the corpses of man and horse. Their boots sloshed in the flowing blood now draining in streams across the grounds and trampled the slit intestines and split brains.

Sepoys bravely scaled the interior wall stairways and walkways. They soon fell, too, from enemy fire as their superior and dangerous positions were exposed. Gunther left the firing lines, his attention distracted by the fort's main tower. He'd seen many Lancers charge up the stairs on horseback into the main building. Now, riderless horses, bloodied and wild-eyed, staggered and stumbled back down these steps. Some fell, tumbling and rolling to the ground.

He, too, dashed up these stairs, dodging the panicked animals, into a place where just a few hours ago he ate mutton like a gentleman and drank the wine of a connoisseur. Now he arrived as a killer, a slayer of everyone and everything that was put in his way and on the wrong side of him.

Three tribesmen bolted from the open doors, and Gunther cut them down with his .45s. A bullet passed through his coat sleeve, no doubt nicking his arm, but he was not sure. His fingers still worked. Pistols still up, Gunther slid around the doorframe into the headquarters. His jaw dropped. He stuttered. He gasped.

If there was a hell for horses, this was surely the place. The once decorated banquet hall had become a purgatory of human and animal destruction.

Perryweather and the first-line Lancers forced their way up the steps and into the fort's main room and leapt from their horses to do battle, all at great expense to their loyal mounts. The men, the ones still alive, were in the levels above, executing, by all explosive sounds, a ferocious battle. This room below them remained packed with nearly fifty riderless horses, with barely enough room to panic, to rear, to stutter-step, or even fall. But fall some did. There were horses with only three, even two legs, hacked no doubt by the blades of Afghans in the assault. Once downed, they screamed and slid in circles of their own blood and feces on the marble floor, their spasms knocking other horses to the floor, setting others off in a push-and-shove match against the masses. An electric terror was in all their eyes.

Wounded men and the dead were scattered among them, further crushed and pounded by every panicked hoof. There were cries for help from some who spotted Gunther. Pleading, outstretched arms, gasps for rescue, water and even holy redemption. But he could not heed. His eyes glimpsed a tribesman on a balcony above raising his rifle at him! Gunther dropped to a knee as a round pounded into the flank of the nearest horse. The beast bucked and thrashed and Gunther scrambled to escape these powerful kicks. In doing so, he dropped a pistol, reached for it, but a hoof knocked it deep into the midst of the equine mayhem.

He tumbled over and, as he crawled with difficulty to the interior steps, his two long guns strapped to his back interfered with his balance and advance. Gunther saw the Afghan running the balcony for another shot at him. Worse, he now spied, between some ten pounding and passing horse legs, a wounded Afghan on the floor some twenty feet away, prone and raising a revolver to shoot at him!

"Son of a bitch!" Gunther growled, as the man on the floor fired. The bullet hit one horse's knee, bursting it open like a red flare. That horse cried out, then its front half dropped down into their low view. Gunther rolled to his side and pulled his shotgun off his shoulder while holstering his remaining pistol.

With this fallen horse between him for cover and the prone enemy now out of sight for a few seconds, he propped up to one knee and hunted his enemy from above. Nothing. He stood. There he was! Racing through the upper level. Gunther fired. He worked the action, firing again, just as the stone wall exploded behind him about ankle high. The grounded Afghan's gun below missed its mark. Gunther skirted off to the left, hoping more horses would cover him from his downed enemy.

Gunther's first shotgun round missed, but the second ripped buckshot all over the Afghan's face and shoulder. The Afghan dropped his rifle and clutched his head. His face ran red. His expression became confused. Shocked. Gunther fired again, this time shredding the man's hands, arms and head. If he'd screamed, it could not be heard above the shrieks and wails of the horses.

Gunther dropped to his chest, barrel in the direction of the wounded Afghan. But he quickly saw the threat extinguished as he watched horse hoof after horse hoof pound and kick the floored man into a battered pulp. Their eyes met for an instant, passionate yet meaningless.

A monstrous roar above him! Gunther looked up. A wounded horse could no longer stand. It faltered, falling, nearly crushing him! He got a boot up in time to brace against the animal's body and the very momentum of the fall itself shoved him away from the crash. The poor beast dropped in a heavy thud, expelling air, gasping. Gunther lay just a yard from its head. Its breath was deep, growling and labored. Its eyes glared at him, just as passionate and meaningless as the eyes of the dead Afghan seconds earlier. Gunther drew his .45 and shot the beast in the head. The bones cracked open. He wished he could do the same for the whole sorry, dying lot.

Gunther heard the shots and yells of combat upstairs. Placing his boots against the dead horse in front of him, he pushed himself away until his back touched the wall. There he reloaded all his weapons. Then he stood and, with a wary eye, ascended the stairs.

He heard Perryweather barking orders above him on the third floor. But, what of the second floor? The floor where that sheik bastard made his grand dinner entrance? That floor was very quiet, almost still, except for some muffled commands from down that hallway, all from a very familiar voice. Gunther's lip twitched in recognition. It even wanted to curl into a smile. But hate wouldn't let it. Hate. His eyes watered. His breath deepened. His red, burning hate was uncontrollable. He lifted his shotgun chest high and stepped down the hall.

32
Death of a Sheik

Men in robes dashed across the hall from room to room, so pre-occupied they never once detected Gunther's steady march upon them.

One looked.

He died.

The blast was covered in the rumble of war everywhere. Gunther worked the lever action. He advanced.

A tribesman peeked out from a doorframe, then extended an arm holding a revolver. Gunther blasted the arm. Buckshot tore the hand open, the pistol dropped. Buckshot ripped across the face and into the eyes. The man fell backward, clutching his head with his one good hand. His back arched from the pain, his shoulders sliding on the floor.

Gunther advanced. Fired again. Misery over. He worked the lever action.

He ducked into the first doorway. Two men were packing, open suitcases lay on a tabletop. He killed both. He spun to cover the door, jamming more rounds into the weapon. He stepped back into the hall, shotgun held hip high.

Another man appeared, carrying a satchel. He was dead before he hit the ground. Gunther worked the lever action. Someone just ahead…

"Yunslalamanna YUNNNN…" a man screamed, brandishing a curved, thick sword and dashed at him. Gunther fired. Gunther fired. Gunther fired. The shredded swordsman toppled over but not before swinging the sword so close that Gunther needed his long gun to block the edged weapon to the side. The tribesman fell, squirming, babbling. Not for long. Gunther drew his pistol and shot him twice in the head.

Three rooms left. Pistol up this time, he entered the next. Four servants cowered in the corner, three men, one woman. He killed them all. Today, everyone dies. He could not leave anyone alive behind him, no matter how innocent they looked.

He returned to the hall. Advanced. He peered into the next room. Bam! A blast at him. He lurched back. Bam! Came another blast at him. Gunther stepped back, ejected the magazine from his pistol, slid in another, and from his vantage point shot into the open doorway, at nothing. The blast smashed into the room's stone wall, kicking up debris. He took a step, shot again, this time deeper. Step. Shoot. Deeper. Step. Shoot. Deeper. Faster. Step. Shoot. Deeper. He cut a live-fire path with random shots while crossing the doorway, to see into the room and make shooters inside take cover.

And the shooter did duck. When he saw Gunther, he dropped his rifle. It was the sheik. The sheik. Gunther stepped in and slammed the door behind him. The sheik put his hands up and forced a nervous smile.

"It is so very fortunate for me," the sheik said," that I am to be captured by such a man of power and influence as yourself. So that we may barter."

"It is so very unfortunate for you," Gunther said methodically, walking forward while holstering his pistol, "that you should be captured by me."

"You can trade me for much money," the sheik offered. "I am your prisoner."

"You…are a dead man. You skunk fucker," Gunther declared.

The sheik backed away. "Men such as myself are…are never killed. We…we…," that speech wasn't working. Then he reached into his robe and produced that curved, bejeweled dagger, the one he showed Gunther last night.

Gunther smiled. "You know what?" He pulled his Bowie knife from his belt. "You see this big rascal?" He turned the huge blade in his hand and it flashed silver from the rising sun beaming in through window. "I think I am going to cut the teeth right out of your mouth, just like you ordered the Koklanare to do to the Star of Africa."

The sheik gasped and lunged his dagger at Gunther, and Gunther sidestepped, cracking the big blade over the sheik's weapon arm.

"Shanamare KA!" the sheik cursed. He switched hands.

Gunther stalked the man about the room. Feinting, faking, slashing, and stabbing with his big knife. The sheik did the same. Gunther grabbed a metal candleholder.

The sheik stabbed forward. Full-body lunge. Gunther stepped to his left, the knife passed between Gunther's torso and arm. Gunther wrapped the arm with his right arm, bringing the tip of the Bowie around under the sheik's chin.

The sheik punched out at Gunther with his wounded right arm, but the Texan wrapped that arm, too, and his empty hand clutched the sheik's robes near his throat.

Now both the sheik's arms were caught. The tip of the Bowie was under the sheik's chin, and he had nowhere to go. Gunther grimaced inches from his face. He smiled.

Panic now showed in the sheik's face. Thoughtless, animal panic. He stammered, "Enoll, su canna feladouala…"

"You ain't got time for a prayer," Gunther growled.

The sheik stopped.

"Adios, fucker," and Gunther plunged the knife into the man's throat, under his chin. Deep. He worked the handle side-to-side. Twisted it. The sheik's eyes went wide, wide like the dead and dying horses on the floor below them. Mouth open. He gurgled. Gunther saw his own knife inside the mouth. The sheik's dagger dropped and clanged to the floor behind him.

Gunther extracted the knife. He let loose the arms. Lifelessly, the sheik dropped to the floor. He kicked the corpse and then spit on it.

Banging on the door. Men called out the sheik's name.

Gunther kicked over a table, kneeled behind it and rested his shotgun on the edge with his left hand on the trigger guard. He drew his pistol with his right and also rested this forearm on the edge.

"Well, come right on in," Gunther shouted. As if they could understand his English. With more foreign babbling, they threw open the door and charged in to rescue their leader. "Come on in, all ya'll fuckers!" He hollered louder.

Three brandished rifles and charged in. Gunther's first shotgun blast caught all three in the doorway, but killed only one, wounded one, and grazed the third. The dead one fell back. The wounded one stumbled forward, firing, and the third broke for the far corner. Gunther shot the grazed one twice as he dashed across, and this freshly grazed man ran full speed right into the wall, then dropped his rifle and fell to his knees.

The second wounded man fired at Gunther, but two rounds hit the thick tabletop. Gunther shot him next, twice in the face, then pointed his gun to the tribesman at the far wall. Still on his knees, the man's chest was against the wall, his face against the stone. He was mumbling. Praying? In a kind of shock? As Gunther walked to the door to close it again, he shot the man in the back of the head. He peeked down the hall to see it was empty. He picked up their rifles, then kicked their lifeless limbs from the doorway. He slammed the door and shoved the table against it.

He reloaded and looked out the window. He saw a raging battle below. His view was behind the enemy. He retrieved his Mexican rifle from the sling across his back, took aim, and began killing each tribesman he saw.

33
George Hall's Relief

The gun wagons gathered back at the base camp. George Hall was relieved to be alive. His hands were still numb from the machine-gun vibration. His damp, sweaty clothes clung to his body. His tongue felt swollen and leather dry. The drivers shouted orders to prepare for the coming retreat. He felt exhausted yet exhilarated as he leapt from the wagon.

"Hey!" cried several voices and he looked up to see some twenty soldiers, American and sepoy, jogging toward him, holding canteens and bandages. They were all smiling and shouting, "Hooo-ahhh!" and "Great work!" and "Smashing job!"

Hall stepped to the side to let the soldiers greet and help their brothers, but a Hindu trooper stepped in his way and handed him a metal canteen.

Hall smiled and took a long swig of warm water. "Thank you kind, sir," he said, handing the canteen back.

"Thank you, soldier, sir," the man said.

"Not a soldier, old chap, I…"

The man winked and with a quick hand wave, saluted Hall. The rest of the men did not ignore Hall as he thought they might. They pumped his hand vigorously, pounded his shoulders and back along with all the others who toughed it through and survived the dashing machine-gun wagon raid. Hall had indeed been a member of the force that had completed a dangerous mission.

"Prepare for the retreat!" a sergeant declared. "Cover fire positions!"

The wounded and dead were carried off. Replacements rushed

into their positions. Fresh ammo boxes were loaded.

"Mr. Hall!" came a woman's voice. He turned to see the fair-haired Marilyn, the nurse who had rescued the choking Afghani at the dinner just the night before. She was tending to the wounded from the wagon but, when she spotted him, she ran to him.

"My aunt! Mr. Hall! Have you seen my aunt? The woman I was with last night? The one who stayed there when we left?" She was breathless. She'd been crying and looked to do so again.

He held her forearms in his hands. "No, I haven't. I am sorry. But I haven't been inside the fort, just around it."

She shook her head with worry, nodded, and returned to the wounded.

Hall turned to the fort. By now the sun was up and the carnage before him fully evident. Hundreds of tents still burned or smoldered. Bodies of enemy men, camels, goats and horses covered the grounds. A few were alive and wounded. Some were skulking about. Koklanare dogs, riderless horses, and camels randomly trotted around the area.

"Bloody hell," he whispered slowly. Gunther's plan of surprise dynamite and overpowering machine-gun fire had worked. But in the distance, a full battle still raged in and around the stone fort. Smoke poured from its windows and blown tower, and the reports of firearms were so thick and steady, it sounded like a thunderstorm in the valley.

The base camp troops ventured out among the tents looking for survivors. Sporadic gunfire split the air when a tribesman was found. One round zipped and whistled right by him. Hall ducked, yanked his rifle off his shoulder, and held it at the ready. The soldiers spread out and cautiously plodded past him. He found himself stepping with them, inexplicably drawn back into the heat.

He passed a rough group of British soldiers, copying their stealth moves and scanning the area with their eyes.

"We'll do some clearin' of the roadway, so the lads can make a clean escape," a sergeant whispered over his shoulder to him.

"Of course," he whispered back.

34
Mesha and the Dogs

"Ahhhgggh!" Mesha screamed. She had not spied any of the wolf-like dogs prowling around her, so she yelled out in shock when a Koklanare dog suddenly snapped his mouth shut on her ankle from behind. It must have found her running figure irresistible. She tried to yank her leg free, but couldn't. She fell into some corpses. The snarling pack swarmed her. One snatched her left arm and yanked. She gasped and wrestled between the two.

"RRRRRGH!" roared at her ear, her face. The slobbering mouth of another dog buried his huge teeth in her hair, grinding open her scalp. She felt herself lifted off the ground with the power of the three dogs pulling savagely from three directions. Panic overcame her. The dogs clutched her, growled. The dogs around her barked. She cursed. Gunther's big revolver tumbled from her blouse and fell onto the ground.

Still cursing she grabbed it with her free hand and fired at the dog near her head, striking the oily, gray breast, and it released her hair with a yelp. Her face crashed to the rocks. The explosion rippled through the pack, and they all sidestepped away and ducked. The dog at her arm let go. She blasted the dog on her leg, the bullet pounded into its ribs with a punching thud and kicked the animal down on its side.

"You all want to die!" she screamed. "To die!" She scrambling to her side and fired at another. The dogs fled at a run.

She lay across two dead men, catching her breath. She began to cry, but it was a cry of anger. Her calf was torn open. Her arm was torn open. She looked over the dead men, gasping for breath. Her heart drummed in her chest. She found a body wearing a white shirt, and another with a curved knife hanging from a belt. She pulled out the bandages she had shoved into her blouse earlier and delicately wiped out the wound with strips she tore from the roll. Then she dressed the wound with more strips careful to tuck the loose, flapping hunks of flesh into their holes before she wrapped the wound. Then she cut the shirt and wrapped strips around the bandaged wound to secure it. She did all this while seated on a dead camel. A wild, wounded horse galloped past so close, it nearly knocked her to the ground.

Her pain was not great. Not yet. She stood, using the carcasses around her for support. There! A Koklanare pistol! She snatched it. With two pistols in her hands she limped toward the fort, searching the grounds for her new master, the cowboy from Texas.

35
The Mastiff

Not a single tribesman fired upon his window, yet Gunther counted thirty-seven kills from this elevated perch, picking off the enemy as his troops advanced across the grounds of the fort. Running out of long gun ammunition, he picked up the Afghan rifles from the dead men in the room and methodically emptied them into the unsuspecting backs and heads of his opponents. He held the last rifle with its last bullets in his hands.

A crash behind him! He spun around. A bashing at the door! It sprang open. A huge man, near seven feet tall holding the leash of a monstrous, growling dog had shouldered into the door, broke the lock, splintered the frame. She shoved the overturned table aside that Gunther had used as support.

Click.

The rifle was empty. The man froze expecting the next round to tear through him.

Gunther drew his .45 from the hip. Shot. The first round hit the warrior in the chest. The next higher, the next higher and in the face, the kind of target needed to stop a giant. It did. The man clutched his face and toppled backward. But, the leash fell free from his lifeless hand. The brown beast charged.

Click.

The pistol was empty.

The massive dog hit Gunther with the force of a train. The pistol flew from his hand. His body left the ground. His head and back smashed into the stone wall and floor. He blacked out, but only for a second.

The nightmare creature slobbered all over him, its teeth locked onto his left shoulder, and he thought he felt the bones crush. Its eyes were the size of a horse's. Its teeth as long as rifle rounds. Its wet, ghastly breath pumped in and out over his face. He fell into shock, babbling in pain as he felt the creature twist at his shoulder trying to tear it free. Would it come clean off? He punched vainly at the animals coiled body. It now straddled him. He grabbed at its throat, but the dog's neck felt like that of a muscular horse. Its teeth sank deeper in his shoulder. It lifted Gunther's upper torso, rocking its head and tearing him open as it hauled him several feet, his legs dragging lifelessly behind.

He saw his own blood shooting up on the dog's face with the pulse of each rapid heartbeat.

I am dying, he thought faintly.

I am dying here in this room.

He blacked out then faded in again.

I…I am being eaten alive by a monster.

And…I will kill it. He grabbed the handle of his Bowie knife on his belt, pulled it, and jammed it into the dog's body. All the way to the hilt. The dog stopped and looked down at him with a face of surprise. He stabbed it again. Again. The dog let go of his shoulder and while the intense pressure ceased, the teeth were buried so deeply, his torso would not come free. So he stabbed again. Again. The wounded beast howled, shook his head free of the bite and snapped at the knife hand. Gunther circled the knife under its chin and stuck it in the throat. He cranked the blade side-to-side. Its hot blood rained down upon him, onto his face, into his mouth, over his chest.

The dog fell on top of him, grunting, panting. The weight crushed Gunther's lungs. He pushed. He rolled. With great effort he cast the monster off his chest.

Stillness. Gasping. Breathing. He crawled back. His left arm was numb. He lay smothered in guts and blood. Man or beast? His knife clanged to the floor.

He coughed, then vomited.

He tried to…

A tremendous explosion rocked the building, not unlike the blast that decimated the tower.

He coughed. His face touched the cold stone floor. He needed this cold. The cold began to spread down his neck. His back.

He thought about getting…

But instead, he lay there.

"I am…dying," he whispered.

36
Hopscotch Retreat

The blast punched through their ears and shook their lungs. Lieutenant Kerry and his men dropped to their knees. The explosion tossed debris straight at them as well as bounced rocks, jagged pieces of cement of all sizes down the interior walls. They were enveloped in a blinding, powerful wave of dirt and rocks that he guessed would not hit Gunther's men fighting on the other side of the main building. When Gunther's troops first charged in to the left of the main gates, Kerry took his men off to the right to outflank the interior forces. Kerry charged inward, ordering a steady stream of fire upon the tribesmen. The enemy retreated behind the many corners of the pockmarked main building, backing up, howling, cursing and shooting as they dropped deeper into the fort.

"Adv—" Kerry tried to declare, but gagged, spitting out dust. "Advance!"

Still somewhat stunned from the explosion, wiping their eyes and coughing, firing their rifles methodically into the swirling clouds, he and his men rounded the last corner. In the fog, Kerry glimpsed the worst possible event in this battle thus far unfolding in the far west corner of the fort.

"The bugler!" Kerry shouted in desperation. "The bugler! Get the bugler!"

The call for the man echoed through the troops behind him. Within seconds a soldier with a bugle strapped to his side ran to him. The dust was settling.

"Sound the retreat, Corporal," Kerry told him. "They've blown a hole in a back wall." Kerry and all his men squinted and craned their necks to see the Koklanare and their allied tribesmen pouring though the giant hole to escape the confines of their capture in the fort. Hundreds of them! They shouted and shook their rifles in the air in celebration.

"They will surround us in here! They will own the outside! Sound the retreat! Sound the retreat. All of you! Back outside the gates! Fields of fire on both sides of the road outside the gates. Pass this on to everyone you see! Sergeants, take command of the firing lines!"

The bugler blew the retreat as he dashed to the front courtyard so that all the troops could hear the call. Ducking and shooting, Kerry followed and reached just inside the main gates, alerting each passing unit of the events.

"Come on. Come on," he said, waving the men by him, "They are moving outside! Retreat! Retreat!"

Captain Perryweather, helmet gone, hair disheveled and brandishing a sword, appeared on the front steps of the main building. His arms flew up as if to ask of Kerry, "What? Why the retreat?"

"They have blown a wall in the back!" Kerry shouted to him. "They are getting outside and surrounding the fort. Get out! Get out!" Kerry knew Perryweather instantly understood the quandary.

Kerry heard Perryweather declare, "Mount! Mount up!" to the Lancers inside. He winced as they wrestled with their panicked horses inside the main hall. In a moment, Perryweather mounted his horse and trotted down the front stairs, followed by a ragtag group of battered and bleeding Lancers, either on horseback or on foot. They tossed their wounded and dead on whatever available horse they could find and jogged beside the animals. Kerry felt inspired and impressed by their quick and gallant presence as the unit galloped past him into the road. Perryweather lingered at the gates as they rambled by. He nodded at Kerry. Kerry mustered a busy half salute in return, but a salute nonetheless. Perryweather could damn sure set a horse and lead men in combat.

As the expeditionary forces evacuated the fort, Kerry could not help but search the faces as the men dashed by. Gunther? Where was Gunther? He looked to the open doors of the main hall. He took a step toward them, but was called.

"Lieutenant!" Sergeant Grimsley beckoned from the street. "Heavy enemy fire from the right."

"Grimsley," Kerry said waving him near, 'Take three men and make a quick look for Gunther. Look in the building, too. Do not stay long. A quick look!"

"I'm on it, sir!" Grimsley said.

Kerry turned for the main road to lead the hopscotch retreat through the center of the village and back to the camp. The fire-fight was thick around him. He wondered how anyone could still be standing.

The battle rolled past her. Mesha crept into the fort. At times she cowered behind rubble or dropped and played dead among the corpses. Stragglers remained from both sides. They too limped by her, or ran in small groups carrying wounded comrades. At times, they even saw each other and ignored the sightings to save them-selves and their friends. Mesha struggled past them, searching for Gunther.

She stepped into the great hall, littered with wounded and dead horses and men and climbed the stairs. Blood drained out the doors and down the stairs. She studied each body. She grabbed the banis-ter and pulled herself up the stairs. With the wall for balance, she maneuvered down the hall. She peeked in each room. In the last room…

"Sahib, Gunther!"

Forgetting the pain in her leg, she ran to him. "Sahib? Oh..oh… oh." She saw his wounds. The shoulder of his left jacket and shirt was torn apart and red with blood. His shoulder, throat and face looked as if a lion had chewed on him. She dropped to his side and saw blood oozing from his neck in tiny pulses.

"Oh…oh..oh.." she babbled as she cut cloth from one of the dead men around them with her Afghani knife. "Is this what hap-pened to you?" she asked as she kicked the carcass of the beast to Gunther's left.

"Sahiiiibbbb!" she shouted inches from his face. Gunther

moaned. "Oh…oh…" she stuffed and patched his shoulder. She tied off his wounds, hoping not to choke him, but the blood loss must stop.

She looked about the room, spotted and grabbed a wooden chair. She dropped it on its back on the floor beside Gunther. She grabbed his torso, rolled him over until half his back rested on the back of the chair.

"Oh Sahib…oh…" she lifted his left leg over the seat and his right leg next.

More wraps! More wraps…she cut more pants and shirts from the dead. With these strips, she tied his right ankle to the right chair leg, then his left ankle to the left chair leg. She ran a long strap across his chest and through the back of the chair. She grabbed the back of the chair and lifted. Nothing. She wiped the blood from her hands and tried again.

"Oh Sahib," she said yet again and, with great effort and a groan, lifted. Gunther's back came off the ground. She balanced him on the two rear chair legs.

She pulled him to the doorway, scraping the two rear legs on the stone tiles. In the hall, the chair dropped from her grip.

"Ahhhhh!" she cried out and tried again, her leg wound aching.

Out of the room.

Down the hall.

The chair fell again. This time on its side, but the straps and ties held fast. Gunther remained in the seat. She lifted again, wailing at the thought of descending the stairs. She cursed in exasperation.

Down the stairs, each step a hard bounce on Gunther, his head bouncing lifelessly when the chair legs landed. Her grip and angle precarious.

They fell. Both of them tumbled backward down the curved stairway, she on her back. Gunther and his chair tumbled wildly.

"I have slain him," she cried, crawling to him. He was still tied to the chair. She lifted the chair back yet again. "I have slain him. I have slain him."

"Help me, lady!" a man called out.

"Me!" said another.

She hauled him around the carnage and across the great hall to the open courtyard: down the wide, front, stone stairs, slippery and drenched in blood, cluttered with body parts and debris.

"Dear God!" came a voice behind her.

She turned. It was the British man George Hall. Hall ran to her side and for a few seconds froze at the sight of the lifeless Gunther.

"Is he still alive?" he asked. He felt under the Texan's face, leaning near.

"He…alive…what…I…" she gasped for breath. "Help me."

"I think he's a bare bit alive," Hall said in astonishment.

Hall grabbed the back of the chair and pulled Gunther across the courtyard as Mesha tried to keep up. She fell. She rose. She kept up. At the front gates, they stopped. Mesha and Hall spied down the main streets.

"We have got to get him to our camp," Hall said while surveying the situation.

The main battle now raged further down the road, yet smaller skirmishes lingered closer.

"Perhaps…" Hall said, "perhaps we can get him down the road a bit and then behind some of the buildings. My old office is just over there. Then get him back down some alley."

Mesha nodded.

Four shouting Koklanare on horseback galloped past the front of the fort and turned down the street.

"Hey!" came an American voice from the courtyard. It was Sergeant Grimsley and three soldiers, crouched and rifles at port arms. They ran near.

"He dead?" the sergeant asked, gasping for breath.

"Not yet," Hall answered. "She's bandaged him proper."

In the distance the American machine guns opened up as planned, echoing throughout the valley to cover, as best they could, the retreat from the village.

"Cut him loose and toss 'im over your shoulders, boys," Grimsley said to his men. "Maybe we can find a loose horse or two. We've got to get out of here."

37
Escape

Gunther coughed. Or, was it was more like gagging. Or was it his head banging on the wood that woke him up? He felt horribly sick to his stomach. And jostled? How? How was he jostled around? He bounced into another person lying beside him.

"Where am I?" he asked, trying to sit up.

"Yer tryin' to get away, sir?" came a familiar voice.

"Away?" A world of savage sounds rushed at him. Horses. Hooves. Yells. Dust. Bullets.

"Yer smack dab in the middle of a mess!"

"A…mess," Gunther drawled. He sat upright. He was in the back of an open army buckboard. The buckboard rattled in the middle of a small Army, his Army, fleeing in wagons, camels and horses at breakneck speeds across a valley.

He was in the middle of two men. One up shooting. One down dead?

They were in the middle of the Khyber Pass.

They were in the middle of a life-or-death chase.

At their heels galloped the Koklanare and other Afghan tribesmen. These men fired rifles and pistols at them. They were in the middle of something else—a fight for their lives.

Gunther shook his head in dizzy disbelief. He looked to the left, to the man answering his questions. It was Rosie!

"Rosie!"

"Sir, these sons a bitches have re-grouped and are chasing us, like you 'spected them to. We killed more n' half agin' of 'em. What's left of 'em now is madder than a hornet's nest, and they's a chasen' us back." Rosie held a rifle and was shooting the pursuers.

Gunther slapped at his gun belt holster. It was empty! He reached for the belt of the prone man. No weapon. This man was wounded, maybe dead, his head wrapped in white cloth and covered in blood.

"Where…"

"We are in a wounded wagon, sir. We is wounded? But, we ain't dead yet." He fired again. Rosie handed Gunther a pistol. Gunther looked at it and focused his vision. His left arm didn't work! He saw his bandaged shoulder and upper arm. He forgot why.

"Have I been shot? Where am…" Gunther mumbled again.

"You is where you is, sir, and it stinks!" Rosie yelled. "Come about yourself and get busy!"

Two horsemen ran their animals full gallop right behind their wagon and closed in fast. Gunther turned the pistol at one of them.

"We ain't dead yet," Gunther repeated in a growl. He got to a knee and fired on one rider center mass. The bullet hit the man's chest. The attacker let go of the reins, dropped his rifle, and fell right off the horse in a second.

Rosie leaned forward and fired his rifle at the other close tribesman. The round kicked the man right off that horse. But there were plenty more behind them. Hundreds in fact.

Dizzy, Gunther dropped to all fours. A stabbing pain cut through his left shoulder, and he cried out. It stabbed the breath out of his chest.

"Major!" Rosie yelled. "Major, we have more shootin' to do."

Tears of pain burned Gunther's eyes, but he sat back on his haunches and fired again at the mass of men and horses close behind them. A wild round hit a horse's head, and the beast dropped headfirst, tumbling in a chaotic roll, tossing its rider at them. But this horse did even more significant damage. It's flipping carcass cut out the legs of at least four other horses behind it. The horses tripped, pitching their riders airborne.

"Rosie, the horses! Shoot the horses!" Gunther shouted.

They blasted away. Each fallen horse took out another four to six horses and riders. At times he and Rosie would bounce clear off the wagon floor.

Rosie opened a saddlebag between them and handed Gunther boxes of bullets. Gunther could hardly open them with the pains in his wounded arm and the severe bouncing of the wagon as it rattled full out over the rocky terrain. Still, he reloaded his pistol. Other men in nearby wounded wagons fired back into their pursuers but not enough to stem this insidious tide.

Gunther noticed that the wounded wagons, not built for combat speed, seemed to be the last group in line in this sloppy, every-man-for-himself escape.

"Where in hell are the machine-gun wagons?" Gunther shouted out to no one as he shoved rounds into his handgun's cylinder, glancing up at the angry faces a few feet away. "They should be… should be taking up the rear!"

"Good idea, major," Rosie shouted, "but you was asleep when they gave out the orders of the day."

A wagon to their left hit a deep rocky gulch and fell apart from the rough ride, its wheels rocketed off to the sides, the bed hit, slid, and disintegrated into wooden planks and splinters. The wounded inside bounced like thrown dolls across the terrain. Its two drivers up front hung onto the reins as horses tore free from the tongue. The team pulled the drivers on their chests for a few seconds until they could no longer stand the pain and let go. The tribesmen fell upon the men and slaughtered them with swords.

To the right! A tribesman leapt off his horse and onto the wagon. He hung on the side, up to his armpits with both arms inside the wagon wall. A curved knife was clenched in his teeth, his eyes wide. Gunther slammed closed the loaded cylinder of his pistol as he kicked at the arms. The man swung a leg over the side.

"Adios, you fucker," Gunther growled and shot him in the face. He spit the knife into the wagon. The stunning blow took effect, and the man slowly lost his grip, slipping out of sight.

There he is! Gunther spotted him. "There he is!" Gunther said to Rosie! It was Latissimo himself astride a horse just behind them and to the left. His fat face full of rage. His long, black hair streamed back in the wind. He held no reins, controlling his horse with his knees! As if guiding the animal was even a possibility now, for it was a madman's dash straight into hell, and this horse knew the way. The colonel clutched a revolver in one and a sword in the other. His sword, the curved sword of Red, White and Blue in color. He shouted orders to his throng, words Gunther could not hear.

Latissimo saw them, his eyes zeroing in on Gunther's face. He had the savage look of hate and death. Barbaric.

Gunther lifted his pistol as Latissimo raised his. The wagon bounced a good six inches, and Gunther was knocked forward to all fours. Or, all threes, as his arm was numb. Without it he tumbled shoulder down, face down to the wagon floor, His shoulder was not numb! It felt like an axe hit him!

From the deck, he pleaded, "Shoot him, Rosie. Shoot him!"

Rosie swung his rifle to the left.

Gunther held down a fit of vomit, as the events around him slowed down and the harsh explosive sounds quelled. He watched as Rosie took aim. The wagon bounced again, and Gunther thought he heard Rosie curse. But this veteran scout, this horseback-shooting expert timed the bounce. Rosie took aim again. He fired. Gunther pushed himself up to see, eyes wide with anticipation.

The rifle round hit Latissimo in the neck. His neck erupted. A look of shock covered Latissimo's face. He lost control of his seat on the horse. He began to bounce. He dropped the sword. He dropped the pistol. He clutched his neck. Rosie fired again into the torso. Latissimo's shirt flapped when the round hit. He slowly slid off the animal and dropped out of sight, trampled by all those in a dead run behind him. His horse, this great animal, never faltered and continued riderless at full gallop.

Gunther vomited. "What is wrong with me?" he asked aloud, and grabbed the rear wall of the wagon. His handgun fell to the wagon's floor. "I've got to…"

"Help up front! Help!" a voice called from the front seat.

Gunther turned to see a Koklanare on the buckboard front, crawling and fighting with one of the two drivers. The wild man stabbed one of the drivers multiple times and pushed him.

Gunther snatched up the pistol and crawled forward. He took aim at the enemy. He shot him twice in the chest. The man propped up and glared down at Gunther. The wounded driver kicked furiously at him and knocked the attacker right off the wagon, but the driver almost fell, too. A sudden bounce knocked him further still. Gunther dropped the pistol, grabbed the driver by the scruff of his neck collar, and hauled him back into the wagon bed.

"Welcome to the wounded," Gunther said, looking over the knife wounds.

"Are they bad?" the driver asked.

"Hell, if I can tell," Gunther added.

"We is the shootin' wounded, I might remind ya!" Rosie complained over his shoulder, still blasting away at the pursuers.

Gunther grabbed at some medical supplies in the corner and laid a box on the driver's chest.

"Fix yourself," he ordered the driver. Then he realized under his own crude bandages on his chest, was his shoulder holster and German Luger. He painfully dug into the brace of cloth straps, got the handle and pulled the gun. He passed Rosie's revolver to the driver. "Fix and shoot." Then, Gunther started blasting away again at the Koklanare.

Bugles? Bugles! Cheers?

Gunther stopped shooting and looked forward.

"The cavalry has arrived!" The driver up front proclaimed.

"The cavalry?" Gunther repeated. He crawled to the front.

"Looky! Looky!" the driver pointed out with glee.

British soldiers on horseback! Running the other way? Running into the Koklanare. Hundreds of them. Crashing into the tribesmen. Fresh men. In clean uniforms! Gunther recognized Scottish uniforms. Did he hear bagpipes in the distance?

Angry Scots cleaved their way into the enemy. Gunther got a good hold on the wagon wall and watched. The wagon slowed! All the wagons dropped to a trotter's pace, then stopped, as they were swarmed with Scots afoot and on horseback.

Firepower and men ravaged the enemy, cutting them down every man, horse and camel. Gunther spotted Sergeant McGillacutty among them. McGillacutty! The sergeant from the fort Gunther sent back to India for help. He got the re-enforcements. They made it back here! They made it. He spotted Lieutenant Kerry among the charge, and then Perryweather as the expeditionary forces joined the Scots in the counterattack.

Gunther burst out in tears of pain, exhaustion and exhilaration. "McGillacutty!" Gunther shouted. He sat back in the wagon and wiped his nose on the sleeve of his shirt.

"Rosie, my friend, we have escaped from the very jaws of death," Gunther said. Jaws? Jaws! The monster dog! It had bitten clean through him. The dog. "My shoulder!" He grabbed for his shoulder. "This is from a damn dog!"

"You don't say," Rosie smiled in astonishment, "You almost done in by a dog. I was almost done in by a scorpion. Come this far, the both of us…to be bit damn near dead by a bug and a dog."

"Ain't that the way of it?" Gunther said, dizzy again. He lay back down.

"Ain't it though," Rosie added.

"Sahib!" came a voice from outside the wagon.

"Mesha?" Gunther asked. He could see just her head over the side. She looked worn and torn, but smiling nonetheless.

"Mesha, the Scots need help," Gunther mumbled with slurred speech, while he grabbed for a handful of bullets loose on the wagon floor. "We…"

Explosions. Screams. Bagpipes and then…Blackness.

38
Back at the Final Intoxication

Awake! The slow rocking of the wagon nudged Gunther awake from a nightmare. Daytime. Bluest of clear blue sky. Cold air. He heard some men singing. British accents? Irish? Scottish? His face felt cold. He was wrapped in thick blankets. To the right were enormous, steep, rocky mountain ridges. His body gently jostled side-to-side. He drooled from his bottom lip.

On a ridge way above him something moved. He squinted to see it. A beast! His jaw dropped. "Jefe!" he called out for help, but he realized his best friend was ten thousand miles away in Texas. "Jefe," he repeated again softly. "The ridge! There."

A horse? A giant, unsaddled, wild horse. It was monstrous. A unicorn? No. It stopped and looked down at them. Right at him.

"The horses!" he shouted out. "The giant horses H. G. Wells told us about! They are here! Tell the president."

A face bent into view. Mesha wiped his cheek. She opened his mouth with a finger and shoved a wet rag into it.

"Chew," she said.

"Horses," Gunther mumbled.

Mesha smiled, but Gunther knew it was a false smile. It wasn't right.

"Why are you so sad?" Gunther asked her, "Are you okay?"

"Chew," she said.

" I…I am numb all over."

"Chew."

Blackness.

Page 351

Gunther's eyes opened. His head pained him greatly. His left arm felt numb. He saw Mesha's face emerge inspecting him at close range. The wagon had stopped. He was in a wagon? He looked around and saw the walls of the buckboard.

"Suffering…." he tried to speak, but the words wouldn't work. The lips quivered. "Wounds…" With a right hand on the side of wagon interior he pulled his chest up to better witness the commotion around him. Mesha helped him prop up. "And fame alike," he finished his rambling sentence.

Back at the edge of civilization! The Final Intoxication pub! Club patrons greeted the returning American, British and Indian soldiers. Cheering and hollering, Scottish Regiment soldiers from the pub carried glasses of beer and passed them to many of the troops. In among his dizzy sickness, Gunther managed a smile.

A Scot walked up to Gunther with a mug, "Ere ya go, Laddy."

Gunther smiled and said, "Suffering wounds and fame alike." He took the tall glass, trying a sip. "It's warm," Gunther mumbled.

"Well a course it's warm. Where the hell da ya think we are, Laddy? Glasgow?"

Gunther chuckled and sipped some more. Mesha helped him hold the glass with her hand over his. Two gabbing horsemen approached, and Gunther tried to focus on them.

"Well, well, well," Rosie proclaimed to his riding partner, Gildy, "The major ain't awake five dern minutes, and he's a drinkin' already."

"Healed up, Rosie?" Gunther asked feebly.

"Healed, sir. But I got a scar and bump like a baby cactus were that nasty shelled bastard stung me. It's like a hump on a buffalo."

"I here ya struck a mighty blow fa tha queen," the Scot said to them with great sympathy while looking the wounded men over.

"That we did, sir," Gunther replied and handed the glass back. "And we suffered wounds and fame alike. Good day to you." He suddenly dropped back down into his bedding, sick to his stomach. George Hall's face appeared before him next, leaning over the side of the wagon, Gunther saw only blue sky behind him.

"Where is Lydia?" Gunther asked him.

"She's dead, Johann."

"Dead?"

"Not in the battle. The cancer. She died two days ago. On the road back."

"Dead."

Another head in a brown hat appeared over the sideboard, "Hello, Major!"

"Lieutenant Kerry. Where is Marilyn? Where are the photographers?"

"They're in your other wagon. They're fine, sir. Lydia found Silas Verne's missing daughter, Amy, in the harem. She's with us. We're bringing her home."

"Amy. I don't…."

"You'll remember the story one day, sir. You need lots of rest."

"And you're fine?"

"Fine, sir."

"…and all in one piece?"

"Completely in one piece," Kerry said with a broad grin, waving the gloved fingers of both hands. "You've been unconscious for eight days. Mesha has been force-feeding you water and mashed food."

"And beer is not the first thing you should drink when you wake up," Mesha complained.

"I am suffering from wounds and fame alike," Gunther babbled again. He touched his right hand pocket, feeling for the smooth round lump that was The Star of Africa's tooth. It was still there.

"I am sick. I am here, and I am not," he said as his head slumped, and then the clouds, the sky and the faces above him spun. His vision faded into a blur. He blacked out.

39
Adios Amigo

"Shall we?" Hall invited.

"I guess I have to," Gunther groaned. With both hands gripping the sides of the hospital sunroom's Queen Ann chair, Gunther stood with a wobble. A pain in his patched and healing left shoulder cut like a knife, even five weeks after the bullmastiff attack.

Hall waited in the doorway, as he had done each day for the last two weeks, coaxing the Texan into his exercise routine—a stroll down the park path of the Ganghi River, right behind the Colonel Kitchner Indian and British Military Medical Hospital.

"Yes, you do, sir," Hall replied. "Doctor's orders."

Gunther walked to the sidewalk of his own volition and stood beside Hall. He looked about and sucked in a deep breath, "Damn, it stinks here," he said, shaking his head. He waved off a bug.

The pair turned south. The warm wind whipped though his billowy Indian, white hospital pajamas and robe. To their left on the riverbanks women, submerged to their thighs, washed baskets of clothes in Ganghi. They slapped the wet garb over and over on the surface of the river, then pulled them up to twist in a drip-dry wrenching. Upstream an old man urinated in the river. Children swam. Teenagers fished. Religious men chanted.

"Perryweather left for London," Hall mentioned.

"Hero that he is. Hero that he will be," Gunther noted.

"I got a glance at his battle report. You are indeed mentioned in it old chap, but as one might imagine, not quite as much as you should be," Hall said.

"One might imagine."

"There'll be a preposterously huge painting commissioned for a wall at regiment headquarters of the glorious scene, and somewhere in it will ride a Texan in a white hat and buckskin jacket."

"On a white horse."

"A white horse. Such as it is. But they do take care to paint in the significant people. Your visage will be included. Probably charging with the Lancers."

"Once again they'll have me making a charge on horseback when I did not. At San Juan Hill in Cuba, we charged up that son of a bitch on foot. But the newspapers depicted us mounted on glorious horses."

Hill nodded. "We do love a great cavalry charge," Hill added. "But, they have taken fine care of you here. Perryweather did see to that. And, the beggar came here almost every day while you were in the coma. He gave you a little pep talk in your ear each visit. Not a bad chap in the end. I think this bit of business… aged…him."

"Like fine wine. And I'm no younger for it all either."

"He knows that your layered use of the machine guns was a brilliant plan. I fear if we had not killed so many of the devils in their sleep, we would not be alive today. You will receive a token from the queen. A medal of some sort," Hall added. "Will you receive something from your president?"

"Just a hardy slap on the back," Gunther said.

"Yes. Hopefully on the …right side."

They strolled on.

"All the Yanks have shipped back. The girl, Amy, the daughter of the reverend? She's off to her relatives in the States."

"Yes, Amy. That is amazing. I wish the poor reverend were around to see it. Leave it to Lydia. Was…was her death a painful one?"

"No. Both your American doctor and the British doctors treated her with painkillers at the end. She died next to you in your wagon."

Gunther stopped. "Next to me? He said softly. "I did not know."

"Yes." They continued on. "She asked to be there. She also

whispered in your ear words of encouragement each day."

Gunther choked a bit, not quite strong enough yet to hide his feelings. "Well then, God bless her," he found himself saying.

"Yes," Hill agreed. "May God bless her. Your two favorite scouts, Rosie and Gildy, came by to see you in your room. Kerry and Marilyn were here to check on you, too. Quite close. I smell a marriage."

"I would have arranged their return together on a cruise ship, had I been awake."

"You lost a keg of blood, Gunth. But, you'll be back in Texas in a month, so the good doctor reports. What's in store for you there?" Hall asked.

"Oh, imagine I'll return to my office and get a case or two to work on."

"Yes, your Remedies business. Gunfighter cases?"

"Noooo," Gunther said with a chuckle. "Times are changing in the Wild Wild West you read about in England, Mr. Hall. My cases are…more complicated than just simple gunfights."

"Like this little misadventure to Afghanistan."

"Yeah, sorta'. A gunfight would be…quicker. And, a helluva lot easier. What is next for you, George? Another district officer position somewhere?"

"No, actually mate, something else." They took a few more slow steps. Hall shook his head, smiled, and continued, "Do you remember that starry night back in Tasheebo? Right before the battle? When I asked you about what I should do? Stay there and fight? Or leave the valley?"

"Ahhhh, whew! Kinda', yeah." But he didn't.

"You told me that the only thing worse than a crazy man with a gun, is a good man with a gun who won't stop him.'"

"Oh, yeah. I do remember that," Gunther said.

"I must tell you ol' chap, that really hit me. I took a good look at myself. And in almost a second, I found something…a courage in me that I did not think I had."

"Since you rescued my ass, I'm mighty glad you did."

"You told me that you were going to charge into that fort and try to kill everyone in there. With such a bravado. Such…such stiff upper lip, confidence." The two men stopped and faced each other.

"I have had that upper lip of mine busted wide open a few times," Gunther said. "It bleeds like a stuck pig."

"I…I have read, or heard about all that patriotic rot…you know…in books and speeches. But that night, right there on the rocks. I felt it all. For real. It's very real, isn't it?"

Gunther saw Hall's eyes tear up. Hall sucked in a breath to quell himself.

"It can be, amigo," Gunther said with a sigh, turning away from the emotion. He started the walk again.

"I have signed up for a different duty than the diplomatic department," Hall said.

"You did?"

"Bit different than being a district officer. Military intelligence. There is great deal afoot in the world, Gunther. The Germans— your bloody relatives—are committing espionage in my England. The Russians are building a new fleet of ships powered by oil from the ground. The Middle East is in a horrible mess…"

"Military intelligence," Gunther repeated. "A spy?"

"Yes, rather much like a spy. In the Foreign Office section."

Gunther suddenly stopped. "Whew! That's about as far as I can go. We'd better turn back."

Hall nodded and put his hand under Gunther's right elbow. Gunther leaned toward him for support.

"Little shaky," Gunther added. "Damn hot here. Whew! So, you will become a spy."

"Yes. Going back to Britain. They will sharpen up my marksmanship. My wits. Box a bit more. Brush up on my jujitsu. The world is in turmoil. The British Empire is losing its hold. A massive war is brewing over here, Johann. I think I can help. I am off first to Turkey, they tell me. There is a great Jihad movement under way there, and they need agents."

"Well, sir, I think you can help."

They walked on in silence, with Gunther leaning on Hall's sturdy arm. An English ward nurse greeted them at the sunroom doors.

"I dare say, that was quite the walk, Mr. Gunther," she said. "Jolly good for you."

"Yes, jolly good for me," Gunther repeated, feeling feverish and eyeing the couch on the porch intently. The nurse wrapped her arm completely into Gunther's, and Hall stepped back. She guided him to the couch that overlooked the river. Mesha appeared carrying a tray with a teapot, cups, and tea biscuits.

"Ohhh boy," Gunther declared. "It's tea time at the ol' corral."

Mesha poured some tea in cups. She looked to Hall, who waved off the offer.

Hall walked to the doorway and grabbed a long wooden box. He propped himself on the edge of the couch with the box on his lap, flipped some latches, then looked up at Gunther and smiled.

"Whatcha' got in there, limey?" Gunther asked.

Hall lifted the lid and with two hands extracted the contents. It was the curved sword, all red and white and blue of it. Latissimo's sword.

"Seems while the lads were cleaning up the battlefield, one of them stumbled upon this artifact. Perryweather saved it for you."

He handed it to Gunther, who took the weapon and turned it in his hands. "I can tell you now, I will eventually give this to the president of the United States. And it will rest in a museum with Teddy's other things. But, there won't be a plaque telling the story behind its acquisition."

Hall nodded. "Just record it as a gift from a foreign dignitary."

"Just a gift it is. But I will keep it for awhile."

"You have lost almost everything, Sahib Gunther," Mesha said, taking the sword and replacing it in its box. Your hat. Your deer-skin jacket. Your knife. Your guns are gone..."

"I still have my Luger."

"And some small things from your pockets. Like jewelry. Now you have this great sword."

"Yes. Small things. Jewelry," Gunther muttered, as Mesha rested the box against the wall.

"Well, Johann, I must go," Hall interrupted. He stood.

"See you tomorrow?"

"No, afraid not, ol' chap. I must take your leave for Mother England. My train to the coast leaves in two hours. Then the ship in the morning."

"Oh?" Gunther tried to stand.

"Keep your seat, old man," Hall's hand rested on Gunther's good shoulder. "You seem to get about the world and find yourself in the most terrible jams. If you ever need any help? You know how to find me. Any British Embassy will find me."

The men shook hands. Hall smiled, tipped the brim of his hat to the nurse and Mesha, and left with a, "Cheers, Johann! Mesha!" shout over his shoulder.

"Adios, amigo."

The nurse handed Gunther his cup of tea, which he accepted with the trembling fingers of his recovering left hand. The cup rattled against the saucer.

"I feel like a dead drunk and without the joy of whiskey," he commented, trying to steady his grip.

"Mr. Hall seems to be a fine sort," the nurse said, whimsically.

Gunther watched Hall walk away.

"He'll do," he said quietly.

Epilogue
Small Things, Like Jewelry

The monkey flipped through the air and caught the red velvet ball. Jefe's children squealed with delight, which seemed to further invigorate the monkey. It chattered and mimicked the squeals, then pitched the ball straight back at them. The office lobby of Remedies was often a playground, now it was a zoo.

Gunther rounded his stately, carved desk for the first time in ten months and dropped back in his brown leather chair. Jefe remained in tow with a nonstop diatribe; halfway through which Gunther lost track of his reported events.

"You teacher girlfriend, Annalee?"

This caught Gunther's attention.

"She married," Jefe said.

"Married! In ten months!"

"To another teacher man. I told you, I told you. You are not smart enough for her. She was a college lady. West Point does not count with a college lady. What you do there anyway? Shoot guns and march around? College ladies like real college men. Anyway, she happy. I see them walk around downtown, and she spins and spins her umbrella, laughing and smiling. Big-teeth smile." Jefe batted his eyelashes and showed his teeth. "When she sees me? She waves. She likes me. I graduated the University of…"

"Manila…" Gunther interrupted while shuffling papers on his desk.

"That's right, Manila, not some bang-bang soldier school. She likes me, but I don't know about you!"

"Not anymore! Well, good for them," Gunther said. He actually hadn't really given her another thought after leaving Washington, D.C.

"You look like coyote shit, you know. Look at your skinny neck in your big collar. How much weight you lose?"

Gunther shook his head. Mesha brought in a cup of coffee and slid it carefully in front of Gunther, then hustled out of the room.

"Oh, I don't know. Fifteen pounds? Twenty?" Gunther said. "I'll get it back."

"Face look like cow skeleton. We do Filipino stick exercises. I will bring that arm back for you with left-hand stick work." He dashed out of the office for some unknown chore.

Gunther stuck several fingers into his starched collar. He'd indeed lost weight, probably thirty pounds or more. He picked his coffee mug up with his left hand and tested its turpitude. No shake. No shimmer. He smelled and then sipped his favorite Indonesian blend. Mesha was learning her new job fast.

A manila envelope lay on the desktop before him. It had the maroon, wax seal of the president's office. With a small knife, he opened the telegram. It was addressed:

To my abominable blunt instrument STOP
Lieutenant Kerry STOP
That is our new CAPTAIN Kerry briefed the War Department on events STOP
Praise the Lord you are alive STOP
Profoundly impressed and in your eternal debt STOP
Fill me in with your observations in Montana hunt next Spring STOP
Yours Truly, The President STOP

Gunther rocked back in his chair. The children and monkey ran from the lobby, and in the new silence, he could hear the horses and coaches passing on the brick street outside his building; saw their familiar shadows flowing from the windows down across the wooden floor. Was he really home? Gunther rubbed his face with both hands.

Reaching into his pocket, Gunther extracted a tiny, precious object, this small jewelry as Mesha called it back in India, now worth more than anything in the world to him, even more than the thousands and thousands of dollars the Army had wired to his bank account for his ten-month duty on the top of the world. Turning it over within his fingers, an indescribable ache burned in his lung, or was it near his heart, or in it?

Her nightmare death. At times the vision of the bags filled with human feet passed through his head, and the Koklanare mounted on their horses. He knew two of those feet belonged to the Star of Africa. The way her feet looked when she walked around him in her bedroom now haunted him. The texture of them bare and brushing his with soft lingering strokes between his calves as they lay together lingered in his senses. He shook his head free of the memories. Opening his desk drawer, Gunther placed the Star of Africa's bejeweled tooth on its green, velvet lining.

But his mind wandered off again and flashed to so many faces and places. Rosie and Gildy. The brave Lydia. Young Captain Kerry— would he marry Marilyn? Poor, poor Kelly Homestead, pitched over the rail of a cruise ship. The mad dash to save the photographers from the notorious Stranglers of India. He thought of the sunny afternoon he sat beside Lieutenant Satin on the flatbed trailer as they approached Kabul, riding the rail outskirts of the markets. The weaponry and the warriors. Then the descent into hell itself: the war—the carnage. The horror. The yellow, giant teeth of that damn monster dog. The mere thought of it caused him to shift nervously in his chair. The jagged rocks and peaks, the magnificent valleys of the Khyber Pass and beyond. And, the face of the Star. The feel of the Star. The Star. She was an exotic woman unlike any other.

"We got company!" Jefe appeared in the doorway. "A Texican rancher from the Mexico border. He say there is a small revolution and Mexicans have promised to murder every white man they can. Dis man? He have five sons, and he wants us to protect them." He winked and rubbed the tips of two fingers together to signal the client was wealthy.

Gunther slid the drawer closed and said, "Send him in."

Acknowledgements

Special thanks to:

Jane Eden – Editor, Layout
Leanna Ellis – Contributing Editor
Loyd Fitzpatrick – Special Consultant
Thomas R. Pentzer – Special Editor

Be Bad Now!
By W. Hock Hochheim

In the 1980's a recession stampedes Texas. The oil industry dries up, laying high rollers low and sending the entire state of Texas into a tornado-like downspin.

Northern mobsters invade these cracks in the Lone Star State. Their schemes: corruption, loan sharking, gambling, extortion, drug and human trafficking, and murder for hire -- all backed with strong arms swinging bats, psychos pointing guns, torture, violence and death.

The city of West Forge, a stone's throw from Houston, is Sgt. "Jumpin" Jack Kellog's town. And when organized crime seeps in, Kellog's brand of justice knows no bounds. He tracks, fights, kicks and shoots his way through conspiracies, threats, ambushes and showdowns. Pushed to near-madness by angst with informants inside his agency and lurking everywhere, Jack tackles the thugs, bosses, lawyers, politicians and businessmen on the Mob payroll, in a battle that takes him from the swamps of Louisiana, to the ghettos of Houston, to casinos in Vegas and even through the Halls of Congress in Washington D.C. Can Kellog beat the Yankee Mafia? Beat the Cowboy Mafia? Their Crime Confederation? How bad is bad enough when you must...Be Bad Now?

Blood Rust - Death of the China Doll
By W. Hock Hochheim

Once an NYPD detective, Rusty was a rising rock star in the Organized Crimes Unit. Then, Mob members and corrupt cops lure Rusty to Grant's Tomb and shoot him in the head. The detective in Rusty dies. The meat puppet Rusty is all that remains, now a brain damaged, paranoid, criminal, psychopath terrorizing the streets of Newark, NJ.

Years later, Alphonso "The Crepe hanger," one of the hit men who lured Rusty to Grant's Tomb, reveals the old China Doll case Rusty solved was an elaborate con, executed by the Mob in an international drug smuggling conspiracy. Soon the State will execute Steverino Downing, the man convicted, for a crime he didn't commit. And shooting Rusty was the Mob's way of clearing up loose ends.

This news ignites something deep in Rusty's exploded brain. He must find a way to free Downing. His obsession leads him to the Freedom Science Foundation, a group run by the internationally renowned Dr. Sad Prevell and Peter, a former SAS South African commando. Both cut their teeth on such cases during African Apartheid. Rusty's quest will take him from New York to the shipyards of South Africa and Shanghai.

Can Rusty nail the pieces of his shattered mind back together? Can he beat the Mafia, corrupt cops, a Chinese Triad and Somalia pirates in time to save Downing's life, and still somehow redeem his own?

(Available by special order at all major bookstores, via Nook and Kindle and at: www.LauricPress.com)

www.ingramcontent.com/pod-product-compliance
Lightning Source LLC
Chambersburg PA
CBHW061621210726
48287CB00001B/231